RAGE

ALSO BY CORA CARMACK

Roar

RAGE

Cora Carmack

TOR TEEN

A TOM DOHERTY ASSOCIATES BOOK

NEW YORK

RAGE

Copyright © 2019 by Cora Carmack

A Tor Teen Book
Published by Tom Doherty Associates
120 Broadway
New York, NY 10271

www.tor-forge.com

Tor® is a registered trademark of Macmillan Publishing Group, LLC.

The Library of Congress Cataloging-in-Publication Data
is available upon request.

ISBN 978-0-7653-8636-6 (hardcover)
ISBN 978-1-250-19402-2 (international, sold
outside the U.S., subject to rights availability)
ISBN 978-0-7653-8637-3 (ebook)

Our books may be purchased in bulk for promotional, educational, or business use. Please contact your local bookseller or the Macmillan Corporate and Premium Sales Department at 1-800-221-7945, extension 5442, or by email at MacmillanSpecialMarkets@macmillan.com.

First U.S. Edition: August 2019
First International Edition: August 2019

Printed in the United States of America

0 9 8 7 6 5 4 3 2 1

For anyone who has ever felt
like they were lost in a storm,
and for the people who held my hand
as I walked through my own.

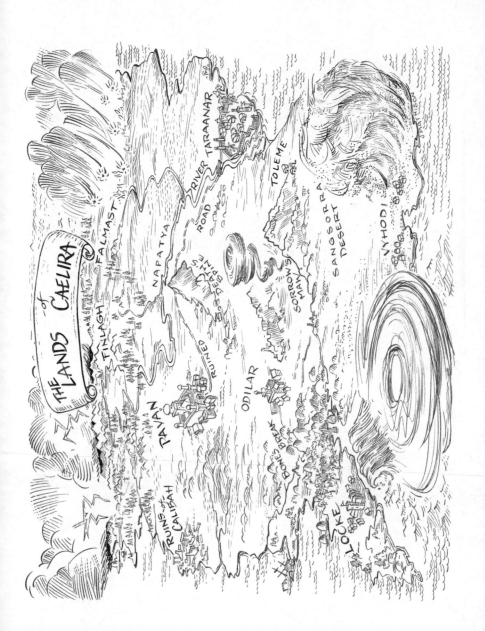

RAGE

PROLOGUE

Thirteen Years Ago

He did not understand the day they took him from his mother.

He did not understand why the soldiers behaved so cruelly, or why his mother did not object. She only watched with tired eyes and turned away as he kicked and screamed and bit at the soldiers' wrists to tear himself free. When he managed to break away, he ran and slid the last distance on his knees, his threadbare clothes doing little to keep his skin from scraping against the stone. He ignored the sting, and clutched at his mother's legs, burying his face in the fabric of her skirt so he did not have to see the way she still kept her gaze from him.

Cruze had known he was not like other boys. There was no large, happy family waiting at home for him. But he had had his mother. Until the king's soldiers peeled his scrawny arms away from her knees and dragged him away. She never looked back at him, no matter how he screamed, not even so he could memorize her face one last time.

Once his fingers were wrenched from their last hold on the doorway to the room he and his mother shared, there was no stopping the men who carried him. He was hauled down the stairs and marched outside the ramshackle building. The other women he had grown up around watched warily, but did not speak a word on his behalf, not even the kind ones who had offered him refuge in their rooms while his mother worked. They watched from their doorways and windows as he was shoved into the back of a wooden wagon. The soldier threw him, and he landed on his side, his hip striking painfully against the floor of the cart. Before he could regain his footing, they slammed and barred a wooden door, locking him away in the darkness.

He beat at the door. Even once he felt the cart jerk and the horses began to move, he rained fury upon the wood with his fists, shouting for his mother, as though she might still hear him as he moved farther and farther away. And when that did not work, and his voice began to grow hoarse, he broke and he shouted his father's name too. Even though it was not a name he was ever supposed to say aloud.

His sire did not come either. And the wagon kept going and going, long past the time his voice gave out and he had only his fists with which to speak.

"Enough," a soft voice said, floating toward him from somewhere in the darkness. "You have hurt yourself enough."

He stood quickly, and spun to plant his back against the door. "Who's there?"

There was shuffling in the darkness. "Someone like you."

It sounded like a girl. A scoff curled in his throat and he said, "I doubt that."

"We're locked in the same cart, aren't we? That's one thing in common. And I can promise there's at least one more thing that makes us alike. Neither of us are ever going back to the lives we had before."

The boy absorbed that knowledge. It was a reasonable conclusion, especially given the soldiers and his mother's reaction. He thought he ought to be more sad to have lost his whole life. But he had always thought it was a rather abysmal life anyway. His mother rarely let him leave their small one-room home. There were no other boys or girls around to play. His father used to visit on occasion when Cruze was younger, but he had stopped coming several years ago. And if not even his mother had cared to keep him, why should he care to stay?

"Maybe we'll have better lives," he insisted.

The darkness stilled around him, and the girl did not reply. After a while, he realized that was her answer. His fists had begun to throb, so he slumped down on the floor and cradled them carefully in his lap. Gradually, the gentle sway of the wagon lowered his defenses, and sleep helped him forget the pain.

He was shocked awake sometime later when the doors were opened and another boy, this one even younger than he, was tossed inside. The boy cried for his father all the while, his eyes red, and his nose running freely, pathetically. "Papa, papa, papa," the boy wailed—his cries a chorus that swelled inside the small wagon, no matter how small the boy's voice grew. Cruze wondered if he had looked that pitiful. In the brief wash of sunlight before the doors crashed closed again, he saw the girl—she was a year or two older than him with dark, unwashed hair, haunted eyes, and a horrible purple-red mark around her throat that made the wounds on his fists look like child's play. Their eyes met, and he knew for certain that wherever he was being taken, it was not somewhere better.

By the time they reached their destination, there were eleven other children crammed into the wagon. He and the girl ended up side by side. The stench of dirt and sweat collected around them and the trip seemed to go on forever and ever.

After a while, the girl leaned over and whispered, "What got you here?"

His brows furrowed and his lips pursed. "How should I know?"

"You don't have to pretend. Everybody here is like us. It's why we were all taken."

"Like us?" Cruze asked.

She shifted in the dark, and he was not sure how, but he knew she was tracing that line on her throat. He wanted to ask how it had happened, but he could not push the words off his tongue.

"We're all . . . different," the girl whispered into the slim space between them.

Cruze thought that over for a moment. He had never been normal, that much was certain. But he'd always assumed that had far more to do with his bloodlines than anything else.

"Who are your parents?" he asked the girl.

"It does not matter."

Then what did matter? Why had they all been taken?

He did not get an answer. Not when the wagon finally stopped what felt like hours later. Not when the children were dumped out into wild, jungle terrain and held back at sword-point when they tried to move. Two soldiers kept them controlled by fear, while two others barred the doors of the now empty wagon. Within a few breaths, the soldiers had loaded into the wagon and given the horses a hard whip that set them off at a gallop.

Some of the children ran after them, wailing and weeping, falling quickly behind, and losing them completely when the wagon turned around the first bend. But Cruze stayed behind, surveying their surroundings. They were near a river; the soldiers had done them that courtesy at least. But there was little in the way of shelter or protection. The leaves and vines were so thick on the trees overhead that they blocked out most of the sky, making it difficult to determine where the sun hung overhead, or if it did at all. They had to be far, far away from the city. Not even the great looming castle that sat atop the gloomy ocean-battered cliffs could be seen from wherever the soldiers had left them.

He set about exploring, mostly so none of the others would see the way his eyes turned red, and his lip shook with every breath in and out.

"This is better," Cruze told himself. He would make a better life for himself. He could. He might have lost his mother and his father and what little home he had. But he had his wits, his strength, and he had the goddess. His father, before he had stopped visiting, had always told Cruze he was goddess-blessed.

And the goddess would protect him now. He believed it.

He had to.

Because as he climbed up a tree in order to kick down a few coconuts for the group to share, he realized it was not the canopy that blocked out the sun overhead. It was a storm. Dark clouds unfurled like the wings of some beast of the night, and he heard it roar on the wind. Cruze did not know how, but when he looked on that tempest something in it seemed to look back at him. Icy awareness trailed up his spine and then he heard a voice—not in his mind, nor in his heart, but everywhere in him and nowhere all at once.

"Destroy," it whispered. "Death. Decay." Again and again, the words took up residence inside him. "Destroy. Death. Decay. This is the will of the goddess."

"Did you say something?" a voice called out below, jerking his attention away from the clouds.

The girl hovered below him, her arms full of the coconuts he had already freed, clearly waiting for more.

"What?" he asked.

"Did you say something about the goddess?"

Cruze's mouth went dry, and he refused to raise his eyes again to the storm overhead. Instead, he slid carelessly down the tree, earning what would prove to be several monstrous bruises later, no doubt.

When his feet met solid earth, he looked at the girl and said, "There's a storm coming. We need to find shelter, or we die."

From that point on, the seasons changed. The bounds of winter could not be controlled, nor could the hope of spring always break through. There was merely the time when the storms slumbered, and the time when they raged.

—*The Time of Tempests*

1

Sweat gathered along the back of Aurora's neck as she followed her fellow storm hunters through the swaths of people to the growing settlement that edged the city of Pavan. The air hung heavy with impending rain, but that was not what made Aurora struggle to pull in a breath.

It was the souls.

They assailed her from every direction—they pulled at her from the earth, laying invisible tangles for her feet, and pressed at her from the air, prickling over her skin. Overlapping whispers clashed with louder bellows and pleas to form a cacophony that ground nearly all her thoughts to a stop. It was difficult to discern the difference between the crowd of living people around her and the swarm of spirits that came with them, but she knew it was not normal for this many unsettled souls to gather in one place.

Either a great many people had died here in recent weeks, or these souls had followed their surviving loved ones here after they fled their destroyed homes as remnants. Perhaps it was a combination of the two.

The remnant camp clung to the exterior walls of the city of Pavan like a wounded arm bandaged close to the body. This place *felt* wounded too. It was in the air, in the earth, in the creeping puddles of water that made mud of the places where people had done their best to create homes from whatever they could salvage. Aurora felt the spirits of the dead most clearly, but in the last few weeks her ability to sense living souls had grown as well. The desolation here had a taste, a bitterness that she did not even have to search for. It was there every time she opened her mouth to breathe.

People had made tents and lean-tos from whatever materials they could scavenge. Ripped and patched blankets passed for roofs in places, while mismatched pieces of wood, tied together with string or torn fabric, were the nearest thing to walls. Most hadn't bothered with walls, opting instead to focus on sheltering themselves from the sky as much as possible, but Aurora knew with certainty that none of these structures would hold up in a storm. In fact, she had the feeling that this little community had been rebuilt on its own bones more than a few times. There was more despair in this place than any one patch of land should ever lay claim to; that it was in a place she used to call home shredded something inside her.

"Roar?"

She pulled her gaze away from the remnants, and found the deep brown eyes of the man who had followed her across the wildlands without a word of complaint, no matter that she had yet to tell him why. She had yet to tell him so many things, and her heart clenched at the uncertainty of what would happen when she did. Would he still be willing to follow her anywhere when he knew how many lies she had told?

Kiran, the man she had first known as Locke, stopped where he had been walking ahead of her, backtracking until he stood in front of her. "You do not look well," he said.

She did not feel it either, but he was tense enough already; the last thing she needed was to trigger one of his overprotective fits. "Such flattery. Stop before I swoon."

Kiran's dark eyebrows flattened into fierce lines, but the straight press of his lips twitched up on one side, cracking the otherwise gruff mask he wore. He stood firm for a few moments more, then he dropped his folded arms, his shoulders softening into an arch as he bent down to graze his lips across her temple before dropping lower, to her ear. He whispered, "Do you want me to flatter you, princess?" The question was a low rumble that sent shivers across her skin.

Skies, his obsession with that nickname would be the death of her. It produced the most bizarre mix of nostalgia for their time together in the wildlands and festering guilt for the truth she had yet to tell him—that she truly was a princess, or at least she had been, before she had left Pavan at the mercy of its enemies. Now she was not sure what she was. Did it matter that she was a princess if her kingdom had fallen to another?

He stepped to her side, offering his elbow, and Aurora took it gratefully. She tried not to lean too much on him as they walked, reluctant to give away her discomfort, but she was nonetheless relieved to have him strong and steady by her side. "A man does have a lot of time to think while traveling for days on end," he continued, his voice a low murmur. "So if you did want some flattery, I have had ample preparation time to think about all my favorite aspects of your character."

"My character?" Aurora asked.

"Among other things." He shot her the most mischievous grin. Her cheeks flushed with heat, and she tried to laugh it off, but at that moment they approached a particularly populated area of the camp, and the crush of souls made the air close off in her throat.

She clutched Kiran's forearm, her nails digging in harder than she intended. Immediately, he jerked to a stop, pulling her to fully face him. "I knew something was wrong," he hissed. "What is it?"

Aurora took a few hard blinks, trying to focus, and scraped in a raspy breath, followed by another. She did not know how to explain to him the way it felt to be this surrounded, this *inundated*. She imagined it to be like swimming deep into the ocean, the heavy pressure of the water pushing at her lungs and her ears harder and harder until they felt as if they might burst. No, no, that was not quite right. It was more like sensory overload, as if her sense of hearing had increased, and now everything was too loud, too close. Only what she sensed was so much more complex than sound, or sight, or smell.

She felt . . . yearning and regret and wave upon wave of hopelessness. She saw fragments of memories and lives and loves. Spirits, new ones especially, had a tendency to dwell on their passing, so again and again and again she plunged into the misery of their deaths, dragged unwillingly along for the ride. Even when she managed to put up a block, there was such painful energy here that it made her feel raw and worn out. Which left her with too little strength to block the other souls she could feel—the ones that were not grieving or coping or following loved ones—the ones that had long ago let go of their human lives and become something else entirely. Mangled by fury and knotted up in lust for power and revenge, these souls were not as close by, but it did not matter. Their presence loomed so large and dark and *magnetic*—she knew if she dared to use her power to call a storm now, it would be one of those souls that would answer. She was not sure she would be able to stop them.

"Roar. Answer me, or I am going to make a scene."

No. They absolutely *could not* draw attention to themselves. She had noted on their arrival the blue Locke flags that now flew atop Pavan's city walls. But it was not only flags that enforced the change in rule; Locke soldiers stood on guard at the gates and occasionally made sweeps through the camp. She had yet to recognize anyone she knew, but that did not mean they would not recognize her if they saw her.

"I am fine. Only . . ." She cleared her throat, knowing she had to give him something or he would never give up. "You remember Avira?" she asked, referencing the spirit witch he had sought out when Aurora had taken the heart of a skyfire storm in the Sangsorra desert and fallen unconscious for days. That night in the desert, she had manifested the incredibly rare ability to take the heart of a storm not by the traditional means of defeating the storm to capture the relic Stormheart it leaves behind, but by literally taking the storm into herself. Kiran did not talk about it much, but she knew that night had been traumatizing for him, not to mention her remaining unconscious for days with a mimicry of a lightning storm where her heart should be. It was a wonder he had not run for the hills before now.

"Of course I remember her. She gave me back my name." He squeezed her arm gently and grimaced. "And I will never forget the way she was always looking around, as if she was having ten different conversations I could not hear. It was unsettling."

Aurora fought not to wince, and in her fatigue just ended up giving a long, slow blink.

"Roar?"

She forced heavy-lidded eyes open, suddenly exhausted. "Hmm?"

"What about Avira?"

"Let's say she would have a lot to work with here."

His eyes left her to scan the camp around her, softening then widening in understanding. "That is why you are so pale? Because you can *hear* them?"

She thought about arguing that she was always pale, but decided it was not worth the breath. "Something like that," she said. "Hear. Feel. Taste. See. It depends on what they are putting off. But yes, they are *everywhere.*"

"This is the nearest you have been to a city since your waking. Is it that?"

She huddled closer to his side, trying to keep their conversation as private as possible. "That might have something to do with it.

But it's also the remnants." She worded her next sentence carefully, hoping he understood. "They have all experienced so much loss. And much of it has followed them here."

Their eyes met, and he looked at her with a knowing grief that made her want to collapse into his arms right there in the middle of everyone. Instead, she let herself lean on him as she took another step forward.

"We can set up camp farther away," Kiran suggested. "It will give you some space. And the Rock is too conspicuous anyway." The hulking metal contraption that passed for a traveling carriage *was* quite unusual.

"But we need to get information, make connections, learn about the guard situation—"

He cut her off. "And we will do that. We can all make trips into the camp for reconnaissance and communication. Yet another reason to set up camp elsewhere—Jinx can grow us food and herbs to trade, and that will be our best way to form relationships in this camp."

Some part of her felt like she should argue because that was their way. Even when they agreed on things, they still argued, examining every aspect of a situation until it had been exhausted. But she was the exhausted one now, and his plan truly did seem reasonable. He was not insisting on the location only for her sake.

She did not want him coddling her. She could not afford that. If the presence of souls was just as numerous inside the city, she would *have* to learn how to deal with the effects quickly, because she could not wait any longer than absolutely needed to get inside the city and find the answers she required. Something had happened to her mother. There was no other explanation for how the Locke flags could be flying. Queen Aphra was a proud and powerful ruler above all else, and she would not part easily with her crown. Not unless . . . Aurora had to stop thinking about the possibilities or she was going to be ill, right there next to someone's home.

She could not let herself waver now. She imagined it not unlike the preparation one took to battle a storm. The other hunters had taught her tricks and put her through training and endurance exercises, but in the end, they said it always came down to which heart was stronger—yours or the storm's. She had to face this the same way. She did not know what waited for her back in the city of her birth; she only knew it was not for the faint of heart.

"Let's go find a spot to set up our camp then," Aurora said. The sooner they got settled, the sooner they could get to work, and she could do what had to be done.

Cassius's mood was as black as the clouds that seemed to ring the city in perpetuity. It did not matter when he dispelled one storm because there were always more waiting just on the horizon. But he had learned from the last time his city had been under siege; he was not so arrogant to make the same mistakes again. This time, he would be ready.

It was not enough to simply fend off the Stormlord's attacks. He was too powerful. The Stormlings here were used to a fierce Rage season with near daily storms, but they had never known what it was like to be beset by multiple storms at once, from different directions that did not play by the rules of nature.

When Locke had fallen, it had been to hurricanes and firestorms and skyfire and snowstorms—bodies had lain frostbitten and burned side by side. He had been trying to prepare the men here for what they would soon face, but none of them truly understood.

Not yet.

But he would make them. If he had to burn or freeze or drown them himself to make them understand the danger that was coming, he would.

When he was halfway down the hall to his room, he began tearing at the buttons to his coat, eager to have the thick garment off his sweaty body. He had come from a training session with the kingdom's most talented Stormling soldiers—a mix of Pavanian men and women and a few of his own surviving men. Perhaps, if he had not lost so many of his own soldiers in the wildlands as they searched for Princess Aurora, he would feel better about their chances. But as things stood, they had a long way to go before the soldiers he was training could prevent the kind of destruction that had taken his homeland.

Scowling, he ripped off his coat, and pushed open the door to his office. He threw the heavy piece of clothing on top of a nearby chair, and attacked the buttons of his shirt next, not bothering to undo them neatly, but pulling the shirt open with one harsh yank.

Then he stilled, noticing too late that his rooms were not empty. He stiffened, ready to reach for one of his knives, before a second person emerged from the bedroom, a silk scarf wound about his fists. Cassius relaxed, but only slightly, then stalked across the room to tear the pretty piece of silk from the hands of his brother.

"What do you think you are *doing*?" he snarled.

His younger brother gave a cavalier smirk, but loosened his hold so the purple fabric came free easily. Casimir said, "Just trying to figure out why you still live in this place, rather than taking rooms of your own like the rest of us have."

"I like these rooms." Cassius said, his tone clipped. He started to fold the scarf, but the scrape of a chair behind him reminded him that there was a third person in the room. Not wanting to give away more than he already had, he wadded the silk up and tossed it aside in the same manner he had his coat.

"You could at least change things up," his brother added. "Bleeding skies, the wardrobe is still filled with dresses."

He ground his teeth together and swallowed the answer he wanted to give—that Aurora would be back, he would find her, no matter how long it took. Instead, he sneered, "I have been too busy to redecorate. Impending doom, and what not."

Casimir crossed in front of him and threw himself lazily onto the settee in the middle of the room, kicking dirty boots up on one end without a care. "You are not the only one working around here, brother. I ferreted out a rebellion rat just this morning. He was caught stealing supplies, and I cut off his hands to set an example. His head too, of course. But the hands first, so he could watch. Made quite a pretty display out by that gaudy palace gate. It really livened up the place, I think."

Ignoring his brother's sadistic boasts, Cassius let his eyes drift to the far side of the room where his father sat coolly at Cassius's desk, his fingers steepled and the slightest smile tugging at the corner of his mouth.

"And you?" Cassius asked. "What have you been doing?"

"Overseeing things, as a king does. Casimir has made quite the impression in his assignments so far. How goes your training?"

Cassius's stomach turned sour. This was always how things went with his father. He saw everything as an opportunity to manipulate, and he would pit the brothers against each other again and again until one or the other was dead most likely.

"Badly. They are ill-prepared for the strength the Stormlord will bring."

His father sat up straighter. "Then *make* them prepared."

"Don't you think I am trying?" He scowled. "I don't want to be here when another kingdom falls. But I cannot do it alone, and there simply is not enough skill among the Stormlings that remain to survive a siege for long."

"Then figure out something else," his father snarled.

"It's not too late to leave," Cassius suggested. "If the Stormlord followed us here as you believe, maybe it would be better if we disappeared for a while."

The king rose abruptly, knocking the chair back against the

bookshelf. "That bastard will not make me leave. I am a Stormling. I am a king. I will not flee because some aberration with a measure of magic thinks he will change the way of things."

"Technically, you already did flee once."

Cassius should not enjoy the sour grimace that crossed his father's face, but he did. The man was an arrogant fool, and father or not, Cassius had no plans to die for him.

"We simply have to do things differently this time," the king said, wandering from the desk to graze his fingertips over the spines of the books that sat on Aurora's bookshelves. Cassius fought the urge to snap at his father for touching one of the few things remaining that gave him some sense of connection to his almost-bride. He did not like either his father or his brother being in these rooms. It made his skin itch deep beneath the surface, where he could not reach to scratch.

Eager for them to leave, he said, "That is my intention, if I can find Stormlings strong enough to back me up. I do not want to simply wait and prepare for the Stormlord's eventual siege. I want to take the fight to him. He might bring with him a multitude of storms, but he is still only one man. If I can fight him face-to-face, I know I will win."

Finished with the conversation, Cassius removed the shirt he had undone upon his entry, and used it to wipe the sweat from his face and chest.

"Now if the two of you are done invading my privacy," he said, "I would like to bathe and rest before the next storm comes. Unless, that is, one of you would like to take a shift?"

Casimir was the first to head for the door. "Sorry. I have things to do. The remnant population outside the city has grown out of control. And I still have some leads on the rebellion to run down." Casimir looked around the room one more time and added, "You really should consider letting go of this obsession with the Pavan girl, brother. You are better off without her."

Then he was gone, the door left ajar with Cassius shirtless and annoyed, facing off against his father. Rather than wait for his father's next prod, Cassius chose one of his own. "How is Mother?"

The king shrugged. "Well, I suppose."

"You suppose?"

The two had never been a love match, but they had shared an interest in power, and that had been enough to sustain their marriage all these years. But since their arrival in Pavan, Cassius's mother had become withdrawn and disinterested in even the manipulative games her husband played with their sons and their new subjects.

"If you are so concerned, go find out for yourself." With those words, his father left, closing the door to his rooms behind him as he went.

Cassius stood there for a long moment, thinking of his mother. He did not love her, not the way he knew children were supposed to love their mothers. But he wondered if she thought too much of home, the way he sometimes did. He had never been an affectionate or loving child. He never would have expected to feel homesick. But he missed the sea, the smell of salt on the air, the way you could hear the waves long before you could see them. His home had been alternatingly cold and brutal and dangerous, but sometimes . . . sometimes it had been beautiful and warm and soft. And Cassius missed it all—the brutal and the beautiful.

It was a place where he fit, and he supposed that was what made it home.

The soul is accustomed to being one half of a whole. Without an earthly body to cling to, it will seek out something else to fill that void. Some find peace in the wind, others lose themselves in the rush of the river, and still others find solace in the darkest of companions—storms.

—from the personal journal of spirit witch Avira Croixell

2

Kiran was used to being the first one up in the morning. It was part of his routine. He liked having that slightly different perspective on the world from everyone else. He learned a lot about people by seeing them first thing. And lately, with Roar sleeping in his tent, he had particularly enjoyed those soft moments of early-morning quiet, when everything was dark and calm, and he could watch the flicker of the skyfire storm upon her chest rage with silent beauty.

But this morning, she was not in the tent when he woke up. He felt a pang of longing that scared him more than any dark sky ever had. She was coming to mean so much to him, eclipsing anything and everything that had come before her. He had no feeling to compare this to, other than the simultaneous thrill he felt while hunting storms, and the unforgiving pain that sometimes came along with his choice of profession.

He dressed quickly and climbed out of the tent, finding Roar tending to a small fire near the Rock in the wooded area they had chosen as their camp. They had left a decent distance between themselves and the city, so their fire would not attract wanderers, and they had waded into the forest some to avoid the constant trickle of remnants that were still arriving via the road. Their horses were tied up nearby, grazing lazily in the early-morning light.

He sat down near Roar and asked, "How long have you been up?"

She shrugged. "Not long."

From the way she had tossed and turned last night, and the smudges beneath her eyes, he feared she had slept hardly at all.

"Any better today?" he asked. They'd had a long conversation the night before about her experience in the remnant camp.

She took a drink of water, and then shrugged again. "Maybe. Maybe not. I suppose we will see when I go back to the camp today."

His stomach tightened uncomfortably, and it took all his restraint not to demand she go back into the tent and rest more before trying any such thing. He knew Roar, and he knew where that would get him—exactly nowhere. But it was not long ago that she was lying limp and unconscious on a cot, with him unsure whether she would ever wake. His protective instincts told him to take her somewhere remote and far away where it would just be the two of them, and no one could harm her. Perhaps it was more than just his protective instincts that wanted the two of them alone together. But anything would be better than where he had brought her— back to the very place from which she had run, a place that was clearly in the midst of tremendous turmoil that they needed no part in, not to mention that the royal family he despised had seemingly escaped the destruction of Locke to set up here. In fact, if Roar's information was correct, then the *entire* Locke family had been in Pavan before she had left for the wildlands with them.

Kiran did not know whether whatever gossip she had heard could be trusted, but she seemed certain. If she did indeed turn out to be right, that would mean that the cruel, corrupt king who had ordered the hanging of his sister when she was a mere child had again escaped any form of justice to live rich and free as the oppressor once more. It was not as though Kiran were *rooting* for the Stormlord. Skies, the madman had leveled an entire city, taking who knew how many innocent lives. And if the stories they had heard so far from the remnants were true, he had been destroying smaller villages in the wildlands as well, pushing nearer and nearer to Pavan. But if the universe were fair at all, the Locke family would have gone down with the city they ruled. That was a sentiment he could feel no guilt over.

"We should split into pairs or small groups," Kiran told Roar. "At least until we get the lay of the camp, and get to know any risks and vulnerabilities."

He was learning to choose his battles with her. For whatever reason, she was determined to return to her home. He could not talk her out of it, so the best he could do was be there with her. Hopefully with the crew's help, she could do what she needed to do, and get out of here as fast as possible.

"Sounds fine." She took another sip of water, her thoughts clearly elsewhere, so he let her be. Instead, he started packing up a few things he thought they might trade today to begin making inroads with the remnant community.

A while later, the sun was firmly piercing through the trees, and the rest of the crew had crawled from their beds to begin the day. Kiran had packed three separate bags with extra supplies and equipment and the fruits and vegetables born from Jinx's earth magic the night before. They could split into pairs, and each take a bag and use it to learn what they could.

He offered Jinx the first bag, since as the resident earth witch she was responsible for creating a good portion of its contents. He would have offered the next to Ransom, but his burly friend had already stepped up beside Jinx, towering over her short frame. The witch rolled her eyes, but did not complain, so he turned to the rest of the crew.

"Someone should stay with the Rock," he said, wishing it could be Roar, but knowing she would never go for it. "Duke, you all right with holding down the camp?" The old man deserved a lie-in after the frantic pace they had set to cross the wildlands.

But Duke stood, his posture firmer than Kiran had seen it in years. "No, I will be going. I have been coming to this city longer than any of you have been alive. There's a better chance I might recognize someone who can help us."

Kiran blinked, but did not argue. He had in many ways taken over leading the team in recent years because Duke did not go out into the storms as much as he used to, but the man would always be in charge. Whatever he said went.

"Okay. Then it'll have to be you, Bait."

Immediately, the lanky, ginger-haired teen was on his feet. "Oh come on, I'm not the novie anymore."

Ransom snorted from his position behind Jinx. "You'll always be the novie. *Novie.*"

"That is *it*," Bait declared. "Next time you fall asleep, that beard is mine." He mimed snipping motions with his fingers at the hunter, who was wider than two of him put together.

Kiran sighed, both annoyed and relieved that at least some things could be depended on to stay the same. "Roar might be our newest member, but it makes no sense for Roar to stay since she's the reason we're here. Now, you can whine to Sly and see if she will swap with you, but somehow I doubt your tears will move her."

Speaking of Sly, he looked around for the quietest member of their group and found her at the edge of the trees, one of the bags of trade goods already in her arms. He looked down to where he had set the third bag at his feet. Sure enough, it was gone, and he had never noticed a thing.

"Well?" the dark-skinned, stealthy hunter asked. "Are we ready?"

"Almost. Be careful out there. We do not know exactly what we are walking into. Do not go off alone. If someone feels off, get out of there. We can always go back to certain people or areas with larger numbers. Be careful with your questions. Do not push too hard too fast or we might draw the wrong kind of attention. Just glean what you can without being too obvious. When you are done, come back here, but make certain you are not followed."

Jinx slapped him on the shoulder and said, "Good speech, *Kiran.*" His new name, or old name, rather, had been an adjustment, but Roar and Jinx had pretty much drilled the rest of the crew into using it. Jinx handed her bag off to Ransom, gave Kiran a silly salute, and set off through the trees.

He watched his friends disperse, and Bait gave him a wave, no doubt grumbling beneath his breath as he climbed inside the Rock. Finally, Kiran let himself turn to look at Roar. She had been silent through the entire conversation, but that did not mean he could not feel her, her presence as charged and powerful as the storm she held inside her.

"You ready?"

She did not look ready. She looked . . . pale. But again, he bit his tongue, knowing what she would say if he commented. She would make some joke to put him at ease, or find something to poke at him with to shift the conversation. And he knew that kind of pretending took energy he did not want her to waste. So he simply offered her his hand. She stood, taking it, and he grasped the bag of goods with his other hand.

Their walk to the remnant camp was slow, in part because they had chosen their own spot a significant distance away, but also because Roar did not seem to be in a hurry. He watched her take deep breaths, and knew she was working hard mentally to set up barriers as they had discussed the night before. Duke and Jinx and Sly had all weighed in with advice, and Roar seemed confident that she could do a better job today of shutting out what she felt from the souls around them.

He could not imagine what she was dealing with right now. The thing he despised most about storm hunting was the possibility that his mind might be manipulated by a storm's magic. That loss of control terrified him. But it was very, very rare that he faced a storm strong enough to catch him off guard. Roar, by contrast, was under siege constantly. The threat of that kind of invasion into one's vulnerabilities would be exhausting one time, let alone in endless stampedes.

Gods, she was strong. It was no wonder he loved her. He had never stood any chance.

When the city came into view, and the camp along with it, he finally broke their silence. "Before we get there, is there anything in particular you want to ask about?" He cleared his throat and added, *"Anyone?"*

She paused, her steps faltering. "What do you mean?"

He sighed. "There has to be some reason we are back here, Roar. I am trying not to pressure you. But you have to know how dangerous a situation we have walked into. I assume there is someone inside the city who you worry is caught up in this danger. Am I right?"

Roar's teeth bit into her bottom lip, worrying it back and forth. Finally, she said, "It is complicated. But yes, yes that is part of it. My mother is inside."

Kiran's jaw went slack, and he gaped at her. "Your mother?" He had always assumed she was orphaned in some way, like the rest of the crew. He did not know why. She had never said anything outright about her parents. But he had gotten the impression that she had been in quite dire straits before she ran away, essentially on her own.

Roar nodded, and his thoughts finally managed to catch up to the situation. He released her hand to cup the back of her neck and pull her in to the side of his chest. "Oh, princess. You should have said. We will get you to your mother."

Her face crumpled into a painful expression, and he did not know what to do except hold her tighter. So he did. And after too short a time, he pulled away and said, "Let's go make some new friends."

If Aurora thought it had been difficult to concentrate before, it was nothing compared to how she felt now with the aching pit of guilt roiling in her belly. She had not technically lied. She *was* desperate to get inside the city and find out what happened to her mother, hopefully find the woman herself, if she was still alive. But it did not feel like any less of a deceit when Kiran had taken her in his arms, looking sorry to have pushed her on the subject.

She was a terrible human. A terrible, awful, selfish human. All of this—it was her fault. She looked at the remnants around her, wondering how things might have been different if she had stayed. Would these poor people be out here, vulnerable and afraid, if it were not Locke flags flying atop the castle walls?

The terrible truth was . . . she did not know.

Oh, she hoped things would have been different. That her mother, that *she* would never have let it get this far. But then Aurora remembered the multitude of reasons why she left in the first place—including all those papers she found on her mother's desk, fines and expulsions over minor infractions, the piles and piles of denied applications for citizenship. It all seemed so very cold and cruel, and nothing like what she had naively thought her kingdom to be.

But she had a chance to make a difference now, even if it was only in a small way.

Aurora broke away from Kiran to approach a group of women who were watching a few small children play in the dirt. The little ones were resourceful; they had made toys from branches and rocks, knotting them together with twine to create figurines, and they were using them to fight, creating the sounds of what sounded like thunder and wind with their chapped mouths.

Aurora stepped closer to the women and raised a hand in greeting. "Hello. May I sit with you?"

The women looked at her, silent for a long moment, but eventually one of them nodded, and Aurora took a spot on a medium-sized rock that seemed to have been hauled to this spot for just such a purpose.

"We only just arrived," Aurora told them. At this, their eyes left her to gaze above her head, to where she guessed Kiran had taken up sentry. "We came very far. We have not heard much news of what has happened here. Have you all been here long?"

Aurora was unsure if she was going to get an answer, but then one of the children distracted her with an incredibly dramatic roar. He threw himself back in the dirt with his toy, flailing and yelling in as deep a tone as he could manage. The girl across from him held her hands up high in victory, declaring, "I have defeated the Stormlord!"

One of the other women jumped up quickly, taking the little girl by the arm and shushing her firmly. The atmosphere grew tense, as though the mere mention of his name might bring a tempest down upon them.

The children, however, were oblivious. As soon as the woman returned to her seat, they carried on playing, though this time in quieter tones. One or two would pretend to be storms while the others fought them off with the help of their homemade toys.

Aurora smiled, knowing exactly how it felt to play such a game. When she was little, her older brother used to pretend to be a twister, spinning around her ominously, sometimes even catching her up in his arms and whirling her around as fast as he could. Eventually though, he would always let her win.

An old, familiar ache opened up at the thought of her brother, stinging at the fresh exposure. She missed him, would always miss him, but after all this time, there were so few memories she could remember clearly.

"Weeks," a velvety-smooth voice said beside her, and they had sat so long in silence that it took Aurora a moment to realize the woman was answering her question. "We have been here near three weeks."

Aurora swallowed hard. Three weeks? And nothing had been done to help them? No one had provided them with shelter or let them inside the city? Did that mean the Lockes had been in control for at least that long? Or was she right in her earlier fears? Could her mother have still been in control when this started?

"Weeks. Wow. You must know quite a lot then."

The woman shrugged. "Nothing to know. With the storms how they are, the best we can do is be as close to the Stormlings as possible."

Aurora nodded. "Right. It's awful how many villages have been destroyed. Did you live nearby?"

"In the lower plains," she answered. "Between Odilar and Pavan." That made sense. From what they had heard, the Stormlord seemed to have laid a path of destruction from Locke up toward Pavan, lingering especially in those areas where Locke soldiers were patrolling. Of course, it was her those soldiers had been searching for—yet another stone of blame that weighed upon her chest.

"Had you been to Pavan before?" Aurora asked. "I heard rumors about a power change or something along those lines. Something to do with the Stormlings. Do you know anything about that?"

The woman stiffened a little and looked around, but after a moment, she seemed satisfied enough to say, "That was before our arrival, but yes, it is true. The Lockes are the Stormlings in these parts now."

Aurora's heartbeat was a riot in her chest, as though it only now realized how very close she was to the life, and the man, she had run from not long ago. An image of Cassius Locke rose in her mind—dark and menacing and unforgiving. Her mental barriers faltered, and she felt the press of thousands of other souls against her own, abrasive and clingy all at the same time.

It was not new information, that the Lockes had taken over Pavan, but the way the woman said it, with such matter-of-factness, as though the two families were simply interchangeable, gutted Aurora. She fought down the urge to push for as many details as possible, and instead took a moment to look to Kiran and the bag he carried.

"We brought some goods to share." She looked back to the group of women. "Some fruits and vegetables."

Finally, one of the other women spoke up, the one who had shushed the little girl before. "What is the catch? What do you want for it?" Her hair was blond, though not the bright, skyfire-white of Aurora's hair, more the golden color of straw. Aurora self-consciously touched the scarf that wrapped her own head, making certain her hair was still hidden, even though she had been extremely careful this morning to tuck it all tightly away.

"No catch, other than company. As I said, we have traveled far." Aurora could tell the woman still did not believe her, so she reached back, plucking a clump of fresh berries still on a vine. "I promise. I think the children will like these." She held the berries out in offering. But when the women still hesitated, she plucked off a berry for herself, popping it in her mouth and letting the flavor burst between her teeth.

Then the first woman, the only one who had spoken openly with her, reached out and took the offered berries. She gave a sharp whistle, and the heads of multiple children popped up from where they were at play. They all came running over when she held up the berries, shrill peals of excitement carrying along in their wake.

"What is your name?" Aurora asked the woman.

"Nazara," she said, plucking berries off the vine to hand out to the children. "And you?"

Aurora hesitated, no longer sure which name to give, but stuck with, "You can call me Roar."

It wasn't until the berries had all been divvied up that she realized that hidden amongst the small group of children was the lingering spirit of a child the same age. She froze, waiting to see what the spirit would do, but it did not seem to be concerned with her. Instead, it watched the other children eating berries with a sad, simple longing that made tears prick at her eyes.

Needing a distraction, she turned back to Kiran, gesturing for him to hand over the bag. His mouth pressed into a reluctant line, but he gave it to her. "This is Kiran, my . . ." She trailed off, completely at a loss for what to label him. *Friend* seemed far too trivial, partner did not reach deep enough for what she felt, but every other word that came to mind felt too personal.

"Husband," Kiran supplied, settling on the ground beside her and nodding to the women.

Aurora could feel her cheeks heat and dared not look at him, simply smiling at the women as though he had not just shocked her to her very core.

He had probably chosen the word because it was the least suspect explanation for why the two of them would be traveling together. Better that than play her brother. But still, the word crept beneath her skin and made her shiver. Did he want that? Part of her *wanted* him to want that. But it only made her feel more guilty for all the secrets she was keeping.

They stayed with the women for the next hour, cooking vegetables over a small fire. They shared a small meal as they spoke. Kiran took over the questioning for a while, his protective side coming through as he asked about the guards—how many there were, how often they patrolled, if any of them were dangerous.

The women were reluctant to speak about the last, but did offer Roar one piece of advice. "Do not be caught anywhere alone with one of them."

They did not have to give specifics for her to understand what kind of danger that implied; she could guess.

Nazara added, "And if the prince visits, it is best to be wary."

Aurora's mouth went uncomfortably dry. "The prince?"

"He wants us to leave," one of the other women volunteered. "He will arrest you or worse if you give him reason."

The guilt inside Aurora began to boil into anger. Bloody skies, the world should not be this way. *Her home* should not be this way. It was not fair. If she did not already despise Cassius Locke, this would be more than enough. These women, these children, they deserved so much better. They deserved compassion at the very least, dignity and respect. They deserved—

Her walls shattered in one terrifying crash, and she was bombarded with hundreds upon hundreds of different sensations at once—none of them her own. She gasped for breath, struggling to stay afloat in the deluge. She tried to focus on one thing, picking the spirit of the little boy who was right in front of her now. He was sad but curious; she saw in his thoughts that he had been hovering among the other children while they played, hoping that somehow he might feel some of what they felt. It hadn't worked. He had not felt joy in so long.

She wanted to give him that; she tried, but there was another presence smothering her—sickly and dark, it latched on to her, and she felt the gruesome taint of its touch deep inside her.

Destroy, it whispered, slithering deeper inside her.

That was all the warning she got before the enchanted crystal she wore beneath her clothes burned blazing hot, and the sky cracked open with light overhead. Aurora did not know where the skyfire hit, only that it was nearby. The smell of char was sharp and sudden in the air, and the hair on the back of her neck rose in warning prickles.

The dark soul pressed on her again, and before she could draw up the strength to re-form her walls, the world was thrown into chaos. People were running, *sprinting*, not caring what or whom they knocked over in the process. Kiran had ahold of her and was pulling her along, but she could hear children screaming, adults too. She tried to find Nazara and the others, but she was swept up in the tide of bodies now, all of them hurling themselves toward the city walls as more screams and cracks of thunder battled for supremacy.

Smoke made the air hazy, and Aurora held onto Kiran as hard as she could as they were lost to the mercy of the crowd. Eventually, the people reached the walls and there was nowhere left to go, but they continued to push and climb on each other, each vying to get as close to the city as possible.

She craned her head back to peer over her shoulder, and saw multiple streaks of skyfire strike the ground. This time, there was a burst of fire, not just smoke. The screams around her were hoarse with desperation, and bodies repeatedly slammed into her own, crushing her tightly into the people in front of her, who had nowhere to go. Kiran was shouting something at her, but she could not hear him, not over the rush of noise inside and outside her head. She had never felt such an outpouring of emotion—panic and fear and hatred and hopelessness. She felt like she might explode from the swell of it all. And all the while, that tainted soul was creeping closer and closer to her own. She could feel it, entangling itself inside her, and she wanted to be sick. She would not be the first—the stench of fear and urine and vomit was all around them, and it only worsened as the skyfire strikes grew closer and closer to the people huddling like rats for survival.

Then, finally, something shifted in the air. The crushing pressure eased, and the dark spirit she had been struggling to push away felt a little farther removed. A strangely familiar swell of power filled the air. The next strike of skyfire hit an invisible barrier above them, and shattered like a glass star.

Around her the screams turned to sobs, and the press of bodies eased, giving her room to take a deeper breath. Immediately, she went back to work on her shields, knowing she would not survive long this open and vulnerable to contact with the multitude of souls. She was not sure how much time had passed when she opened her eyes, but Kiran was still with her, even though most of the crowd had dispersed. The sky above looked a pale, innocent blue, as if it hadn't just rained down such cruelty.

Together, she and Kiran made their way back through what was left of the remnant camp. They did not bother searching out the bag of supplies. It had likely been trampled or burned, and if not, whoever found it was welcome to it.

What Aurora needed now was . . .

Well, she needed *home*.

But home did not look or *feel* much like home anymore.

She had Kiran though, and that was close. She leaned heavily into his side as they walked, wanting to run away to their tent and hide from the world and forget everything that had happened. But she knew she would never forget those screams. Not for as long as she lived.

Nature is the cruelest of masters.

—The History of Stormlings

3

The next day they were back in the camp at dawn. There had been a long thunderstorm that lasted most of the night, and the camp looked even worse than when they had left it the day before. Flooded and burned and smashed, it was hard to see anything of the meager existence the remnants had created. The plan today was twofold. They would help as much as they could while continuing to gather information, and they planned to spend the day observing the guards, making notes, looking for patterns.

The group had gleaned a fair amount of information the day before, but none of it specific enough to help them do the impossible—break into the city. And that was what they would have to do. Duke had managed to find out that the previous guard that the crew used to bribe for entry into the city was dead. And none of them thought it worth the risk to approach any of the Locke soldiers.

So instead, they would watch and learn and wait for their opening.

They set about helping to restructure what had been demolished, but mostly they were just gathering debris, sorting through to find what was usable and what was not. Aurora had been working just long enough for a sheen of sweat to gather beneath the layers she wore to hide her identity and the distinctive skyfire storm that showed on her chest, making her uncomfortable despite the morning chill, when she began to sense that something abnormal was happening.

She, like everyone else, had been surreptitiously watching the soldiers that guarded the gate. She pondered where they had gone yesterday during the madness of the skyfire attack. Had they been caught up in the crush of bodies too? Or had they managed to slip inside the city walls somehow? If so, that might be an option they could look at for entry. A storm certainly provided a natural diversion.

At that thought, the large city gate began to open and a surprisingly large contingent of soldiers marched through. She waited, wondering if anyone here would be desperate enough to make a break for it while the gates were open, but when the soldiers kept coming, twenty at least, she knew it would be suicide for anyone to try.

She paused at the pile of debris she was sorting, watching as the men came to a halt in a block formation outside the gates. Then she saw the man who followed them and felt as if a crater opened up inside her. He too wore blue, but his dress was much more sophisticated than a standard soldier's uniform. His hair was near black, with natural curls, and she remembered that the last time she had seen him she had thought him charismatic. He looked far from that now, with his lip curled in distaste and his eyes narrowed dangerously. He was shorter, leaner than his brother, but that did not make him any less intimidating. Instead, he had the severe edge of a man looking to prove himself, and in his family, she did not want to know what that looked like.

Casimir Locke's eyes scanned over the camp, and she hurriedly looked away when his gaze neared her, feeling her heart pound frantically in her chest. She did not know exactly what would happen if the Lockes found her, but she had read enough novels of political intrigue to know they likely would not be keen to have anyone around who might challenge their rule. If they found her, she was probably looking at imprisonment at best, a myriad of different deaths at worst.

By the time she chanced a look back in Casimir's direction, he had moved, as had all the soldiers. For a moment, Aurora thought they were helping as they waded into the camp, picking up pieces of the wreckage, but then they started piling it up in an area where she now saw Casimir waited. She heard a commotion, and turned to see Nazara protesting as a soldier ripped down a tent that had been newly constructed. He shoved Nazara back, and she toppled onto a pile of debris. The soldier did not stop though, only gathering up his find and marching toward his leader like the rest. Soon the soldiers were swarming, taking all the pieces that were already set aside as salvageable.

Aurora did not fight when two men came toward her. She kept her head down and backed up, afraid one of them might recognize her, despite her efforts to disguise herself. They took her collection too, and while they did she felt a steady warmth at her back and a hand at her waist that she knew was Kiran.

Once the pile near Casimir had grown to the height of several men, the soldiers made their way back into their block formation, and the prince stepped forward. He gave the onlooking crowd of remnants an almost cheery smile before lighting a match and setting the materials on fire.

It was a testament to the strength and endurance of the people around her that not one of them made a sound. They did not cry or scream or give Casimir whatever other reaction he had hoped for. They only watched as the last of what they had burned.

Smoke made Aurora's eyes tear up, but she did not look away. She would not.

When the fire built to a large inferno, Casimir stepped in front of it, as though he had been waiting for it to reach its full height before using it as his backdrop.

"Whatever it is you were hoping for, you will not find it *here*. So go back to wherever you came from. You will not bring your scourge into my city."

Aurora jerked at his words. Kiran had told her how some reacted to remnants, that they called them a scourge and treated them like a disease that would somehow bring bad luck along with them. But to hear it spoken by someone who should have known better was disgusting. Casimir was a Stormling. He knew the workings of storms better than anyone here, and he knew that these people held no blame in what happened to them. Storms were indiscriminate in their destruction. Or rather, natural storms were. The ones the Stormlord brought were an entirely different matter because they answered to *him*, but *still* these people were clearly just cannon fodder in a larger war. A war that had seemingly started in Locke, and now had made its way here.

And that he had called Pavan *his*?

Seething, she turned around to face Kiran and found him staring at the Locke prince with a hardness in his eyes that she had never seen before. It was possible he hated that family even more than she. Aurora said, "We need to find a way inside the city. Fast."

Two nights later it was time to make their move. They had left the Rock hidden deep in the woods, hoping that would be enough to keep it safe. Aurora had cried as they released their horses to the wilds. Honey had tried to follow her to the remnant camp, but listened when Aurora ordered her to stay. For so long, that horse had been her only company, her only solace. She hated leaving her behind. But it was impossible to take her with them.

The night died a thousand deaths as they waited for the perfect moment. Again and again, the dark sky lit up like the world itself was splitting at the seams. Perhaps it was.

Aurora wore a thick cloak, but when the night was dark between bolts of skyfire, she could still see the faint glow of her own heart beneath the fabric. It flickered faster, reminding her with every frenzied heartbeat that she was about to go home. She was about to get all the answers she had been desiring and dreading. She was not the same girl she had been last time she stood this close to her home. She'd left powerless with nothing more than hope in her hands, and she'd come back with a storm wrapped around her heart.

The skyfire storm approached from the southwest, and while it was not directly upon the city yet, she could already hear the voices of the remnants carrying on the wind, begging at the city gate for admittance. She ached to go back to them, to *do* something, but as soon as she turned her head in their direction, Kiran was there. His voice was a low whisper as he said, "There's no time. We must go now, while there's a distraction."

She understood that, understood that Kiran and the rest of the hunters were doing this all for her, and she hadn't even gathered the courage to tell them why. But she had not realized that once she came home with magic, she could still feel as utterly powerless as before.

She opened her mouth to argue, but it was Duke who stopped her this time. "We can't fight the storm either, Roar. This is Stormling territory. We would put everyone in greater danger if we tried to interfere."

For the thousandth time, she wanted to throw back the hood that covered her hair and declare to the world that she *was* a Stormling, that she was *home*. That she wanted to make things better.

But just as she had been shaped into something new by the wildlands, Pavan too had changed.

Aurora had done what she could to help in her time among the remnants. Kiran kept scolding her for giving food and supplies away for free rather than trying to barter, arguing it made them stand out too much. But after that display by Casimir, she knew these people had nothing to trade, and even if they did she would not take it from them. Each hour had heaped more guilt upon her shoulders, until she wondered how she could still walk upright. Once they were inside the city, she would tell Kiran the truth. She would tell them all the truth. Even if it meant they all left her behind.

Tonight, she had led them through what remained of Pavan's famed wheat fields. They were largely scorched or otherwise destroyed by storms, and in the few untouched areas, they clearly had not been tended to in weeks. The land was overgrown with weeds and other plants.

She could no longer hear the remnants over the rumbling storm by the time they stopped at their destination, a point on the city wall far out of sight from the gate where the soldiers' attention was now focused. She had been sad to observe in recent days that when a storm hit, the men on duty seemed more concerned with keeping remnants out than being on alert should the storm slip through the city's Stormling defenses, which meant the only other worry they had were the soldiers stationed in each of the high towers facing the cardinal directions. So they had chosen a spot equidistant from the two nearest towers, and thus their best chance at scaling the wall unseen.

It was a gamble. But no one expected them to have an earth witch on their side.

Jinx knelt in the dirt, and reached into the breast pocket of her leather jacket, pulling out a single seed. She pushed that insignificant seed into the soil, planting each finger around it like the roots of a tree.

It took only a few breaths before a tiny green leaf broke through to open air, unfurling as though taking its first breath. The leaves grew and multiplied, followed by reaching vines that moved quickly over the earth until they found the stone wall that surrounded the city of Pavan. Faster, the vines began to uncurl, reaching higher and higher, winding about each other to reach the top. Roar recognized the plant as Rezna's rest, the same plant she'd relied on for weeks in the wild to knock her out when she lost her emotions to a storm. The plant seemed to whisper as it climbed, gasping and growing in a way that reminded her too much of the people who were even now grasping the front gates in fear, begging for mercy, hoping just for a reprieve from the onslaught of this dangerous world.

When the vines had grown thick and sturdy, Jinx sat back, her normally tawny face dotted with sweat, and her skin several shades paler than usual. "That should work," she said in a whisper. Ransom was there a moment later to pull her to her feet. Jinx brushed him off with a cavalier smile and turned to look at the others.

"Who wants to try first? It's completely safe. *Probably.*"

"Probably?" Bait asked, his eyebrows raised in exaggeration.

Roar stepped forward, her voice quiet but firm as she said, "I will." She saw Kiran about to object out of the corner of her eye, and she held up a hand. "I'm doing this." After all, they were all only here because of her, because she asked, and because they now counted her part of their team. Her stomach clenched, and she refused to let herself think about how they might feel differently soon.

Before anyone else could object, she marched up to the thick vine and grabbed hold. She lifted her foot, finding a sturdy notch in the vines, and then pulled herself up a little with her arms. She wanted to take it slow, to step cautiously, but she knew there was too much at risk to be anything but quick and efficient. When she reached the top, she was relieved to find that Jinx had grown the vine not only up the wall, but down the other side. For one brief second, she allowed herself to look out over the city of Pavan. There were hardly any lights to be seen, and the streets were deserted. She knew all the people were likely hiding in shelters, but it didn't stop the unease she felt at seeing her city so lifeless. If she dared to lower her shields, she could probably feel the souls of the people below, maybe even pick up a bit of their emotions, but it was too dangerous to risk her walls being breached.

She felt the rustle of the vine as someone else began their ascent, and quickly threw her legs over to continue her climb down. When she was a few feet off the ground, she jumped, the sound of her landing swallowed by a boom of thunder that seemed to shake the skies.

Kiran was there by the time she found steady footing, having dropped from the top without bothering to climb down at all. "And you call me reckless," she whispered. "You could have broken your leg."

He didn't answer, simply closed the distance between them, curled his hand around the nape of her neck, and pulled her forward into the softest kiss he had ever given her. It lasted only a moment, but they stayed close, heads bent together, lips a whisper away. And slowly, the frenetic beat of her heart eased, the tension in her fingers loosened, and she felt all her fear slide somewhere farther back in her mind, pushed away by the intensity that always rose up between them.

She could do this. *They* could do this.

This man had taken down hurricanes and lived through firestorms, and he *loved* her. She would tell him the truth, and he would understand. He had to, because she wasn't sure how she could get through the next few days without him. If she searched for her mother, only to find out the worst . . . she did not know what she would do then.

Kiran whispered, "I can feel you tensing up again."

A thump signaled another hunter's arrival on this side of the wall. Roar gave Kiran the best smile she could manage and promised, "Later."

She had been promising *later* for days, but this time she meant it. She pulled him down for another hard kiss, and when they pulled apart, he looked more worried, not less.

"I promise I will tell you everything—"

He cut her off. "But first, we have to find your mother. I understand, princess."

She winced, and hoped he did not see it in the dark. "I also need to find out about what has happened since I left."

"We all do. We need to know what kind of trouble we are in here."

Trouble she had dragged them into. Goddess, she was selfish. If she had any honor, she would tell them right here, right now and let them leave before they got involved any further. But the greedy part of her was not going to make it any easier for Kiran to leave her. If she could just prepare him, and say the right words at the right time, maybe she did not have to lose everything she had gained in the last few months.

Kiran laid his palm over her heart, and she felt the zing of sky-fire rise up to meet his touch. She didn't think he could feel it, but it always made her feel as if her heart were too full, as if it might burst under his attention.

"What are you two up to over there?" Bait asked. Roar hadn't even heard him descend. He continued, "Am I going to see something inappropriate the next time the sky lights up? Because some of us have virgin eyes. Not from lack of effort, mind you."

Kiran rolled his eyes, and blew out a steady breath before pulling away. "Nothing to see. Your purity will remain intact."

"Too bad." It was dark, but somehow Roar could feel Kiran's glare fix on the novice hunter, and by the way the redheaded teen threw up his hands, he could feel it too. "What? I'm only saying you could both stand to loosen up. You act like we're breaking into a hostile city in the middle of a violent storm during the dead of night and could be caught and jailed at any moment."

No one replied for a long moment. By skyfire's streaking light, they saw Jinx step down gracefully from the vine and head toward them.

"What? No laughs for that one?" Bait frowned. "*I* thought it was clever."

"Now's not the time to be clever," Jinx said.

"It's always a good time to be clever."

"No, it isn't," Duke said from halfway up the vine.

The old man took longer than all the rest, and Roar watched him as best she could in the fractured darkness. She would tell him second, after Kiran. She was fairly certain he already suspected her secret, but she would need him on her side if she were going to convince the crew to stay and help her put things right here. If that could even be done—the unknowns were unraveling constantly in her mind, threatening to pull her into a panic.

Of course, Duke was not the only one among their group who suspected Roar had been untruthful about aspects of her past. Sly, who had somehow appeared on this side of the wall without Roar ever glimpsing her on the vine, stood leaning against the stone. With her arms crossed over her chest, and her eyes as sharp as ever, Sly scanned the abandoned city around them. Roar was relieved not to have those keen eyes on her for a change.

Ransom was the last to come down the vine, his large body moving with surprising agility. Roar supposed she shouldn't be shocked—he was a hunter, after all.

Once everyone had cleared the wall, Jinx crossed back to the vine. With a brush of her fingers and a few whispered words of peace, the vine grew dry and brittle, and broke apart in the wind. After a few gusts from the storm, there was no evidence of their break-in to be found.

"We need to move," Kiran said, stepping into the circle made by the others. "The Stormlings shouldn't need much longer to take down this storm. We need to get to the Eye before people start peeking out of their shelters."

She and Kiran had agreed that morning that the secret black market where storm magic was bought and sold should be their first stop. The Eye was the only place she knew she could get an honest accounting of what had happened to Pavan in her absence. It had taken some explaining as to why they should not search for her mother first. She had not technically lied when she told him she did not know her mother's whereabouts, though it felt like one all the same. But she could hardly walk up to the palace gates, declare her identity, and ask after her mother without knowing what awaited her on the other side.

They moved on swift and silent feet through the empty city. Kiran with his long strides took the lead, and Roar stayed at an even pace with Jinx directly behind him. They darted around corners and through alleys, and she was struck by the realization that Kiran knew Pavan far better than she ever had.

She didn't recognize their route, but as the homes and buildings grew more derelict, she sensed they were getting close. They turned onto a familiar street at the same time that the skyfire storm overhead reached the edge of the city. Roar craned her head back, watching the deceptively beautiful display of light as the skyfire rained down, shattering against an invisible barrier over the city. Shimmering silver-white light ran in what looked like rivulets over the barrier. They reminded her of great salty tears, as if the goddess were up there somewhere weeping over what her world had become.

She was too distracted by the display overhead to notice immediately what was wrong. She felt the sting at her nostrils first, and blamed it on the lightning overhead. She had experienced the same singeing sensation in the remnant camp a few days prior and also in the Sangsorra desert when she had been right in the center of that skyfire storm. A phantom pang lanced through her lungs at the thought of that day, and she put a hand to her chest as if she could soothe the storm that beat beneath it. But the skyfire was too far away for it to be the cause. The Stormling barrier was thick and powerful, and even when she tried, she could only detect the dull presence of the soul inside the storm. She tore her eyes away from the silver lights overhead, black spots dancing in her vision as she attempted to focus on the street in front of her, where the other hunters had all gone still.

For a moment, she thought it was just the play of darkness over the street that made it look so ominous. But as more light shimmered overhead, she began to make sense of the blackened, hollow husks and the stench that forced her to blink watery eyes. The entire rest of the street appeared as if it had already undergone a skyfire storm. The scent of char hung in the air, and the streets were littered with burned boards from collapsed buildings. When she opened her mouth to speak, she tasted ash on the wind, and the words dried in her throat. The buildings that had hidden the Eye were decimated, nothing left but rotted stairs and tumbled walls. She could see the area that used to house the black market; even the remains of a few stalls were identifiable in the ruins.

None of the other surrounding streets were destroyed. It did not look as if anyone had even tried to clean up whatever happened here. It was as though the entire area had been scorched by a skyfire storm, then left behind as if . . . as if in warning.

Like the one Casimir had given the remnants a few days ago.

Kiran's eyes were dark, his brows set in a grim line as their gazes met. She saw his worry, and the way he tried to hide it beneath his taut jaw and clenched fists. She knew he would rather be anywhere else but here, under the dominion of the family that had destroyed his. But he didn't say that, didn't tell her that it was stupid to come here.

Instead he asked, "What now?"

She looked out at what remained of their only plan. She hoped the inhabitants of the Eye were all safe, that the damage had occurred when the markets were empty. But she feared that was not the case. On their journey through the wildlands, they'd encountered a funeral pyre, and the stench of burned flesh was one she would never be able to forget. And though the damage here did not appear recent, a nauseating scent clung to the carcass of the market.

She turned away, slamming her eyes shut, and biting hard on her lip to keep from being sick. She should have *realized* that the Eye would be compromised. After all, she had found it by following Cassius there. She had not expected him to destroy it, for he seemed to have a use for it once upon a time. But obviously, she knew even less about the Prince of Locke than she had believed.

She did not know what to do next, where to go, or whom to trust. Before she could respond to Kiran's question, the barrier overhead suddenly dropped away. Roar took a gasping breath as she was assaulted by the dark, seething soul that churned high overhead. Its presence felt thick, like oil, even through her shields, and the singed feeling from before was nothing compared to the way her eyes and nose burned now. Tight bumps pulled up on her skin in reaction to the enormous power in the air. Then the light blazed bright and fierce, blocking out the entire palace it hovered over. She clapped her hands over her ears as the wind shrieked, and she bent her elbows to her knees, using all her strength to block out the soul that was lashing out in every direction above. She struggled to breathe under the battery of rage it unleashed, and she swore she could feel oily tendrils of its power trying to catch hold of her, to find *refuge* in her.

Then with a deafening roar of thunder and a blinding explosion of light, the night died and went quiet for a final time.

Slowly, Roar straightened, rolling her stiff shoulders back. She cast her eyes from the palace dome, to the scorched road, to her trusting friends.

What now?

She wished she knew.

Meeting at dawn.
Z

      —a note that was burned after reading

4

Aurora could not sleep, which was why as dawn approached she was on the roof of the inn where they had taken refuge the night before. Everyone had been so weary that they had all gone straight to bed. Aurora had tried to do the same, glad to finally have a real bed again. But no matter how she tossed, she could not stop her brain from turning over thoughts about her mother and Kiran and Cassius and the Stormlord, and how all of this was going to come tumbling down any moment.

She was staring at the slowly brightening sky, blooming with pinks and oranges and blues that brought the smallest measure of peace to her chaotic heart. Her thoughts, her emotions, her *everything* had been straying too often of late. She'd come to the roof for that very reason, hoping to knit herself whole before doing what had to be done today.

Then movement down the street caught her eye, and she ducked behind the roof's ledge, a gasp lodging in her throat as a group of soldiers came into view in the dawning light. She reached for her hair on instinct, and despite finding it covered, her heart still raced uncomfortably. Her heart did not simply beat anymore, not since that night in the desert. Rather, it rolled through her like thunder, and she felt the erratic streak of skyfire all the way down to her fingers. Sometimes she felt as if she had no blood left, only skyfire sizzling in streams beneath her skin, and she wondered if she would even bleed the same. If anything would ever be the same . . .

A deep, emphatic voice from below cut through her thoughts, bringing her to the very real and potentially dangerous present.

The sun had barely cracked open the sky, and soldiers were patrolling in the neighborhood where she and the others happened to have found lodgings. Could it be a coincidence? Was this happening all over the city? Or were they here for her?

She rose up on her knees, peering over the roof's ledge at the men in blue prowling below her. One tall, dark figure spoke to the rest, sending them off in pairs in various directions. They fanned out through the streets, moving at a leisurely pace, stopping to peek in windows and doorways. When the leader was left alone, he turned his head up toward the new sky, and Roar's stomach plummeted.

She knew that face—the short, nearly shaved hair, warm brown skin, and prominent brow combined with the perpetual frown. He had been her teacher, her guard, and something very near a friend. And yet, despite being certain of the man's identity, her brain still struggled to comprehend. Taven, the man who'd taught her how to throw a knife, was wearing Locke blue.

She took a sharp, painful breath. This did not make any sense. Out of everyone, she would have trusted Taven the most to be loyal to her and her mother. Was it possible there was something she was not understanding? Were things not as bad as they seemed?

Taven sighed and watched in apparent apathy as the last of his men disappeared down various streets and alleys. Aurora wanted to open her mouth to call out to him, but a thread of wariness held her back. And she was glad for it a moment later when his disinterest disappeared between one blink and the next. His tall frame taut with tension, Taven glanced around, then turned and strolled quickly down the road that led back toward what remained of the Eye.

She waited one quick breath, then another. She shook her head, knowing that it was reckless even as she swung her leg over the edge of the roof.

Three floors. Too far to jump. She kicked at a metal downspout, and decided the pipe was sturdy enough to get her to one of the lower windows at least. She could have used one of Jinx's vines right about now.

She only gave herself time for a short inhale, then she swung herself down over the roof, feet scrambling for purchase against the wall as she held tight to the downspout. Heart thundering, she began an ungainly slide down the side of the building. The pipe creaked under her weight, but held long enough for her to drop down to the ledge of a second-floor window.

A glance showed that Taven was nearly out of sight. She decided that there was no time to be cautious. She crouched on the ledge, and then leaped.

She landed with a jolt, pain shooting up her legs, but she let her momentum carry her forward into a roll, and she came up walking, her ankles tender, but otherwise unhurt.

She checked to make sure her hair was still covered by her hood, then darted down the road after Taven, only limping for the first few strides. She stuck to the shadows, and tried to ignore her warring thoughts. She could be making a grave mistake, but she was also tired of feeling hopeless. This was the first time since seeing the destroyed Eye that she saw a clear path forward. Taven could tell her everything she needed to know . . . if she could trust him. And this might be her only chance to catch him alone.

After a few streets, she had caught up enough that she could slow her pace. She breathed heavily, and her ankles protested, but her eyes remained on Taven. When her former guard passed the charred ruins of the Eye he did not even glance at the destruction. He walked past it with cold indifference.

Aurora wished she could do the same. But as she skirted by the blackened husks of the market stalls, she could not stop her imagination from turning dark and bleak. There had been dozens of people inside the market each time she had gone. Where were all those people now? Had they survived? She did not feel a stronger than normal presence of souls in this area, but that did not mean there had not been casualties. She was so focused on her imagined horrors that she nearly missed Taven's sharp turn down an alley strewn with trash and debris and muck of questionable sources.

She stuttered to a stop moments before she would have stepped out into plain view. A quick peek around the corner revealed Taven stopped halfway down the alley. A broken, swinging sign hung over an abandoned apothecary. The windows were boarded up, and the front steps sunken in rot. Hope began to unfurl. This was not the first time she had followed someone to a seemingly abandoned location only to find a different reality. Perhaps the Eye had just moved?

Aurora leaned farther around the wall, trying to get a better glimpse of what was happening. She felt something brush against her arm, and a moment later someone whispered, "I always have your back, novie. But this seems . . . shall we say, *unwise.*"

Fear clutched her heart for a long moment, and the distraction made her mental shields waver briefly, sending an overload of sensation into Aurora from the spirits around her—living and dead. She turned and her eyes fixed on Jinx's familiar grin. After a stabilizing breath Aurora asked, "How did you find me?"

"I saw you fall past my window."

Frowning, Aurora whispered, "I did not *fall.*"

"The roll at the end was a nice addition. Looked *almost* purposeful."

Aurora did not care to argue, not when Taven might overhear them. But she whispered, "You followed me."

"Good thing too. Kidnapping that guy will be much easier with two of us."

"Kidnapping?" Aurora's eyes widened, and she shook her head fiercely. "No one is kidnapping anyone." After all, the last kidnapping she planned had come with extreme, unforeseen consequences.

"Are you sure?" Jinx tilted her head. "His information would be incredibly valuable. Plus, if he is anything like the Locke soldiers we met before . . ."

"He's not." At least, Aurora hoped he was not. "I . . . know him. *Knew* him. When I saw him walk past the inn, I didn't think. I just followed him."

Jinx's eyes narrowed, and she hummed behind closed lips. "How well did you *know* him? Because I have a feeling Kiran is about to get his first taste of jealousy if this soldier is the reason you've been so secretive."

"It was not like that. He was . . . a friend."

"You were friends with a Locke soldier?"

With quiet, clipped words, Aurora answered, "He did not used to be one. His name is Taven, and he's . . ."

She glanced around the corner to make sure they wouldn't be overheard, and her stomach sank.

Taven was gone.

Aurora cursed and entered the alley, scanning again and again for where he might have gone, but she could see no avenue for escape. She pushed her fingers into her temples, a sudden ache unfurling in her head.

"No need to look so lost, novie."

Aurora turned around to face Jinx, and found the witch standing beside the entrance to an old storm shelter, overgrown with moss and weeds. As she watched, the witch bent down, and in one sweeping motion, tore the greenery away from the shelter door. It came up in one large sheet, like a blanket, and Jinx dropped it to the ground, her nose wrinkling.

"I didn't even need my magic to tell those plants weren't real. They're little more than cloth counterfeits."

And sure enough, now that the greenery had been removed, Aurora could tell that the shelter door had brand-new hinges. She darted forward, kneeling by the door and pressing her ear down against it.

She heard the breeze whistling around them, the rumble of thunder in the distance, but no sound from within the shelter. She sat back on her heels, and looked up at Jinx.

"What do you want to do?" her friend asked.

The smart thing would be to wait and watch for Taven to leave. But a storm was rolling in, the thunder coming more frequently by the second. She could feel it. The air was humid and thick. But more than that, an uneasy feeling scraped up the back of her neck, and something dark and oppressive lurked just past her shields.

What if something happened and they lost him? Or he did not come out until the storm passed? She was not sure she could handle another day without knowing what had happened to Pavan in her absence. The uncertainty of that combined with her anxieties over revealing her secrets to Kiran were too much to contemplate.

A creak sounded, and Aurora looked over to see a grinning Jinx holding the shelter door open enough to peek inside. The witch shrugged and gestured for Aurora to join her.

Aurora quickly ducked her head near the opening. It was pitch-black inside. The sliver of light from the crack revealed the top rungs of a ladder, but it was swallowed up by the dark before they could see the bottom. Aurora could hear voices. A woman—her voice smooth and rich with an edge of command. A man's voice echoed a moment later, but she could not discern the words, only the muted sounds.

She pressed her lips together, pondering the risk of stepping down into an unknown environment. Then she thought about Jinx calling her *novie*, about the fact that she'd traveled through the wildlands of Caelira, and stared into the heart of a skyfire storm, and survived to return home. Now more than ever, she needed to be brave.

Decided, she tugged up a piece of cloth that was already knotted around her neck and used it to cover her face. She gestured for Jinx to lift the door higher, and carefully she swung her leg over the ledge and found the first rung of the ladder.

More sunlight poured in, illuminating a small, empty room with dirt floors. She caught glimpses of debris, a few wooden supply barrels, and a small darting shadow that she guessed was a rat. She moved quickly and quietly down the rungs, not wanting to draw attention. Jinx appeared to have the same thought as she lowered the door until only the barest crack of light shone through. Aurora paused to let her eyes adjust to the limited amount of light. The room smelled dank and stale, as if it had not been touched by fresh air in months. The sound of her heartbeat in her ears reminded her of a stampede, and Aurora could only hope that her descent down the ladder was quiet enough to go unnoticed.

Finally her foot hit earth, and she stepped down and turned around. The voices had stopped, and she struggled to listen for movement in case she needed to hide or run.

She began feeling her way around the wall, careful not to run into anything. Then she had an idea.

She wore a leather vest with a connected high collar, closed by a series of belt-like clasps. She undid the straps and opened the collar just enough so that the flickering light of the skyfire in her chest lit up the darkness. It worked, allowing her to see enough to explore more quickly. She moved toward the barrels first, finding them empty. She quickly scanned the rest of the room, only finding a few rotted boards and piles of degraded linens. Finally, she made her way to a wooden door. She could see the barest hint of light escaping from beneath the door. Pressing her ear against the wood, she heard the stifled murmur of voices.

She managed to make out the words *weapons* and *storms* before she heard a shout aboveground, and the shelter door dropped closed with a loud thud.

"Jinx?" she whispered as loud as she dared. Her only answer was a loud crash as something was slammed onto the door. Suddenly, she heard voices coming not from above, but from deeper in the shelter. She ran across the room, using her hand to flatten her leather collar over her chest, smothering the skyfire light, and then hurled herself behind the supply barrels moments before the door she'd been listening at flew open.

Aurora pressed her back into the wall, doing her best to slow her breathing. The silver-blue glow of a skyfire lantern cast shadows on the wall. She crouched lower, and quickly strapped her collar back into place. The thud of multiple sets of feet were drowned out by more noises overhead. Before Aurora could wrap her mind around anything but hiding, the shelter door was pulled wide, washing the room in daylight, and revealing a large brute of a man with one thick, inked arm curled threateningly around Jinx's small throat.

Aurora slapped a hand over her mouth to stop her gasp. Jinx, on the other hand, looked nonplussed, almost *bored*, despite the fierce grip of the man who held her. Aurora ducked lower as the man's eyes roved over the room, and she saw that Jinx was careful not to let her eyes wander.

"Brax!" a deep, feminine voice called out, mere feet away from Aurora. The man's eyes snapped to attention. The woman asked, "What have you brought me?"

Aurora listened as Jinx was transferred down the ladder from the first man to another. After a series of heavy footsteps down the ladder, the room dropped into darkness once more, save for the skyfire lantern.

Aurora peeked around the barrel enough to see the woman. She was medium height, but plump, with womanly curves. Her sandy brown skin had an otherworldly gleam in the skyfire's light.

The man called Brax cracked his knuckles and answered, "Found her lurking about outside, fiddling with the plants you use to hide this place."

"Is that so?" Silence hung in the air after the woman's question; a dangerous intensity wove through the room. Her voice was layered and deep, but precise and crisp. She took one slow step forward, then another, until she was face-to-face with Jinx. Then she tilted her head to the side, her long dark hair sliding over her shoulder, and said, "Now *who*, exactly, are you?"

Aurora saw Jinx smile in the glow of the skyfire, utterly fearless in the face of whoever it was they had stumbled upon. Jinx shrugged casually and replied, "No one you need concern yourself with. I mean you no harm. I just . . . have a fondness for plants."

The woman laughed, the kind of laugh that would have drawn every eye in a room, only the men around her stayed still and stiff at her side, like soldiers waiting for her command. "That's darling," the woman replied, circling around Jinx, surveying her like a predator. "*I* have a fondness for sharp things."

At her words, Aurora heard several blades pulled by the surrounding men. Her stomach clenched with nerves. She should have been more careful. She never should have taken such a risk.

"Take these, for example." The woman held up a hand near Jinx's face. She wore a shiny, red leather glove that was more like armor, tipped with dark sharp points that she lightly trailed down the side of Jinx's throat. "I took these from a wildcat that made the wrong choice in prey. That's actually her you feel at your feet. I took her claws as punishment, but let her keep her teeth as respect for one predator from another."

Aurora hadn't noticed before, but sure enough, a spotted cat with pointed ears wove between Jinx's legs, tall enough to rub its cheek against her thigh.

"How intimidating," Jinx said, an exaggerated shiver in her voice. "A cat! How ever will I keep from spilling all my secrets?" Despite the blades pointed at her, the brazen earth witch bent just enough to scratch the wildcat between the ears. She murmured something that might have been, "Sweet kitty," then straightened and asked, "Is this the part where I should beg for mercy?"

Skies, Aurora didn't know how Jinx did it—stayed so calm. She was a mess of nerves, and she had not even been noticed.

Brax, the man who had captured Jinx, took a menacing step forward. "Are you stupid or something?"

Jinx smiled, her eyes crinkling at the corners. "Or something."

Then the earth buckled beneath their feet, and a chorus of shouts rang out as the room began to shake. Roots and plants of every kind burst from the dirt floor and walls. Vines twined around people's limbs. Jinx swung her arm, landing an elbow to the face of the man holding her. Jinx shoved the woman back into a grasping web of green and yelled, "Now, Roar!"

Aurora leaped up from her hiding place. A large man turned, looming in front of her. His skin was nearly the same shade as the shadows that swathed the room. A vine caught him around the ankle at the perfect moment, and Aurora shoved him off-balance. Jinx was halfway up the ladder, calling for her. Darting after her friend, Aurora cleared the first few rungs in a leap. The plants rose ahead of them, pushing the shelter door up and up, dousing them all in bright sunlight.

Then . . . something went wrong. The plants around Aurora began to turn brown and dull. They continued moving as Jinx's magic commanded, but they grew dry and brittle, and they snapped under the strain.

Aurora too felt strange. Her vision flashed with shadows despite the sunlight overhead. Her mouth felt as if a dust storm had rolled over her tongue then settled into a desert in her throat. A gnawing pain began at her temples and the base of her neck. The world started to wobble, the ground tipping from side to side below her. A fist curled around the belt at her waist and jerked her backward. Her fingers broke from the ladder like the brittle vines beside her. Dust flew up as she landed flat on her back, and the pain shattered the remaining control she had over her mental shields.

Sensations swamped her, foreign and overpowering, but even lost in the deluge it was the ache in her throat that bothered her most. Dizziness kept spinning her mind around as she tried to focus. A dark form came into view, and her vision cleared just enough for her to see.

The woman. The one with the claw-tipped, red glove—singular, for her other hand was bare. She was striking, and not just because Aurora felt like the air had been knocked from her lungs and refused to return. She had thick dark hair that trailed past her waist and was decorated with braids and curls. Her eyebrows were dark and straight over piercing brown-black eyes. Her cheekbones were sharply defined, and her skin a gold-touched brown. The woman wore fine clothes made of rich, draping fabrics that flowed around her shape as if at her command. She radiated power.

The dark spots in Aurora's vision began to stretch and merge, blocking out even the sun that streamed through the open hatch above. When she dangled at the edge of consciousness, the woman bent down toward Aurora's face, a shrewd look in her narrowed eyes.

"I can make it stop," the woman said, her voice soft—just shy of kind. "*If* you tell me who sent you."

Aurora tried to answer her, but her tongue was thick and dry and useless in her mouth. The woman reached out and pulled away the cloth covering the lower part of Aurora's face, then tugged at the hood covering her hair. Aurora's heart gave one heavy, panicked thump, but she was too weak to fight back.

A voice in her head shouted, "Stop!" And she tried to make the word herself.

"Stop!"

The word surprised her, for it came not from her mouth, but from somewhere outside her narrowed vision. She heard it repeated—a deep voice, a man's voice.

Someone grabbed the woman, dark hands on her pristine garments, shoving her back and away from Aurora. The terrible crushing pressure on her chest eased, but she was hit by another wave of nausea so extreme she rolled to the side and retched. Nothing came out despite the desperate, painful heaving of her stomach.

"Help her. Please, Zephyr."

Someone pulled on her shoulder, rolling her back and pushing away the sweaty hair that hung across her face.

"Why should I?" Aurora heard as her vision cleared enough to make out the stern, serious face of the man who had once been her guard.

Taven's eyes were wild and panicked like she had never seen them.

"Because she's the rightful heir to the kingdom of Pavan."

Under the will of the goddess, and my own power as a Stormling king, I offer my services to the city of Pavan as its protector and ruler in its time of need.

—declaration signed by King Cruzef Locke

5

Novaya woke to hands on her person, and her magic screaming in revolt. She shoved blindly, and ended up slammed against the rough stone wall for her troubles. Her bones clashed painfully with the stone, and liquid fire churned in every joint.

It was a soldier who held her against the wall—his palm planted on her chest to keep her pressed backward.

In her mind's eye, she saw that hand burst into flame, and she knew she could do that with the raw magic inside her, was tempted to simply let it out, to pour all her frustration and fear and fatigue into the fire, and burn it all away.

But then the man spoke. "The prince wants to see you."

Her eyes flicked to the door, expecting to find the dark, sinister form of her only visitor in the doorway. But it was empty. And . . . *open*.

She raised her hands in a show of supplication, and the man stepped back, taking away the hand that had felt like a brand on her chest.

Metal clanked, and the soldier held up a pair of iron manacles. "Put these on."

He shoved them toward her, and she took the irons with shaking hands. They were heavy, so heavy it sapped all her strength just to hold them. She was not sure she could put them on herself, but she forced herself to try, knowing she would prefer her own touch to that of the soldier.

Her wrists were so thin, she thought she might be able to slip them off later when no one was looking, but then the soldier invaded her space, moving a bar to make the manacle openings smaller, trapping her skin right up against the iron. Then he tightened it with a small tool just to be certain.

The soldier used a length of chain attached to the manacles to pull her toward the door. She stumbled, her feet dragging clumsily against the stone. The man was impatient as she regained her balance, but made no move to touch her again, for which she was grateful. She shuffled behind him as they stepped out of the cell, and her heart pumped with manic hope as her bare feet cleared the threshold. "Where are you taking me?"

"Wherever Prince Cassius wants you."

They shuffled past a few more dark stone cells. She tried to discern if there was anyone else being held down here with her, but if there were other prisoners she saw no trace of them. Nor had she ever heard anyone in the dungeons but the guards who brought her food on occasion.

She stared at the back of the guard's head and wondered at how callous human hearts could be. How easy it was for a man just to avert his eyes in the face of someone else's pain or fear. What had the prince told everyone about her? Did they all truly believe her to be the criminal mastermind behind the princess's kidnapping? Her best friend? Or did it matter to them if she was guilty or innocent? She was not a Stormling, so perhaps in their eyes she had little worth at all.

They came to a set of stairs, and Nova was surprised to find that she was beyond exhausted already. Her legs quaked with weakness as she took the first step.

The soldier jerked on her chains. "Come on. It will be nightfall again before we get there if you move this slow."

She felt some of her fire leech from her skin into the manacles, and quickly pulled it back. As satisfying as it might be to see him scalded by the chain he held, it was too reckless. There was too much she didn't know. Even if she incapacitated this guard, she had no idea what waited on the floors above, or if she could even reach them on her own.

She might only get one chance to escape. And she knew timing would be everything.

By the time the soldier jerked her up the last step to the landing, she was near tears from fatigue, and the weakness made her heart swell with fury. At the prince, at this world, at herself. And yes, at Aurora too.

They entered the main floor of the palace, and the familiar sounds of her former workplace and home slowly came back to her. They were near the entrance to the kitchens, and she could hear the clang of pots and the murmur of voices. The smell of fresh baked bread made her stomach clench painfully. When had she last eaten more than a few scraps? She could not recall.

A gasp stopped her escort in his tracks, and with far too much effort, Nova tipped her head up to survey the scene.

She saw the familiar face first, and it took several long moments for her mind to recall just how she knew the young serving girl who stood slack-jawed in front of them.

Renia. They'd shared a room together. Nova used to lie in bed listening to Renia prattle on about the details of her romantic life. It had always been a grand distraction for Nova, who had no desire for romance of her own. Not with her secrets. But listening to Renia had been a glimpse into another, simpler life.

Those days felt so far away now, like they existed in another world.

"What are you looking at?" the soldier sneered.

Renia quickly concealed her horrified expression and ducked her head. "My apologies."

The soldier tugged on Nova's chains, and she stumbled forward. Her eyes met Renia's as they passed, and the girl quickly averted her eyes.

Nova could not blame her. If the situation were reversed, she would have done the same, desperate to stay safe and keep her secrets unknown.

She kept her chin up on the rest of their trek through the palace halls, refusing to cower. The world, it seemed, kept moving as it always had despite her absence. It was alarming to know that her life could be upended so completely, and yet all the people she had once known continued on in the same day-to-day drudge.

Finally, after another set of brutal stairs, the soldier led Nova to a part of the palace she knew all too well—the royal wing. Nova eyed the soldier with confusion and distrust as she was led down the hall to the rooms that had once belonged to the Princess of Pavan. The soldier opened the door and shoved her through.

The first thing Nova noticed was the plush carpet beneath her feet, so soft against her calloused, broken skin. She almost wanted to give in to the urge to collapse, just so she could feel that kind of softness all over her skin. Then there was the smell—the scent of ink and old books and fresh air teased her senses and brought tears to her eyes.

For a moment, Nova could see this room as it used to be. The windows had always been open, the room washed in sunlight and teased by a breeze. Aurora used to leave books on every surface, piles of stories she had read and read again. The memories stole what little breath she had, and pulled painfully at her heart.

Now the room seemed stale, as closed off and cold as the man who had apparently claimed it as his own. The quaint writing desk Aurora had used had been replaced by a large desk of gleaming, dark wood. Behind it the prince sat, his back to her, facing one of the many bookshelves that held the princess's books.

He turned, his dark hair disheveled and his eyes sunken and dark.

"Sit," he ordered, his voice a whisper, but filled with command.

The prince waved a hand at the soldier, who stepped from the room and closed the door.

They were alone, and Nova had no idea what was happening. The prince's visits to her cell had slowed of late. Based on the number of storm sirens she had heard, she assumed he was busy with the Rage season.

The prince stared at her through the silence, his mouth a slash of frustration. They sat so long that Nova's fatigue began to pull at her attention. The chair she sat in felt so soft in comparison to stone. She thought she could slump there and sleep for days. Not even her fear was a strong enough opponent to overcome her exhaustion.

"Do you think she's still alive?"

Nova blinked. They'd been through this before, when the queen had broken down over her fears that Aurora had been killed by her kidnappers. Nova had never been able to get word to her of Aurora's true intentions.

"Is this about the queen? Is she well?"

Cassius's frown grew flatter, his gaze hard.

"That's none of your concern. I want to know if the princess is alive. Am I wasting my time searching for her?"

Nova shook her head. "I do not know."

His jaw worked, teeth clenching, and he took a deep breath.

"The circumstances of Pavan have changed dramatically over recent weeks. I have put as much time and attention toward the search as I am able, but a time is approaching . . . the time is *here* when my priorities have been forced elsewhere. If you know anything, if you care at all to see your friend again, you will tell me what you know now before it is too late."

The last was said in an exasperated growl. It was clear the prince was obsessed, and that obsession had worn down his regal facade, letting the darkness inside him show through.

She observed him carefully—the clench of his fists hinted at how close he was to the edge. She did not care to know the depths of this man's depravity. Nor did she want that for Aurora.

Nova had had much time to wonder over the days and nights whether she had done the right thing in assisting Aurora's escape. Goddess knew she'd sat too often in the dark, grappling with the possibility that she might have helped her truest friend into an early grave. For what could the wildlands be for a girl without storm magic except for a death sentence? She hoped—hoped with every spark of fire that burned beneath her skin—that her friend was somewhere happy and whole.

Her own weariness had her counting the days, wondering when Aurora might return, and if she could undo all the damage that had befallen Pavan in her absence. But as someone who had walked beneath the crushing weight of a dangerous secret, she wanted Aurora to have a life free of lies, free of peril, free of the Locke prince. Forever.

And so she told him one part of her truth. "I do not know for certain, but in the dark of night, when worries press too close to ignore, I fear the queen is right. Aurora Pavan is gone. For good."

The first few moments after the declaration of Aurora's true identity were like the calm before the storm, and then the silence broke with a cacophony of voices and a flurry of movements that only made Aurora more dizzy. She felt like she was dying—as if everything inside her was shriveling up like old fruit. And her thoughts were a jumble—some not even her own—as she tried and failed to rebuild her mental walls.

Taven's deep booming voice shouted above all the rest. "Zephyr, please! Have I ever done anything to make you mistrust me?"

Aurora could not see the woman's response; she could see nothing except a very small tunnel in the center of her vision that showed Taven kneeling over her.

Zephyr answered, "You pledged your life to our cause—if you are lying, I'll not hesitate to take it as penance."

"I pledged my life to her protection long before your cause. She is who I say she is."

The woman did not reply, but almost immediately Aurora felt the rush of something cool on her skin. It wrapped around her like silk and then sank beneath her skin. She could feel it spreading inside her—like ice melting the burning pain. Her vision began to clear and her chest stopped aching and slowly she felt herself come alive again, as if she'd hung over the abyss of death by only her fingertips. She was able to swallow, her throat burning at first, but easing as the strange power worked through her.

By the time she sat up and looked at the woman called Zephyr, she felt as if she'd been born all over again. Her words were raspy when she asked, "Who are you?"

Zephyr stepped out of the shadows, emerging into the sunlight.

"I am the one who has been fighting for your people in your absence." She held up her arms and waved at the shelter around them. "Welcome to the rebellion."

Aurora looked to Taven, and then down at the blue uniform he wore. *Now* she understood. She wanted to demand he tell her everything, but there was something else she had to know first.

"What are you?" she asked Zephyr.

Jinx, whom Aurora had forgotten in the chaos, dropped down then from her place at the top of the ladder. Dust rose at her landing, swirling around her feet in a way too perfect to be natural. Her eyes were on Zephyr as she said, "Water witch."

Zephyr crossed her arms over her chest in response, cocking her hip casually. "Earth witch."

They studied each other for a few moments—Jinx with narrowed eyes and Zephyr with a purse of her full lips. Then one after the other, they turned to face Aurora.

It was Jinx who said, "And a princess too. Who knew?"

Jinx's tone was even, but it was missing the warmth and effervescence with which she always spoke.

"I can explain," Aurora croaked, her throat still parched from what she was only now realizing had been a dangerous case of rapid dehydration, courtesy of Zephyr's magic.

But when she opened her mouth to continue, the words dried in her throat. A tingle of foreboding skipped up her spine, and she tilted her head back to look up through the open shelter door at clear sky. She took one breath, then two, then another soul's consciousness slammed into hers.

Malice curled around her like the tentacles of some monster from the deep. She pushed at the soul's presence, but the day's events had weakened her, and by the time she'd shored up her defenses against one intrusion, another was already coming. She gritted her teeth as fury—hot and thick as tar—clogged in her veins. A thirst for vengeance stole across her tongue, and she only had time to say, "Someone close that door!" before the sky ruptured and bled out fire.

There were no sirens, nor Stormling barriers. Beneath her clothes, her crystal necklace burned in warning, but the first flaming embers were already scorching through the sky. At least a dozen slipped through the opening overhead, which no one had been quick enough to close.

All of Aurora's focus was on enforcing the boundaries around her mind, and she only avoided getting burned because Taven took hold of her elbows and dragged her back into a corner.

Aurora heard screaming, and was horrified to realize that it was not coming from anyone inside the shelter, but from the city above. The screams built and grew into an agonized chorus, and the scent of char rapidly tainted the air. Zephyr used her magic to douse a pile of burning debris, and Jinx resurrected one of her vines to make the perilous journey up to the surface where it wound around the handle to the shelter door. Jinx pulled with all the strength of her small form, and the door crashed down, immersing them in darkness.

The only sounds were the sizzle of dying flames. The pale blue glow of the skyfire lantern cast them all in ghostly shadows. Aurora shoved her fist against her mouth to keep from sobbing. She could still feel the storm—though her barriers were strong enough to keep her thoughts her own. But now it was the other souls that fed her agony. She could feel them dying—by the dozens.

A siren sounded. Too late. Far, far too late.

Desperate to do something, anything, to stop the horror and pain that bombarded her with the arrival of each newly departed soul, Aurora jerked up the leather necklace that held her tiny bottle of firestorm powder.

Locke had told her to use it in the event of a firestorm. It would not protect her completely, but it would temporarily make her impervious to flame.

She yanked out the cork with her teeth.

"Don't!" Jinx yelled, throwing out a hand to stop her.

"Why not?"

"That powder is rare. Firestorm hearts aren't exactly easy to capture. Don't waste it when you're already safe."

Aurora cringed. "Waste it? Do you know what is happening out there?"

Jinx held her ground. "I do. And I also know that you cannot do anything out there that you could not do in here."

She meant for Aurora to soothe the storm. While much of her newly realized power was still a mystery, she had spent their journey back to Pavan quietly soothing unsettled souls and preventing them from becoming storms. But those souls were relatively normal—lost and wandering from their inability to disconnect from their former lives. The soul that seethed above them now had been twisted and marred into something foul and unrecognizable. There was no soothing that kind of rage, not without a Stormheart to bring the storm to heel.

"I can't," Aurora whispered. "It's beyond my skill."

"What do you mean, beyond your skill? I thought you were the most powerful Stormling to grace the Pavan line in generations?" This question came from Zephyr.

Aurora grimaced and shook her head. "I'm not."

"You're not the most powerful?"

She was not a *Stormling*. At least, that's what she had always believed. Now, she was not sure what she was.

"It's . . . complicated."

Brax, the overgrown guard who set this all in motion when he caught Jinx, plopped down onto the ground and said, "I have time."

"Well, I don't," Aurora replied. "I cannot sit in here while people are dying out there."

She pushed Jinx's hand away and raised the bottle to her lips. Then a familiar haze emerged between Aurora and the storm's consciousness. This time she knew for certain that the power she felt in the air belonged to Cassius. It had the same cold, menacing potency as his presence the first time she met him. It filled the air like his deep voice filled a room. And while she loathed the Locke prince, the presence of his magic over the city eased the pressure she felt against her own barriers.

She returned the cork to the bottle and the necklace to its home against her sternum. "Never mind. It's no longer necessary."

She didn't bother explaining further before she crossed to the ladder and scaled to the top. She shoved back the door, and the sound of screams came back with a vengeance. High above, a near-translucent barrier quaked from the impact of falling embers. Flames licked at the magic, and it looked to Aurora as if the sun had fallen from the sky and stopped mere moments away from crashing into the city.

Smoke filled up the space beneath the barrier, and even though the embers were no longer razing the city, that did not stop the current fires from spreading out of control.

She turned, intending to call for Jinx, and was surprised to find all the inhabitants of the shelter standing just behind her, gazing out at a blackened, burning city.

Zephyr was the first to jump into motion. "I'll do what I can, but I cannot create water from nothing. There's only so much I can pull from the air."

"I can help with that," Jinx replied, peeling back one side of her jacket to retrieve a jar of storm magic from a holster near her ribs. She held out the jar, the inside of which was swirling with torrential rain.

"A hunter?" Zephyr shared a knowing look with a tall, dark-skinned man whom Aurora could not recall speaking a single word since his appearance.

"Two hunters," Jinx replied, glancing at Aurora.

A rush of gratitude filled Aurora's chest. Jinx had every right to be furious with Aurora's lies, but she still included her as one of them. For now.

Zephyr's smile was filled with satisfaction as she jumped into action. She turned to the dark-skinned man first. "Raquim, you and Brax focus on search and rescue as I work on dousing what I can." She cocked her arm and threw the glass jar of storm magic against the building in front of them. Wind and rain surged in every direction, whipping at their clothes and hair. Zephyr gave a shout of triumph. But before she focused on her magic, her gaze trailed to Taven. "I suppose you will be reporting for duty."

He nodded, his eyes straying first to the tempest still fighting overhead, then to Aurora. He hesitated.

Zephyr did not, setting out at a run toward the city center, where the blaze loomed the largest.

Selfishly, Aurora wanted to keep Taven here to tell her everything she needed to know. But she knew he was needed elsewhere.

"Go," she said. "I'm not going anywhere."

His eyes were torn. She knew his sense of duty was telling him to stay with her.

"Will you meet me here tomorrow at first light?" he asked.

She nodded. "I will. I promise."

He waited another beat, staring at her as if she still might be a dream, then he turned sharply and began to run.

"Wait!" she called, sprinting after him.

He slowed, but did not stop. "I've already been missing too long. My unit is likely searching for me. If any of them survived. But if you want me to stay, you only need to ask, Your Highness."

"Please don't call me that." He slowed to a walk, and she avoided his serious gaze by looking at the palace instead. It was hard to see between the smoke and the rain, but she could see the shape of the large golden dome. "I'll let you go, but first, please, what of my mother?"

Taven stiffened, and his long strides stopped abruptly. Horror knifed through Aurora's middle. "Is she—did they . . ."

He gave a sharp shake of his head. "She's very ill. But she lives. Though she does not believe the same is true of you."

It is thought that the first magic users were given gifts not unlike the gods themselves. They had the magic from which all the world had been created and with which all the world could be destroyed.

—*An Examination of the Original Magics*

6

Thirteen Years Earlier

Cruze tried to keep track of the time, but during a tempest, the whole world slowed down and sped up all at once. The downpour soaked past the skin, until the cold felt like it would never let you go. First, you wanted to move constantly in an attempt to create heat. But after a while, you realized that creating heat means losing it, and then you didn't want to move at all. You wanted to sleep. But it was too cold for that too. The unexpected changes of the wind kept you on high alert, always wondering if there was something worse than wet and wind coming next. If you were the other children, you cried and cried and cried.

Cruze did not cry, not even when the voice in his head came back—the voice that whispered of destruction and death. He waited for something more to come of the voice, for madness to take him fully, or the voice's owner to present itself. But the whispers remained whispers, just skimming the surface of his thoughts; sometimes he even had to strain to hear them over the sobbing of the other children. They cried for mothers and fathers he knew would never come.

Only one other child seemed to understand that they were on their own out here—the girl with the bruise across her neck. Together, she and Cruze had done their best to build a shelter in the time before the storm hit. They found a set of boulders close together, and piled long sticks over the top, followed by fern leaves. When they had finished, it had looked like a makeshift hut, and Cruze had been proud.

But it had done next to nothing to protect them from the rain when it came. The leaves grew heavy and curled downward, leaving gaps in their would-be roof. The earth beneath them grew into sodden soup that stuck to their feet and legs in muddy smears and clumps. The others huddled closer and closer around him, until Cruze could feel their shaking limbs against his own. And with that whisper still in the back of his mind, he had a sudden urge to shove and shove until he had space, until none of that weakness touched him.

Instead, he hurled himself forward and up, crawling out of their pitiful shelter and submitting to the fury of the storm outside.

"Where are you going?" a voice asked, small and high-pitched.

Cruze did not stop to answer. He kept putting one foot in front of the other, and he did not stop until his clothes were soaked through and his skin was slick with rainwater. Thunder howled overhead, trees quaking at its roar, and he stopped to listen, to feel fear, to perhaps finally cry like the others.

But still . . . it never came.

Because for the first time possibly ever, Cruze felt free.

He was not locked away in that house where his mother lived with the cloying perfumes and noises at all hours and the people coming and going that never included him. He had never done anything but stay. Stay behind. Stay quiet. Stay unseen.

"What are you doing?"

Cruze whipped around and found the girl. She'd followed him, but somehow she seemed less touched by the elements. She wasn't dry, to be sure, but it was as if she stood beneath a tree that guarded her from the worst of the rain. But there was no more shelter where she stood than he, and he could hear the steady patter of the rain and felt it fall against the back of his neck.

"Nothing."

"You'll fall ill if you stand too long in the rain," she said.

"So will you."

She did not reply to that, only tilted her head slightly and looked at him with more focused eyes.

"What happened to your neck?" he asked, tired of wondering, and too far from his mother to care what was and was not polite.

She grabbed the collar of her shirt, pulling it up to hide the mark, but then dropped it, as if she changed her mind.

"I made a choice," she answered.

"What kind of choice?"

She shrugged and did not blink as she continued, "Not to die."

He did not know what she meant, but she was the only person out here he felt even the slightest connection toward. "What's your name?" he asked, aware that he had made no effort to get to know any of the others before, while they had all told story after story of their families and lives back home.

"You can call me Kess."

Kiran Thorne burst out of the smoke-filled inn, his heart galloping at a painful speed.

She was not here.

They had evacuated the inn as soon as it was safe to go outside. Firestorms made for a particularly violent dilemma—stay in the building as it burned or run out into the storm that caused the fire? Usually it came down to guesswork, and most often it led to injury or death regardless of where one stayed. Unless, of course, you carried magic like the firestorm powder he had already taken.

When he had not found Roar in her bedroom on the third floor, he assumed she had already made it out. But when he could not find her with the others, he'd charged back into the burning building, determined to find her. Ransom followed close at his heels, for Jinx was missing too. But no matter how much they searched, the girls were nowhere to be found. When the third floor was smothered completely in flames, they'd finally given up and retreated back outside.

Now Kiran paced back and forth, every muscle in his body pulled taut like a bow. The arrow, he felt, might be lodged in his lungs, for no matter how much air he gulped down, it seemed to leak out faster than it should.

She couldn't be inside. She just *couldn't* be.

They'd not traveled safely across the wildlands only to have her die in a Stormling city just like his sister. His skin began to crawl, the way it sometimes did in cities, as if the memories were about to burst through his pores so he could ignore them no longer.

Out of nowhere, a downpour of rain began a few streets over, quickly expanding to reach over the inn. He turned his head up to the sky, and welcomed the wash of cold over his face and down into his clothes. He never felt clean in cities. It was good that hunting kept him in the wilds the majority of the time because he was already restless, and they had barely arrived.

He watched the flames atop rooftops sizzle and steam under the fall of rain, waiting for the inn's fire to subside completely. Pushing his soaked hair off his forehead, he resumed his pacing. He was not sure how many times he marched back and forth in front of that inn, refusing to think about what he might find inside, before Ransom called out, "Kiran!" His friend gestured down the road where two silhouettes were beginning to take shape through the torrent of rain.

The taller of the two had a hood pulled low to cover her face, her form little more than a moving shape in the distance, but he would know Roar anywhere. He had memorized everything about her—the too-graceful glide of her walk, the way she hunched her shoulders to make herself seem shorter when she wanted to go unnoticed, and how it was utterly impossible for him to ever not notice her.

She was moving gingerly, as if in pain, and before he knew it, he was sprinting toward her. She was dripping wet, but somehow a streak of soot still marred her pale cheek. When he was almost upon them, she turned and shared a long, unreadable look with Jinx.

What were the two of them doing that took them away from the inn?

He cast the thought away. None of that mattered, not when he'd been so afraid that she was . . . He shook his head, refusing to dwell another moment on the possibility.

Kiran slowed as he neared, covering the last of the distance in a few long strides. Then he caught her face in his hands and kissed her.

He did not care that it was raining, or that the tips of his fingers were burned from a brush with the flames inside the inn. He rarely cared about anything else when Roar was around. She melted against him, and did not try to stop him when he pushed back her hood and tangled his uninjured hand in her short, skyfire-white hair.

Despite the cold fall of rain, her lips were fire beneath his own. She met his desperation without a moment's hesitation, as if she knew that he felt like his heart might burst if he did not pull her as close as possible.

"I couldn't find you. I thought . . ."

She quieted him with the soft brush of her lips against his jaw, then his cheek, before resting her forehead against his. She murmured apologies between light, teasing kisses, and Kiran could do nothing but hold her tight within his arms.

When his heart finally slowed to a bearable pace, he pulled back and asked, "What were you doing out at this hour? I thought we agreed the city was not safe." The words came out harsher than he intended, but one glance around them made clear those words were true as ever. Fear knotted his insides all over again. Even though she was safe. Even though she was in his arms. He was somehow still deathly afraid.

Was this what it meant to be in love? Would he live the rest of his days in a constant state of fear that this one slice of perfection he'd been given would be torn away like every other good thing that had come before her?

The corners of her lips twitched down in a frown before she gave him her practiced blank expression. Sometimes he loathed that look. He never wanted to see her withdrawn and emotionless. And it irked him that he'd had the same expression once upon a time, until she came into his life and smashed it into pieces. Now his emotions were always too near to the surface.

She stepped back slightly, out of the circle of his arms. "I had something I needed to do. Plus, Jinx was with me."

"I don't like the idea of the two of you out alone. There's too much we don't know about the state of the city."

"You don't have to like it."

As his fear faded, he found frustration filling up the space left behind. "What I don't like is the fact that you keep hiding things from me. We're either in this together or we're not. It cannot be both."

Roar laid her hand on his chest, directly over his heart. She exhaled and closed her eyes. He wondered if she could feel the way his heart beat harder just at the proximity of her touch.

"I know," she answered. "I want that. I do. That's why . . ." She hesitated, squared her shoulders, and continued, "That's why we need to talk. Tonight."

Something in her voice wavered, a sliver of vulnerability breaking through. And even though he'd been longing for her to open up to him for weeks, he now found himself a little . . . unsettled. Curiosity had been strangling him from the moment he first laid eyes on Roar. He had tested every limit of his patience in recent days in an attempt to give her the time she needed. And now that she was ready, he realized he might not be. Whatever Roar was hiding, he had a feeling it would change everything.

The crew spent the afternoon helping the inn clean up what damage they could. It was lucky that only the top floor of the building sustained significant damage, and the rest only suffered from a layer of soot on every surface and the lingering scent of smoke. Many other areas of the city had not been so lucky.

Apparently Jinx had been the one to supply the rainstorm that saved this area from the worst of the damage. But in other parts of the city, they were focusing now on cleaning up the bodies, not just debris.

Aurora and Jinx had been the only ones to occupy rooms on the top floor. So when night fell and they'd done as much work as they could for the day, the hunters gathered to discuss their lodgings for the next few days. Jinx suggested the girls all bunk in Sly's room. When Roar started to respond, Kiran touched the back of her hand.

He leaned toward her, pressing his lips to her hair first before whispering, "Stay with me?"

She squeezed his hand and nodded in answer, and he found himself wishing they were alone in his room already. He did not know where the urgency came from, except that Stormling cities always made him anxious.

He felt more at home in the wildlands, dangerous though they were. There was something comforting in knowing the danger that lurked around you, in calling it by name. But in this city, in all Stormling cities, he was acutely aware that humans could cause just as much damage as the fiercest of tempests.

He and Roar excused themselves from the group, but not before he noticed another pointed look pass between Roar and Jinx.

That urgency rose another notch. It did not help that Roar had been unusually quiet through the whole day, and the same was true now as they climbed the stairs up to Kiran's room. Her brows were furrowed and her lips pursed. He wasn't even sure she was paying attention to where she was going—her thoughts were so clearly turned inward.

"This doesn't have to mean anything more than you want it to," he told her.

Her eyes jerked up and over to him, and she shook her head. "I'm sorry. What?"

"Staying with me," he finished. "I didn't ask because I wanted—I asked because I want you with me. That's it. No more, no less."

Roar slowed in the hallway, and turned to face him. Her hand lifted and one delicate finger traced over the leather straps of the supply harness he wore.

"You're a good man, Kiran Thorne."

He scoffed beneath his breath. Most people would take one look at him and call him trouble, danger at the very least. He was glad she saw differently.

"I'm a man, that much is true. And I want to be good for you more than I want anything else in this cursed world."

Her tiny finger curled beneath one of his leather straps and drew him closer, slowly, temptingly. At the same time, her head tilted to the side and she looked up at him with blue eyes that broke his heart and put it back together again.

"You *are* good for me." She lifted up on her toes and stole another piece of him from the corner of his lips. She kept doing that—chipping away pieces of him he did not even know were loose.

She turned and led him the rest of the way to his door, pushing her way inside, finger still wrapped around his harness strap. But as soon as she stepped inside the room, she halted on a gasp, and her hand dropped away. Kiran followed her inside, closing the door behind them, and found her kneeling next to the bag containing her belongings, clutching it tightly to her chest and staring up at him with tears in her eyes.

"You saved my things," she said through choked tears.

"Of course I saved them. When the storm first started, I went straight to your room. You weren't there, but your bag was."

She made a noise somewhere between a sniff and a laugh. "I— I've been so worried all day that I forgot completely that I'd left this in my room. I would have been devastated if it had burned."

Kiran swallowed the lump in his throat and murmured, "I would have been devastated if *you* had burned."

Roar pushed her belongings off her lap and rose to her feet. She came to him, snaking her arms around him and tucking her head beneath his chin. He returned her hold, and they stayed like that for a long while. Together they reminded him of some kind of tourniquet—like the pressure each of them exerted on the other held all their wounds closed.

"I never want to feel like that again," he spoke against her hair, his voice scratchy. "I never want to imagine a future without you."

Roar did not answer, but pressed her face closer to the hollow of his neck. He thought she might stay there forever, and he found he did not much mind the idea. But eventually she did speak, whispering, "I need to tell you the truth about my past, about my life before I left with you."

He swallowed, and it was suddenly difficult to remain still. He needed to pace, to do something with his hands, to do *anything* to keep himself calm through whatever was coming next. But somehow he stayed right there, still folded together with her like the pages of a book.

"I am going to tell you everything," she continued. "And then tomorrow, I have to meet someone. I'd like you to come with me, if you still want to when I'm done."

Skies, he hated the anticipation of not knowing, of fearing the worst. Though, honestly, he truly did not care about her past. He did not care who she had been before or what she'd had to do to survive. He only cared about who they were to each other moving forward.

Slowly, she pulled back to look him in the eye. "Before I tell you. Can you do one thing for me?" she asked.

"Anything."

"I just need one moment where the rest of the world does not matter. I need one moment that's only about you and me. I want . . . a pause. I want the eye before the storm continues."

"And how do I give you that?" Kiran asked.

She smiled, a full smile—not the nervous one he'd seen all day. "That's simple. You kiss me."

Kiran searched her eyes, the brilliant blue hue swimming with emotion, and then he stepped back and moved toward the door.

"Where are you going?" Roar's voice wobbled a little.

He stopped next to the door and looked back at her. Then he reached up and turned the lock.

"I'm pausing the world."

Aurora's breath caught in her throat at the warm look in Kiran's eyes. He looked at her like . . . like a man who loved a woman, and all at once, she felt very grown up. When she had left Pavan, all she had was a lifetime of waiting—waiting for her magic to manifest, waiting to come of age, waiting in fear of her secret getting out, waiting for some day in the future when she could finally be the true Aurora.

And now . . . here she was. She had discovered so much about the world and herself. She'd faced danger and taken control of her own choices. She'd seen deserts and mountains and walked unfamiliar roads. She knew what it looked like when someone loved her. In some ways, Aurora had lived more life in her few short months with Kiran than all her previous years combined.

She looked at him now—the dark hair that fell to his shoulders, the strong, stubbled line of his jaw, the broad expanse of his chest. He was stunning in the glow of the room's lanterns. His body was big and strong, and she could not help remembering all the times she'd been pressed against him—so, so close, but never close enough. Would tonight be the night that they took things one step further?

Her thoughts were abruptly interrupted when Kiran crossed toward her—two long strides eating up the distance between one blink and the next. He didn't touch her, but he stood toe to toe with her, his head tilted down toward hers.

"What were you just thinking about?" he asked.

She knew a flush was rising in her cheeks, could feel the heat, but she met his eyes anyway. She was not embarrassed, not with him. When she thought she would have to marry Cassius, she'd been overcome with nerves at the thought of being intimate, being *vulnerable* with a man she barely knew. But now, the swooping feeling in her stomach was not nerves, but anticipation. She trusted Kiran with her heart. She was about to trust him with her greatest secret. It was surprisingly easy to trust him with her body as well.

"I was thinking about you," she said.

"What about me?"

She didn't hesitate. "How good it feels when you touch me."

He hummed beneath his breath, and she knew he wanted to smile, could see the tension around his mouth as he tried to hold it back.

He raised his hand and caressed her cheek with his thumb. "When I touch you here?"

She leaned into his hand. "Yes."

"And here?" he asked, trailing his fingers down over her jaw to dip beneath the leather collar she wore and graze the sensitive skin of her neck.

She tilted her head up, giving him more room, and he failed to fight off his smile this time. "You already know the answer," she told him.

He chuckled, and a languorous heat unfurled in her belly. It really was as if the world outside had ceased to exist. There was no more worry, no more frustration or urgency or guilt. It was if they had all the time in the world.

"I do," he said. "But I like hearing it all the same."

"You mean your ego likes it."

He snaked an arm around her middle and yanked her forward until she crashed into him.

"All of me likes it."

And then he kissed her, and time couldn't move fast enough.

The kiss ignited immediately, going from slow and soft to deep and passionate. He pulled her up on her tiptoes, and she wrapped her arms around his neck. But when that wasn't enough for either of them, his hands curled around her hips and pulled her off her feet completely. Her legs wound around his waist, and then he was walking her toward the bed.

Aurora broke the kiss to pull at the leather straps that kept on the collar and vest she wore. She had the top two undone when Kiran tossed her on the bed. She squealed in surprise, and he laughed as he crawled onto the bed beside her.

"You could have warned me," she said, her hands moving quickly to undo the rest of the straps.

"Where would be the fun in that?"

When she finished with the last clasp, Kiran helped her remove the protective vest, leaving her in a linen shirt and pants. He removed her boots, followed by his own. Then he lay back and rolled onto his side to face her. She did the same.

They stared at each other, and a flicker of nerves surfaced. Maybe she needed to tell him now, before things went any further. She had gotten her pause. It would never be long enough, but it had calmed her spirit. It would have to be enough.

Kiran interrupted her thoughts by rolling her back and coming to hover over her. His upper body was propped up by his hands, and his legs were tangled with hers.

"I thought we were paused," he murmured. Lowering himself until his body rested lightly against hers.

"We are," she said, lifting her chin to graze a kiss along his jaw. "But it can't last forever."

"It can last until I'm done kissing you."

"And how long will that take?"

He slid one of his hands past her waist, down over her hip, and to the cradle at the back of her knee. With one good tug he had her leg curled around his hip, and their bodies pressed more firmly together.

"Only one way to find out."

He lowered his mouth to hers. He gave her every kind of kiss that night. He began with the painfully slow ones that caused pleasure so sharp it nearly hurt. He kissed her fast, as if they had to fit a whole lifetime into this one night. He kissed her hard and soft and everything in between.

Aurora waited for him to ask for more, but he never did. She almost asked herself, but found she did not mind the endless kisses that led nowhere except to the next one and the next. It made her feel like this was simply one night of a thousand more they had to go.

Finally, sometime between the dead of night and the early morning when the lantern had burned low enough that they could only see each other, their kisses slowed and they lay content in each other's arms.

And finally, Aurora knew the time had come.

Her head was laid against his chest, his heartbeat steady and sure in her ear.

"And now the world goes on," she murmured.

He stiffened slightly, but kept his arm tucked around her. "So it does."

She didn't want to, but Aurora sat up and scooted off the bed to stand. Her nerves were back in full force, and she could not lie there on the bed with him and get out the words she needed to.

She walked to the room's one tiny window and stared out for a moment. She could just see the top of the palace dome over the neighboring buildings, gleaming in the moonlight. She thought about her mother in there somewhere, ill and believing her dead.

She was alive. That was something. But for how long? How sick was she?

Aurora had the best of intentions when she left, but something along the way had gone terribly wrong. And if her mother had never received her letter from Nova explaining the truth of her supposed kidnapping, it likely had been wrong from the very start.

"I do not know where to begin," she finally confessed.

She heard the bed creak as he moved, but she did not let herself look at him, too afraid she would lose her nerve.

"Start with the simplest truth."

The simplest truth. She could do that. She took one last look at the palace in the distance, and then forced herself to face him.

Then she confessed to her first lie.

"My name is not Roar. It's Aurora."

We are not free when ruled by fear.

—leaflet dispersed by the rebellion

7

Aurora.

It was a pretty name. But something about it set Kiran's heart racing.

Aurora.

"Why lie about your name?" he asked.

Roar—no, *Aurora* winced. "It's not completely a lie," she answered. "Most of my life I've gone by Rora. Roar was just . . . a clean slate."

He could understand that. After all, he had spent half his life going by a name he hated simply because it was where he had grown up.

"And why did you need a clean slate? What were you running from?" And more importantly . . . was she in danger by being back in this place that she'd once seen fit to run from?

She took a deep, almost ominous breath and said, "I was supposed to be married."

He was standing and halfway across the room before he'd even realized it. He made himself stop. His heart was hammering, the sound in his ears rivaling any storm he had ever faced.

"*Married?* To whom?" A tangle of emotions rose in his chest—anger and jealousy and fear. And then . . . horrified realization. The pieces began sliding into place. She was educated, *very* educated.

She always spoke with such surety and command. She'd been so secretive about her life in Pavan. She wanted to come back for *her mother*. Everything in him slowed, as if he were trying to claw himself free of time so that he could stop the words from leaving her mouth.

"I was supposed to marry Cassius Locke."

He recoiled. He'd lived with the name Locke himself for so long, but now he thought he might vomit if he even thought it again. He took one step back, then another. Then he made himself look at her. One glimpse of her skyfire-white hair, and he wondered how he had not seen it before. He felt stupid and sick to his bones.

"Say something," Aurora whispered.

"What am I supposed to say?" His voice was gravel, stripped down to stone, and the hurt in her expression immediately showered him with guilt. But he could not apologize. He was too busy desperately drawing on every ounce of control he had to stop from losing his mind.

Royalty. She was bleeding *royalty.*

He turned toward the door, suddenly desperate for space. His mind was calling up every suspicious word or moment in their history, seeing them in a new light, and he needed it to stop. Everything was unraveling—both the past they'd shared and the future he had envisioned.

She was royalty. He was, for all intents and purposes, a criminal.

"Where are you going?"

He did not answer, and as he reached the door, he felt her hands on his back.

"Wait, please. Let me explain."

He kept his eyes fixed on the wooden door in front of him, tracing the grain to keep from looking back at her. "I understand, perfectly."

"No! You don't." She slammed a hand on his back, none too gently. "Look at me."

"I can't," he breathed, pressing his eyes closed. He'd said he wanted to be good for her. And somehow she had looked him in the eyes without laughing. In what world would an orphaned renegade be good for a future queen?

She slipped around him, sliding between his body and the door. "I am still me."

"Are you? Nothing I know about you is true."

Everything was a lie. From the moment they had met in the Eye, everything he thought he knew—all false.

She took his hand, holding it between both of hers and pressing it close to her chest. "We are true. I did not lie about any of that."

He did not think she did. That was part of what made this so scorching hard. He loved her. She loved him. But it would not matter, not in this world.

Unless . . .

He cupped her cheek with his free hand. "We could leave," he said. "Go anywhere on the continent. We'll make a new life."

That he could do. He might not be able to give her a palace, but the riskiest hunters could name their price. He'd get her as close to a palace as was possible in the wildlands. Skies, the two of them together, they could carve out their own territory to protect. Who needed Stormlings at all?

She was already shaking her head. "I cannot do that. Look at what's happened in my absence. My mother is ill, the city is under attack, and a ruthless family has taken over my kingdom."

The words hung in silence between them. *Her kingdom.* He had simply been a reprieve from this life, this place. He had been a *pause*, the same as she had asked for tonight.

"And how, exactly, do you plan on regaining *your kingdom*?" he asked, his stomach lurching painfully. "Will you marry the prince?"

"*No*," she insisted, horrified.

"You should," he answered, bile rising in his throat. "It's the simplest way to make things right."

"If I cared about simple, I would not have staged my own kidnapping and run away with *you*."

Skies above, he had forgotten that part of the princess's story completely. The soldiers they had encountered in the wildlands had said she was kidnapped. What would have happened to his crew if she had been discovered then? What would happen to them if she was discovered *now*?

He pulled away from her, crossing the room to put distance between them as his temper flared to life. "Do you have any idea how much danger you've brought on the rest of us? I *told* you what the Lockes did to my sister. They took a *child* to the gallows for being in the wrong place at the wrong time. What do you think they will do to the people who took away the prince's intended bride?"

Her bright blue eyes were covered in a sheen of tears as she answered, "You did not take me away. I took myself."

"That won't matter much when there's a noose around our necks."

This was his fault. It was his responsibility to protect his crew. Sly had *told him*, told everyone that there was something not right about Roar's story. But he'd been too blinded by what he felt for her.

"I know," she whispered, a single broken sob cracking through. "I know how selfish I have been. But I promise I would never let that happen."

"Are you paying attention, Aurora? This isn't the home you left. Things have changed. You can't just waltz back in and demand your crown back, not unless you plan to marry to do it."

"There are other ways. Yesterday, I saw an old member of my personal guard. I followed him."

"You did *what*? Bleeding skies. What if he saw you?" Gods, even now there could be soldiers out there looking for her. He turned back toward the bed, his mind already turning toward packing up, deciding they should move locations to be safe.

Aurora's voice stopped him. "He did see me. Jinx and I followed him, and he ended up leading us to a secret hideout for members of a rebellion. They can help me find out what happened and fight to undo it."

Kiran pressed his hands against his head, trying to soothe a brutal ache that had started down the center of his forehead. "I don't understand."

"I'm supposed to meet him again in the morning," she said. "I had hoped you would go with me."

"Not that," he snapped. "You left this place, left everyone in it. You were so desperate to leave that you followed strangers into one of the most dangerous situations imaginable. And now you want to fight and possibly die in some revolution for this place?" His voice was growing louder, his frustration harder to tame. "Even if you win, there's a madman outside those gates somewhere probably planning to level this city into nothing but dust and ash like he did the last one. We could be back in the wildlands tomorrow, back to hunting storms and living however we want to live."

She crossed her arms over her chest, and Kiran hated how vulnerable she looked. "You want me to run away?"

"Yes!" he cried. "You did it once before, what's the difference?"

"I never planned to *stay away*," she yelled, her breath coming in heaving pants.

He stared at her, and for just a moment, he *hated* her. His life had been so simple before she came along. He fought storms, made money, and lived each day however he wanted, as if it might be his last, as if it *should* be his last. Then she had cracked him open, and made him *feel* and *want* things he had never let himself want. He began to think of what it might be like to plan past the present, to dream of a future. And now he knew that was all a lie. There was no future here. Not between them. She was a Stormling. He was *nothing*.

"Kiran," she murmured, stepping toward him.

He held up a hand to stop her. "Don't. Don't touch me."

He did not know what he might do if she did. He would never hurt her, not on purpose. But he had never felt this many emotions at the same time. He did not know if he wanted to cry or yell or beg her to leave with him. And he hated feeling so out of control.

He needed to leave. Now. He crossed to the bed and jammed his feet into his boots. From a chair in the corner, he pulled on his supply belt and a coat.

"Kiran, please. It was never my intention to hurt you."

"What was your intention then?"

She shrugged, her eyes glistening with tears. "I wanted to be happy. I wanted to choose my own life, rather than having it chosen for me."

"Is that not what is happening now? You feel guilty because you left, and now you are going to get yourself killed for it. If you go against the Lockes, they won't care who you are. Princess or peasant child—they will cut down anyone in their way."

"I left so I could become the woman I needed to be in order to protect my kingdom. And now it's time for me to do that."

"You're a Stormling. What more did you need?"

She touched a hand to her heart, where Kiran could see the furious flashing of the skyfire storm in her breast through the fabric of her shirt, and the last piece of the puzzle clicked into place.

"You needed magic," he said.

She nodded. "Mine never manifested, at least that's what we all believed. It's why I was supposed to marry Cassius. He was powerful enough to make up for my . . . flaws. But then I met you, and everything changed. I realized that I did not have to remain helpless."

So they had always been a stepping stone for her. A means to an end. She would have used them to gain power and then left them to return home, the conquering Stormling.

"I see."

"You saved my life that day, Kiran. You kept me from making what would have been the biggest mistake of my life."

"Did I? Sounds to me like I was the mistake. If you never met me, the city would not be in upheaval, you would still have your crown, and you would be with your mother and your friends where you belong."

"I belong with you." She sounded so earnest, so sweet. And it only made him want to run, far and fast.

"But I don't belong here, *Princess*." His lips curled into a bitterly sad smile. "I never will."

Then he opened the door, and he left.

Aurora stayed at the inn as long as she could the next morning, waiting for Kiran to come back. Jinx was with her, and the two had barely spoken. They did not need to. Aurora and Kiran had woken most of the inn with their argument. And while the others had no idea what had caused all the yelling, Jinx knew without having to be told.

Finally, when she could wait no more, Aurora said, "You don't have to come. This is my mess. I won't drag the rest of you into it."

She met the witch's eyes, and flinched at the wary look she found there. Jinx might be here, but it was clear she had misgivings.

"Why didn't you tell us?"

Aurora shrugged helplessly. "My whole life, my mother drilled into me that I could not trust anyone but myself. Secrets are what I know. Besides, it was difficult enough to get Kiran to agree to let me join the crew. If he'd had any inkling of who I was, he never would have allowed it."

"That was then. In all the weeks that followed, did we not do enough to earn your trust?"

A stone sunk in Aurora's middle. For a girl made of flesh and bones, she felt like she had wreaked more havoc than one person should be capable of.

"Of course you did. But by then, it was too dangerous. Soldiers were looking for me, and my magic was out of control. Truth be told, there were days I thought about being Roar forever."

"I think that's the problem. All of us are loners in some way. We don't form attachments easily. But you were one of us. Nothing matters more in a crew than trust. We would all be dead a hundred times over if we didn't have it. We invited you into the closest thing we all have to family, and for you it was temporary. How are any of us supposed to react to that?"

"I don't know," Aurora answered, her insides feeling shredded. "It is not as if I could have anticipated any of this. I did not know I would fall in love with Kiran. I did not know how much I would love you all."

"But once you did, you still kept your secret. You never let us in the way we did for you."

"I made a mistake. If I could go back and change it, I would. Because I've never been happier than the time I spent on this crew. But how could I live with myself if I turned my back on these people now? I would die a little every day knowing what fate I had left them to. I'm dying now knowing there are remnants vulnerable and suffering outside these gates. I know that Stormlings are not known for their compassion, but that's something I would like to change. Something I *will* change."

Jinx shook her head. "You even sound like a princess."

"And that's a bad thing?"

Jinx reached out and took Aurora's hand, giving it a firm squeeze. "No. Everybody wishes they could change the world. You actually can. I hope you do everything you want to do and more. I genuinely believe you can. But if you do this . . . you have to put those people above everything else—your own needs and wants and fears. It won't work any other way. And that's what Kiran knows. He knows you will belong to your people more than you ever will to him."

Aurora nodded, hearing his final words from their argument during the night.

I don't belong here.

Strangely enough, she had felt the same way her entire life. Even now . . . she would never be a *normal* Stormling. But she loved her home, and she believed it could be better.

"Just give him some time. It is a lot to process for all of us, *Your Highness*," Jinx gave a teasing half-bow.

Aurora groaned. "Please don't start that. It's been so nice to be treated like a normal person."

Jinx tapped her finger on her chin. "I loathe to be the one to break it to you, but you are far from normal."

"Says the woman who waged a full-on battle with vines she conjured from nowhere."

"That was incredibly impressive, true."

"It was," Aurora said with a smile. "You always are."

Jinx groaned and waved her hand in the air dramatically. "Enough with the mushy talk. I don't want to catch your emotions." She covered her mouth as though the weepy feeling in Aurora's throat was contagious.

Feeling a spark of lightness for the first time all morning, Aurora threw her arms around Jinx for a hug. The witch protested loudly enough for the neighbors to hear, but her arms folded around Aurora without hesitation.

Aurora had not realized how close she'd been to breaking until the hug eased her back from the brink.

"You might be a princess," Jinx whispered, "But you're still a novie to me, *novie*." Jinx pushed her back, dusting herself off as though the hug had left behind residue. "We're going to be late to your meeting."

"We?" Aurora asked.

"Of course. Like I would let you have all the fun."

The sun had already broken past the horizon. Taven would be wondering where she was. If she did not get there soon, he would start searching for her. She pulled up her hood, and together she and Jinx set out at a clipped pace.

The streets were busier today already. The damage from yesterday's firestorm appeared extensive. And with the sun's rise, people had risen too to repair their homes and comb through the wreckage. As badly as she was hurting, the sight of all this destruction only made her feel more certain that she was making the right decision. She would not let Pavan become like Calibah—nothing but stories and myths left to haunt the ruins. She had read the story of Calibah's siege and Finneus Wolfram's last desperate attempts to save his people more times than she could count in her childhood. She had seen herself in the outsider that was Finneus—a noble Stormling by birth, but an adventurer and sailor by calling. He had not been what society expected of a noble lord, but in the end it was he who rose up in the city's darkest moments.

It was Aurora's turn to do that now. She had not been a particularly good princess. But she belonged to Pavan, and Pavan to her, and she would fight for it until her dying breath, as her childhood hero had done upon the seas.

When they reached the location of the rebellion's hidden shelter, Taven was waiting for her, visibly distressed.

"Thank the goddess," he said. And then he bowed to her right there in the street.

"Stand up," she hissed. "Someone could see."

Jinx only snickered behind Aurora.

"I do not care," Taven answered. "You are alive. Better if the people know. They'll be more inclined to fight back."

It was not like Taven to be so careless, or so emotional. But of course, she had no idea what he had been through these months. She was about to find out though, and her stomach tossed with dread.

"Let's get inside. There's a great deal to talk about before we get to that point."

He removed the fake plants covering the door, and gestured for the girls to go first. Then he followed down after, pulling the camouflage back in place as he closed the door.

Today, there was a lantern already waiting in the first room. Taven picked it up and led them to the door on the right side of the room. The door, it appeared, was kept locked, for he knocked—three times in rapid succession, followed by a pause, and two more slower knocks. Aurora heard a lock slide, and then the door opened, revealing a man standing guard, armed with a wickedly curved blade. Beyond him lay a shockingly long corridor lit by skyfire lanterns. There were a few rooms off to each side; most appeared to be stockpiled with supplies. Taven continued past them all to a closed door at the end. This time there was no secret knock, merely a few quick hard raps.

Aurora heard deep, throaty laughter inside that could only be Zephyr—the water witch. Aurora barely had time to process the news in all the ensuing fallout. Of course, Jinx had told her that witches of numerous powers existed, but Aurora had been taught for so long that witches were extinct that it still stunned her anew every time those lessons were proven wrong.

The laughter moved closer, and then the door swung open just in time for them to catch the show of Zephyr's head slung backward in mirth—her wild hair as dark as the space that stretched between stars.

She turned her head and smiled at them and said, "Come in. Come in."

Aurora stepped inside first, and her heart lurched so hard she lost her breath.

"I am told you know each other," Zephyr said, appearing at Aurora's side. "I was quite shocked myself when Locke found me last night." Zephyr winced and added, "Excuse me. Kiran. Or do you prefer Thorne?"

"Either is fine." Kiran's deep voice was a punch to the chest.

"That will take some getting used to," Zephyr added.

Aurora couldn't move. She certainly couldn't speak. Her heart felt smashed against her rib cage, like someone was trying to push it out through the gaps.

"He told me quite a tale," Zephyr continued, stepping past Aurora to return to her desk in the center of the room, upon which Kiran leaned as if he'd been there a thousand times. The witch paused briefly to scratch the head of the wildcat who lay curled up on a plush pillow in the corner, before retaking her seat. Kiran's expression was empty, matter-of-fact, and Aurora found herself struggling not to cry.

"Rescued from kidnappers in the midst of a storm. Goodness, you are one lucky girl." Zephyr laughed again, and this time it did not sound quite so effervescent.

He lied for her? She had not necessarily intended to tell the whole truth, especially not to this Zephyr woman. But his gaze met hers with a hard intensity, and she found herself nodding along with his story. "Yes. Very lucky, indeed." She could not help but add, "I could not be more grateful to have met him."

He averted his gaze, and she did her best not to let the hurt show on her face. "How do the two of you know each other?" Aurora asked.

Zephyr smiled, and took a seat at her desk. "We have similar interests."

Aurora's stomach pitched, and she thought she might be sick. He left her the night before to come find this woman. *Why?* She was so hyperaware of the exact distance between the two of them that she hardly noticed when Taven closed the door and pushed her gently toward a chair.

"Zephyr was the proprietor behind the Eye," Kiran said. "Though she tended to keep that secret. I did a special hunt for her a few years back."

"Yes, it's a pity the Eye is no more," Zephyr said, her full lips pursing into a frown. "We have your almost-husband to thank for that."

Finally, Aurora found her nerve to speak. "So it was Cassius who destroyed the Eye?"

The water witch shrugged. "His brother technically led the raid, but since Cassius oversees the military I am sure it was done at his command."

"How did you know where to find her?" Aurora asked, turning her stare back to Kiran, hoping he could not see the hurt shining in her eyes. If he had known how to get in touch with the leader of the Eye, why hadn't he done that to begin with?

For a moment, she thought he might ignore her completely, but then he shrugged. "Jinx mentioned the leader of the rebellion was a water witch. I only know of one in Pavan, so I went to a tavern where I knew I could get her a message."

A quick look to Jinx confirmed this. But Aurora still did not understand. He had been so against her taking part in a rebellion, and then he went straight to the woman who led it? What was he playing at?

She wanted to bombard him with questions, but she would not do it here in front of the woman whose eyes traced over his back as if he were a particularly impressive work of art.

So instead, she forced her eyes to Taven and said, "Tell me everything."

She listened for the next hour as Taven told the story of her kingdom's fall, starting with the day of her kidnapping, and the exhaustive search that followed. She immediately felt guilty, for it was clear that Taven had taken her disappearance incredibly hard. It was why he had involved himself in the Locke military, so that he could be part of the search for her. The news was worse than she feared. It was more than the remnants outside who were suffering. The Eye had been burned in a show of force when the Lockes first took over. The only reason there was not massive loss of life was because Taven had managed to get a message to Zephyr in time for them to evacuate. That had been the beginning of his relationship with the resistance. He spoke of fellow soldiers killed for refusing to switch sides. He told her about the increasing number of volatile storms appearing nearly from thin air, and the people who suffered when the Stormlings were not fast enough to provide cover.

"And my mother?" Aurora asked. "How could she let this all happen?"

Taven shook his head mournfully. "When the queen found out you were taken . . . it was not as though she had lost hope, but as though she had none to begin with. She was devastated, reduced to ruins by her grief. She took to her bed, and she has not left it since."

"You've seen her?"

Taven nodded. "She looked right through me."

"And she is there still?"

"As far as I know."

Now Aurora knew her first priority. She had never known her mother to be overly emotional, but if she had never received Aurora's note, she would have believed that Aurora really had been kidnapped for her Stormling abilities. And since Aurora had had no such abilities, kidnappers might indeed have found her worthless.

Aurora cleared her throat to make sure her voice did not crack. "And Novaya—is she well?"

Taven's mouth dropped open slightly, and he stared. "Your Highness, I assumed you knew."

She winced at the honorific, but pushed on to the point. "Knew what?"

"That she helped orchestrate your kidnapping."

Aurora leaped from her seat. "That's not true."

Taven's eyes widened. "She was investigated. They found a large sum of gold in her room, and the Stormheart that Prince Cassius gave you as a gift."

She turned on instinct, and found Kiran's jaw tightened into stone, his eyes fixed menacingly on the floor.

"I gave the Stormheart to her because it meant nothing to me. She did not steal it. And she had *nothing* to do with my kidnapping," Aurora answered.

"You are certain?" Taven asked.

"Of course!"

He frowned, and his eyes turned solemn. "She's in the dungeons. The prince put her there the day you were taken."

Aurora nearly lost her footing. In fact, she did lose her footing, and the only reason she was not sprawled out on the floor was because someone had caught her.

Kiran.

She could feel him at her back, his large hands curled protectively around her waist. She wanted nothing more than to turn around in his arms and beg for comfort. But she steadied her footing and stepped back toward Taven.

"We have to help her."

"That's why we're here," Zephyr drawled. "To help them all. It's not only your friends and family hurting."

"I know that," Aurora snapped.

"Then what are you going to do about it?" Zephyr asked.

Aurora lifted her chin and stared first at Zephyr, then Taven, and finally Kiran. She saw no hint of emotion in his expression, but he did not look away. This was the problem, and they both knew it . . . she wanted to help, but she did not have the first clue how.

She might have been good with a knife and decent at hand-to-hand combat, but she was not a soldier. Late at night, she still seethed with grief for the soul whose magic now lived in her breast. And that was a storm, a life already lived. How could she possibly think to fight a real *war*?

"I do not know," Aurora finally answered.

Zephyr rose from the desk and walked toward Aurora. "The first thing you must do is decide where you draw the line."

"What line?"

"How far are you willing to go to save your people and recover your crown? What are you willing to compromise? Give up? Betray? How dirty are you willing to get your royal hands?" As she asked the question, Zephyr raised her own hand, the one adorned with the menacing red glove.

Aurora wished she could respond immediately, assert that she would do whatever it took, but she knew there was far more than her own life at stake in this decision.

"And once I decide that line," Aurora said, "what comes next?"

"Then we use one problem to solve another. There's no point defeating the Lockes only to be destroyed by the Stormlord. Nor will there be much use in deposing the Lockes if there is no kingdom left to rule. From what Taven has told us about the Stormlord's interactions with Locke soldiers in the field, he seems particularly fixated on this family, even taunting them with his kills. If we are lucky, they are all he wants. So, the logical solution is to deliver the Locke family to the Stormlord, either by stealth or violent insurrection."

It was a sound plan, even if it made her stomach turn. She wished a great many things on the Locke family, but did she wish them dead? Or worse, perhaps? The Stormlord was said to be mad and cruel. If it truly was the Lockes he wanted, what would he do with them? And what was to say he would stop once he had the

Stormlings he wanted? But it was a plan, something tangible they could work toward, which was more than she had. That would have to be enough for now.

"How do we begin?" Aurora asked.

Zephyr laughed. "What's to say I even want you involved? You are just another Stormling who will stomp all over the rest of us. This is *my* revolution. If you want to be part of it, you will need to prove your worth."

Aurora tipped her chin up, and met Zephyr's gaze with a hard stare of her own. "And if I decide I would rather start my *own* revolution? Taven will side with me, won't you?" The soldier looked uncomfortable, but he gave Zephyr one solemn look before nodding his head.

"My life is to protect yours," he replied.

"Not to mention," Aurora continued, "I spent eighteen years exploring the halls and rooms of that palace. No one knows it better than I. And the skyfire that runs through my veins will open the palace gate."

That point was a bit of a bluff. She hoped that the skyfire in her chest would work just as well as a normal Stormling affinity, but she did not know for sure.

"You do drive a hard bargain," Zephyr said, her pretty, dark-red lips curling.

"I have not offered you a bargain, yet. But I am prepared to."

Zephyr's eyebrows raised, and the lazy, uninterested slouch disappeared from her posture. "Do tell."

Aurora took a deep breath. "Help me save my kingdom, help me restore the Pavan throne, and you may reopen the Eye, this time as a legal venture, safe from prosecution."

Everyone in the room stared at Aurora as if she'd grown a second head.

"You will, of course, still risk prosecution for the darker endeavors that sometimes go round the market. Cutthroats and thieves and any other purveyors of violent crime shall be tried according to the law. But I promise that magic will no longer be viewed as a crime."

Zephyr appeared almost dumbstruck for a moment, but she recovered with a quick blink and stuck out her gloved hand, claws first. "You have a deal, Princess."

And just like that . . . Aurora had joined the revolution.

Not our king. Not our refuge.

—painted by a rebel on the city wall

8

That night Aurora told the entire crew about her identity and her intent to involve herself in the rebellion. She had been prepared for the worst, for them all to hate her for lying and luring them back to Pavan. But to her surprise, no one yelled or raged as Kiran had done.

Bait was the first to throw in his support. "Does this mean we get to fight? *With magic?* You do not know how long I have been waiting to put all that storm magic to a use that does not include powering the Rock or weakening another storm. As long as I get to blow some things up, count me in."

Aurora was thoroughly surprised when Duke was the next to rise from his seat. He had not been shocked by her announcement, but he looked at her strangely, as though he saw an entirely different person standing before him. "I don't know how much use an old man would be, but I have never been part of a revolution. Seems like something I should do before I die."

Aurora swallowed a lump in her throat, suddenly all too aware of how frail the wise old man seemed. His hand clasped her shoulder, and she laid hers on top of it. He gave her shoulder a squeeze, then looked past her to the hunter looming against the far wall of the room.

If possible, Kiran looked more angry than he had the night

before. It showed on his face as clearly as a thunderstorm building on the horizon.

"Are you really planning to legalize magic besides Stormling magic?" Jinx asked. "*All* magic?"

"All magic," Aurora affirmed. "I've seen what you can do, Jinx. And while I might not know as much about it as I would like, I'm certain that all the lies I was taught as a child are just that. What you do is not evil or against nature any more than what I can do. So whether our abilities came from the goddess or something else entirely—we should be treated the same, you and I."

"Then count me in," Jinx said.

Surprisingly, Sly was the next to follow. She still did not appear any friendlier toward Aurora than she had been to Roar, and she did place a condition on her participation. "No more lying," Sly insisted. "From this point on, we deserve your trust and your truth."

"You will have it," Aurora promised.

Ransom was the last to speak, and he too glanced at Kiran before he answered. "I was getting a bit bored anyhow," he said. "Little bit of treason ought to break things up nicely."

She waited, unsure if she wanted to address Kiran in front of the group, or wait until they could be alone to talk. But he surprised her by stepping forward and addressing the group as a whole. "Well, now that you have all agreed. You should know I volunteered our remaining magic supplies to the cause when I met with Zephyr last night."

Aurora's mouth dropped open.

"You did what?"

He'd been vehemently against her taking part, and now he volunteered his own services? She had not thought he could be more infuriating than he'd been when he first started training her, but this surpassed even that. All the torment he'd put her through the night before, and now he was simply on board?

But when he looked at her with those same cold, unfeeling eyes, she knew that he wasn't doing this for her.

"I have been waiting a long time to punish the Lockes for what they did to my sister. To punish Stormlings for what they've done to thousands of families just like mine. This seems like it might be my best chance."

If Aurora's heart had not already been broken, that would have done the trick. He looked at her as if she and the Lockes were the same. And after the way she had acted, thinking only of herself, and not what would happen to her mother or Nova or the hunters she had made her unwitting accomplices—perhaps she deserved that.

"Well then," she said to the group. "We meet the rebellion under the cover of the next storm. So be ready."

Thirteen Years Earlier

The first child died of a fever after a few days of endless rain and wind. She was young, too young, and when Cruze had gone to sleep the night before, curled into the hollow of the rock he had claimed as his own, she had been delirious and shivering, but alive. When he woke the next morning, she sat with her arms wrapped tightly around her legs, her head laid against her knees, and her eyes flat and unseeing as she stared out at the forest.

Kess tried to wake her, but at the slightest touch, she fell over, her limbs stiff and locked into place the way she had died. Another girl, a friend perhaps, tried to pull her out of the knot she was in, but her body was stuck in her final position—huddled for warmth that would never come.

That had set off a round of wailing and blubbering that made Cruze's head ache and his eyes twitch, so he once again stalked off into the woods, searching for something, *anything* to distract him from the situation.

Cruze was not worried about dying, though perhaps he should have been. Instead, he dreaded the slow march toward death he would have to endure with the others. It was clear to him that these children would not last long in this harsh environment. There was no doubt it was their captors' intention, to let nature dole out the cruelty for them. But he refused to be dragged down by the weakness of those around him. The dark whispers had advanced in frequency, and he found himself fighting off bursts of temper. He worried that he would snap if he had to listen to them cry for another day.

He had to find a way to survive on his own.

That was when he felt it—another of those provocative whispers that had been trailing him since his arrival. This one was closer though, more like a brush of the wind. This time, he did not ignore it. Instead, he sought it out.

He spun around, searching the jungle around him. There was green everywhere he could see—in the vines and leaves and trees overhead, along with the undergrowth at his feet. The trunks of the trees stretched on and on, until his eyes blurred when he tried to focus on any in the distance.

"Who is there?" he called out.

The whisper curled around his ear again, murmuring indistinct words of passion and determination that made something in his chest rise up in response.

"Where are you? *What* are you?"

No voice answered, not this time. But a tickle crawled up the back of his neck and then he saw a flash of something in his mind's eye. It was this same forest, but *not*. In the image, skyfire burst overhead, trees were toppled around him, and there was screaming, so much screaming.

The sight lasted only for a moment before the present came rushing back, and he spun around searching for the source as the screams still echoed in his ears.

Another vision came, this one longer. There were children running, sliding in the wet mud, desperately trying to escape *something*. The vision panned backward, as if he looked over his shoulder, and he saw the trees, alight with fire that flew like a flock of birds from branch to branch, chasing him, crackling an awful warning the closer it got. He ran and he ran, but the fire was faster. Then trees started dropping; great towering beasts older than he could imagine slammed to the ground, rattling the very earth. The fire spread like a monster's breath, lighting up the undergrowth and decay that sat beneath the canopy like it was nothing more than kindling. Before he knew it, the flames were in front of him and beside him, as well as behind him. He turned and turned and turned, certain that somewhere there was a gap, if he could only find it. But the smoke was getting thicker, and his head ached and his lungs burned with every breath. He huddled in the middle of the small clearing with a few other children, back to back, as the fire encroached ever closer, waiting.

Waiting to die.

Cruze pulled himself from the vision with a start, pressing his hand to the nearest tree to be sure it was standing. He felt the wet bark against his palm as he struggled to regain his breath, and was embarrassed to note tears tracked down his cheeks. He shoved his knuckles roughly over his skin, wiping away the weakness, and surveyed the area around him more carefully, noting downed trees over which shrubs and moss had grown so completely that Cruze could only guess that lifetimes had passed since their falling.

"Did you die here?" he murmured, knowing volume did not matter, not in this strange, haunted place he found himself in.

A rush of emotion poured over him, stronger than the torrent of rain they had endured in the days since they had been stranded here—grief, regret, fear, but most of all—fury.

"Were you left here like me?" he asked. "Left to die?"

He received another flash of images, this time of a carriage like the one that had transported him and the others to this place—something more suited to moving livestock than children—followed by a flash of the city by the sea he used to call home.

Locke.

Cruze made a promise to himself then. He would do whatever it took to survive this savage place. And someday, no matter how many days it took, he would have his revenge on the people who did this. Not just to him, but to all those who had died in this place before him.

After a few more meetings, the plans were cemented, and under the rumbling distraction of a thunderstorm, Aurora began her first mission for the rebellion. She was covered head to toe, her identity hidden but for her eyes—a necessity for the night's work. Had she not worn thick leather, anyone would be able to see the strange light that was no doubt pulsing erratically in her chest alongside the anxious beat of her heart. And that was one secret she intended to keep for as long as possible.

Aurora's sharp blue eyes scanned the top of the palace walls. The posts above should be deserted; during a storm, the soldiers typically retreated to the towers stationed at each of the cardinal directions as secondary levels of defense for the Stormling fighting from high atop the palace's dome. But all the same, her gaze darted up to scan the walls just in case. She could hear Jinx's light footsteps falling close behind her own, and her heart careened between each unsteady breath. The other rebels were watching from afar, waiting for her signal. As were her fellow hunters, who had followed her blindly into this chaos even though she did not deserve their loyalty.

Tonight, the rebellion would infiltrate the palace that had once been her home. And Aurora would be the one to open the door. Or gate, as it were.

Aurora slowed to a stop and met Jinx's eyes; the witch nodded her readiness. Nothing but confidence shone in her friend's face. Having Jinx by her side calmed some of Aurora's nerves, but she would have felt better with Kiran there, and worse all at the same time. Things with him were . . . *complicated*. They still appeared to be part of the same crew, for now. They had made commitments to the same rebellion. They even slept under the roof of the same inn. But that was all that remained the same.

Their eyes rarely met, and when they did, his were unreadable. He avoided being alone with her at all costs, disappearing quickly after meetings with the rebellion or with the other hunters. The girls were bunking together as originally suggested, and that night she had spent in Kiran's room felt more like a dream than a memory. It was as if the weeks they spent together in the wilds had never happened. He had written her out of his life as though she were nothing more than a footnote in a longer story.

So it was for the best that he had been designated part of the infiltration group. She was worried about him, about the risks the rebellion was taking, but if he was off with the rebels, he wouldn't be around to interfere with her own plans. It had been decided in their meetings that Aurora was "too valuable" to contribute anything to the mission except the barest essential—hence she and Jinx's current approach toward the palace gate that could only be opened by someone of Pavanian lineage (or someone who wielded skyfire magic as they did).

But she was no longer the Aurora who had grown up in Pavan, constrained by fear into letting others make her decisions. She was done seeing her value as a prize to be kept away and guarded and played like a game piece at exactly the right time. Aurora still had a great deal to learn, but of one thing she was certain: the value of a person remained unmeasured until they did something worth measuring. Sometimes the most important thing a person could do was to simply show up. And Aurora Pavan had been missing long enough.

Tonight she would help the rebellion's mission, but she would also take on a mission of her own choosing.

"Ready?" Jinx asked, breaking the silence. Aurora nodded. She had been ready to do this for days. Only reason and fear of repercussions had stopped her from storming into the palace days ago.

Knowing the thunder rumbling overhead would serve as the best cover for their mission, they waited until the next rolling crash began, then they set off at a hard sprint. They came around the curve of the wall, and as Taven had promised, only one man stood guard at the palace gate; all the others had gone to their respective stations for the storm. By the time the soldier turned his eyes from the sky to them, it was too late. Jinx held out her hand as if to blow a kiss, and instead a fine powder danced from her palm like mist. The soldier gulped in air to yell, breathing in the powdered and enchanted Rezna's rest, and before his tongue had even curled thought into sound, he slumped into a deep sleep, his limbs sprawling awkwardly across the wet grass.

Aurora glanced quickly at his face, but did not recognize him, so with Jinx's help, they carried him closer to the wall and gently laid him out in the shadows. Jinx had made a large enough dose that he should be out for several hours.

The sky overhead looked as if the stars were weeping, giant glittering tears falling against an invisible barrier. Aurora gave a low whistle, the signal that all was clear. The sound was barely discernible above the din of the storm, but somewhere out there, fellow rebels were running to join her. The plan was to enter the palace and kidnap at least one of the Lockes to use as a show of trust in their attempts to contact and reach a bargain for peace with the Stormlord.

Aurora tried not to think about that, about the fact that they were giving a human being over to a madman who had laid waste to villages across the continent of Caelira, who had wiped the city of Locke from existence as thoroughly as the city of Calibah had been destroyed two decades before. The Lockes had done unspeakable things to the people of Pavan, to her city's soldiers, possibly to her own mother, certainly to Nova.

It was them she had to fight for now.

And more than that, she tried not to think of the Stormlord at all, for thinking of him made fear leech in from the shadowy places inside her. They shared a gift—she and this madman—and if she let herself think too long on that she began to worry that his fate would one day become hers. *That* was a fear for another day.

Aurora stepped forward to survey the palace gate, its skyfire clockwork as dazzling now as it had been to her as a young child. She began to hear the soft thud of footfalls, and knew that the others were sidling up behind her, keeping tight to the shadows.

"You sure you can deliver, hunter?" a low, feminine voice drawled.

Aurora looked over her shoulder, meeting ink-black eyes rimmed with long lashes. The rest of the speaker's face was covered by a cloth mask. Long, dark braids spilled over shoulders fitted with thick, black leather armor. Even without those clues, Aurora would have known who questioned her.

Zephyr.

Aurora opened her mouth to reply, but then caught sight of a familiar pair of brown eyes just behind Zephyr, and she forgot her intentions. Those eyes had been so many things to Aurora— infuriating, enticing, and above all comforting. Now, they were just another part of the chaos, another thing she had to work to shield herself against. The silence must have gone on too long because Jinx answered for her, "She'll come through."

Aurora wished she were so confident. It was taking all her concentration to keep the storm above from bleeding into her thoughts and emotions. The magic barrier overhead was different this time, lighter, keeping the worst of the skyfire at bay, but allowing the rain to slip through. Oddly, the rain did not fall straight through, but instead gathered across the barrier like dew on a leaf and slowly dripped through in heaping droplets when the water became too heavy. Every now and then, a large splash would hit her arm or head or back, soaking her skin or hair or clothes. The lighter barrier also let more of the storm's consciousness creep through, and she could feel it crooning to her, crackling in the air around them.

Shut it all out.

Aurora stepped up toe to toe with the gate, eighteen years of doubt and anxiety roiling in her belly. She could not recall how many times in her life she had stared at the skyfire workings of this gate and despaired that she would never be able to use them, to wield the power of her ancestors.

Everything was different now. *She* was different now. In every way. But she hoped that the skyfire storm that beat in her chest, unusual as it was, would still allow her to open the gates. In fact, she had already promised the rebellion it would. And if it didn't, there was no guarantee they would not offer her up as their next bargaining chip.

She concentrated, focusing on the foreign energy that resided in her chest, and laid her hand flat against the cool glass and metal that comprised the gate. The storm in her chest was not entirely separate from her, nor was it completely woven into her own makeup. But when she reached for the magic, it filled her in an instant. She sucked in a breath, overwhelmed by the intensity of otherness that crashed through her. The feeling turned to alarm as she felt an answering flare of magic from the storm overhead. The thunder exploded above; even the ground beneath her feet seemed to shake. Skyfire streaked across the sky, calling to her. She tilted her head back, gasping for breath. She could feel *so much*—the churning clouds in the sky and the trees shaking in the wind and all the little souls hunkered in their homes wondering if today would be the day that another storm broke through the Stormling's barrier.

"Anytime now," Jinx whispered under her breath.

Right. She had a mission. *Two*, technically. Slowly, Aurora came back to herself, focusing on the here and now instead of the expanse of the world around her. She built up her mental walls to quiet the true tempest, and concentrated on the one sparking frantically inside her. She imagined pushing it into the gate, using the magic to turn the clockwork wheels that would unlock it.

A glow began in the corner of her vision, at the bottom of the gate, and then she heard the metallic grind of the first cog beginning to turn.

Her excitement grew. She was doing this. She was truly working storm magic. She pushed harder, and the process sped up, adding a second cog, then a third. The gears of the door moved faster than she had ever seen. She opened herself up, pouring out more and more of the magic, watching the wheels whirl at a wondrous speed. Tears gathered at the edges of her eyes, sheer joy and surprise and relief all wrapped around her. She might have even laughed.

Then she felt it.

Something in her, something vital, shifted out of place. It did not hurt, not like a bone slipping out its joint, but she felt a hollow where one should not have been. She felt a stark, swallowing emptiness, and it was only when a whisper of magic from the thunderstorm overhead curled beckoningly inside her that she realized what she had done.

Hold tight to your own soul, the spirit witch had advised.

Aurora yanked her hand back, stumbling on legs that felt not quite her own. Then she pulled, on her magic, her consciousness, on anything and everything that was *hers*. The moment her soul slid back into place, she fell backward and began to weep uncontrollably. The sobs were not rational, she could not stop them, no matter how hard she tried to think them away; instead they came from somewhere deep inside her that she had not even known existed. She felt . . . uprooted, as if she had lost something essential that tied her down. Jinx was with her in a moment, her face shoved in front of Aurora's. The vision of her friend blurred through Aurora's tears.

"Quiet," Zephyr hissed.

Aurora knew she was making too much noise, but she could not stop the panic welling up inside her.

"Breathe," Jinx told her.

Aurora met her friend's eyes, trying to convey without words what had almost happened, what she had nearly done. Was it possible to lose your own soul? To just let it go? A new round of gasping sobs overtook her, and Jinx pulled Aurora against her in a hug.

"What's wrong with her?" Zephyr demanded, eyeing Aurora with suspicion.

Jinx said, "She opened the gate. That's what you wanted. Go on with your mission, and I'll take care of her."

Zephyr hesitated, her calculating gaze settling on Aurora in a manner that made reason begin to seep back in for the princess. She had spent her whole life keeping secrets, never letting anyone too close, and it appeared she was not through with that yet. There was much she still did not know about what she was and what she could do, but she knew that having some of the same identifying markers as the Stormlord could prove problematic if the wrong person found out.

Zephyr began gathering her crew to set off, and Aurora was counting the seconds until she was out of sight.

"Thorne?" Zephyr asked. "You're with us. Don't you remember?"

It was only then that Aurora realized Kiran stood directly behind her, less than an arm's length away. She looked at his feet, at his knees—she made it as far as the utility belt around his waist armed with storm magic before she ducked her head and forced her eyes down.

"I have her," Jinx whispered.

Then Kiran strode off after Zephyr without a word. Aurora pushed her forehead hard into her knees and fought off another round of sobs. Grabbing onto each breath as though it might be her last, she focused on the in-and-out, in-and-out. When she was calm enough to look up, everyone else was off to their positions for the mission. It was only she, Jinx, and the drugged soldier lying in the shadow of the still-open gate that remained. Jinx's expression was racked with concern. "What happened?"

Aurora shook her head. They did not have time to puzzle over the specifics of her abilities right now; they had other tasks to attend to. "I'm fine. Pushed too far, too fast."

Jinx nodded, but the witch still worried her bottom lip between her teeth. "Maybe we should—"

"No." Aurora cut her off. "I cannot wait anymore."

If Jinx was still worried, she did not object, not when Aurora rose to her feet or when she led them both through the palace gate, or when they darted through the royal courtyard toward the north wing that housed the royal suites.

Aurora knew all the secret passageways and tunnels in the palace, but she wanted to get to her mother as quickly as possible, so they'd decided to use Jinx's magic to scale the wall next to the queen's balcony. Then they would use the passageways to move about the palace and hopefully find Nova.

The courtyard was eerily silent under the reign of the night's storm. Puddles had begun to form in the grass, and their feet splashed as they ran, but there was no one around to hear. Aurora found her own room first out of habit, and was shocked to see light coming from her window. Did her mother visit her room sometimes?

But no, it could not be that. Taven had said she was bedridden.

Ill. Beyond help. She shook off the curiosity for another day and ran the last few paces to the space that lay beneath her mother's chambers. The queen's room, by comparison, was dark. There was a faint flicker of what she guessed was a candle, but nothing like the light that had been coming from her own rooms.

Jinx immediately set to work with her vines, digging a small hole in the earth and dropping a seed inside to make her magic easier. The plant bloomed quickly, climbing fiercely up the wall like a warrior to battle. Aurora went up first, her hands and feet moving faster than they ever had.

She landed on her mother's balcony with a heavy thud, but thunder rolled through the heavens a moment later, eclipsing the noise she and Jinx made. Aurora peeked through the curtains that lined the windows leading to the balcony, and she could see nothing inside the room except a lone candle by the bed, and a dark, huddled shape beneath the blankets. She rushed inside and went straight for the bed.

The first sight of her mother stole her breath and broke something inside her. Aurora had always known that her mother was aging. She'd had Aurora past her prime, and that had been eighteen years past. But Queen Aphra had always seemed so regal, powerful beyond measure—more like a goddess than a mother. Her silver-gray hair had never seemed a sign of her age so much as her power. But the woman lying in that bed looked old and frail. The skin of her face sagged as if she were in pain, even in her sleep. Her fingers clutched at the top of her blankets, knuckles wrinkled like prunes. She looked more than breakable. She looked as if she'd been broken, and no one had been able to put her together again quite how she used to be.

Aurora held one hand to her mouth in horror, and the other she reached out toward her mother. She touched a hand—the skin felt thin and too soft.

"Mother?" she whispered.

When no reply came, she tried again, "Ma?"

Carefully she held her mother's shoulder and shook. "Wake up. It's me. Aurora. I'm home."

Her mother did not move. Aurora shook her a little harder. Still no reaction. Jinx came around the bed then, and she took over with an emotionless efficiency that Aurora could not match. The witch touched Aphra's skin and checked her pulse and lifted her closed eyelids. Then her lips drew down in a heavy frown.

"What? What is it?"

"She's been drugged," Jinx answered. "My guess is heavily and for a long time."

Aurora stifled a cry and covered her mouth with both hands. She briefly slammed her eyes shut, letting the guilt and revulsion roll over her in one consuming wave. This was *her* fault. She had let this happen. The shame pierced her for a moment, through and through, then she pushed it away for another day.

"Is there something we can do? Is there any way to wake her up?"

"Not quickly," Jinx answered. "I have to be honest with you, Aurora. I am not positive she will wake up. It depends on what has been given to her. Only time and rest will tell."

A horrible wailing horn blared through the silent room in several quick bursts, but this was not any storm siren that Aurora recognized. It stopped, then started again. The sequence repeated. A rumbling sound began, followed by shouting, that grew louder when the door opened, revealing a distracted maid carrying a pitcher of water, and beyond her a glimpse of soldiers moving down the far hallway at rapid speeds, shouting about a breach. The maid bumped the door closed with her hip, turned toward the bed, then froze at the sight of Aurora and Jinx. She opened her mouth to scream, but Aurora beat her to it, shoving her into the wall and snarling, "Don't make a sound."

The maid began crying, little whimpers escaping her pursed lips. "Are you one of the ones who has been drugging the queen?" Jinx asked from behind Aurora.

The maid tensed, and her crying stopped immediately. "I—uh . . ."

"Tell the truth," Aurora demanded.

"What have you been giving her?" Jinx asked.

The maid stiffened her lip, lifted her chin, and replied, "I don't know what you mean."

Aurora pushed her hands harder against the girl's shoulders, pinning her to the wall. "Don't lie to us."

"I'm not ly—"

"Enough!"

A jolt of crackling magic shot from Aurora's hands into the girl, whose body jerked back against the wall. She cried out, her eyes fluttering wildly, then in a whining, wheezing voice said, "I don't know. He gives me the vials and a coin, and I don't ask questions."

"Who?" Aurora asked.

But it was too late. The girl had begun to slump against the wall, her glazed eyes falling shut. Aurora was tempted to let the girl drop, but instead she eased her to the ground, and then took two careful steps backward before shoving her fists against her eyes in frustration.

When she lowered them, Jinx was kneeling by the girl, her eyes trained on Aurora. "That was . . . *new*," the witch said carefully.

Rora looked down at her hands. Was it terrible that she had not even spared a thought for what she'd done? It all mattered little in comparison to what had been done to her mother.

"It was not intentional," she promised her friend. "I only wanted her to tell the truth, and the skyfire came unbidden. She's . . . she's not—"

"No," Jinx answered, standing. "She only got a bit of a shock. She'll be fine. But we need to move. She will have quite the story to tell when she wakes. We need to be lost to the winds by then, your mother too."

Together they heaved the queen's deadweight from the bed, dragging her too-thin arms around their shoulders as an anchor. Then they each wrapped an arm about the woman's waist and hefted her up between them. Aurora was more than half a head taller than Jinx, which left most of the queen's weight on her. Rora was fine with that. She'd carry her mother across Caelira if she had to.

She said, "We need to go out into the hallway. There's a tapestry there with a passageway behind it."

Jinx left Aurora holding her mother, and opened the door just enough to peer outside.

"Any soldiers?" Aurora asked.

"None that I can see."

"They must know the rebellion is inside the palace. Hopefully, they will be preoccupied with them long enough for us to find Nova and get out."

They shuffled into the hallway, the queen's feet dragging helplessly against the ground.

"That one," Aurora said, jerking her chin toward a tapestry woven in rich blues and blacks. It depicted the day the Time of Tempests began, when the very first storms poured from the goddess's hands out on the land below.

Carefully, they peeled the tapestry away from the wall, revealing a latch that opened and slid back a door to show a narrow stone passageway. Maneuvering slowly, Jinx slipped in first, followed by the queen, and finally Aurora, who returned the tapestry to its normal place as best she could.

Aurora looked at the dark corridor, wondering how they were going to get down the long and winding route to the royal storm shelter where this particular passage led.

"Maybe I should go on alone," Aurora said. "You could stay here with my mother, and I'll bring back Nova."

Jinx gave one firm shake of her head. "We stay together. If something happened, and I lost you, Thorne would throw me out and let the fog have me."

"He would not," Aurora huffed.

"Perhaps we should get your mother free, and try for your friend another time."

"No," Aurora snapped. Then, softer, she said, "No. Novaya has suffered too long for my mistakes. I am not leaving without her." She hitched her mother higher, and began the long trek down the cramped tunnel. She had to hunch because she was too tall. She'd been hunching in this particular tunnel since she was twelve years old and hit a particularly strong growth spurt. But everything was different this time. Her ears were attuned to every sound, and she could feel each scrape of her mother's unresponsive feet against the stone as if they were her own.

"So . . . dungeons next?" Jinx asked. "Do you know how to get there?"

Aurora pulled in a quick breath, ashamed. She did know where the dungeons were, having explored the location on a few occasions as a child in an effort to do something *scary*, but she did not know how to get there using unseen passageways. At some point, they would have to take to the main halls, which would leave them vulnerable.

"I do. But it won't be easy. I still think we should split up. You could stay with the queen, and I—"

"I said no, Roar."

Rora's breath caught at the name, at the familiarity in Jinx's voice. She wanted so badly to keep both versions of herself, both lives. But she did not know if it was possible. She shook the thoughts away, one thing at a time.

"Then we might need to hide my mother somewhere safe, and come back for her after we retrieve Nova. Otherwise, we're too conspicuous."

"Is there somewhere safe?"

That was a question with no answer. The tunnel led to the storm shelter, which even now could be in use by the Locke family. The tunnel itself could be safe, but it was impossible to know. There had been unused rooms and studies, but how much had changed in Aurora's absence? A great deal politically. She couldn't be sure how much had changed around the castle.

"I don't know."

"Then I'll go alone."

Aurora readjusted her mother's weight, pulling her limp arm farther across her shoulder, and shook her head. "No. You don't know who you are looking for or where you are going or who not to be seen by. I won't have you being caught because of me."

Jinx gave that wild-eyed, witchy smile and said, "Together it is, then."

The two moved as fast as they were able down the tunnel with the queen's weight between them, and found the storm shelter at the end deserted. They took a chance, and left her in one of the bedrooms there. Aurora chose a small maid's room, not one of the larger royal rooms, hoping that if someone did come looking they would not think to check there.

Together they laid the queen's frail body out over the small bed frame, and Aurora did her best to plump a flat pillow beneath her mother's head.

"I'll move fast. Like lightning made flesh," she promised. Aurora pressed her lips to her mother's dry cheek, and closed her into the dark room, praying to the goddess she would still be there when they returned.

Fog, while less destructive to property, is one of the most precarious storms to encounter in person. Its magic, like the low cloud's slow creeping invasion, is insidious and subtle. In the same way that the dense clouds can obscure an entire mountain from view, so too can it obscure a person's thinking to the point of imminent danger.

—*The Perilous Lands of Caelira*

9

Cassius was accustomed to hearing sirens. They sounded when he ate, when he worked, when he slept—or tried to. Sometimes he wondered if the Stormlord had some untold-of magic that allowed him to see into Cassius's mind, to know when he was the most distracted or vulnerable, because that was always when his storms came calling. It would be more realistic for him to move his living quarters into the dome itself so that he had quicker access to the skies.

But Cassius was a selfish man. He had never denied that.

So like many times before, he was in his office, the princess's former study, when this siren sounded. He had recently finished dispensing a thunderstorm, a mere annoyance more than anything, and had kicked off his boots and coat to relax for however long he could.

Never long, not anymore. He was so damned tired.

But when the siren sounded, it took even Cassius a few moments to realize that this siren had nothing to do with tempests.

He stood abruptly from his desk, knocking over a bottle of ink in the process. Black liquid spread across his papers like unholy blood, but there was no time to stop it, not even time to be frustrated with himself for his clumsiness.

They were under attack.

Not by storms, *but by men.*

He hastily pulled on his boots, inserting a spare knife into each one, then grabbed his sword. By the time he entered the main hallway, the edge had left his movements and his steps had grown into a sprawling stalk. This was where he thrived. Give a predator prey and he came alive, no matter how close to death he might feel. His vision sharpened, the exhaustion disappeared, and a hunger rose from deep in his gut.

A fight was exactly what he needed—and not with some faraway magic, but up close, hand to hand, face-to-face, blood drawn. He needed to feel victory. Needed to serve up a defeat that was permanent.

When men died, they stayed that way, unlike the enemies he normally fought.

The hallway swarmed with soldiers, all clearly taken by the chaos. He grabbed the highest-ranking officer he recognized and spat, "Tell me what you know."

"A breach, sir. The main gate."

Bleeding skies. How had they gotten through *the main gate* without anyone noticing?

"Where is the fighting located?"

"We don't know, sir."

Cassius froze, his eyes narrowing, and his jaw went tight. "What do you *mean,* you don't know?"

"We have not found the intruders."

His heart slowed, forgoing its beats as his mind raced—not in anxiety, but in deference, as if one knew the other was more needed. What would intruders want? Where would they go? What would their goals be?

One blink, and he knew.

"I want soldiers on every member of the royal family, now." He was surprised there had not been an attempt at overthrowing them before now, frankly. "Once my family is protected, then every other remaining soldier is to scour this palace until the intruders are found, do you understand?"

An affirmative chorus rang out from the soldiers in blue, and then everyone was in motion, chattering about who would be seeking out his father, brother, and mother. The room emptied quickly of everyone except Cassius and a handful of soldiers who stood behind him.

"I did not mean me," he growled.

The soldiers hesitated still.

"Go!" he barked. "Find them. Now."

Then, blessedly, he was left alone, the siren still wailing on occasion, the only company for his scattered thoughts.

He should have gone after them, should have put himself in the thick of things, but instead he turned and headed back the way he came, down the royal wing where the Pavan family had stayed.

He was the only Locke to call this wing home. He was not certain why, but he bypassed his office and went for the door at the very end of the hall, the queen's rooms. He listened for a moment, but heard nothing inside. He knocked. Again, he could not say why. The woman rarely ever woke, not since his father had started bribing the nurse to add something extra to her tea.

But sometimes when he looked at this door, he had this feeling in his stomach that he didn't recognize, a feeling he didn't know how to name. And it told him to knock before he went inside. When no answer came, he turned the knob and entered on his own. First, his eyes saw bare ankles, and followed them to the unconscious form of the nurse who cared for the queen. Her arms were askew in front of her, and her face lax, but a quick press of his fingers to her neck told him she was not dead. He lifted his eyes farther and found only rumpled sheets where the queen should have been.

Something in him rose high, pressing right under his skin, the part of him that liked to hunt and hurt.

He had been just down the hallway. Had someone managed to steal the old queen right from under his nose? Or did he somehow have even less knowledge and control than he thought? Could she have walked free herself somehow?

He had sent all those soldiers off searching and here was the breach right under his very eye. Where he slept and worked. Humiliation burned deep in his gut, and he charged toward the bed, pulling at the sheets as if he might find some clue there to how he had allowed such a blunder.

Could this be the Stormlord? Another prong in his plan? The meager resistance his brother had been cheerfully exterminating to impress their father? Or something else entirely? There were too many pieces on the board for him to win this game. The board was too damned big for him to even know what the game was sometimes.

Quickly, he searched the rest of the room, searching for any advantage, and he found it in the poorly closed balcony door. Outside, he discovered a peculiar crawling vine that had somehow made its way from the ground up to the queen's balcony even though he had never seen it on any of his walks around the grounds. He touched the leaves, bright green and crisp—*fresh*. And something else about them—they were real, to be certain, but they hummed under his touch, as if they brimmed with something that was nearly familiar to him.

Cassius knew what he was seeing, knew it by heart from years of engrained warnings and fear. But his father had done such a thorough job of eradicating the practice and the people from Locke, it had often seemed more myth than malevolence.

But here before him was proof.

He rubbed a newly birthed leaf between the pads of his fingers, and plucked it free from the vine. He waited for it to wither or turn to dust, but it stayed—both a truth and a lie all at once.

There was a witch in Pavan.

And whoever they were, *wherever* they were, they had the Pavan queen.

There had been an itch somewhere beneath Kiran's skin from the moment he'd left Aurora sprawled out and weeping before the palace gate, and he knew it would not go away until he saw her again. It distracted him throughout the entire mission, as they crept through the halls, each time they quietly dispatched an unsuspecting guard. He kept waiting for an attack to come out of nowhere, and for a sword to pierce him clean through, because he could do nothing but think of that look on her face. Try as he might to convince himself that he did not know this *Aurora* at all, he knew down to his bones that she had been terrified.

And he had left her there.

He hated himself for that almost as much as he hated her for lying, for making him believe something was possible when it wasn't.

They had nearly reached the wing where the Locke family resided, and the group began to split apart, so that they could surround the wing and cut off escape.

He and Ransom had naturally been paired together, as they were the ones to initiate the next part of the plan. Zephyr and her lieutenant, Raquim, were the last pair to leave. She asked, "Ready?"

Kiran only nodded.

"This is important," she added.

"This family killed my sister," he snapped. "Trust me, I know the importance."

She began to turn, looking satisfied, but then a loud, blaring siren cut through the air, shattering the stillness that had been their friend up until this point. A door swung open in the hallway beyond, then another, followed by a woman's voice.

"Onto plan number two," Ransom growled, ripping a glass jar from his utility belt and throwing it around the corner into the hallway where they hoped at least one royal family member would be. The shattering of glass was followed by a quiet *whoosh* of noise and the spread of moisture in the air. Kiran knew thick tendrils of fog were unfurling from the broken jar, spreading to consume the hallway.

Each of them reached for a small vial containing powdered fog Stormheart, and threw it back. The powder melted in seconds on Kiran's tongue, tasting like some odd mix of mist and ash. Their supplies had been low, so they only had enough to give each member of the rebellion a small amount. It gave them a limited window of time during which they would be immune to the fog storm's particularly potent effects of confusion and sedation.

Duke, the one member of their crew who had remained back at command for this mission, had been unable to say exactly how long they would have, so they needed to get in and out as quickly as possible. They had intended to use this method for escaping the palace. Now they would need to make it last through the capture too.

He and Ransom entered the now eerily clouded hallway with Zephyr, leaving Raquim out as a fail-safe in case something went wrong. Hopefully, the rest of their group would be making their way back too now that the plan had been upended. There were ten of them in all, and he thought they were likely to need every single hand to get out alive.

The first step into the fog was a leap of faith. Both Ransom and Zephyr held back a breath, but Kiran charged forward. He had lived his whole life running straight at danger, arms open wide. There had been a brief time there when he thought that would need to change, that he would need to find some other way to live. But now he knew better. This was who he was, who he would always be. The one who stepped forward first.

The fog parted around him, clinging to his shoulders, surrounding him. When he took a second step and then a third, he knew that the powder had done the trick. He waved his arms out in front of him, trying to push away as much of the dense cloud as he could, for it was hard to see anything at all. In fact, he didn't even notice the broken jar until his boot crunched on top of it.

The noise brought Ransom to him, and Zephyr a few seconds after that.

"Come. We don't have much time," Zephyr murmured, pushing past him and taking the lead.

They came upon a few soldiers first, one still with his arms up, as if to protect his face from either the shattering glass or the incoming magic. He was not frozen, per se—more like he had forgotten the reason he had put his hands up in defense to begin with.

Of all the storms he had faced—twisters and firestorms and hurricanes—fog unnerved Kiran more than any other. He would rather die in a fiery blaze of chaos than waste away wandering under a storm's enchantment, lost to himself. It was why it was one of the only affinities he had not sought for himself. When it came time to steal the heart of a storm, you were betting your heart was the stronger of the two. And he had always been willing to do that with the fiercest tempests from which others shied away. But to take the heart of a fog storm required strength of mind as well as heart. You had to not only empty yourself of the fear of death, but of the fear of living on, caught by the storm, a slow, torturous, forgotten death.

"Over here!" Zephyr yelled.

Kiran left his thoughts behind and followed her voice to find her kneeling by a middle-aged woman with honey-brown skin and expensive clothing, who was sprawled facedown on the floor. She appeared to have fallen in the chaos, and now she looked chillingly unaware, laid out that way, her eyes wide but unseeing.

"This is the queen. I would rather have one of the men, but she will do if we cannot find anyone else," Zephyr said.

A lump rose in Kiran's throat. He hated the Locke family, hated everything about them, and every single thing they stood for. But a woman? In all their planning for this mission, he had never imagined they would kidnap a woman, regardless of who she was. He glanced over at Ransom, and the hard set of his friend's jaw told him that they shared the same thoughts.

"We'll look for someone else," Kiran said, immediately turning to search farther down the hallway. Ransom's heavy footsteps followed behind.

"Wait!" Zephyr cried. "That siren had to be about us. It was not the usual storm signal. They will be searching for us. We have to go. *Now*."

Neither hunter replied. They only kept trudging through the hallway until they reached the end. When they found no more enchanted victims waiting for them, the two looked at each other again, unsure what to do.

"Doors," Ransom offered.

Kiran jumped on the suggestion, and they each took one side of the hallway, throwing open every door they passed.

Empty.

Empty.

Empty.

Kiran had just thrown open his fourth and final door when he heard a shout behind him, followed by a heavy crash. He spun fast to see Ransom heaving himself up off the floor, a broken piece of pottery smashed all around him. His attacker, a lean young man with curly black hair and skin just a shade darker than the queen's, was frozen in place by the door, his face a mask of cruelty, teeth gritted in determination, as wisps of fog tangled around him in a slow, sly dance.

Zephyr appeared in the doorway, her expression grim. She

lifted one arm and touched a claw on her gloved hand to the man's cheek. "Casimir." She tapped her claw twice, and dragged it down to his chin, leaving a pale line behind. "I watched from a nearby building when he had the Eye burned. I think he *enjoyed* it." The man did little more than blink, his thoughts locked away somewhere inside by the fog storm's magic, as Zephyr gripped his jaw hard and smiled. "You'll do nicely, *Casimir Locke*."

Aurora's uneasiness grew with every empty hallway they traversed and each step that carried her farther away from her mother. Her heart beat a heavy repetition in her throat, making it difficult to swallow or breathe, let alone whisper the required directions to Jinx following alongside her.

"Wait," she said, the words more like a gasp. They slowed to a stop as they neared the center of the palace. Through the next archway, they would be in the Great Dome, and it would be much harder to conceal their presence if any soldiers were about. The official entrance to the dungeons was where the dome met the south wing, where most of the military was housed and organized. But Aurora knew a second passage existed in the Hall of the Ancestors near the stairs that led up to the back of the ballroom. Neither seemed like a safe avenue, but they were the only options.

She checked her hood and mask, making certain she was as covered as possible, then she sidled closer to the archway. She could hear a commotion, shouting and the slamming of boots against the ground, and then . . . the clash of swords.

She hesitated. That had to be the rebellion. They'd been found, perhaps surrounded. Kiran could be in danger; Ransom too. Aurora took one step toward the fighting, but Jinx pulled hard on her elbow.

"No. They can handle themselves, and we need the diversion."

Her friend was right, but the metallic clang of sword against sword reverberated inside Aurora's skull, and she did not know how to walk away.

"What happens to the rebellion if you're caught today?" Jinx asked. "Your mother will never be free, nor will your friend. You'll be used as a pawn to quiet the malcontents, and—"

Aurora had heard enough. She never wanted to be anyone's pawn, not ever again. So she ignored the pull she felt to the fighting at the front of the dome, and instead darted out from the archway and toward the servant's halls used to serve the ballroom during large events.

Her shoulders bunched tight, and her head ached from her clenching teeth. She kept waiting for a disruptive noise, a loud voice, some signal that they'd been seen, that the fight had moved their way, but Jinx was right. The fighting gave them the perfect diversion. The more steps she took, the farther away the voices drifted, and soon she had rounded a corner and pushed through a door into the servant's hallway. It too was empty, so she took the opportunity to run, covering the narrow, dimly lit space in a dozen long strides.

She must have held her breath nearly the entire way, because Aurora was dizzy by the time she stepped into the ornate hall that housed paintings and sculptures of her Stormling ancestors. There were two golden altars to the goddess on each side of the room, but they were small, and more like decorative antiques in comparison to the monstrously elaborate and expensive pieces that had been commissioned for her ancestors. Aurora fixed her eyes on the far altar, a tumble of confusing emotions sluicing through her belly at the sight.

She'd left this place so naive. And while she knew so much more now about the world than when she left, she was more confused than ever with regards to her thoughts on magic, and the goddess. She knew now that naivety of the world did not disappear with age, only the willingness to admit one's own unknowing. If her magic revealed anything to her, it was that the world was far more complicated than anyone could possibly know, and it was only the truly naive who tried to pretend they understood it.

"This is . . . bleeding skies, Aurora. How rich are you?"

Aurora turned to find Jinx fixated on a painted and gold-filigreed statue of her mother. It was as tall as the room, high enough that her mother's outstretched hand towered above their heads. It was her mother, yes, the same skyfire hair and tall build, but if her mother had been well enough to walk beside them, the statue would have dwarfed her too. None of these depictions were about truth; they were about power.

"You forget none of this belongs to me anymore," Aurora answered simply, then she knelt by the altar of the goddess.

"Is now really the time?" Jinx asked. "To each his own, of course, but we're not entirely out of danger here."

The altar had a half-relief carving of the goddess. Her arms were the only thing fully sculpted, and they stretched out, holding a bowl meant to symbolize the day she poured out the tempests upon the earth. Aurora placed her hand flat in the bottom of the bowl, pushing down first. The arms did not budge, but when she placed a second hand in the bowl to push, the arms began to slowly lower until she heard a click, then Aurora pushed forward and the relief carving of the goddess slid back into the wall far enough that there was a gap to crawl past.

Jinx gave a low whistle. "You royals are too rich for your own good. But I must admit to being a fan of all the secret passages. Much better use of the coin than . . . *that*." Jinx waved her hand vaguely in the direction of all the expensive statues and paintings.

Without replying, Aurora crawled past the goddess, and then waited in the dark tunnel for Jinx to do the same. When they were both inside, she pushed the goddess back into her rightful place, and heard a heavy clunk as the secret door closed behind them. In the dark, she rested her hand against the back of the altar and sent up something like a prayer, not to the goddess necessarily, but just outside herself.

Be safe. Please, please be safe.

A faint glow flicked over the stone walls when Jinx dug an eternal ember from a bag at her hip. "You must have had the most amazing childhood," Jinx whispered, waiting for Aurora to take the lead.

After a few feet of crawling they were able to stand upright, and Aurora answered honestly. "I did not have much of a childhood at all."

They continued on in silence for a few steps, but Jinx was never one to leave things alone.

"And who is Nova to you?"

Aurora sighed. "A friend. The only one I ever had really."

"A princess with one friend? That's not how I ever pictured it."

"What do you mean?"

"You do know most little girls dream of a life like yours, don't you? Myself included, once upon a time."

Aurora swallowed something between a laugh and a cry. "I suppose we have that in common then, because I dreamed of a life like yours. Don't misunderstand me, I know how blessed I was to grow up in a place like this, with food to eat and a safe bed to lay my head, and a mother who would protect me at all costs. But . . . there *were* costs. My brother, the original heir, died when I was a child. And when we realized that my magic was not coming, at least in the way we expected, I had to isolate myself in every way. Each word I spoke had to be turned over and over again in my mind before it could leave my lips, lest it give me away. I was a nervous, emotional child, especially after my brother died, and I—I could not be trusted to keep my own secret. So instead, it was me that had to be kept. Away from the world, from other people, including my one and only friend."

"So that's why you left."

Aurora met Jinx's eyes in the flickering ember light and nodded. "Part of it. There was also my looming marriage to Cassius Locke. It was the only way my mother could see for me to keep the throne and have a Stormling present to protect the city. But . . . he was cold and cruel. A life tied to him would have been like a life bound to the tempests we fight."

"To hear Kiran talk of the Lockes, they're like monsters."

Aurora shrugged. "My mother kept me too sheltered to know much, but I learned enough to know they had a cruel edge I wanted no part in. With my secret, I felt very much like I was bleeding in a pool of sharks. Now I know they were even worse than I feared."

"So that's when you decided to kidnap yourself?"

"Nova helped me escape, even though she thought the idea was mad. She did not hesitate, despite the fact that I'd pulled away from her years before. Truly, I do not deserve her."

Jinx said, "You don't have to feel guilty for wanting to be free. It's hard to live under the weight of that kind of secret. I left my home for a fresh start too."

"Yes, but you did not leave an entire kingdom at the mercy of a carnivorous family and your best friend to take the fall for your disappearance."

Jinx stopped asking questions after that. Either because she had the answers she wanted, or because the passageway began to turn in sharp circles as they wound down into the lowest levels of the palace. The air had grown cold and slightly sour by the time they reached the end of the passageway.

And it did in fact end. One minute, they were walking through the darkness with only the glow of the ember to help them, and the next they had come upon a brick wall that allowed them no way forward.

"Now what?" Jinx asked.

Aurora swallowed once, and then again, because she did not

know. She knew the passageway existed, but she had never actually followed it all the way to its destination. Was it always like this? Or had the Lockes discovered it and cut it off to prevent infiltrations like the one she was attempting?

Aurora laid her palms flat against the brick and pushed, but nothing happened.

"Roar?" Jinx whispered.

Ignoring her friend, Aurora pushed again, harder this time, sliding her hands to different spots, searching for some weak or special area, but again, the wall did not budge. Her thoughts began to race inside her head, flipping and turning over on themselves, twisting until the inside of her mind felt loud and churning, like the rapids of a flooded river.

"I don't know," she finally admitted. "I don't know what to do next." The words came out scraped and raw. She *had* to get Novaya out. She could not even fathom how long she had been locked away down here, could not bear to think of what she had endured, all for Aurora's frivolous freedom.

Jinx, as always, was undeterred by the snag in their plan. She laced her fingers together and cracked her knuckles. "Let's see what we have." She too began to examine the wall, running her fingers across the bricks and along the grooves between them.

"It's enchanted," she murmured. "Like the front gate. It requires magic to open."

Aurora's eyes widened. That made sense. The purpose of this particular passageway was for use in the event of a hostile takeover. Should the ruling Stormling be locked away in the dungeon, they would have a built-in way of escape that would only work for them.

Quickly, she closed her eyes, calling up the skyfire storm in her chest, and slammed as much energy into the wall as she could. It shook, dust raining down around them, but it did not open.

Jinx pulled back, hissing, shaking out her hands. "Warn a witch next time before you go throwing around skyfire."

Aurora might have mumbled an apology, but she was more focused on trying again. This time, the whole tunnel around them rattled and her hair rose up with the amount of electrical charge she funneled into the brick.

But still . . . nothing.

Aurora growled in frustration. "Goddess burn it. Why won't it work?"

For a long moment, there was silence, then a voice came from the other side of the brick.

"Hello? Is someone there?"

Aurora knew immediately who it was. Relief surged through her so strong, she was nearly sick from it.

"Novaya? Is that you?"

There was no answer. Had there been a guard? Goddess, it was the dungeon—of course there was a guard. What if they'd just brought all the soldiers directly to them?

"Nova? Are you alone? Are you well? Please, please be well."

This time the voice came back louder, and clearly shocked. "Aurora? It can't be . . ."

"It is. Stand back. I'm getting you out."

Aurora did not know how yet, but this wall would not stand between her and her friend. Nothing would.

"Maybe it's not skyfire that unlocks it," Jinx offered. "What other magic does your family have?"

Aurora frowned. "None that I can control."

"Then it's good that you're not the only one on this crew with magic."

Aurora gasped and spun around. The words hadn't come from Jinx, and the two of them were no longer alone in the passageway. Leaning against the stone wall a few paces back was Sly, looking as though she'd been there all along.

"What are you doing here?" Aurora whispered.

"Following you," Sly whispered back.

Jinx pierced the tense moment with a chuckle.

"*How?* You followed us the whole way, and only just now showed yourself? And we never noticed?"

Sly shrugged off the wall, her posture casual. "I might have lost track of you for a bit with that last secret passageway. But I figured it out eventually." She clapped her hands together and continued, "Now, let's see about getting past this wall."

Man, unlike the gods, is limited in what he can see and know and understand. And so it came to be that those with magic began to hunger for more than the tremendous gifts they had already been given.

—An Examination of the Original Magics

10

Novaya had always feared this day would come. All the time alone in her cell, the enormous effort of keeping her magic in control, the devastating melancholy of having no end in sight, not to mention her long battle with anxiety—it was bound to catch up to her eventually.

That had to be what this was—these voices. There were three of them now. One that did indeed sound exactly like the Aurora from her memories, so much so that it caught her off guard every time she heard it. Nova's heart broke a little every time she had to remind herself this probably was not real.

The other two voices were unfamiliar, the accents foreign too. She tried to match them to some other voice that she had heard once upon a time, wondering if her mind had pulled it from a memory. That had to be the only explanation for why she would be hearing voices from the solid stone wall of her cell.

It wasn't as if she had never called out in the middle of the night, hoping that someone outside these four walls would call back. But this . . . this was too impossible, too good to ever be true.

But every time she convinced herself to block it out, Aurora's voice would ring out again, telling her to hold on. It may have been impossible, but . . . she didn't think she had imagined the shaking of the walls. It had showered dust and dirt on her already charred and ruined bed. Again and again, there were frenzied conversations she could not quite understand, followed up by a firm rumble of the wall.

Maybe it was an earthquake? Some other natural phenomenon, and her traumatized brain was simply weaving imaginary tales to keep her from falling apart. She had always been a girl divided. Her mind was too easily ensnared by worry and guilt and fear—so much so that it betrayed her too often for her to ever trust it. And since her magic had manifested when she was a girl, her body had become her enemy as well. Realistically, she had known those divisions would tear her down eventually. She supposed imprisonment was bound to speed that along.

"Nova? Nova! Can you hear me?"

She almost did not reply. It could not be real. It would hurt too much if she believed, and it wasn't.

"Oh goddess, what if she's unconscious? Nova?"

"I-I'm here," she returned, already regretting it.

"Thank the skies," the Aurora voice said back. "Listen, we can't get through the wall."

And there it was, Nova thought, the beginning of the delusion. This wasn't a rescue, it was a siege. These voices would take up camp in her head, and she would lose what little control she still had left.

"But we're coming underneath it, so you need to move back."

Nova blinked, uncomprehending.

"Did you hear me? Move back from the wall."

"I hear you," Nova called back. She was already pressed against the far wall, since the bed had been burned beyond use during one of the prince's questionings.

She waited and waited. There were no more voices. No more shaking walls or showers of dust. But after a moment, she began to feel something strange—a tingling warmth in the atmosphere around her. Suddenly she no longer felt tired, and the flame that always churned beneath her skin was crackling hot and right at the surface.

The dirt floor of her cell began to vibrate so gently it was almost a hum. Then, as if it were the most natural thing in the world, a hole began to open up in the middle of her floor, revealing a staircase carved from earth, and the face of an unfamiliar woman. Her face was all brazen angles surrounding wide-set brown eyes. Her hair was shorn on one side, but long on the other, and she wore leather battle gear.

She was . . . *magnificent.* All of it was, which only made Nova pinch her arm as if to clear a dream. But the vision didn't disappear, it expanded. From behind the mystery warrior woman, a blond head appeared and Nova gasped, her eyes immediately filling with tears before she could even catch sight of Aurora's face. But that *hair.* No one had that color hair but Aurora Pavan.

"I hear you are long past due for a rescue." The words came from the woman in front, and they only made Nova cry harder.

"This is terribly rude, but I am going to have to ask you to save that crying for when I'm not holding up an entire wall with my magic. Think you can slide forward for me? Once you reach the steps, you can move past me to Aurora, and we'll get you out of here as fast as possible."

Somehow, Nova listened. She stifled her tears, and scooted herself across the floor to the opening that had not been there a few moments ago. A part of her was waiting to find it all an illusion still, but as she drew nearer, her foot went into the hole and landed firmly on the top step.

"Good. Keep coming."

Her legs shook like a newborn colt's, but Nova pushed herself up enough to walk the rest instead of slide. That tingling warmth from earlier surrounded her as soon as she entered the tunnel, and when the flame inside her answered again, Nova remembered the woman's last words.

Holding a wall up with *magic.*

No storm magic she had ever heard of could do that, which meant that *this,* that the warrior woman had . . . *earth magic?*

The next thing Nova knew, she had been seized in a tight grip, pulled hard into a hug that was the closest contact she had had in months. She froze, scrunching up her face and preparing to lock down her magic with all her might, but . . . the need never rose. It was there, present and close to the surface, but it didn't ache to be free the way it did when others touched her. After a few long moments to be certain, Nova lifted her arms and returned Aurora's hug, relieved to finally know her best friend was alive.

That was when all hell broke loose.

Nova pulled back with a gasp as something between her and Aurora became sizzling hot, even by her standards.

Aurora's familiar face contorted with an emotion she didn't know—terror, pain, or something worse. Her friend let out a low agonized groan, and at the same time the entire world seemed to shake, the passageway around them raining down dirt and rocks. The soft touch of Aurora's hands on Nova's arms became tighter and tighter, nails digging in until Nova could feel the skin break.

It was like something out of a nightmare, worse because not even Nova's traitorous mind could ever dream up something this cruel. She yelped and squirmed, trying to get free from her friend's grasp, but the hold was too tight.

Storm sirens blared outside, but Nova would have known a storm approached from the howl of the wind alone; it sounded like a monster. As if in reaction to the building storm, Aurora's grip grew painfully fierce. In Nova's panic, a burst of flame rose up inside, ready to rescue her, and Nova cried out louder in response, not sure how long she would be able to hold her instincts back.

A girl she had not seen before with short curly hair and dark skin appeared out of nowhere, pressing one hand to each side of Aurora's head and commanding, "Your shields, Aurora."

The princess squeezed her eyes shut, and breathed, "I'm trying."

The other girl continued, "Separate your soul. *Now.* You know what is you, and what is not. Separate. Make space. And enforce your shields."

Nova had no idea what was happening, but after a few moments, Aurora's grip did ease enough that Nova could break away. The warrior woman was there to catch her as soon as she stumbled back.

"Easy, there. Breathe." Nova tried to do what she was saying, but her anxiety was in control now. Her heartbeat was loud in her ears, her skin clammy, and her vision blotted with dark spots. "You are safe. I promise. I promise."

Other words were said, but Novaya did not hear them. Her eyes were fixed on her best friend, watching the look of fury fade from her eyes and confusion and shame take its place. Goddess, she knew that look. She had worn it so many times herself.

Aurora met her eyes and said, "I'm sorry." But Nova could only read the words on her lips because the sound was lost to another rumbling crash as the entire palace shook again.

Aurora stood, somehow still regal despite the dirt and dread that covered her. "It's the Stormlord. He's attacking the palace. We need to get out before it's too late."

It was not until Nova felt a gentle push at her back, urging her forward, that she realized the warrior had been touching her this entire time, and not once had her magic risen in response.

Skies, they were lucky. Kiran and the rest of the infiltration crew hadn't met resistance until they had been almost completely out of the palace, and even then they'd had the numbers. The fighting had been minimal, just long enough to gain the advantageous position, then Kiran lobbed another jar of fog magic, and they made a run for it.

The palace gate was closed, but they were prepared for that. They no longer needed stealth, only speed. So they hurled a grappling hook over the wall and made quick work climbing over and lifting up their *cargo*.

The fog they'd left to consume the palace entrance bought them time. Anyone who came that way to look for them would be ensnared for some time. But the sooner they disappeared, the better. Zephyr had been the first over, and her lieutenant, Raquim, was to be the last. When only he, Kiran, and Ransom remained, they were caught off guard by the sudden approach of a figure at full sprint.

Raquim was quick to pull his weapon, but Ransom waved him off.

"He is one of ours."

It was Bait who approached, winded and with his red hair plastered to his face by sweat or rain. He'd been assigned as lookout, and should have already been on the other side of the wall by now.

"What is it?" Kiran asked.

Bait winced, and looked at Ransom instead when he answered. "After you lot left, Sly noticed something."

"Noticed what?" Kiran asked.

Again, Bait kept his eyes fixed on Ransom, avoiding Kiran. "Jinx and Roar did not return to headquarters after they completed their part. Instead, they entered the palace grounds."

"They did *what*?" Kiran growled.

"Sly followed them," Bait rushed to reply. "To make sure they did not run into any harm, but, uh, she still has not returned. None of them have."

Kiran's vision tunneled until he could see little more than the worried and fearful expression on the novie's face. His world was so narrowed, his mind so focused on the idea of Aurora and Jinx and Sly, and all the things that could have befallen them, that he did not notice when the air changed, when the pressure dropped, and the world went quiet.

It wasn't until everything burst wide open into color and light and pain that his hunter instincts kicked in and he realized what was happening.

A hole had torn open in the sky and flame rained down in enormous torrents, changing everything in an instant. The first ember hit his forearm, burning through several layers of skin before he batted it away, earning another scorching wound on his hand. The next skated by his face, searing his cheek on its way down.

He could not seem to think in the right order. He should do something about the storm, about the immediate threat, but his mind was caught up over the threat to Aurora. Ransom had to pull the firestorm powder from his utility belt for him and hold it directly in front of his face before Kiran even began to think rationally. He pulled the cork and emptied the powder on his tongue, trying not to think of how many of their resources they had depleted in this one mission alone. That was far from the most important thing right now. The next ember that hit him hurt, but didn't burn, and that sharpened his focus.

He looked to his left to see that Raquim was already gone, the rope too. No matter; there was no way Kiran was leaving without the rest of his crew.

"Where did they go?"

They followed Bait at a sprint to the vine that Jinx had grown up to the queen's balcony, but it had already burned down to ash in the ensuing firestorm. Parts of the palace were burning too, and no one seemed to be doing anything to fight the storm.

Kiran thought of the fog storms they'd left scattered around the palace. They might have grown by now to fill even more space, incapacitating even more people. What if they had unknowingly left the palace, and the entire city of Pavan, vulnerable to attack?

That, he knew, was something for which Aurora would never forgive him. So even though it went against his every instinct, even though it physically hurt him not to go after her, he turned and faced the sky instead.

"New plan," he declared. "We deal with this, then we find our girls."

Kiran was the only one among them with a firestorm heart, so he pulled that from his belt. But the other two had their own ways of helping.

"I'll work on the flames," Ransom said, pulling a jar of rainstorm magic from his belt. Kiran noticed that Ransom too was looking low on supplies.

Bait pulled his lone Stormheart from his belt and said, "Distraction duty. I'm on it."

Ransom and Bait timed their actions perfectly so that the appearance of the thunderstorm from Ransom's jar might be confused for the Stormheart Bait was infusing with his magic, tricking the storm into thinking another real tempest was in its midst. The first downpour met the flames with a loud sizzle, smoke filling the sky until it was hard to tell what was storm and what was smoke.

Kiran chose that moment to attack, pushing his energy through the Stormheart he held and at the churning, rotating beast overhead. He managed to break up the formation, catching it by surprise, but then an awful howling sound came on the wind, and the rotation snapped right back, faster this time, pushing lower to the ground, closer to the palace.

The wind changed again, this time at his back; he felt a sharp updraft, matched by the rising heat from the flames, and his ears filled with a loud, guttural rumble that shook the ground beneath his feet. He looked up and backward just in time to see a funnel cloud dipping lower and lower before tearing a chunk away from the side of the famed golden-domed roof of the palace.

Bleeding skies. This was it. This wasn't just a single storm. This was one of the onslaughts of multiple tempests that could not be natural. It was happening. The Stormlord was coming for Pavan, and too many people he cared about were still inside.

Four women from different worlds crawled out of the secret tunnel, and Aurora breathed out in relief to finally be on the ground floor. The tunnel had shook and shifted around them every step of the way, and though none of them had ever spoken a word, she knew they all had feared its eventual collapse.

Now that they stood in the light, Aurora could not keep her eyes off Nova. Her friend had lost weight; her once-round cheeks had unnatural hollows in the middle, matched by sunken skin beneath her eyes. Her steps remained unsteady, even once they stood on flat ground.

Captivity's mark was clear on her, and Aurora wanted to reach out in comfort, in aid, but she couldn't. Not after what she had let happen down in the tunnel. Not with the way another soul was trailing her own at the moment, as if waiting for a momentary lapse in her strength.

It should not worry her that no barrier had been thrown up to guard against the storm yet. What did she care for Cassius Locke? She meant to bring him to justice in the end. But time and again over the last week, no matter how many times a storm broke through, it had never been long before she felt his icy barriers go up, before his fighting gave her a much-needed reprieve.

But there was no barrier now. Nothing to stop whatever storm this violent soul controlled, and she feared what they would find if, no, *when* they made it outside the palace. They hastily crossed through the Hall of the Ancestors and the servant's hall, but when they swung the next door open, Jinx slammed the door before the thick cloud on the other side could leech inside.

"Fog," Sly was the first to supply. They all knew it was part of the infiltration's plan. But none of them had the supplies to walk through it unharmed, as they were all supposed to be out of harm's way.

Aurora did not have time for this. They still had to get back to her mother. This task had seemed so . . . well, not simple, but *direct* when they had begun. But the problems just kept unspooling further and further until she lost all sense of the thread.

She had to stay focused. She said, "We either need to find a way to neutralize the fog, or we need an alternate route." The fog outside the door was collected magic, and thus had no soul for her to influence. She turned to her fellow hunters. "Either of you happen to have any fog Stormheart on you?" They both shook their heads.

Sly reached for something on her belt and slid it free. She held out her palm, revealing a gray cylindrical stone.

"Wind?" Aurora asked.

"If we can't negate it, we move it," Sly said.

"And do you have wind magic on hand?"

"No, but you do."

Aurora's eyes skipped to Nova, who looked too exhausted to have caught the hunter's meaning. And even if she had, Aurora could hardly insist on holding back secrets from her friend, not after all she had been through. If there was a way her abilities could get them through this, she would do it.

She held out a hand, and Sly slapped the Stormheart against her palm. As always, she did not feel the call other Stormlings felt. She could sense no connection to the defeated storm it came from, nor would it enable her to channel the natural magic that other Stormlings manifested as children. Those gifts had never come for her. But she knew now that did not mean she could not utilize it for magic of a different kind.

She took a deep breath. Then another. She looked to Jinx and

Sly and said, "I have to lower my shields. I'll do my best to keep the tempest at bay, but if it should take me—"

"I have a little powdered Rezna's rest left if you go full assassin on us." Jinx shrugged nonchalantly, as if having to incapacitate a friend was simply part of her normal day. "But try not to go full Rage Roar. We've already got one unconscious body to carry; two would make things very difficult."

"I will do my best."

Sly opened her mouth as if to say something, but then closed it and simply nodded.

"What's happening?" Nova asked.

"The way out is blocked, but I'm going to try something. It . . . I might have a *reaction* like I did before, when I squeezed your arms. I'm sorry for that, by the way. I promise, I will explain everything later when there is time."

Aurora hated the fearful expression on her friend's face, but Nova nodded all the same, loyal despite her misgivings.

"Why don't Nova and I stand back to be safe?" Jinx offered. She took a pouch from her belt and held it out to Sly. "Sly can be your second. She brought you around pretty fast down in the tunnel." Jinx shifted her focus to the other hunter and added, "If she becomes more than you can handle, just a tiny pinch of powder is all she needs to breathe in to be subdued. Any more and she'll be out for the night."

After a bit of shuffling, they were all in position, and it was just a matter of Aurora dropping her walls enough to choose a soul to summon a storm. It was not something she had mastered by any means, but the process was basic enough. It reminded her a bit of threading a needle. Aurora could feel spirits around her always, some distant and meandering, some close and suffocating. She merely had to choose one and pull it through the Stormheart she held in her hands, and the soul took on the life of that storm.

It was simple.

"Very, very *simple*," she mumbled to herself, and then slowly began to lower the walls she'd erected between her own spirit and the world around her. She imagined taking away one stone, only one, letting in just a sliver of the outside.

Even that small opening seemed like a floodgate, filling her mind with noise and feeling and sensation that was not her own. It felt like an invasion, foreign and overpowering, and her instinct was to try to claw it away like a spider's web she'd walked through unsuspectingly. Instead, she held still, trying to adjust. The world outside was loud and unfocused and chaotic, and it enflamed her own thoughts until they too were loud, competing as if to say, *I still exist.*

"Don't panic," Sly said, her voice quiet and commanding next to Aurora. "You will only waste your energy."

She was right. Aurora could not fight her own mind in addition to the world outside. Somehow, she had to trust—that she could do this, that she would find her way back. She inhaled, imagining the breath pushing all her own thoughts deeper inside her, safe and separate. Then on the exhale, she focused on that opening and took down a second stone, widening her exposure.

The storm's consciousness rolled over her, and she felt it like a disease—thick and cloying and searching for its next victim. The soul was old—so much so that there was little humanity left in it. No memories, no yearning ache from its former life. She wondered if souls like this one even remembered why they still clung to this world, or if they only held on out of habit and hate.

She pushed it aside and tried to search for another soul, for one not so tainted, one that would help them and submit to her control without causing any harm. She closed her eyes and let the pull she felt inside drift where it wanted to go, but it was hard to navigate the chaos of the living souls outside the walls who were filled with desperation and panic and fear.

Aurora pulled back and tried to start smaller. In her immediate vicinity, she felt the lively presence of her friends, the unique buzz of each of their spirits. Beyond that, past the closed door, she found more living souls, though these were more subdued—caught in the fog's snare, she guessed. She reached farther, searching for a gentle spirit mingling with the earth or the air, but they all had scattered in the presence of the monster ruling the skies.

When she searched as far as she could without losing touch with herself, she decided to risk opening herself up more. She began lowering her defenses, stone by stone, until she could reach out in every direction.

I need help, she thought. *Pavan needs help. Please, if you're willing, come.*

She felt a few answering nudges, tentative and wary. She sent out feelings of warmth and compassion, and a plea for courage. It was such a cruel irony how much the spirits she touched differed. Malicious and power-hungry souls gravitated toward storms naturally. They often felt they were owed something by the world they'd once lived in, and they took that payment in destruction. And the rest—they were soft, more than vulnerable, like one might expect when a person's truest self is shoved into the harsh world without even skin and bones for armor. It was these souls she had to coax and comfort. While they had not been able to let go of their old lives enough to move on, they had done their best to adjust, settling into the seams of nature where life and death were constant and less complicated.

Aurora thought of her magic like a song—soft and soothing—and she poured it out for those souls, asking for their aid. She found one, huddled low in the earth, avoiding the storms overhead. It sent her images of fire and chaos, and she sucked in a breath.

A firestorm wreaked havoc outside. No wonder the city was in such turmoil.

She promised the spirit shelter and guidance and urged it toward her. It came, but slowly. This soul was no fighter, not like the one that inhabited the firestorm. But she did not need it to fight, she could do that. She only needed it to submit.

She had it out of the earth and almost to the palace when suddenly another soul appeared. This one came from somewhere up above, as if out of nowhere. It moved fast and needed no cajoling from her. In her surprise, she released the other soul, which immediately scurried back to its hiding spot, so she faced the newcomer in her mind's eye.

This soul was . . . *different*. Bold, eager, but not at all childish like the skyfire storm she'd encountered in the Sangsorra desert. This soul projected a sense of duty, and she wondered if he or she had been a soldier once upon a time.

You are here to help? she sent the thought its way.

It did not send anything back, no images or words; it only rushed closer, crowding her space.

All right, then. Thank you. I promise to release you as soon as I've cleared the fog.

Again, it pushed closer, a sense of impatience filling her, the first real communication she had received. Definitely a soldier, she thought.

Aurora lifted up the wind Stormheart, cradling it between both her palms, then with an indrawn breath, she took hold of the spirit before her and simply drew it through the heart.

Aurora had been going for a gentle breeze, but this spirit was so strong that she received a gust instead. It blew the heavy wooden door in front of her wide open before she even had the chance to gather her thoughts.

The others did not seem to mind the hurry. They rushed up behind her, and in moments the four of them were out of the door and into the open hall.

Aurora focused, directing the wind at the heavy clouds of fog that hugged the walls ahead of them, and the thick white masses rolled back like waves under the assault.

Once the hallway was clear, the soul returned, swirling around her with delight and approval. The wind seemed to move through her, brushing away the fear and lifting up her spirits. The air tugged at her clothes and her hood, ruffling through her hair. She could not resist the urge to join the whirlwind in a spin. It felt almost like they were dancing.

"How is she doing that?" she heard Nova ask Jinx, drawing her back to the moment.

Neither of them ever got the chance to answer because a bellowing growl mixed with a nightmarish shriek pierced the air. Aurora winced and covered her ears moments before something cracked and crunched, and that sound that had seemed too loud before became deafening.

The next moments unfolded faster than she could process. Things began falling around them—plaster and wood and stone— and all of it covered with fire. She tilted her head back to see what was happening, but then a gale of wind seemed to wrap around her middle and haul her backward, sending her toppling onto her backside and sliding only a few paces away from the fiery beam that crashed down right in the spot where she had been standing.

Aurora heard screaming and looked up to see Nova and Jinx on the other side of the flames. Sly had been blown backward by the same gust of wind as she, leaving their group separated. Aurora dragged herself to her feet, her back aching from her collision with the ground. As soon as she was standing, she nearly toppled again as she felt the magnitude of two giant storms roiling in the sky overhead.

It was a twister that had torn open the top of the dome, and it had sucked some of the firestorm's embers into its rotation, hurling them with frightening force inside the palace walls.

Part of Nova's threadbare cloak had caught fire, and Jinx was trying to stamp it out with her bare hands while Nova shoved her away, yelling something that Aurora could not hear. In fact, she was struggling to hear almost everything around her because the souls above had taken to her mental walls like battering rams, and she felt like she might lose the contents of her stomach. She dug her nails into her temples until the point of pain and groaned.

Sly appeared at her elbow, trying to force her hands away from her face, but the pain was the only thing keeping her sharp at the moment, keeping her in control.

Then, a third storm arrived. Aurora did not know from where or what kind, only that it was swift and sadistic, and it was going to break her. She wouldn't last. She looked to Sly, gasping. "Do you—do—Rezna's—do you have it?"

The hunter's face fell and she shook her head. "I don't. I dropped it when the beam fell. I don't know where it is now."

Aurora smashed her lips together hard and screamed into her closed mouth, willing herself to hold out.

Sly took hold of her shoulders and in the most soothing tone Aurora had ever heard from the girl, she coached, "Focus less on them, on keeping them out. Instead, direct all your energy at knowing the boundaries of your own soul. Know yourself, know you are incorruptible. Be so bright that they cannot even look upon you, let alone touch your spirit."

Aurora ached from soul to skin and back again. "I am not sure I know how."

"You have to."

So that's what Aurora did. She stopped trying to construct a wall that had already crumbled. She stopped desperately shoving and pushing at the intrusions she felt and turned inward instead. She did not know what the *boundaries of herself* were, her journey through the wilds had made that much evident, but she tried anyway. She focused on her love for her mother and for Nova and Jinx and Sly too. She thought of her memories in this palace, good and bad. She thought of her brother, who had been so brave and bold. And even though it hurt, she thought of Kiran, and the confidence she had gained in being loved by him. Aurora might not know everything she was, but she knew what she was *not*.

She was *not* going to let these storms take control from her, not when she still had a mission to complete. She was *not* going to leave this city vulnerable and broken and caught up in a war that was not theirs. And she was *not* afraid to do whatever it took.

Ever so slowly, Aurora felt herself drawing back from the brink. Her bunched muscles loosened, the fingers she had gripped tightly about her head fell away, and she opened watery eyes to take in the hallway around her.

The world was still a tumult of fire and fear, but she was not losing herself, not today, not now. She approached the beam that blocked her from Jinx and Nova to see that their situation had only worsened during her temporary distraction. Nova's clothing was no longer alight, but now they were surrounded by four soldiers in blue Locke uniforms, soldiers she had probably freed from the grasp of the fog storm only minutes before.

She turned to Sly. "Rainstorm? Do you have any? Heart or magic, I'll take either. We have to get to them."

Before she could answer, four more soldiers arrived, doubling their number. "Hurry," Aurora demanded. Impatient, she reached for the windstorm she'd had before. It would not put out the flame blocking their path, but perhaps she could redirect the fire just long enough that they could leap over.

Once again, Sly tugged on her elbow. "We can't. We need to go while we still can."

"*What?* And leave them? *No.* I'm not leaving either one of them."

Aurora turned and charged for the beam, but Sly latched on and pulled her back hard. Sly was a handspan shorter, and a good deal lighter, but somehow she continued muscling Aurora backward no matter how hard she fought. And it only took a few moments for Aurora to expend what little energy she had left.

For the briefest moment, Aurora's eyes met Jinx's through the leaping flames before the witch spun, executing a complicated move to block an oncoming soldier with one blade while swiping at another to keep him back.

Aurora thought she heard her shout, "Don't be stupid, novie!" but she could not be certain because Jinx did not meet her eyes again. She was too busy holding off attackers.

"Please *no, no*. This is not how this is supposed to happen. We cannot leave them," Aurora begged.

"Maybe you should have thought of that before you went on a rescue mission without a plan."

A sob caught and burst in Aurora's throat. How did she always do everything wrong? No matter her intentions, no matter that she wanted to make things better, she only seemed to make them worse.

"Enough," Sly snapped, whirling Aurora around a corner and slamming her none too gently against a wall, not a hint of a comfort in her tone. "Life happens how it happens, and you either move with the maelstrom or die wallowing about the change in the winds. You still have your mother to save. Not to mention ourselves. This whole place could come down if those storms aren't handled soon."

Aurora and Sly had never been friends exactly. The hunter had mistrusted her from the moment they met, rightly, Aurora supposed. Sly had seen through her persona as Roar and knew that it had not been the whole truth.

Truth, she realized, was the only thing Sly dealt in. And it was what she needed to hear in that moment. They would get her mother, then maybe in the chaos of the storms there would still be time to go back for Nova and Jinx. Maybe she could still make this right.

Maybe.

Maybe.

With renewed determination, the two traversed through the palace and back to the storm shelter beneath the royal wing. Aurora could feel the skyfire storm in her chest sending frantic bolts of energy from her fingertips to her toes as they neared the room where she'd left her mother. She held her breath as she pushed open the door, and relief blazed from her every pore when she saw her mother's prone form still laid across that tiny bed.

Goddess, so much had gone wrong this day, but this was still something. She would get her mother free of these people, and she would make certain the queen woke. She had to. Because Aurora did not know if she was capable of being what Pavan needed right now.

Aurora leaned over her mother, pressing their foreheads together for just a moment before she pulled the older woman up into a sitting position. Almost simultaneously, she felt a sudden release of pressure from her mental shields, a dark weight dissipated.

"The firestorm is down," she told Sly.

Aurora still had not felt Cassius's familiar barrier go up, so someone else must have dealt with the fiery beast. A vision of Kiran appeared in her mind, and she sent up a silent hope for his safety.

The firestorm's defeat would make their escape less dangerous. She had been trying not to think of how she would carry her mother from the palace in the midst of the raging tempests outside without taking them all directly to their deaths. But at the same time . . . if the storms were being controlled, she had far less chance of getting back to Jinx and Nova.

But maybe they had got out on their own. Jinx was a warrior, an earth witch, one of the strongest people Aurora had ever known. *Maybe.*

The trek up the secret passageway to the royal wing was far more difficult than the way down had been. The incline was steep, and the queen's unconscious form hung heavy between Aurora and Sly, whose differing heights made the job even more challenging. Normally Aurora would have taken the majority of the weight, but the day had begun to take its toll on her. Her feet felt like lead as she forced them up and up the path, and the mental and physical exhaustion had begun to blur into one heavy weight that lay atop everything else, slowing her down.

It did not even matter when she felt the second storm unravel, and then the third. The damage was already done. She was beyond depleted, and the only thing she knew to do was put one foot in front of the other again and again.

She would have kept walking right out of the passageway and into the open hallway if Sly had not stopped her, and held a finger to her lips.

There were voices in the royal wing. And as soon as she began paying attention, her skin broke out in bumps at the familiar deep voice she heard just a few steps away.

"No," Cassius Locke snapped. "Don't kill either of them. I want to question them. And don't put them in the dungeon either, not until we know how they got the girl out before. Go. I'll follow shortly. I want to be the first to speak to them."

Aurora locked eyes with Sly and her stomach sank. She heard the heavy footsteps of the departing soldier, but nearby a door opened and closed quickly. She took the chance to undo the latch and slide open the wooden door of the passageway, and she curled her fingers carefully around the tapestry that hid their position.

A quick peek revealed an empty hallway, but only moments later the door to what had been her private rooms for eighteen years opened sharply, and the tall, dark form of Cassius Locke emerged. His hair was longer than the last time she saw him, less regal, edging on unkempt. He wore all black, just like she had remembered, but patches of his tunic had been singed away, revealing reddened, burned skin. His hard face was smeared with ash, but his eyes were set with determination as he closed the door to her rooms and stalked down the hallway.

To interrogate the friends she had left behind.

She released the tapestry as though it had caught flame like so much of the rest of the palace, and clamped her palm over her mouth until her lips ground painfully into her teeth.

When the hallway had grown quiet, Sly said, "We should go."

Aurora did not have any other answer. She was tired of leading. Clearly, it was not something she did well. So she did as the other hunter said, and they slipped into the hallway and moved quickly into her mother's room at the end of the hall.

Luckily, it was empty. No waiting soldiers. No unconscious maid.

No Jinx either.

Aurora held up her mother while Sly ducked out to check the balcony and confirm what they feared—their escape route was long burned. Sly came back, and her eyes fixed on the bed.

"The bedclothes will have to do. We can use them to wrap your mother and lower her down."

Aurora nodded, still feeling numb, but she carried her mother over to begin the process. Sly laid out one linen blanket on the floor, and Aurora carefully positioned her mother on top. Efficiently, Sly rolled the queen onto her side and said, "Pull her knees up. We need her as small as possible."

Aurora blinked, but did as she was told, swaddling her unconscious mother like a child. In minutes they were ready to try their escape. Aurora would lower Sly down first, then send her mother down next. Together, they carried her mother to the balcony door. As soon as they stepped outside, the smell of ash and rain filled

Aurora's senses. She looked up and saw pillars of smoke rising from the city beyond, and all at once that numbness went away, reality coming back in a sharp slice.

"Wait," Aurora gasped. "Wait. I have to do something."

She did not let herself think or worry or fear as she charged back through her mother's room and to the door. She listened only for a moment before she returned to the hallway, Sly's quiet objections lost as she closed the door behind her.

The hallway was still empty, which was good. She strode forward until she reached the door that had once been hers, then pushed it open and ducked inside before she could change her mind.

She blinked, taking in the mix of old and new before her. Her books remained, as well as the small love seat where she used to curl up and read, where she had sat beside Cassius as he discussed their impending marriage and decided that she would do whatever it took to make her own future. But other things were different. A large black desk lay in front of her bookshelves, covered in papers and ink and books—some of which she recognized and others she didn't. There was a burned and bloodied coat slung over a wooden chair—neither of which were hers. There was a rack of weapons in one corner, with two discarded pairs of boots nearby.

Aurora shook her head in disbelief. It was not enough that he had taken her kingdom and drugged her mother, Cassius Locke had *moved into her rooms*? She had a sudden urge to destroy it all—his, hers, it did not matter anymore—but there was no time for that. Instead, she made for that monstrosity of a desk and grabbed a piece of parchment and a quill. And she did the only thing she could think of to possibly save her friends.

Aurora wrote Cassius Locke a note.

She scrawled the words quickly, but with a firm line of ink. When finished, she stared down at the words, hoping she was not making another mistake, but knowing she had to do *something*. She took one last look around her old sitting room and slipped away, returning to her mother's room.

"Finally!" Sly cried. "Hurry up."

Aurora's brow furrowed in confusion as she emerged onto the balcony to find the linens with her mother inside them already gone.

"Go, up and over," Sly urged.

Still confused, Aurora leaned over the edge of the balcony and she found her mother, safe in the arms of the man she had loved and lost. Kiran was covered in soot, and a bright red burn streaked from cheek to chin, but he cradled her mother effortlessly and with great care. Ransom and Bait were huddled close, keeping watch for soldiers no doubt. Tears began gathering in her eyes as she and Kiran looked at each other, but she knew there would be time for her gratitude later.

So Aurora crawled over the ledge of the balcony, her feet dangling, and she let go.

And so the first magic users turned themselves over to destruction. They took from the land more than they gave. They ransacked that which was plentiful and violated what should have been sacred. And the goddess repays their sins a thousandfold with each new dawning of the Rage season.

—An Examination of the Original Magics

11

Terror was a strange thing—it at once brought her every fear and worry to the surface, bubbling like hot oil, yet it was so consuming, so immense that it eclipsed them all. Novaya could not get sucked down the well of thoughts about the future or tangled up in the past, for this moment, this horrifying moment loomed so large that there was nothing but this, nothing but her and another witch, whose name she still did not know, back-to-back against more soldiers than she could count.

The other witch had given her a short dagger, but Nova did not have the first clue what to do with it, other than to hold it out as a warning.

"Come now, pretties," she heard a man say. "You are outnumbered. Don't make us hurt you. Some here enjoy that kind of sport, and I can't promise they will stop when you're subdued."

"Ah, yes," the other witch replied. "I have met some Locke soldiers like that before. In the wildlands. I regret to inform you, they met a grisly end against a twister in the Sangsorra desert. Though I rather thought they deserved it. Have you been to the Sangsorra desert? It's named for the red sands, supposedly the blood of the first tribes or some such nonsense. But it was very clear that day that the red sand was much lighter than actual blood."

Someone lunged, and the next moments happened as fast as a

skyfire strike. Nova heard the clash of swords, saw a menacing male face come toward her, then felt herself swung around by her elbow just in time for the other witch to stop the sword that had been arcing toward her. Without thinking, Nova jabbed her dagger forward, slicing through the raised arm of the bicep that her partner held off. The man's sword clattered the floor, and she quickly picked it up, even more at a loss with the larger weapon than she was with the smaller blade.

"Well done." The earth witch smiled before planting their backs together once more.

A little bird of hope stretched its wings inside the cage of her chest, and Nova wondered if they might somehow make it out of this situation alive. Even if they could just stall, maybe Aurora would be able to send in reinforcements.

Then the men seemed to think better of their strategy, and they all rushed in at once. She was torn away from her partner in moments, both weapons falling uselessly from her hands. Two soldiers caught her arms, hauling her back.

But the warrior witch proved to be a far greater foe than Nova. She spun and lunged, her dark hair whipping around her like a third blade. She was surrounded, but her feet moved so quickly that she managed to keep pushing them back and back, creating a small pocket in the middle for herself as she fought. When three men charged all at the same time, Nova could not see how the witch would fight them off, but then the earth lurched, the palace floor shaking and the walls rumbling, more of the damaged ceiling crumbling overhead.

Nova stumbled, as did the men holding her, and for a few brief moments, she ended up free and on her knees near a pile of burning debris. She spied a mound of firestorm embers that had piled up during the storm, and she reached, grabbing two just before a soldier took hold of her again. Nova let the soldier pull her back to her feet, then she shoved her hand at his neck, until she heard the sizzle of the still-burning ember make contact with his skin.

The man's scream was piercing, and so close to her ear that it echoed painfully inside her head long after he had stumbled away. Novaya didn't look down at her hand. She could feel the pleasant warmth of the ember against her palm. It did not burn her, but instead whispered to her magic, like something familiar and foreign all at the same time, like a dear old friend she could not remember. It was fire, and yet it was not. It was . . . more.

Another soldier came at her, and this time Nova did not hesitate, throwing one burning ember straight at the man's chest, where it burned through the uniform in a near-perfect circle before hitting the skin beyond. The soldier dropped his weapons, his hands patting down his rapidly disintegrating uniform as he screamed in reaction to the ember's unseen path beneath. Nova spun, scooping up as many embers as she could hold, and then she began launching them at the men who were ignoring her in favor of the warrior witch.

Her first throw went wide, missing the group entirely, but she hurried forward, and her next throw made contact, causing another soldier to peel off, clawing at his own back where an ember had struck him between the shoulder blades. Again and again Nova threw her embers, picking off men on the outside until she'd left the other witch with only two foes.

Novaya was out of embers, so she rushed to a nearby wall where the winds had pushed a drift of the smoking stones. Grabbing as much as she could hold with two hands, she stood and suddenly heard the world go quiet.

The strike of sword against sword disappeared.

No one spoke or groaned or grunted during the ensuing fight; in fact, she could hear no signs of fighting at all.

Over the hammering of her heart, she realized that she heard·

no signs of the storms outside either—no howling winds or rumbling thunder.

Slowly, she turned, and she saw the warrior witch with her arms raised, and a wall of soldiers that blocked out the rest of the room. Nova let the embers drop, and they scattered around her feet like scorching little skipping stones.

From among the wall of soldiers emerged a tall form—light brown skin, dark hair, eyes nearly as black as his heart.

Cassius Locke.

It appeared reinforcements had arrived.

They simply were not hers.

Kiran had always prided himself on thinking quickly on his feet, but the moment Roar—no, Aurora—landed with a soft thud from the balcony overhead, his thoughts scattered, and all the plans he had been making fled with the wind.

He was so relieved to see her whole and safe, but the weary, shamed expression she wore as she met his eyes made his skin feel too tight against his bones. Or that could be the burns, which were aching something fierce under the pressure of the weight he held. It was a person, that much was clear, but Sly had not told him more than that when she lowered the cargo to him over the balcony's edge. Whoever it was, they appeared to be alive at least, based on the warmth he felt and the occasional subtle breath.

Sly made a quiet landing a few moments later, and Kiran managed to tear his eyes away from Aurora for a moment to look at her as she approached. His old friend wore a dark and serious expression. "We need to go. The grounds will be crawling with blues soon."

"Where's Jinx?" he asked, then hesitated, lowering his head to look at the covered form he held. Jinx, he was certain, was far shorter.

"Not here. We got separated."

"Separated?" Ransom cut in, his voice gruff.

There was a long moment of silence, and when Sly's expression gave nothing away, Kiran shifted his gaze back to Aurora. Her eyebrows were furrowed, her cheeks hollowed, and her lips pursed as moisture gathered in her eyes. "It's my fault," she whispered. "I took her in there. And now they have her."

"Have her?" Ransom growled.

Kiran cut him off. "Who has her?"

"Locke soldiers. When the twister hit, we were in the dome, and part of the roof collapsed. Sly and I ended up on one side, and Jinx on the other with my friend Nova. We would have found a way through, but soldiers came on their side, and . . . and . . . we had to leave before it was too late."

"Speaking of too late," Sly said, "is there a way out of this place that isn't going to be guarded by a legion of soldiers? Otherwise, we might all be captured."

Kiran kept staring at Aurora, feeling like he was being pulled in two different directions. He was furious and horrified at the capture of his friend, at the fact that she had been in needless danger at all, but he knew, *knew with every bit of certainty there was in the universe*, that he would always want Aurora to save herself if she could. But that did not stop the shredding feeling inside him, like he was being pulled not so cleanly in two.

Feelings would have to wait. For Sly was right; they could do little for Jinx now. They needed to get to safety, regroup, and plan. He had a grappling hook and a rope; they just needed to find an isolated spot and hope they could get all of them over the wall without being seen.

In the end, they used his hook and one of the steel-arrowed anchors they used sometimes to keep their footing during high winds when hunting. He threw the hook over the wall, pulling until he had solid leverage, and then he shot the arrow into the uppermost section of stone. It only sunk into the rock a bit past the arrow's head, but that would have to be enough. Together, the two ropes allowed them to move quickly, and it helped him and Ransom carry the added weight of their extra passenger. They were lucky that the sky was still shrouded by smoke from the firestorm; it made the city dark and hazy, and they were over the wall after a tense period without drawing any unwanted attention. But the danger was not over once they had made it onto the city streets.

People were beginning to venture out of their homes, striving to save the parts of the city that still burned, because it was clear no one from the government cared enough to send help. Kiran knew that desperate people, especially ones whose homes had just been damaged or destroyed, would not think twice about giving their descriptions to anyone who came looking if the information garnered them coin or some other much-needed good fortune in this miserable place.

The lot of them could hardly traipse through the city back to their inn carrying an unconscious person wrapped in bed linens without standing out in someone's memory. They needed to find somewhere close and safe to lie low until the danger passed.

He looked to Aurora then and raised the bundle in his arms slightly. "Do I get to know more about this now? Any chance our guest will be able to carry their own weight soon?"

Aurora's face grew troubled, and she shook her head. "I can carry her if you need a break," she said, drawing nearer.

"No, it is not a problem," he insisted, despite the ache in his shoulders. The burns had mostly grown numb by now anyway. "Just curious as to who *she* is?"

Aurora lifted a hand, running it lightly over what must have been the person's foot.

"She's my mother."

He looked at her, wishing he'd heard the wrong words, that his tired ears had somehow mixed them all up. But he knew that wasn't the case. It all made sense now. Her secret journey into the castle against the rebellion's wishes, and why Jinx would help. The earth witch had lost her mother shortly before joining the crew, and the loss still plagued her.

Holy raging goddess. Kiran was holding a godsdamned queen.

Now, more than ever, they needed to get off the street and somewhere private. There was only one place he could think of, and it would not go over well, but he did not think they had much of a choice.

So he hefted the queen higher in his arms and said, "Follow me."

"Where in the bleeding skies were you while the kingdom was under attack?" Cassius snarled, slamming the door to the throne room behind him as he approached his father. It did not close properly, undermining his anger, but the hole in the ceiling and the pile of half-charred furniture and curtains and rugs in the center of the room underscored his point well enough.

His father straightened, slowly, lifting one hand off the table he leaned on, then the other. His black hair was scattered with gray, and the wrinkles in his tanned skin settled into grooves as he sneered. "I was busy. I had assumed you had things under control. It seems I assumed wrong. Perhaps I should listen to Casimir. He thinks you've lost your edge. Maybe it is time for a little healthy brotherly competition."

Yes, his father would love that. The brothers had spent their childhood more like animals his father trained to fight each other than a true family. His father had a certain cruel curiosity when it came to pushing his sons.

Cassius turned that same cruelty back onto him as he said, "That might prove difficult, seeing as Casimir is missing."

That news caught his father's attention, wiping the bored sneer away in an instant. "What do you mean, *missing*?"

"I mean as soon as the palace was infiltrated, I sent men to protect each member of the family, but they were too late. The residential wing had been ransacked and bombed with fog magic. Casimir was gone, and my mother, *your wife*, was laid out on the floor as though she'd been crawling for help. Not that you likely care. The fog left her confused and frightened, and she has been asking for you, and no one knew where you were either until moments ago, when I was notified that you showed up here. So, where *were* you?"

His father avoided the question and asked instead, "Are you saying your brother has been kidnapped?" The Locke patriarch marched across the room as he asked the question, but his feet didn't cooperate, carrying him in a wobbly diagonal instead of a straight line.

"Gods. You are drunk," Cassius snapped. "And getting more pathetic by the day."

The king's face reddened, and he puffed up his chest. "You will not speak to me that way. I am your father. Your *king*. I *made* you."

Cassius knew those last words had nothing to do with parentage and everything to do with brutality. His father had made him cold and hard and hungry for victory and violence in equal measure. His lip curled in disdain, knowing one day that urge would turn on its maker. Cassius did not regret being ruthless. It was necessary in this world. But if he was to be a monster, he would be his own, not his father's.

"And what a failure you are in those roles now," Cassius said. "King of a city that no longer exists and father of a son you did not even know was in danger."

With a growl, his father lunged, and it took surprisingly little effort for Cassius to spin his momentum around until his back crashed into the nearest wall. Dust and ash floated down around them, and a loose, half-burned plank of wood toppled from the ceiling to join the debris scattered about the floor.

"I should leave you here," Cassius growled. "How long do you think you would last against the Stormlord without me? How long before he would have you? Do you think he would kill you slowly? Keep you around to torture and play with? I hear he's viciously mad. Maybe you will get lucky and he'll take your head in one clean cut, and mount it on the battlements to make a display of you like he has done to so many of our soldiers. I'm done being your pawn, old man. I should have gone my own way the day you got our home destroyed."

His father swallowed, lifting his chin to meet his gaze head-on. His eyes were watery—from the drink, no doubt, not from emotion. Cassius knew his father had few of those.

"You are wrong if you think he will stop at me," the king spat. "The things you have yet to learn about this world could fill an ocean."

"Then perhaps it is time for me to venture out and see if I can swim. Good luck keeping your head above water without me."

Cassius stormed from the throne room, out into the hallway of the dome beyond, fury stirring in his blood. Soldiers and servants alike were working on cleanup, and he wove between them, determined to put as much distance between himself and his father as possible.

Cassius was not, by nature, someone who second-guessed things. He made a decision, and he charged forward. But in recent weeks, he found his mind forging the same paths again and again—asking the same questions.

What if they had never come here? Would the Stormlord have thought them dead? Or did he have some way of knowing? Of tracking them? Was it only his father's greed for another kingdom that had brought him upon them once more? Cassius liked power, but he was not naive enough to think becoming king was the only way to gain it. There were a hundred different lives he could have lived if he had done as he threatened, if he had split from his father on the day his homeland fell. With the magic he possessed, he could have gone anywhere, seen anything, but instead he was here, doing this all over again—watching the world fall, piece by piece.

Perhaps this time he would not stick around for the end. What did he care for this land, for these people? And thanks to his father's careful raising, he had never grown too affectionate of anyone else in his family either—emotions were vulnerabilities, after all. There was nothing at all tying him to this place.

When he re-entered his rooms, he ripped at the buttons on his shirt, needing the fabric off and away from his burns. He hissed as he pulled the fabric free, opening up wounds that had already clotted.

Let it bleed. The pain helped dull his rage.

Cassius grabbed a glass and poured a drink from the sideboard, and moved to his desk. He was about to sit when he noticed a piece of parchment directly in front of him. He tended to be rather meticulous with his belongings, and he did not recall doing any writing recently.

With two fingertips, he dragged it closer to the edge of the table where he could read it more clearly. After the first read, he sank into his chair, tossing back what remained of his drink. Then he pulled the parchment close to his face and read the words again.

I have my mother.
I'll be coming for my kingdom next.
And whatever cruelty you've shown to Novaya, I'll make
*   sure is visited upon you a thousandfold.*

Aurora

Cassius sat back in his chair, a burn on his shoulder stinging at the contact with the wood. One corner of his mouth pulled upward in a ghost of a smile.

It seemed he still had one thing tying him to this place after all.

Those with the gift of water were often lonesome creatures, for they knew the depths of the ocean and the farthest reaches of the world in a way no other could.

—*An Examination of the Original Magics*

12

Thirteen Years Earlier

Cruze was not sure of the days any longer. More than a dozen had passed, of that he was certain, but sometimes the days and nights blurred during tempests and it was difficult to know the difference when dark clouds blocked out the sun for endless lengths of time.

The numbers of those he had been stranded with were beginning to dwindle quickly, and he did not allow himself to think too long on the loss. His father used to tell him that only the strong survived, and the rest did not matter. That was back when his father still visited . . . before he decided that Cruze was not one of the strong ones.

But Cruze would show him. Someday. He would start by proving himself here in this jungle.

Of those that were left, there was him and the girl Kess, the one with the bruise on her neck, though that had nearly faded away completely now. There was also a tall boy with dark skin, and a younger boy he had taken under his wing. One other girl remained, with dark red hair and a mottled purple-and-red mark around her eye that Cruze had assumed was a terrible bruise in the early days. But the color had remained exactly the same, so he guessed now it was a birthmark of sorts.

It was her, the one with the mark, who made Cruze finally

understand why all the others had been taken. He saw her save herself in a way that should not have been possible.

It had rained so much and so often over the past few days that the river they depended on had swelled past its banks, swallowing up the rocky shelter they had claimed as their own. What had once been a calm and winding provider of sustenance became a ferocious blend of rapids and debris that rose with unexpected swiftness. Half their party had disappeared in the initial floods, never to be found—mostly the younger children who did not know how to swim, or those who had already grown too sick and weary to battle the rapids.

But she—the girl with the mark—Cruze had seen her hold out a hand and stop a wall of rushing water in its tracks, giving her the extra seconds needed to climb up into the same tree in which he was already taking refuge.

Even after they had relocated, the danger did not end. Animals had come after the floods. The rising water had displaced them too, so they were all on the run—everything from small, harmless creatures to wild boars to the large, predatory cats that stalked the jungle. It was the latter that had taken another member of their contingent.

Kess had been the one to find the body. She and the marked girl had taken to wandering off together for long periods of time, sometimes to collect firewood or other supplies, sometimes for no reason at all. Cruze had sent one of his ghosts to follow them, in part because he was curious about the other girl's abilities and because out of everyone, he felt a certain connection to Kess.

He had had a great many visions since being stranded in the jungle, and he was learning to tell the ghosts apart, to communicate without words. In fact, he interacted far more with the invisible whispers and stirs of emotion than with the other children at the camp. When he heard Kess screaming, he feared the worst, and he yanked hard on the connection he had to the spirit watching her. Even from a distance, he received an answer, flashes of Kess, safe but distraught. He still tried not to care about the others, but that did not mean he wanted to be alone. And if that meant keeping someone alive with him, he intended for it to be the girl who was smart enough to save herself when needed.

With directions from the spirit, he had been able to find the girls quickly in the woods. When he came upon Kess in the clearing, she was vomiting against a tree, and he knew why as soon as he saw the half-eaten body of the young girl who had wandered off to use the bathroom and had never come back. Her skin had been torn open in several places, and her insides were no longer where they were supposed to be. Instead they were scattered around her in a grotesque display.

Another body he would have to deal with.

The others were too squeamish, so Cruze had taken on the duty of disposing of bodies when nature did not do it for them. This would need to be addressed quickly or it would bring more predators crawling around their new camp.

"Are you all right?" he asked Kess, who still hovered near the tree, her palms pressed to the bark and her head ducked low.

"I do not know how much longer I can stay here."

"You are not *her*," Cruze told her. "You are a survivor."

"Right now I am. But this place . . . if we stay here, it will take us eventually. Somehow, someway."

"You want to leave?"

"Don't you?" The question came not from Kess, but from the other girl, the one with the mark. Cruze scowled, turning to face her. A swarm of otherness pressed in around him, and he knew immediately what it was. He had made promises in his time here. He had seen deaths both in the present and the past—so many that he was beginning to know the forest by the marks death left behind, by the memories and ghosts that lingered. They had opened themselves up to him, and he could not abandon them.

"You two should go back to camp. I will deal with this," Cruze said, gesturing toward the body, another death. He wondered if he would encounter her spirit at one point too.

"Really though," the red-haired girl continued. "You think it better to stay here than try to leave? Maybe we could make it out of the jungle, find another city to take us in."

Cruze resisted the urge to roll his eyes. He might have lived in a ramshackle house shared with near a dozen women, but one thing his father had done for him was provide the books needed to educate himself.

"The nearest Stormling city is Odilar, on the other side of the Sahrain mountains. We would have to trek north through the entire jungle, then cross the mountain paths. Here at least we have water and some degree of shelter. If we leave, we are at the mercy of both the storms and the land."

The girl lifted her chin. "Then we don't make for a city. We make for the coast. Perhaps we will have some chance there of finding help."

Curious. If she was a witch of water, as he suspected, she would feel more comfortable by the sea. His father had called the original magics evil. When Cruze had asked for a book on the subject, he had gotten a swift slap to his cheek, and an order never to speak of those magics again.

But he did not think his father would approve of the voices he heard and the visions he saw either. Would they make him evil in his father's eyes? After this long in the jungle on his own, Cruze decided he did not care what his father's opinion would be. He had his own ideas on the subject.

"On the coast, we will be a vulnerable target for the next hurricane. This is not a world in which one *finds help*," he said.

"So then what do you suggest?"

Cruze was unsure what to make of the girl, the marked one— he had heard the others call her Jael. She looked at him with an expectant glare and asked, "Well? Do you have a suggestion or are you only here to tear apart ours?"

Cruze straightened to his full height and said, "I suggest you keep surviving."

Aurora did not recognize the building to which Kiran led them. It was only one street over from the palace walls, and appeared to be well kept. An intricately hand-painted sign hung over the door declared it THE MERMAID TAVERN. Aurora had little experience with taverns, but this one seemed nicer than most. The building was well painted and quite large—two, maybe even three floors. The inside was dark, but Kiran avoided the front door, leading them through a side alley and around back instead. He nodded to Ransom, and the man stepped up to the door at the back and gave a few hard knocks.

There was no answer, and Aurora looked around nervously, wondering how long they had until the Locke soldiers would be crawling the streets looking for them. The storms had undoubtedly bought them some time, but the longer they spent out in the open, the more vulnerable they were.

And it was all her fault. So many things were her fault that if she let herself think about them, let her mind wander in that direction, she feared she might collapse in on herself. So she treated the thoughts like she would a meddling soul and blocked them out.

Ransom stepped up to the door again, this time knocking repeatedly until they heard movement on the other side. A lock clicked and the door swung open, revealing a haphazardly dressed Zephyr on the other side. She had replaced her rebellion gear for another one of the long, draped and flowing dresses that flattered her shape, but she appeared as if she had pulled it on in a hurry.

"Bleeding skies," the woman muttered. "Inside now, before anyone sees you."

Ransom went in first, his big body narrowly squeezing past Zephyr into the building beyond. Sly went next, and when Aurora hesitated, Kiran jerked his head for her to go in ahead of him. She did, but she hovered near to the door, waiting for him to pass through with her mother. By the time he did, Ransom had already cleared a nearby table of the chairs stacked on top, and Kiran swept forward, laying out her mother atop it with care.

Aurora rushed over, hearing the slam of the door and the turn of multiple locks behind her.

"What did you do?" Zephyr growled, pushing through the group until she stood facing Aurora across the table. "I already know you went against my orders."

"I don't take orders from you," Aurora shot back.

"You do if you want to be part of this rebellion. There are lives at stake. Any miscommunication, any alteration in the plan could ruin us all."

Aurora did not answer. She couldn't. Because as much as she hated to admit it, Zephyr was right. Jinx had walked into that palace with her today because she trusted her, because they were friends, and now she had lost her freedom, and possibly her life because Aurora had failed. Aurora could only hope that her note would save her. That the risk of revealing herself would pay off. If only she had not kept her plan a secret, if she had enlisted more help, if they had done reconnaissance rather than rushing in without more details . . . Aurora was no general in an army, nor was she a leader of a rebellion. She was a princess—a naive and defective one at that. How had she ever thought she could make a difference? Could do *any* of this?

"Well . . ." Zephyr finally said, crossing her arms. "Is anyone going to tell me what you have here? Or did the princess simply miss her fancy linens and decided to take them with her?"

Aurora gritted her teeth, and refused to rise to that bait. Instead, she leaned over the table and began folding back the sheets. Her mother's hair came into view first—not quite as skyfire white as her own, more a starburst of pale blond and gray that shimmered in the low lantern light. It covered her face, and Aurora carefully pushed back the strands, tucking them behind her mother's ears until her face was revealed.

The room went deadly silent—not unlike the eerie quiet of a storm's eye. Then things erupted in a cacophony of noise. An awed curse dropped from Bait's mouth, at the same time that another curse, far less awed and more gruff, came from Ransom.

"You kidnapped the queen and brought her *here*?" Zephyr said, somewhere between a shriek and a whisper. "Do you have any idea how many soldiers will be in here tonight, drinking ale, and shaking off the day's battle? And you decided to put everything I have built at risk by coming to my place of business? Do you realize what you've done?"

"We had to get off the streets," Kiran replied. "This was the closest safe place I could think of."

"Safe," Zephyr scoffed. "*Safe?* You are mad. The entire lot of you. This place is a lion's den. *On purpose.* We cater specifically to soldiers and dignitaries and nobility in the hopes that they will let things slip when they are too deep in their cups. If there is ever even any suggestion or whisper that we are hiding something here, all of that goes away."

"I am sorry, Zephyr. I know it is not ideal," Kiran said. "But the alternative was that we risked being seen with her as we crossed the city, or worse, captured. I made a judgment call."

Zephyr stared hard at Kiran, then shifted her gaze to focus on Aurora. "It seems to me your judgment is in question."

Aurora did not know whether that retort was directed specifically at her, or Kiran, or both. She did not particularly care at the moment. She was tired. Her body ached. Her spirit too. And her mind weighed far heavier things than the words of a near stranger.

"I apologize for the disruption," Aurora said. "But my mother is not well. She was being drugged by the Locke family. It's why she sleeps. You may not like me—"

"I don't much like your mother either," Zephyr snapped. "She might be better than the Lockes, but that does not make her a saint."

Aurora swallowed, and the truth tasted bitter all the way down. "I know that. I—I know you do not owe her anything. But you and I, we have an agreement. I take back the kingdom, you get to use and sell magic freely."

"Princess, after today I am not sure I trust you can even *do* that. Perhaps you need mother's help. And what's to say her royal highness won't turn around and prosecute us all as soon as this is over?"

"Aside from the fact that my mother may never *wake*—" Aurora steeled her voice and continued. "—I gave you my word. And I will keep it."

"How can you be so sure?"

Frustrated, Aurora did the only thing left she could think of to do. She reached for the buckles on the neck of her leather vest and began pulling them free with hurried, agitated motions.

"Aurora," Kiran warned.

"It's the only way."

He pushed between her and Zephyr, blocking the other woman's sight, and he laid a large hand over the two of hers where they worked.

"*Don't.*"

Kiran's voice was low and urgent, and it was the closest Aurora had been to him in days. Her hands felt freezing in comparison to his. She tilted her head up enough to meet his eyes. "I cannot run from it forever. I could run from this world into the next and still get no farther away."

His dark eyes bored into hers, and the intensity coming off him melted away some of her fatigue. She gently shook his hand off, and began working on the buckles again, less frenzied this time. "This is who I am. I either accept it, or live forever as a fragment of a whole. I told you on the night it happened I would never wish the world smaller, not even to make it easier. My mind has not changed."

She finished with the line of fastenings and peeled back the leather until a faint white-blue glow lit the space between them. She met his eyes once, firmly, and it was clear he still disagreed. But he had given up his right to have an opinion when he ran from what they had at the first sign of difficulty. He might be content to spend the rest of his life running from the truth, but she was not.

So Aurora stepped around him and into the open. The flickering of the light grew stronger as she met Zephyr's gaze, and she pulled the leather down enough that the skyfire branching out beneath her skin became visible to the woman.

"You can trust my word because I am not like the other Stormlings. I am what happens when the magic of a spirit witch combines with the lineage of a Stormling."

For the first time since they had met, Zephyr looked uncomfortable, perhaps bordering on afraid. She did not look away from the storm that resided in Aurora's chest as she said, "You—you are like him? Like the man outside the gates?"

"Not like him, no. But I *can* do what he can do. I can call a storm to do my bidding if I so choose."

Her jaw slack, Zephyr shook her head and asked, "Then why do you need me? Why bother with the rebellion at all? Just go in and take your kingdom."

"As I said, I am not like the man outside our gates. I have no wish to cause destruction, no wish to bring another unneeded death upon this city. I want to protect it. See it thrive in safety and freedom. If this becomes an all-out fight between my magic and the Stormlord's with the Locke family in between, I am not sure anything or anyone would survive. I don't know the answer yet, but I know throwing another storm into the sky is not it."

Zephyr stared at her for a long moment, hesitated, then took a step closer, leaning to peer closer at her chest. "So, that's skyfire then? *Inside you?*"

"In a manner of speaking, yes. It's the soul of a skyfire storm I took in the wildlands." Aurora kept her chin up, and hoped none of the residual anguish from that experience showed on her face. She might be telling her secrets, but that did not mean she wanted to show all her vulnerabilities. "For another hunter, it would have produced a Stormheart. But for me, because I carry the power of a spirit witch, things . . . happened differently."

"And do you carry other storms too?"

Aurora heard Kiran shift behind her, and somehow knew he was moving closer. She could feel the nearness of him the way moisture collected in the air after it rained. "Not in the same way," Aurora answered. "But I can call any storm I wish with the use of a Stormheart."

"Interesting," Zephyr muttered. "So, if we needed a particular kind of storm magic, you could call that storm and control it long enough for one of your hunter friends to collect significant supplies?"

Aurora considered the idea. "The storm would draw attention, of course. But if we could get outside of the city, into the wildlands, then yes. Yes, I could get you whatever you needed, provided we had a Stormheart for me to use for the summoning."

"Good. Then fasten yourself up, and let's get you and your mother hidden away before it's time to open. I don't want you taken away before we have the chance to make use of your skills."

Relief rushed through Aurora, followed closely by the exhaustion that had been gnawing at her since she had used her magic in the palace. Zephyr led them up two sets of stairs, Kiran following behind again with her mother. She showed them up into a loft area that overlooked both the first and second floors, and placed them in a room connected to her office with a soft bed covered in silken sheets and thick, warm blankets. Aurora saw her mother settled, then seated herself on a plush sofa nearby, sinking immediately into the cushions with a barely contained groan.

"I could use some help getting things ready downstairs if any of you are willing," Zephyr said.

Ransom volunteered. Bait and Sly made plans to return to the inn to fill in Duke, who would no doubt be worrying about their long absence. As the group began to filter out, Zephyr stopped at the door, wrapping her knuckles softly on the frame.

"If you need anything, send Kiran down. You just stay out of sight, Princess."

Aurora did not know when it had been decided that Kiran would be staying with her. Frankly, she was too tired to argue. And she was not sure she would, even if she were fully rested. It had been too long since they had been in the same room alone. Too long since she had been able to just look at him. She wanted that, even if it was not wise.

Zephyr continued, "And thank you, for trusting me with your truth." Then the water witch was gone, along with all the others, and the door closed, leaving her alone in the quiet with the man who broke her heart and a mother who might never wake.

Kiran leaned back against the door, keeping his distance. That was the safest thing to do, really. If he crossed the room like he wanted to, he would begin by checking Aurora over, because he itched to be certain that she was well. And if he did that, if he touched her, he would want to keep touching her, and he would not be able to remember all the reasons it was a bad idea for them to be together. He would forget all the ways in which he was wrong for her, and she for him, and he would offer himself up in any way she would have him—as friend or comforter or lover, whatever she asked.

So instead he concentrated on the feel of his shoulder blades pressing into the door, and he watched. She removed the heavy hood that covered her hair, along with the high-necked leather brace that hid her secret. He understood why she had told Zephyr, but that did not make him any more comfortable. She did not see herself the way he saw her. She was constantly throwing herself into the midst of things—willing to be the shield for others—but she did not know how easily she could be made a martyr, or a pawn, or a commodity to trade. She was not as naive as she had been when they first met, but she still always assumed the best of people, of this world. Kiran knew better. And he knew it would demolish him if something happened to her because he did not protect her when he could have.

But where did he draw the line between guarding her from harm and guarding himself from her? For there was nothing for him in her world except pain; he knew that with the utmost certainty. As she shook out her starlight hair and stretched her tired limbs, he wondered if he was past the point of caring. Did he really think he could leave her one day? Even if she regained her crown, if the Lockes were removed and the Stormlord no longer a threat, could he walk away and leave her to live a life with him nowhere in it?

He was not sure. He could not imagine himself doing that any more than he could imagine himself staying while she drifted farther and farther away, out of his world and back into hers. There were only impossible choices left to him. He had never been one to contemplate the future. With the life he led, it was better to assume you did not have one, live each day as it came.

Aurora was the first to speak. With her hands folded in her lap and her head down, she said, "I know you must hate me."

Kiran stood frozen, the muscles of his shoulders bunching even tighter. The only thing he hated was that he did not know how to act around her anymore. He wanted to reassure her, but he worried if he said more than a few words at a time his heart might come tumbling out after. He might tell her of the way he lay awake at night thinking about her, how he could close his eyes and recall the exact color of her eyes, and the curve of her chin, and the way her nose tipped up ever so slightly at the end. He would just keep going until he turned inside out from wanting her.

So he fell back on old habits, and asked his own question, rather than providing an answer. "Why would I?"

"Because . . ." Her voice shook slightly. "Because Jinx." Her shoulders trembled, and she buried her face into her hands, and he was across the room before he even realized his shoulders had left the door.

He crouched down in the space between her and the bed, but did not move to touch her. "She made her own decision to accompany you into the palace. I have known Jinx a long time, and she does not do anything she does not wish to do. She knew the risk, and she went anyway."

"For me," Aurora whispered, lifting her head. Pools of tears made the light blue of her eyes look almost incandescent. "She took the risk for me. You must wish I had never walked into the Eye."

Did he wish that?

Maybe. Or rather . . . a part of him wanted to wish that. He wanted to be able to go back to his old life, to slip away into the wilds as if nothing had changed, and be content as he had been before, if not entirely happy.

But now . . . goddess, he knew he would find nothing but misery in the wilds. He could not even remember what being *content* felt like anymore. There was only this chasm that existed in the space between being with her and without her. She had stretched him beyond what he had thought himself capable of, and now the world was brighter and bigger and more dangerous, but sweeter too, and once a life had been expanded as his had been, he did not think it could be shrunk down to what it once was.

But the guilt she felt? That . . . that was something he knew intimately. And he knew how to deal with it too.

He stood, squaring off in front of her. She had to lean back into the sofa to see him, and when she did, her eyes had gone wide and wary, as if she was waiting for him to pronounce some terrible punishment.

"Are you one of us?" Kiran asked.

"What?" Her head tilted slightly, wide eyes blinking.

"Are you one of us? Our crew? Would you fight by our side if we needed it? Would you provide help if we asked? Would you risk yourself for one of us?"

"Of course I would."

"Then why would I hate you? You could have died at any moment you were with us. There are a thousand ways to die in the wildlands. Attacked by an animal. A fever. Bandits. Not to mention the storms. We take risks. It is what we do. And all of us are prepared for the day one of those risks does not pay off. Jinx made a choice, and this time the risk won out."

"How can you be so casual about this? I thought Jinx was like family to you."

"Close to," Kiran affirmed. "My point is . . . accepting the bad days is part of being a hunter. If each of us held on to the blame every time something went wrong in the wilds, we would never make it past a city gate again."

"But we are not in the wilds."

"That's true. But it's also not over. You said you are one of us. There will come a time to get her back. I do not know when. And I do not know how. But I know we will keep going until we figure it out, and I know you will be right there beside us, novie. And that is all I need to know."

Kiran finished his speech with his arms folded, and with her in his peripheral vision. His heart thumped unsteadily as he waited for her to respond. Normally, he knew how to lead his team, knew how to soothe the fears of a conflicted novice, but things were so much more complex with Aurora.

"It seems you know a great deal more than me," Aurora said, with a hiccup of a laugh. Kiran turned quickly, unsure if he had offended her, but she was . . . smiling, albeit tentatively, her eyes still red with worry.

He shrugged. "I have a lot of faith in you, that's all."

"I guess it's good at least one person does," she replied, her tone dropping.

"What happened to the girl who was going to travel the wilds and win her magic, no matter what I or anyone else said?"

Aurora sighed. "I am beginning to realize that I traded one kind of naivety for another. I left this sheltered place, looking to learn more about myself and the world, and I did that. I thought I had cracked open some secret and everything would then fall into place. But I forgot that it is not as simple as my single journey from beginning to end, that there are thousands upon thousands of other journeys happening simultaneously. Why should mine be any more important than theirs? We're all connected, and more suffering for one means more suffering for all. At least that's how it should be. But everything is so divided, no one here looks past the parameters of their own wants and needs. Promise me you will tell me if I ever do that—if I put my own wants ahead of the humanity of others. *Again*, that is."

By the end of her speech, she was rubbing the heel of her hand over the place where the skyfire originated in her chest. And he could not help himself any longer; he was drawn to her like waves to the shore. He could try to hold himself back, but as long as he was near her, he would find himself falling again and again and again. She was the irresistible tide.

He sat down on the sofa beside her, slowly, so that she had the chance to object or move away if she wanted. When she stayed where she was and boldly met his gaze, he looped an arm gently over her shoulder.

"I did not want you to be a princess. You know that by now. But if anyone should be admitting mistakes it is me. I was selfish and greedy. I wanted you all to myself. But the world needs a princess like you, Aurora. It needs someone who contemplates the suffering of others. We need someone willing to admit to mistakes, willing to compromise and work alongside people from every background. This world needs your courage and your compassion, and I never should have tried to keep that for myself."

Ever so slowly, her body began to lean into his, until her head nestled into the hollow of his neck and her chest lay along the side of his own. She breathed in deeply, and then turned her eyes to her mother. He felt the soft tickle of her hair against his cheek, and the gentle rise of each breath as it moved from her body into his. And when he went to say something else, anything else to prolong this moment, he realized she was already asleep.

And for the first time in a long while, the knot of longing in his chest began to unwind, and the pain of missing her subsided.

The least studied of the original magics is the power of spirit. Those documented were typically of weaker ability, and their gifts might be nothing more than a sense of knowing—an unusual awareness of both the living and the dead. But it is believed that a powerful spirit witch can speak to the dead as easily as the living, and perhaps command them to do his or her bidding. Some have hypothesized that a similar sway might even be possible over the souls of the living.

—*An Examination of the Original Magics*

13

Nova should have been terrified. And she was, in part. But she also still felt the rush of energy coursing through her from the fight before. Her palms tingled with the seemingly boundless supply of magic she had absorbed from the firestorm embers she had been holding at their final capture. It coursed through her, making her feel alive, and banishing the fatigue and despair that had clung to her for so long. The soldiers did not return them to the dungeons, but instead took them to the wing that housed the military forces, and she and the other witch were placed in a small barracks room meant for a few soldiers to share. The soldiers on guard did a thorough search of the room, removing anything metal or large in size that might be used as a weapon, and then locked them inside. She heard their continued conversation outside, so she assumed they remained on guard, but she tentatively took a seat on one of four narrow beds, her body rejoicing at the first sign of comfort she had felt in ages.

The warrior witch paced the room, stopping to listen to the soldiers' chatter on occasion or pressing a hand to the wall or the floor without explanation. After a while, she seemed to have ascertained whatever she needed, and she crossed the room and sat on the same bed as Nova.

"Someone will be coming to question us soon, and we need to have our stories aligned."

Nova nodded. "It will be the prince. He always questioned me himself after Aurora disappeared. He was obsessed."

The witch tilted her head. "Was he?"

"Yes. He never stopped searching. He questioned me again just last week trying to find something he'd missed. He even stays in Aurora's old rooms."

"Interesting." Her companion nodded. Continuing, she said, "For today, keep things simple. You had no idea we were coming. We are friends, and we freed you in the chaos of the storm. You know nothing about any rebellion, no mention of Aurora, and if anyone asks about how you were able to touch the firestorm embers, you tell them you were given firestorm powder, understand?"

Nova's spine went stiff at the last instruction.

"Yes," the warrior witch continued. "I noticed you pelting my opponents with embers, and I don't recall you screaming in pain. Nor do I see any burns on your hands now." The girl tilted her head, and her dark hair fanned over her shoulder, softening her fierce appearance. "Does Aurora know you are a fire witch?"

Heat crept up the back of Nova's neck, and a little wisp of smoke danced up from her clenched fist. Novaya had always imagined the moment her secret came out would be much more disastrous. She feared punishment or exile or even a fight to protect herself. Instead, it had come with a tiny flicker of shocked flame, snuffed in an instant. The years of agonized fear had prepared her for the worst, and now she was amazed by how freeing it felt not to carry the knowledge alone anymore.

Of course she was still technically being held captive, probably for more serious crimes now, and her position had just become even more precarious, but yesterday Nova had been in this alone. Every day it had been her in that cell with that too-small window, and that burned bed no good for sleeping, and the memories and worries that pressed down until even breathing felt like work. But now she knew Aurora was alive, that she had a whole team of people working to help Pavan, and she had this witch, who was far more courageous and capable than she.

Goddess knew she was still afraid, but she was not alone, and that made all the difference.

"I suppose that's a no?" the other witch asked.

Nova answered, "No one knows. It has been my secret since I moved to Pavan as a child."

"From where?"

"Taraanar. My father was a trade adviser there, before . . . before we had to leave to keep my secret after an incident with my magic."

The earth witch nodded. "I know my manifestation was dramatic. I can only imagine how much more terror you felt to have fire at the tips of your child-sized fingers."

A rush of emotion built up in Nova's throat, and she found herself struggling not to cry. She did not often think about those days, afraid if she allowed herself to go into those memories, she might never crawl back out. She cleared her throat and searched for a change of direction.

"Your name," she finally said. "I don't think I caught it before."

The other witch smiled, and there was something about her presence that made the world feel more in balance. Nova found herself wishing she had been given the gift of earth rather than fire. Maybe then she would not swing between such wild extremes of emotion. Maybe then her parents would not have had to give up everything they had worked for to live a life as servants here in Pavan.

"I am called Jinx by my friends, which you officially are. When you have done battle and been captured with someone, you get to skip over the boring niceties, I think."

Jinx held out her hand in offering, and Nova hesitated. Normally she avoided touch as much as possible, but this witch had touched her down in the tunnel when she freed Nova from her cell, and it had not called up her fire then. And now that she knew more about Aurora's ability, she was beginning to wonder if her unique abilities had something to do with why Aurora's touch had also never bothered her. Perhaps her magic did not react defensively when it recognized a similar ability in the other person. Or maybe she had been so caught up in everything else going on that her magic had been too overwhelmed to rise up. Aurora's reappearance alone could have put her at ease enough to coax her magic into sedation.

There was only one way to be certain. Nova lifted her hand and fitted it against the one Jinx offered. The earth witch squeezed and gave a firm, authoritative shake. Nova waited for some reaction, for the flames to crowd under the surface of her skin, or for the restless energy to prick her anxiety. But nothing came. She smiled, so wide her cheeks pinched as if out of practice.

Jinx grinned in return, and the expression looked mischievous and wild when paired with the leather she wore, and the hair shorn short on one side and long and flowing on the other. Something flipped in Nova's stomach, but it was not fire. It was almost like the way her stomach rumbled when she was hungry, except the day had been too chaotic for her to even think of food. Instead, she just felt a little wobbly on the inside as Jinx released her hand and that reckless smile faded away.

Nova had a sudden urge to ask questions, *every question*—about how Jinx had met Aurora, and where *she* was from, and how she had become a hunter, and what her manifestation had been like. But at that moment the lock of the door slid back with a loud *thunk*. The door swung open fast enough that she only had time to turn her head before her familiar captor entered the space, taking the peaceful balance that Jinx carried with her naturally, and smashing it into a thousand irretrievable pieces.

Cassius had caught the two women off guard, which was good, for he was a bit off-kilter himself. He studied the one called Novaya—

the one he had held in a cell for months, whom he had questioned multiple times, who had always insisted upon her innocence, and yet today was nearly rescued in a highly coordinated attack that had left the palace vulnerable, and his brother missing, along with the Pavan queen.

And then there was the letter, if it was real. He slipped a hand into his coat pocket, feeling the rasp of the parchment against his fingers. His gut told him it was her writing. He had spent enough time in her rooms now that he had seen notes scribbled into the margins of her books, or forgotten slips of paper tucked between pages. He had sat at his desk and studied her scrawl, wondered at the woman behind it, and the strange events of fate that had brought him to her and then taken her away.

Cassius should not have cared, that was the troubling part of it all. Things had arguably worked out very well for him. His family had gotten the kingdom they had come for without even having to go through with the charade of marriage. So why could he not have been happy and embraced his new role fully? Why had he obsessed so completely over her disappearance? And why did the possibility of her being in the city now make him want to abandon everything and search door-to-door until he set eyes on her and confirmed the truth for himself?

He had to know. He had put off this questioning as long as possible. He'd seen his mother settled, sent out scouting parties to search the city for his brother, assigned others to see to the city's most immediate issues from the storm. He had done all the things his father should do but would ignore in favor of another drink, another distraction, another day of running with death nipping at his heels. But now he was done waiting. He needed answers. So he entered the room where the two women were being held, and this time he hesitated before closing the door. He looked to one of the soldiers outside and said, "It is cold in here. Fetch some blankets. And ask a maid to bring up something to eat and drink for our guests."

The soldier hesitated, clearly confused, but Cassius fixed him with an impatient stare, making clear his order, and closed the door. He turned to the women and found another confused expression on the maid Novaya's face. But the other, the one who had single-handedly fought a dozen or more of his men, if the stories were to be believed—she looked almost . . . *smug*. Certainly not an expression he had ever seen before on a prisoner's face. It was almost enough to make him open the door and reverse his request, but then he remembered the note in his pocket.

He did not fear reprisal, but whoever this girl was to Aurora, clearly she was important.

"You do realize who I am, don't you?" he said to the woman, unable to adopt a completely welcoming tone.

The girl snorted, flipping her strangely styled hair as if she were captured every other day.

"I have heard things about you, yes. A great many things. Most of them bad, if you were wondering." She held up her hands in mock innocence. "No offense. Honesty among friends, and all that." She leaned back into the wall with practiced ease, not a bit of fear showing.

"I've heard about you as well. Quite the fighter, it seems. Rebellion, are you?" Cassius asked.

"Hardly. I don't have a say in this storm. This isn't my city. I'm just passing through."

"You mean to say you are not a legal citizen of Pavan?"

"Last time I checked, neither were you, since that wedding fell through."

Cassius's eyes narrowed. "I am a guest of the royal family of Pavan."

"Are you now? And where are they? I would *love* to have a chat with them about the subpar hospitality we have received. Nova, here, is even quite good friends with the princess, I hear. I am sure a moment with the queen would clear all of this up."

No wonder Casimir had not yet stamped out the rebellion despite his brutal tactics, if this was the kind of woman they had in their midst.

"You are quite brazen, aren't you?"

"And you are 'cold and calculating,' 'carnivorous,' and like a 'shark,' from what I've heard. Now that we have had our introductions, can we move on please?"

"Who told you that?" Cassius asked, his eyes tracking to Novaya.

The chatty one snapped, "Not her, so do *not* think about harassing her more than you already have. Don't you think you have caused enough trouble?"

"I? You were the one captured amidst a rebel raid."

"I simply assisted in the rescue of someone wrongly imprisoned when asked by a highly respected friend."

"A highly respected friend?" Cassius jumped on the clue, barely resisting the urge to reach back into his pocket for the note.

"Yes, that's right," the girl said.

"And who would that be?"

"I doubt someone like me and someone like you have the same friends," the girl answered.

"One never knows." He was too eager, damn it, and the girl knew it. He could see a glitter in her eyes, like she knew she had just gained the upper hand, and he had to gain it back. His instinct was to make her afraid by whatever means necessary—pain, most likely. But if his suspicions were correct, if this woman did somehow know Aurora, torturing her into giving him information might backfire in the long run. This required less blunt force, more a precise incision. He backed off a little, crossing the room, breaking the frantic pace of their conversation, before finally saying, "For all I know, your special friend could be the Stormlord."

The girl laughed openly. "If you thought that was the case, we would hardly be in this average-sized room with acceptable beds on a normal floor, with guards *outside* the door. And you certainly would not have called for blankets. And *food*."

Cassius gestured in Novaya's direction. "You clearly were able to breach the dungeons, so I decided spontaneity was in order. And whatever you might think, I am not a monster. You have information I want. Working with me will make each of you much more comfortable. And longer lived."

"Oooooh!" she mocked, half laughter, half ghostly howl. Then she leaned forward with a hand up to one side of her mouth and whispered, "Your evil villain monologue does not work as well when an actual evil villain is laying siege to the city you stole."

Cassius realized suddenly that his casual movement about the room had turned to outright pacing. The audacious little chit had turned the entire conversation around on him, and he'd lost control. He stopped abruptly, planting his feet and glaring at her.

"I could have you executed for my pick of offenses at this very moment if I so chose." He raised an eyebrow carefully.

"You *could*. But I do not think you would."

He gritted his teeth and tried to keep his face passive, tired of this game. He did not have the patience for the back-and-forth of interrogation. Not when it came to Aurora. If she was back in the city, free from her captors, why had she not returned home? Was she still in some kind of trouble? Had the rebellion found a way to retrieve her from the kidnappers? Were they using her for their own ends now? Or had she joined them willingly? Did she not know she could walk right back in and he would welcome her gladly? Maybe his brother's treatment of the rebellion and his father's hasty move to turn over the flags had left her insecure. If he could find a way to get her word, perhaps she would just come home. He would give her back her maid friend if that was all it took. She was nothing, just a means to an end.

If Aurora came home, they would stand a better chance at holding off the Stormlord with their abilities combined. That was what mattered now. She could have the throne. He found he was caring less and less for the idea of it by the day.

Cassius decided to cut through the subterfuge and straight to the point. "You know where she is, don't you?"

"Where who is?" the girl asked.

"My future wife," Cassius said.

"She will never be your wife." The answer did not come from the brazen rebel, but from Aurora's maid friend. The girl had nearly plastered herself to the wall where she sat on the bed, but she had roused herself enough for that impassioned interjection.

"You heard her," the other girl said. "I don't know any wife-to-be of yours."

"I do not care to quibble about the specifics. All I care about is whether she is safe and where she is. I need to speak to her."

The rebel's head tilted to the side, revealing the way her hair was cut shorter than his own on one side. "She is safe. I do not know where she is. But she knows where we are. That is enough."

"And if I want to get a message to her?"

The rebel smiled. "You could let us go. We will be your messengers."

"Not a chance."

"Then I guess your message will remain unsent."

Cassius stalked toward the door and said, "Or perhaps I will tire of bargaining and decide to send a different type of message." He directed a hard look at the maid, who sat quiet again on the bed. Then he stormed out, determined to find another way to reach Aurora Pavan.

When he returned to his rooms, he took a seat and opened a drawer on his desk, withdrawing the still-green and vibrant leaf he'd plucked from the vine he'd found outside Aphra Pavan's room. He ran his thumb along the ridge on the underside. If he could not find Aurora, he would find her witch.

Kiran pulled the hood high over his head. He was glad for the chilly turn in the weather, so he had a good excuse to wrap a scarf around the lower half of his face, besides the fact that the streets of Pavan were crawling with Locke soldiers. He had stayed with Aurora at her mother's bedside as long as he dared, so long that his skin smelled of her and every breath threatened to send him tumbling into painful memories of what he had given up.

He was stopped five times by soldiers between the tavern and his destination, and each time he answered their questions with as few words as possible. He let them pat him down for weapons because he was not wearing any. He had left his belt and storm-magic supplies back at the tavern too. Zephyr had received word from Taven that soldiers would be executing random searches on the streets and of properties in certain neighborhoods.

Luckily, the tavern was not in an area of suspected rebellion activity, so it was not one of the neighborhoods they planned to search at this time, but all the same they had put a plan in place for where to hide Aurora and her mother should such a search occur. It was lucky that Zephyr was as paranoid as a hunter, because the woman already had a hidden passage installed off her office that led down to the basement, where a small window could be lifted to make an escape. How they would make that escape with an unconscious queen, Kiran did not know, but he felt better knowing there was a plan at least.

As he neared his destination, the appearance of soldiers only increased. He knew they were focusing on the poorest areas of the city in their search for the rebellion. But they were not bothering to stop people in the streets. Instead, they were barging into houses, throwing around furniture and beds, making a heinous mess, and seeming to relish it.

He scanned the area, checking for any wandering eyes, but when the only soldiers he saw were preoccupied with their harassment inside people's homes, he ducked into the alley where the rebellion's secret headquarters was hidden.

He undid the latch on the storm-shelter door, pulling it up only enough for him to slip inside and swing his feet down onto the ladder. Quickly, he descended, closing the shelter door behind him. He waited on the ladder for several long breaths, listening for any sign outside that he might have been spotted. When all he heard was silence, he dropped down to the ground and crossed to the locked door at the end of the room.

He did the fancy little knock that Zephyr had instructed him to do, and after a few moments the door opened, Raquim on the other side. Kiran had never heard the other man say a word, but he was a competent fighter and clearly had Zephyr's trust.

Kiran stepped past him into the long, dimly lit hallway and asked, "Where is he?"

Raquim pointed a finger in the only possible direction Kiran could go. Guessing that was all the answer he was going to get, Kiran set off down the hall. Next to Zephyr's office, he found a room with a closed door, a hint of light showing out beneath.

He knocked, heard footsteps, and then the door swung wide to reveal the hulking man named Brax. Kiran knew of him from his previous trips to Pavan. The man was a brawler. He and others like him got paid to fight in bloody, ruthless melees that others bet on. The events were big draws and made a fair amount of money for whoever won—both the fighters and the gamblers.

He looked past Brax into the room and saw the man he had come to see.

Casimir Locke.

He wished it was the other brother, but he would take what he could get.

"How goes it?" he asked Brax.

His answer came from farther in the room. "He's stubborn. And *annoying.*"

Kiran stepped past Brax to see Zephyr seated on a stool in the corner, her legs crossed far too elegantly for what he guessed was an interrogation.

"Who is this bast—" The snarled question died on Casimir's lips before he could finish the word.

"Ah, ah, ah!" Zephyr *tsk*ed. "What did I tell you about annoying me?" She rotated that red-gloved hand of hers, and Casimir shook in his chair, his mouth gaping open like a fish dying on land as Zephyr used her water magic on him.

"Man, I wish I could do that."

Kiran swung around, shocked to find his best friend, Ransom, sitting in another corner. He had not even known the other man was here. He had assumed he was back at the inn with the others.

Ransom met his gaze. "Bait would never get a word in if I could do that."

Kiran huffed an almost-laugh. Ransom returned what might have passed for a smile, were it not for the bleak expression that ruled the rest of his face. His friend's eyes returned to Casimir, and Kiran had a feeling Ransom was thinking about Jinx. Kiran was having difficulty not thinking about what might be happening to her in that palace.

She could be in this exact same situation, only it would be her tied to a chair rather than the smarmy, hateful cretin who sat before them.

"What has he told you?" Kiran asked.

"Nothing," Zephyr answered. "Yet."

At that moment, Zephyr's pet wildcat ducked beneath Casimir's chair, slinking between his legs as if waiting for its owner's command to pounce.

Kiran crossed to the center of the room and bent so that he was at eye level with the Stormling. "Do you know what we plan to do with you, Casimir? We're handing you over to the Stormlord. So anything you tell us now, every moment you prove yourself useful by giving us valuable information about your family, the military, their plans—that's that much longer you stay here with us, instead of out there with that madman. Do you understand?"

Zephyr must have released her hold on Casimir long enough to let him speak because he let out a croaked laugh, his voice dry and ragged. "You don't scare me. Neither does he. *This*," he said, using his chin to gesture at the ropes that bound him, "captivity was a *game* when I was a child. So was torture. My father liked to see which one of his boys would break first. You want to send me to the Stormlord? Go ahead. I look forward to meeting him."

"Even after what he did to your home?" Kiran asked. "He must *really* hate your family. To have reduced an entire city to rubble, to kill thousands, and to follow you here when he realized he did not get the job done."

He waited for Casimir to deny it, to claim the rumors were lies, but he only smiled and shrugged. "We found a new home, didn't we?"

"Yes, how convenient for you that the Pavan princess disappeared and then the queen fell ill."

He wheezed out a laugh. "What can I say? We got lucky. And we could not leave Pavan defenseless. That would be *cruel*."

The look in his eyes at that last word turned Kiran's stomach.

"Cruel is what you are doing to those remnants outside the gates."

"We cannot save everyone."

"From the danger you brought here? As far as I can tell, you and your family are the primary problem."

Casimir sneered. "You are all small-minded fools. Without us, you would not last a week of the Rage season, stormlord or no Stormlord."

Kiran rolled his eyes and looked at Ransom, then Zephyr. "I don't know who you think you are talking to, but we are not afraid of the Rage season. We have lived in the wildlands. I have stood in the middle of a firestorm and lived to hold the Stormheart in my hand. I have faced hurricanes and twisters and men much stronger than you. You, Casimir Locke, are not necessary to this world and its survival in any way. The time of the Stormlings is over here in Pavan. Soon, all magics will be welcomed—the kind you destroyed at the Eye and the kind this woman is going to spend the next few days making you intimately familiar with." He gestured to Zephyr and she stood, coming to stand before Casimir, her shoulders straight and proud.

"I don't know whether to call you mad or stupid," Casimir said. "Idealistic fools. Your rebellion has always been doomed. You will die. Every single one of you. By my hand or my brother's or the Stormlord's—"

The words dried up in his throat, and he jerked in his chair, his face going red, then pale as Zephyr took away the water his body needed to survive.

"I think that's enough talking for now," she said. "Perhaps you should do some more thinking. Think about how thirsty you feel right now. Is your vision blurring yet? Has the headache started? Is the room spinning? Think too about the Stormlord, about what he might do when we offer you up to him, weak and vulnerable. Where will your arrogance be then? Will your brother come for you? From what I have heard, you are not close. Perhaps he will be glad to be rid of you. Less competition. Right now, I control whether you live or you die, whether you stay here in the safety of Pavan or meet the man who followed you here from the rubble of your former home. Think on that, Casimir Locke."

Those with the power over earth could have been the makers of new worlds. Instead, with greed-corrupted hearts they used their gifts to rupture the land and suck the marrow from her bones.

—*An Examination of the Original Magics*

14

Thirteen Years Earlier

Cruze had found a spot of his very own, where he could get away from the others, and where he could listen to the voices without fear of anyone noticing. He discovered a place high in the canopy where branches from several trees crossed and wound around each other, creating a relatively safe cocoon for him to perch without fear of falling. It also gave him a good view of the sky to watch for approaching storms. He had taken to spending most of his days there, only keeping tabs on the camp and Kess with the help of the spirits who had become his companions.

In his time alone, he found himself hungry for more knowledge, about the past and whatever it was that was happening to him now. There was always the chance it was madness, of course, that had him hearing other voices, but as he searched his memories, he began to recall similar whispers during his time back in Locke when he was younger. They'd never lasted as long, not like the ones he experienced out here, and they had always seemed farther away. But he was almost certain that he had felt the sensation before being left in the jungle.

So he focused his energy on expanding his abilities, trying to communicate more effectively with the spirits, learning what he could about their deaths. For some, that was all they could remember. Others could provide minimal information about their lives. But for almost every spirit he encountered, when he tried to ask if they knew *why* they had been deserted in such a way, the spirits either grew quiet, disappeared, or could not remember.

"What are you doing up there?"

Cruze bolted upright, nearly toppling out of the tree entirely. But a strong breeze moved through the canopy at that moment, providing just enough of a reprieve for him to spread his legs and throw out his arms, rebalancing himself on the twisted limbs where he was perched.

He looked down to see Kess on the jungle floor, looking sheepish. "Sorry," she said. "I did not mean to . . ."

"Distract me to death?"

She shook her head. "Definitely not."

He shrugged. "I should have been paying closer attention." Or one of the spirits should have warned him of her approach. He sent that thought out wide, and felt a few answering nudges of apology.

"I was . . . hoping we could talk," Kess said, fretting nervously with the frayed end of her shirt. All of their clothes were little better than rags now. They had taken to ripping them up and remaking them into smaller, more wearable pieces as they all lost weight.

"Yes," Cruze replied. "There are some things I would like to talk about too."

He had been thinking more about the possibility of her being a witch, and the strange experience he himself had had since coming to the jungle.

He made his way down the tree quickly, used to the descent by now. When he was standing face-to-face with her, she seemed hesitant to ask whatever she had come for, so he took the opportunity to ask his own questions instead.

"Do you believe in the supernatural?" he asked.

"Do you mean magic? Of course I believe in storm magic."

"No," he snapped, his teeth grinding at the thought of such magic, and those he knew who wielded it. "Not storm magic.

Other kinds." Stormlings were all-powerful in this world; they made the decisions, created the laws, commanded the soldiers. They had everything when Cruze had nothing.

Kess hesitated for a long moment, but eventually, she nodded. "I-I do . . . believe, that is."

Her hand went up to the collar of her shirt, pulling it closer to her neck.

"What if I told you that we were not the first to be left here, in this same area of the jungle? I have been seeing things, hearing things. There are ghosts in these woods, and . . . and they speak to me."

"You have magic?" Kess asked.

Cruze scoffed. "I don't know that I would call it that. If I showed any true aptitude for magic, I doubt my father . . . well, never mind. I just get these visions, like the ghosts are showing me things."

"That is magic," Kess insisted. "Of the spirit."

Cruze frowned. "What does that mean?"

"It means you can communicate with the souls of the dead."

Cruze felt something hot and triumphant boil up in his stomach. So, it was true. He was not mad, as he had feared. And the visions were real. He had believed it, of course, done his best to convince himself rationally, but to have another confirm it . . .

"How do you know?" he demanded. "What do you know of it?"

Kess frowned and gave a sad shake of her head. "It is why we are here. All of us." She pulled back the collar of the shirt she had been fiddling with, showing what was left of her nearly healed bruise. "I told you that I made a choice not to die. That choice was to use my ability to control air to save myself from a noose." Cruze stared at the girl, dumbstruck. "I did not die when they kicked the stool from beneath my feet. So they sent me here instead."

"Noose?" Cruze growled. "They tried to hang you? But . . . but you are a child."

"As are you. And they left us both out here to die. The Lockes do not care. Anyone who is a threat to them, to their magic, or their way of life, they see as disposable."

Cruze had trouble swallowing after that statement. His heart was beating so hard that he felt almost light-headed. Spirits pressed in close around him, so close—some of them trying to soothe, while others . . . others seemed to feed off his distress.

Kess continued, "That actually brings me to what I wanted to talk to you about. The others—we talked, and we have decided to leave. We've built a raft, and with my air magic and Jael's water magic—"

"So she *is* a water witch?" Cruze interrupted.

Kess's brow furrowed. "Yes, Jael can manipulate water. With our abilities combined, we think we can navigate the river to the coast without much danger. It is the fastest and safest way out of the jungle."

"No," Cruze said. "No, it is too risky."

"No more risky than staying here."

"But don't you see? I can communicate here, with the ones that came before us. I can learn from them. And then—"

"And then what?"

"And then we will take revenge."

Kess's eyes went wide. "We are children. What revenge could we possibly take? I would settle for living. That is more than I thought I would have the day they put the rope around my neck."

"Damn it, don't you see? They got rid of us because they are scared of what we could become. They want us to die out here because we are strong enough to one day challenge them."

"And how do you expect to challenge them when you can only talk to ghosts?" Kess snapped.

Cruze felt like he had been slapped. And for just a moment, a violent urge swelled through him that told him to return the damage, to give as good as he got, better, even. To return tenfold the pain upon whoever dared hurt him. But then the moment passed, and Kess looked at him apologetically.

"I am sorry. But our decision is made. We leave at first light tomorrow. I hope you will come with us."

Cruze let her walk away, knowing he would not. He had finally found a place where he felt at home. Yes, it was among the dead, but they accepted him; they called him their own. And he would avenge them no matter what it took.

"Again," Cassius yelled, and on his order the small contingent of soldiers he had built began the conditioning drill anew.

Since his brother had burned the city's black market in a bid to impress their father, he had no way of obtaining the supplies to allow his soldiers to practice against true storm magic, so he had devised a compilation of the most difficult training exercises he could think of, and he put his men through their paces as often as possible, pushing them harder and harder until they moved with speed and fluidity. Soon, he would begin to test them by allowing them to cover the palace's defenses in shifts. He would be there, of course, in the case of an emergency, but they needed more field training, and fighting the storms that plagued the city was the only option.

Eventually, they shifted to weapons training, and he joined in, trading off with different partners to test their skill levels, trying to determine who were his strongest men.

Someday soon he would need them at his side because he would not react defensively forever. To win they would have to pursue the Stormlord on their own terms, and he would make certain they were ready. Or as ready as they could be.

Finally, when even he dripped with sweat, he took mercy on the men and called for an end to their session. He heard no groans or complaints or other sounds, but he could tell by the slow-gait and tender movements of the men that they were grateful to be done.

Perhaps, they were finally beginning to take this threat seriously. The recent damage at the palace from a firestorm and twister occurring simultaneously had put things into perspective for many. He had been out of reach for only a short time, dealing with the infiltration by the rebellion and the fog magic they had left to spread through the palace that had mesmerized the majority of his men and made them useless, but moments was all it took for tempests of the Stormlord's caliber to reduce something to rubble. It could have been so much worse. They could have lost everything that day, but someone had worked to defeat the storm in his absence.

Another mystery to solve.

It had to be Aurora. His mind could think of no other alternative. She was out there somewhere with a witch as a partner, and he needed to find out everything he could.

Once he made it back to his rooms, he shed the layers of his clothes until his chest was bare, and he wore only his pants. He wanted to call for a bath, but it had been too long since the last storm siren sounded. They had to be due for another soon. So he settled for dipping a cloth in the water basin in the corner and washing himself clean as much as he could without a full soak.

When he was done he returned to his desk and retrieved the book that had been delivered to him this morning. The cover was black leather with no title anywhere to be seen. But when he opened it, the first page revealed the words *An Examination of the Original Magics.*

All books on witchcraft in Locke had been purged long ago, but the laws in Pavan had not been quite as strict. The long existence of the Eye had enabled enough of an underground to survive that works like the one he held still survived, thank the goddess, for he needed its information now.

One of the Pavanian nobles that had taken a liking to Cassius from the moment he arrived and supported his bid for the throne even before Aurora disappeared had mentioned the book to him once upon a time. He was a collector of rare items and had procured it from the owner of a popular tavern, who was said to be quite the keeper of both secrets and unique items. It was only after Cassius had mentioned his own adventures into the Eye that the nobleman mentioned the tavern owner, for it appeared the person had some connection with the old market as well.

Perhaps after Cassius read the book, he would pay a visit to this tavern and see what information the owner could offer him. For now though, he turned the page and began to read, hoping for some insight into the earth witch with whom Aurora had aligned herself.

Three days passed with no change in her mother's condition. On the first, Aurora mostly slept herself, waking up occasionally only to worry over her mother, note the awkwardness of being in close proximity to Kiran again, and fall back asleep in whatever place she could manage. By the second, restlessness had set in, and she had paced the room, stopping far too often to check the temperature of her mother's skin or the rise of her chest. She had been left alone more then, with various hunters dropping by on occasion.

Duke visited, and it was the first time she had seen him since before the mission. She expected him to be disappointed for her part in Jinx's loss, for the friendly lines of his old face to be set in a grim expression, but instead he offered her a fierce hug. She clung to him like a lifeline, and he sat patiently beside her while they waited for her mother's condition to change. He asked her questions, and she told stories about her childhood, about her mother and brother. He reassured her in ways no one else could.

But by the third evening, she felt like the walls had begun to scream at her. She needed to be doing more than sitting here. Surely there was some way to help her mother, to help the rebellion, to help Jinx and Nova. She would go mad if she spent one more day stifled and shut away, watching her mother lying so still and vulnerable, feeling guilty and useless.

So when Ransom left her alone that evening to go down and assist with something in the tavern, Aurora took the opportunity to explore. She found a scarf in Zephyr's office and bound her hair up in a popular knotted style that Nova had taught her, and she donned one of Zephyr's long flowing cloaks that hung on the back of her office door. The material was soft and moved across Aurora's hands like water. Wrapping the mass of fabric all the way around her, Rora stepped just outside Zephyr's office door to the loft area beyond that gave her a view of the tavern below—both the more exclusive second floor and the ground level. She huddled back into the corner, away from Zephyr's door, and observed the movement on the two lower floors.

The inside of the tavern shimmered in a soft blue light that reminded her of skyfire, but Aurora could detect no specific source of the blue tint, for the lanterns around the room and at each of the tables held plain burning wicks. The scent of seawater hung on the air, and a small waterfall fell over a rocky sculpture in one corner, a mermaid cast in bronze lounging on a rock at the base. If she had been anywhere else, Aurora would have thought it some marvel of mechanics, a system of pumps and pipes perhaps, but knowing what she did about Zephyr, she wondered if the woman was bold enough to risk magic in plain sight.

The room was crowded, the main bar full with people standing behind those seated. And most of the tables were full too, both the plain wooden ones on the first floor, and the more cushioned, private tables that were kept reserved for more special guests on the second floor. Aurora spied Ransom carrying a large box back behind the bar, but besides him every other employee she spotted was a woman. They came in every shape and size and look, but each of them wore pastel, flowing skirts that shimmered like the tail of a mermaid might if they were real; they dazzled in the blue light of the tavern. They smiled and charmed and cast coquettish glances at every man they passed, and every man in turn—whether he be a young lad barely old enough to drink or an old general she had seen countless times around her mother's advisory tables—they all seemed to sway to the movement of the women around them, drawn like magnets.

On the second floor, she saw distinguished men meeting in alcoved tables, surrounded by plants for some modicum of privacy, but none of them paused their conversations when the women passed or stopped to refill drinks, and Aurora watched the way the women sometimes lingered by certain tables, unnecessarily dusting at plants, or filling up drinks that were nowhere near empty.

The men never seemed to notice. If they looked at the women at all, it was to stare or flirt or in a few instances reach out and touch. That was when Aurora saw the second male employee of the night. Zephyr's lieutenant—the man called Raquim—was tall with dark skin and eyes that said what his lips did not. He had an uncanny way of appearing whenever a man tried to do anything more than talk to one of the women on staff.

Aurora was not sure how long she had been watching the ecosystem below her, studying the way it worked and thrived, before a tall form cut off her view. "What are you doing?" Kiran muttered, crowding her under his arm and shuffling them both back toward Zephyr's office door. Before Aurora could argue, he had her through the door and shut away again. "You know you cannot be out there. If you are seen, you could be in tremendous danger. I told you that the patrols have been dramatically increased since the palace breach. All it takes is one person to recognize you."

Aurora sighed, trudging through the office and into the bedroom next door. "I cannot stay in here forever. I need to do something."

"Try resting."

She snapped her head around to glare at him. "I am rested."

Kiran held his hands up.

"What about a book?"

"I am tired of reading."

Kiran raised an eyebrow. "You? Tired of reading? Are you ill?"

"No, but it does not help my mood when the only book in my possession is about a royal from a city that fell to vicious storms, especially when he at least got to *do* something. Finneus Wolfram braved an ocean looking for safety. I am braving a bedroom, while those women out there, complete strangers, mind you, risk themselves to gain information for us. I could be doing that just as easily."

Kiran balked. "That's ludicrous. There are some high-level people out there, from both the Locke and Pavan command hierarchy. They have most certainly seen you before."

"I can wear a disguise. Those men are clueless. I watched them. They do not really *see* those women. They see what they want to see. And unlike the women working down there, *I* know what to listen for, and I will know whose conversations are worth my time."

Kiran opened his mouth, his brows already set in a familiar straight line, and Aurora continued, "And don't you dare forbid it. As if you have any right to rule over me because you are male, and I am not. If I am to rule a kingdom, surely that begins with the right to rule myself at the very least."

Aurora stared at him, her chin tilted up slightly, and for a few long moments he said nothing. He just looked at her with the most confusing mix of anguish and frustration and something that might have been pride. Then he inclined his chin slightly and said, "You will have to convince Zephyr, but I am sure you will. You are remarkable in that way."

A raspy voice broke in from the other side of the room. "She really is, isn't she?"

Aurora gasped and spun around, the scarf on her head toppling to the side with the quick movement. Her mother was awake and struggling to push herself up onto her pillows, but her arms kept folding weakly under her own weight. Rora pushed past Kiran, rushing to her mother's side to press her back, urging her to be careful.

"You are awake," Aurora whispered, her throat choked with tears. "Oh goddess, I am so glad you are awake."

Her mother's too-bony fingers wrapped around her forearm, pulling Aurora's hand down and against the queen's cheek. "And you are alive."

There was no stopping the tears then. Aurora could not fathom the pain she had put her mother through, the worry and grief her mother had suffered needlessly, because her plan went awry. If she had been brave enough to tell her mother the truth, if she had not kept so many of her fears about Cassius to herself—Aurora could not think of what might have been. There was no going back to fix her old mistakes; she simply had to do better moving forward. And this time, she knew that trusting people with her truth, the whole truth, was the only way they would possibly make it through.

Sometime in her crying, Kiran had slipped from the room, perhaps to inform the others of the queen's waking. She took one of her mother's frail hands between both of hers—it felt small and delicate, like a tiny bird.

"I have so much to tell you, Mother. Beginning with the fact that I love you so very much, and I am sorry I left you so worried." She could not bring herself to apologize for leaving in the first place, not entirely, though she had plenty of regret and grief over the decision. She could have handled it better, left fewer people in jeopardy, prepared her mother in some way, perhaps. But she would not regret the things she learned and the ways she grew on that journey. She could not. "I had planned for you to receive a note explaining the truth of my disappearance, but things did not go as planned."

Her mother listened through the evening and most of the next day as Aurora filled her in on everything that had happened, stopping occasionally when her mother's body called her back to slumber. Aurora started from the beginning—from the way she had foolishly gotten wrapped up in Cassius's flirtations, and overheard his true plans to control her and the crown. She left out details when necessary. Though she loved her mother, and she hoped by the end they would come to see things the same, she would not risk the identities of her friends and compatriots should her mother cling to her old ways of thinking about magic. They talked of the Locke family, and what occurred in the days after Rora disappeared. Aurora actually had to fill in some gaps for her mother there, using the knowledge she had gleaned from Taven. It seemed her mother had been incapacitated for a very long time indeed. They were sidetracked a few times as the queen asked for news of the kingdom, and how she had come to be wherever she was (which Aurora had refused to tell her). Aurora gave her the necessary information about the Locke takeover and the rebellion, and the Stormlord, but held her mother at bay when she wanted to continue asking questions about the current state of affairs. For one, Aurora was not entirely sure herself, having been cooped up here for days. Furthermore, she knew her mother would be determined to help against the Stormlord's attacks, and she was far too weak to do anything but lie in bed for now.

So instead, Aurora tried to draw her into stories about her time in the wilds. She spoke at length of the changing landscapes, and the storms they encountered, and the emergence of her magic. *That* got her mother's attention. The excitement that flushed over her features was almost enough to make her look healthy again. But Aurora was careful to weave her story slowly, leaving her mother in the dark about the nature of her powers as much as she had been, building to the discovery that she was something more than Stormling, something *other*. Though she hoped her mother could see the error of the prohibition of the natural magics on merit alone, she would make this about her if she needed to. If she had to make her mother choose between Stormling traditions alone and a free and fair way forward with her daughter, she would. Traditions and power and pride should not mean more than human lives.

Finally, when Aurora had told enough of her tale that she decided it was time to hammer home the truth to her mother, to prove once and for all that she would never be the perfect Stormling princess her mother had always desired, she began to unfasten the vest that hid her secret. She laid herself bare in front of her mother, presenting her truth with the light that beat in her breast.

"You see, when I took my first Stormheart, it did not happen for me like the others. The emotions I had been experiencing, the violent bursts when storms were near, they were unintentional uses of spirit magic. The old tribes were right. It is unrestful souls of the dead that truly lie at the heart of a storm, and somehow because I have a natural connection both to souls and to storms, I took the storm's heart, the lost soul, into myself instead of gaining a talisman for use with magic."

Aurora's mother looked at her in wonderment and confusion. She reached out a finger, hesitating before she reached the skin where skyfire streaked underneath. "Does it hurt?" her mother asked.

"Not anymore."

Her mother's eyes lifted to hers. "But it did."

Aurora shrugged. "I took another soul into my own. That kind of conquering comes at a cost."

"But what does it mean?" Aurora's mother asked, gesturing at the phenomenon in front of her.

Rora hesitated, unsure how her mother would react to the next piece of news. "You remember what I told you of the Stormlord? How he is said to have the ability to conjure storms at his bidding?"

The queen nodded. "I am still not sure I believe it. He is probably another one of those hunters, using fear to intimidate in my absence."

"He is not a hunter, Mother." Aurora flexed her fingers, trying to summon the same feeling of urgency she had felt in the palace when she had shocked the maid into giving them answers. At first, she only got a tiny spark, then the hair on her arms began to stand on end, and bright white light shot from the tip of her forefinger to her thumb in one strong, steady bolt. A few smaller branches arced around her fingers, zigzagging back and forth with a series of crackling pops. "He can call storms, Mother. As can I."

To rule fire was to be the mediator of all magics—the closest thing to the law in days of endless chaos.

—*An Examination of the Original Magics*

15

The bed was on fire.

Nova was kicking and screaming, but her limbs were tied down to the posts and the linens were blazing, her clothes right along with them. The entire mattress below her was an eruption of flame, but she could not get away. Nor was she burning. And beyond her watering eyes and the billowing clouds of smoke filling the room, she could see the face of Prince Cassius, cast in an eerie glow by the yellow-orange blaze.

He was smiling.

He knew.

He knew.

"Nova. *Nova.*" She came awake gasping, and bolted upright on the bed, surprised when her limbs came up easily at the slightest jerk. Only Jinx's quick reflexes kept their heads from colliding.

"You are safe," Jinx assured her over Nova's fast, gulping breaths. "You were beginning to make noise. I did not want to bring in the guards."

Nor did Nova. She was grateful that they had largely been left alone the last few days. She had even managed to relax some in the daytime. But she had little control over where her mind wandered during the night, and it never failed to venture toward the worst of scenarios.

Jinx reached out, and Nova jerked backward before the other witch's hand could land on her arm where it had been heading. "Don't," she said. "I am not under control."

Jinx tilted her head, those large eyes of hers seeing too much. "Is that a common occurrence for you?"

Nova closed her eyes and focused on her breathing, on the in-and-out, the way her body moved and expanded. Each time she released a breath and her chest lowered, she imagined the fire being pushed deeper and deeper from the surface of her skin. When it was buried enough that she felt safe, she opened her eyes and looked at Jinx again.

"All is well."

The earth witch maneuvered her way onto the foot of the bed, and Nova pulled up her legs to make room. Jinx sat with her legs crossed, her hands hooked around her knees. She looked less ferocious this way, with her feet bare and the entirety of her body folded up into a surprisingly small knot.

"Can you explain to me what happened there?" Jinx asked.

"It was nothing. I had a nightmare. Sometimes my nerves get the best of me, and when they do, the fire inside rises up. It does not know how to tell the difference between true danger, and the dangers of my unsettled mind."

"So if I had touched you . . ."

"I might have burned you. I am not sure. Better not to take the chance."

"I imagine that is how you have had to live much of your life here. Not taking any chances."

Nova shrugged. "At least I had a life here. I could have been caught back in Taraanar or any number of times since then. It was a miracle each day I sat in that cell and did not set the entire place alight."

"Perhaps you should have."

Nova shook her head hard.

"You don't understand what is inside me. You, your gift is about creation and balance and beauty. Mine is destruction. It is death. Even if it had gotten me free, it likely would have hurt many who did not deserve it in the process. I do not let it out, not ever if I can help it. Every time I do, it only brings worse things upon me and those I care about."

"Surely you cannot resist it completely," Jinx said. "I let out trace amounts of earth magic without even trying. It's a natural reaction anytime I am close to the natural element. I feed off the earth and plants and the trees, and they off of me. I suppose with fire, you are not surrounded as constantly, but I assume you have the same natural propulsion as I."

"I am drawn to it, of course. And the flames do rise closer to the surface when I am near natural fire. Also when I am agitated or emotional, as I said. But I have become quite practiced at burying the magic deep enough that I have at least some control."

"Burying it?"

"Yes," Nova answered. "It is the only way to be completely safe. I do my best to avoid contact with people, but sometimes the soldiers do not give me any choice. I need as many barriers between my magic and my skin as possible to keep from burning them."

"So you do not touch anyone. Ever?"

"I have. It is just easier if I don't."

"But you shook my hand. I have touched you several times since then, and you said nothing."

Nova felt an unfamiliar heat creeping up her cheeks. She checked her magic, but the flames were still safely locked away. It had nothing to do with that.

"I think it is different with other magic users. I was always more comfortable with contact with Aurora too, but I did not understand why. I thought it was because we were friends, and I simply trusted myself never to hurt her."

"That could still be it. Magic is intuitive. It is a part of you.

When engaged correctly it should flow according to your desires and intentions, not against them."

"Perhaps that is how your magic works, but not mine. It has always been the monster in the depths, wreaking havoc no matter how I try to control it."

Jinx peered at her, and Nova had to fight not to squirm under her attention. "You are so afraid of yourself."

Nova smiled sadly. "You would be too if you knew the damage I could do. I saw a man's face burn before my eyes when I was naught but a child, all because he had frightened me, and my magic did what it does best. My child's brain reached out for help, as if seeking out a household pet for a protector, but I came back bound to a dragon instead."

"Flare-ups happen to every magic user. It is difficult to find the right balance."

"I cannot afford flare-ups," Nova said, struggling not to let her voice rise in the dark room, lest she bring the guards upon them.

"Pushing your powers down as if they do not exist will not prevent them. It will likely only make flare-ups more common. You have to find balance between your body and the magic."

"And how am I to do that?" Nova said, clutching her fingers into desperate fists.

Jinx held up a hand, palm up. "Let me teach you."

"Here?" Nova asked, aghast. "You want to teach me magic, here?"

"I want to teach you balance and trust. You will never control your magic if you cannot trust it."

"Then I will never have control, because I cannot envision a world where I can trust what is inside me, where I can trust a brain and a body that always seems to betray me."

The earth witch must have lost her patience, for rather than continuing to offer her hand, she reached out and placed it on top of Nova's balled fist. Spine straightening, Nova froze, but like before, her magic stayed dormant in response to the other witch's touch.

Jinx said, "I know you feel impossibly alone. And I cannot pretend to know what it is you have suffered. But at the heart of every human there is a secret or a lie. Sometimes those secrets are inherited through no choice of our own, like yours and mine and even Aurora's. Sometimes we pile on lies for survival. Or sometimes we are given a lie by someone else, and we hold it tight, try to turn it into the truth, even though deep down we know it for what it is. I have a friend who thinks he does not deserve happiness, that all there is to life is danger and the fine line between life and death. It is a lie, but he has lived with it so long that he has convinced himself it is the truth. I think your magic is much the same. You had a horrid experience in your youth, and it convinced you your magic is something to be feared, which is *a* truth. But it should not be yours. Magic makes you strong, it makes you whole. That fire was given to you for a reason, because it is meant to balance you in some way. And the more you push it away, the more out of balance you will be."

Nova's heart was beating fast. She had never met anyone like Jinx—so sure of herself and her place in the world. She wanted to bottle the confidence rolling off her and keep it with her always so that when she needed it, she could pull it out and bask in it all over again.

"Will you try something for me?" Jinx asked.

Nova nodded, unable to even contemplate telling the witch no.

"Give me your other hand."

Nova did so, and Jinx placed Nova's palms flat against each other, pointing in opposite directions, then laid her hands over the outside of each. She scooted forward until both of them were sitting with their legs crossed, knees touching, Nova beneath the blankets and Jinx on top.

"Close your eyes."

Nova followed her direction, though the steady thrum of her heartbeat had only increased.

"I want you to unbind your magic."

"But—" Nova cracked one eye to find Jinx looking at her.

"It will be fine. Remember, you said it does not react to other witches."

"So far. That does not mean it will not ever."

A wide smile spread over Jinx's mouth. "I will risk it. Now close your eyes and open whatever walls you have set up."

Nova swallowed, but did as she was told, letting go of the tight hold she had on her magic. At first, nothing happened. Then she felt the tempting, yearning heat of the flame rising up inside her. She nearly panicked, but then she heard Jinx give a quiet hum under her breath. "There you are. Tell me. How does it feel?"

Nova squeezed her eyes shut tighter, suddenly nervous to reveal this part of herself to another person.

"Warm. Buzzy. Like there's a swarm of bees inside the cage of my ribs."

"Magic wants to move," Jinx said. "It is probably restless from being locked away."

Nova jerked a little, and Jinx's hands tightened about hers. "I don't want it to move. Then I will not be able to keep it inside."

"It is not meant to be still. Think of it like another working piece of your body. It should circulate the way air does when you breathe. The way blood moves through your body, so should your magic move through you. Rather than focusing on keeping it in one place to stop it from breaching your guards, instead let it move, *make* it move. It has to become an integrated part of you, rather than a separate piece."

Nova thought about the idea, and tried to put it into practice. She started small, only letting the magic move about in her midsection, like her own swirling firestorm inside. When that seemed doable, and did in fact ease some of the overwhelming energy that always bombarded her when her magic was close to the surface, she pushed it farther. First into her legs, all the way down to her toes and back up again. She made that loop several times, and when all seemed well, she braved the final circuit—letting the fire flow into her arms, passing through her connected palms again and again in an endless circle.

She got lost in the practice, following her flame to every corner of her person, exploring herself in a way she had not ever imagined possible. The fire burned away the soreness of her muscles and any lingering fatigue; it energized her with each sweep, and she felt better than she could ever remember feeling. She felt . . . *brand new.*

She had no idea how long she had been circulating the flames by the time something heavy came in contact with her knee. Her eyes snapped open, and she looked down.

A yawning Jinx waved her off. "Keep going. I could not sit up any longer. But it is good for you. I can feel it. Your whole energy has changed. Wake me if you need anything." Then the witch closed her eyes and fell asleep against the lump of Nova's knee beneath the blanket.

Nova stared, in awe that she could fall into slumber so quickly. Then again, she was not quite sure how long they had been at this. She gazed down at Jinx, at the small bow arch of her top lip, and the long straight line of her nose. She barely knew her, but there was a swell of something that happened inside every time Nova looked at her. The sensation got larger by the day, so much so that Nova did not know what to do with herself when it happened. Gratefulness, she thought. The warrior witch had blown into her life like a windstorm and brought with her every kind of hope and courage. She was awe-inspiring. Who would not be drawn to that?

And there was the fact that even now as she studied her friend's sleeping face, her magic was still routing itself through her body, already adapting to the trick Jinx had taught her. A few nights together, and Nova already felt less controlled by her fear, and more in charge of her own fate.

She adored Jinx for that alone. And she desperately hoped that they would be able to find a way out of their current situation, because she had a sudden desire to see the world the way Jinx saw it. Maybe even with Jinx at her side.

For now she knew there were other options for a life like hers besides secrecy and solitude.

Aurora spun around to face her mother and asked, "What do you think?" She wore a false wig of long black hair that made her skin look nearly as luminous as the moon. A shimmering skirt of greenish blue hugged her hips and fanned out at her knees like a mermaid tail. The color made her think of secret coves and far-off island waters. With it she wore a cream-colored top with short, capped sleeves and a neckline that sat just below her collarbone, high enough to cover her secret. In all, it was less revealing than what she had worn for her betrothal ball, but she could imagine how intriguing it might look under the blue lights downstairs. "Would you recognize me?" Aurora asked.

Her mother still did not know exactly where they were, but Aurora had been honest enough about her intentions for the evening. She needed to fool people who had seen her, some of whom had once been among her mother's advisers. She knew her mother had wanted to object at the idea of Aurora risking herself, could see the worry on her mother's face, but for some reason the once-overbearing queen had kept quiet.

"You will certainly draw the eye," her mother said. "Come here. Let me add some more rouge and shadow to your eyes, and then I think you will be disguised enough to fool even me."

Aurora went and sat next to her mother on the bed. The queen was able to pull herself up better now, but her muscles had lain unused for so long that she tired quickly and was far weaker than either of them remembered her ever being.

When her mother was done with the adjustments, she sat back with a deep inhale and said, "There. You are like an entirely different person."

Her mother stared, lips pursed upward in a sad smile, and the words landed heavily on Aurora's heart. The queen sniffed delicately, and Rora quickly caught one of her hands.

"I am still your daughter."

"Oh, I know that, my dear. It is simply that seeing you now, hearing the stories you have told, watching the way your face lights up like it never used to . . . I am ashamed I did not realize how much I had let my fear stifle you." Her mother sniffed again, but it did not stop the tear that stole down her cheek. "I thought I was keeping you safe from harm, but in truth I kept you from becoming this amazing daughter the goddess meant for me to have."

"You believe in the goddess?"

Her mother shrugged. "I believe you are as that young man said . . . *remarkable*. Whether that happened by goddess-divined fate or luck or something else . . . I believe in you. That is where I will start."

Aurora did not think a language existed to express how she felt in that moment. She knew her mother loved her, certainly. And despite the guilt and her other fears, rationally, she knew too that her mother had always tried to do what was best for her. But there was such an innate power imbalance between parent and child, between creator and creation, that she feared she would forever be inadequate, that she would always be choosing between her own wants and her mother's wants, and that would likely mean always disappointing either herself or her mother.

But now . . . now she felt less like someone else's creation, and more like her own. She had never felt so free, albeit terrified.

"Thank you," she responded, even though the words hardly sufficed.

"Promise me you will be careful," the queen said, a little bit of command creeping into her voice.

"I will be."

"And do not be too long. I get bored up here alone."

"I will send someone to keep you company."

"The handsome young man who called you *remarkable*?"

Aurora blushed. "Someone. Perhaps my friend Duke, if he is around. I told you about him."

"Ah, yes, the wise old hunter. I should thank him for taking care of you."

"You should talk to him about magic. He is very knowledgeable."

"Perhaps I will."

Aurora kissed her mother's cheek, then made her way downstairs to speak to Zephyr before the tavern opened. She found the owner by the waterfall, the room already lit in the mystic blue light. She cleared her throat, and Zephyr turned, eyeing her carefully, evaluating her appearance from head to toe.

"Not bad," she pronounced. "I would still keep talking to a minimum, in case someone recognizes your voice. Float the room, clear empty glasses, bring new drinks when asked. Do not push for conversations. Let them happen around you. Best to be invisible."

"What do I do if an important conversation is happening? Is there any kind of signal?"

Zephyr frowned. "Most of my girls do not know enough to know what is important. They listen for names, dates, locations. Frivolous details to them, but it helps us concentrate some of our other efforts. They write down whatever they hear, whether they think it is important or not, file reports at the end of the night, and are paid handsomely for it. If you notice something of importance, do your best to stay nearby. If that is not possible, then you come to me at the bar, and I will organize a rotation to keep things subtle."

"And if something goes wrong?" Aurora asked.

Zephyr's eyes hardened. "Nothing can go wrong. If you are concerned about that, I suggest you take yourself back upstairs to your mother."

Aurora shook her head. "You are right. Nothing goes wrong."

Everything was going wrong.

Aurora was trying to be invisible, but in truth, she was the exact opposite. She had started the evening by dropping a nearly full tray of glass mugs, making a shattering introduction to the occupants of The Mermaid Tavern. That had earned her a glare and a disappointed frown from Zephyr at the bar, and a raucous round of applause and laughter from the young soldiers on the first floor.

From then on, several in the group seemed to keep tabs on her, teasing as she passed, gallantly parting the crowd as she walked, even after she switched from the tray to carrying single drinks in each hand. Others jeered and lunged as she walked by, as though trying to startle her into another accident. Their treatment began drawing so much attention that Zephyr pulled her off the floor and into the back room.

"Let's try this again another night," she said, before the door had even swung all the way closed.

"No, please. Send me to the private area upstairs. It is quieter up there. And it is where I am likely to be of more use anyway."

"It is also where you are more likely to be recognized, and you have not shown me much evidence so far that you are good at blending in."

"Let me try. *Please.* If the slightest thing goes wrong, I will take myself upstairs without a word. I promise."

"Do not expect to get another chance beyond this one. Your value in this game depends on your surviving until the end. If you get reckless because you are restless, it is the rest of us who will pay."

"I understand. I will be careful."

Zephyr sighed, but sent her on her way with a wave of her gloved hand; the glove she wore at the tavern was pearlescent and dainty, not bloodred and claw-tipped. Not for the first time Aurora noted that she was not the only one with secrets around here.

But she left the mystery of Zephyr's gloves for another day, and made her way upstairs to the second level where things were calmer and quieter. The girls still wore the same uniforms and fetched drinks from the bar downstairs, but the guests sat in round cushioned booths with more distance between each. Potted and hanging plants combined with the blue light and sea-salt smell to give the atmosphere of a deserted island beach, where one might divulge the most sinful of secrets with no care of being overheard.

Aurora was certain now that Zephyr was using some of her magic, for though she knew there was naught but wood beneath her feet and in the walls around her, the room made her *feel* as if the ocean were sitting just out of sight. No matter how far she craned her neck, it never came into view. It was bold, indeed, but Aurora could see how at ease the guests were here, and it was more than being in their cups, though she was sure that helped. It likely dulled their senses, made them question the otherness less, explain it away as their mind's reaction to the drink. Suddenly, it made a great deal more sense how a woman as young as Zephyr, who could not have passed more than thirty seasons and might have seen far fewer, could wield such power in the city.

Things did, in fact, move far smoother for Aurora on the upper level. The space allowed her to glide about without having to dodge any moving bodies, and she busied herself helping where she could. For a long while, she heard nothing of true consequence—

discussion of the recent storms, speculation about the Stormlord and the rebellion, but curiously no mention of the missing Locke prince. None of it was new information, merely idle chatter among friends of a wealthier and more influential set. Aurora wondered if she was wasting her time. She had left her mother alone to be out here, and she could pass an entire night without hearing anything of importance. Maybe Zephyr was right. Maybe she was being foolish to insist on involving herself in these aspects when it was clear her role in this revolution lay elsewhere. She got lost in the busywork of cleaning up an empty table while she contemplated these thoughts, the soothing atmosphere of the tavern providing a calm backdrop for her wandering.

She picked up the last empty glass from the table, fitted it between her forearm and her breast along with the others, and then straightened to leave, nearly toppling into a man wearing a blue Locke admiral uniform. Then she let her eyes lift up to see him, and she found the familiar face of one of her former guards.

Aurora quickly lowered her eyes, and mumbled a quiet apology.

"Is this table free?" the man asked.

Aurora nodded and tried to flee, but he called after her, "Grab me an ale, will you?"

She nodded again, and then hurried off. She only let herself glance back when she reached the stairs, and she saw him shaking hands with another man in Locke uniform whom she vaguely recognized as someone who had kept close to the royal family. She descended the stairs before Merrin could set eyes on her again.

He had been her other primary guard, often playing the foil for the far-too-serious Taven. But gone was the cheery-eyed, curly-haired Merrin that she remembered. His hair had been cut short, all the curls gone, and his expression had remained flat, his voice too.

Aurora returned the empty glasses to the kitchen, then thought of taking herself straight up to her mother as she had promised.

Then she remembered that Merrin had asked for an ale. She did not want to make things more suspicious by disappearing without his order. She would take him his drink, then disappear.

She requested the drink at the bar, and while she waited, she decided to do the responsible thing and tell Zephyr she would be leaving. But she could not find her in the back where she had left her, nor was she behind the bar. So she told the woman behind the bar to tell Zephyr that the new girl needed a word.

Then she set off back upstairs. As she drew near the table where Merrin sat, she slowed her stride and lowered her head.

"And this information the prince has . . . is it credible?"

"Very much so, he believes."

"Why would she not return home if she were back in Pavan? Surely she must have heard of how we searched for her."

"The prince is not certain she is free to leave. It is possible the kidnappers sold her to the resistance."

Aurora was nearly to the table, and she did not know what to do. Did she stop and hope they did not notice her? Did she put down the drink and hope they continued?

"And they let her live? What use do they have for her?"

"We are unsure. Blackmail, perhaps. Or they have some intentions for her magic. All we know is there is credible evidence she is in the city. And that is where you come in. Prince Cassius would like you to lead the investigation into her whereabouts."

Aurora turned and sat the drink on the first table she passed, much to the surprised delight of an older man who did not order it. She hit the stairs, and she climbed up and up until she found the loft and then Zephyr's office door. She pushed through it, her breaths heaving, the long mermaid-like skirt catching between her ankles. Her fingers scrabbled at the door handle to the bedroom, her joints refusing to work properly, agitation rising until she finally shoved the door open wide.

Then inside she found her mother weeping, great gusting sobs that shook her thin frame. Duke sat beside the queen *in* her bed. The old man's head snapped up at her entrance, but her mother was too distraught to do anything but cry.

"What did you do to her?" Aurora cried, more than happy to direct all the panic coursing through her system at something, *some-one* else. "Did you hurt my mother?" Aurora demanded, marching across the room.

Suddenly Kiran was there, appearing from nowhere, slamming first the office door, then the bedroom door behind him. "What in the bleeding skies are you doing, Aurora? You left the doors wide open."

"I want to know what is wrong with my mother."

Kiran moved closer, trying to quiet her, and she knew he was right, knew there was a world outside these rooms with very large, very looming consequences. But she had only just gotten her mother back safely, and now Duke had upset her terribly, and she did not need that kind of stress in her condition.

"Nothing is wrong with me," her mother said, her voice cracking with emotion.

"Then why are you crying?"

Aphra Pavan looked far from queenly and surprisingly vulnerable as she shrugged and answered with a bewildered, teary smile, "Because he is alive."

Aurora looked to Duke. "Who is alive?"

Aurora's mother gazed at Duke, the old man who had become something between a father and mentor to Aurora. Tears still flowed down the queen's cheeks and dripped from the regal line of her jaw. "You might know him as Duke. But I knew him as a lord, a long time ago."

Aurora's mother took Duke's hand and squeezed. "You could have come here, Finn. We never would have turned you away. No matter what happened in Calibah."

Duke lifted her mother's hand and placed a kiss on her knuckle.

"I had a lot to live with. It was easier to spread that grief around, not take it with me all to one place. Besides, I came when it was time, I think."

Panic made Aurora's mind slow, like she was trudging through melting drifts of snow.

Calibah.

Finn.

She saw the pieces, knew how they would fit together if life were fiction, but how, *how* could this be?

"Are you saying . . ." She trailed off, staring at her mother.

The queen pushed herself up a little higher in the bed, and wiped her tears. "Aurora, may I present to you Lord Finneus Wolfram of Calibah. Lord Wolfram, I believe you know my daughter."

Finneus Wolfram, nephew to the king, left Calibah that day with a small contingent of soldiers and sailors, intent on finding safe passage to another land. Neither his ship, nor he was ever seen again, and the city of Calibah fell to catastrophic storms two weeks later.

—*The Fall of Calibah and the Mystery of Lord Wolfram*

16

Kiran's head was pounding as the voices in the room swelled to a deafening noise. They were damned lucky it was morning, and there were no customers to overhear them in the tavern below.

He was having a hard enough time grasping the fact that his mentor, the man who had practically raised him from the time he had joined the crew at eleven, was some long-lost, believed-to-be-dead lord. The fact that he had apparently once had an affair with Aurora's mother before the queen was married was a thought he had set aside to examine another day—hopefully one that never came.

Aurora had been shocked by the revelation of the affair. She barely took a breath while berating her mother for never telling her she had known *the* Finneus Wolfram, *really* known him. But that was far from the most dire news of the evening. Once Kiran had finally gotten Aurora to calm down, he managed to get her to explain why she had abandoned the tavern and run upstairs in the first place.

The Lockes knew she was in the city. And they had tasked one of her old guards to lead the search for her.

Kiran had sent notes to the relevant parties, asking for a meeting the next morn, and here they were in Zephyr's office—Duke and the still-healing Pavan queen sitting off to one side, Zephyr pacing behind her desk, Taven standing in the corner with a stern expression, and the rest of his crew looking on, as dumbfounded as he no doubt looked. Aurora stood across the room, her face grim, and her arms wrapped tightly around her middle.

"I do not understand how word got out," Zephyr fumed. "We have been so careful. Taven, have you heard anything?"

"Nothing. I can try to talk to Merrin."

"No," Zephyr snapped. "He is in too deep. It is more dangerous to risk alerting them of your involvement."

"Merrin?" Aurora asked. "*Merrin* is in too deep? What does that mean?"

Taven sighed. "He was one of the first volunteers to go out on a mission to search for you. He went south to Odilar with a contingent of Locke soldiers. All but three died. He has been *different* since he came back. I was never sure enough of his loyalties after that to approach him about the resistance. I do not know where he stands."

Aurora's eyes widened, and she clutched her own elbows tightly. She looked as if she was trying to force herself to take up less space. "So, if he found me, you think he might turn me over to Cassius, regardless of my wishes?"

Taven shrugged. "I do not know, Your Highness."

Aurora scowled. "I told you to stop with that nonsense."

"The point is . . ." Zephyr cut in. "Somehow they know you are in the city, and they are going to be looking for you, which means no more floor time on the tavern. No leaving this building at all. We have to keep you hidden until the time is right."

"And when will that be?" Aurora asked.

"When I say it is," Zephyr growled, bracing her hands on her desk.

Unable to stand any more of the back-and-forth, Kiran cut in, "Would it not be better to get her out of the city entirely? We do not know how far the Lockes will go to find her. They could start raiding neighborhoods indiscriminately."

"You think they have time to do that on a hunch?" Zephyr asked. "When storms threaten daily? Surely not."

"It depends on how sure they are she is here."

Kiran's eyes turned to Aurora, whose face had gone remarkably pale, even for her. Based on her wary expression, he guessed everyone else's gaze had fixed on her too. "Do you know where you might have been seen?" he asked. "Could someone have caught sight of you in the palace?" Aurora hesitated and an awful thought occurred to him. "Or they could have gotten the information another way." His eyes flicked to Ransom, then Duke. "From Jinx, or your friend. Jinx is the most loyal person I know, but we don't know what they are doing to them in there. One of them could have even revealed something by accident."

All of a sudden, Aurora dropped her arms from where they were wound tightly around her waist. "It was not them. It was me."

This time, Kiran's voice joined the cacophony, and Aurora closed her eyes and let the noise spill over her. He wanted to rush over and shake her, then take her far, far away from here.

"What do you mean it was you?" he asked.

Aurora swallowed and lifted her chin. "I was worried for Jinx and Nova's safety, so I made a choice. Before we left, I wrote Cassius a note."

It was like a hurricane swept through his head. Kiran needed to sit down. There were no chairs left, so he ended up leaning against Zephyr's desk, his mind reeling.

"That's what you went back for," Sly popped in, speaking up for the first time from the corner she leaned back in.

"It was the best way I could think of to guarantee they stayed unharmed."

Ransom's gruff voice joined the fray as he said, "You probably did the exact opposite. All you did was tell the prince that they have information on you. They are likely being tortured for that information as we speak."

Aurora's face went ghostly white, and her fingertips found the wall at her back, steadying herself.

"No." Aurora shook her head vehemently. "No, it was not like that. I told Cassius to treat them well."

Zephyr snorted. "And you think that despot will do as you ask? You think he has a heart?"

Aurora gritted her teeth and shook her head. "Of course not. I left him for a reason. But I do think that he . . . he *wants me*. He could have just taken the kingdom when I left. I gave him the perfect opportunity to have everything he wanted. Instead, he searched for me relentlessly. Obsessively. He sent soldiers to die in the wildlands who could have helped fight the Stormlord here. I do not know why, but if he would go to those lengths for me before, I thought I could save Jinx and Nova by tying them to me. To buy us time."

For once, the room fell into quiet. But though the world might have been silent, Kiran was screaming on the inside. To think that *that monster* wanted Aurora made him ill. The fact that she'd had to run away to keep from marrying him made it hard not to resent the vulnerable old woman sitting silently only a few steps away. It made him want to break things, starting with the prince's face against his knuckles.

"Well, that settles it then," he said. "He will not rest until he finds her, not if he knows for certain she is here. We need to either get her into hiding or get her out of the city."

"And we need to get Jinx out of that damn palace," Ransom barked.

"I have connections in a small outpost north of the city," Zephyr said. "We could hide her there for the time being until things die down."

"No," Aurora cried. "I am done hiding. We need supplies to rescue Jinx, right? Did you not mention the possibility of sending me into the wilds to stock up on magic? We could do that. Then I am out of the city, and we are preparing for the next steps. We will come back with everything we need to rescue Jinx and take down the Lockes once and for all."

Zephyr stopped where she was and turned to meet the gaze of her lieutenant, Raquim, who stood silent and still in the corner of the room. Kiran had forgotten he was there entirely. "That could work," she said. "Though you will be in danger in the wilds as well. And I am not sure how long you will have to stay. I can smuggle you out of the city, along with supplies in and out when needed."

"How will you do that?" Aurora asked.

Zephyr gave her a hard look and jerked her chin toward the queen. "I think I have given away enough of my secrets in present company."

Aphra Pavan held up her hands, and the movement was graceful despite her illness. "Please, we have the same intentions. I would see my daughter safe, and the kingdom restored to her guidance."

Zephyr raised an eyebrow. "Not your own?"

"I am an old woman. And if age gives one nothing else, it should be the ability to learn from one's past. It was my decisions that brought the Lockes to this place, that allowed them to enact their schemes. My daughter clearly saw what I could not. I will provide any help or information you would like, but . . ." She trailed off for a moment and glanced at Duke. "The crown is not everything."

"Then it is settled. Tonight at midnight, we smuggle you out."

"And me," Kiran added. "She will need another hunter to collect the magic, while she focuses on controlling the storm. I have the most experience, other than Duke. And he is retired. And *occupied*. I can keep her safe should anything happen while we are in the wilds."

"Any other reasons?" Duke asked, those blue eyes challenging him like they had so many times through the years, so many times when he thought Duke was just another misfit like him, not some *lord*.

"Does there need to be another reason?" he asked.

Taven asked, "Is that acceptable to you, Your High—" He trailed off at the glare Aurora gave him and added, "If you require more guards, I will gladly come."

"We need your eyes and ears in the palace," Zephyr declared. "I want you to try to find out whatever you can about Jinx and Nova—where they are being held, how many guards, when they change shifts. If the princess wants more guards for her sojourn in the wilds, she will have to choose someone else."

"I do not need more guards. I do not need *any* guards," Aurora pushed.

"But you do need another hunter," Kiran said, meeting her eyes.

"I suppose that is true."

"Then are we settled?" Zephyr asked. "Midnight?"

Aurora met Kiran's gaze, and though she looked wary, she did not refuse. She nodded. "Midnight."

"You should sleep."

Jinx's voice drifted across the dark room to Nova's wide-awake ears. She had been trying. But it was one of those nights where she heard every little sound, and her mind magnified it like ripples in a pond. And her thoughts kept following those ripples to anywhere but here—to Aurora out in the city somewhere. Was she safe? What was the rebellion doing now? Would they be coming back for her and Jinx? Her mind drifted to her parents. She had heard nothing of them since her incarceration. Were they worried for her? Had they been spared punishment or had she somehow dragged them down too? Perhaps she had been gone long enough that they had decided to move on, live a life free from the danger she presented. She would not resent them for it. Though she would miss them. Frankly, she would worry less if they were gone, when there was only herself to hurt.

And then there was Jinx. Nova thought about her more than she cared to admit. The obvious things—where she came from, what her life had been like, how she had learned so much about magic. But Nova also thought about less practical things that she had less explanation for. She thought about what Jinx's hair felt like where it was cut short on the side of her head. Would it be soft like the long tresses on the other side, or rough and spiky? Nova had grown used to the *feel* of Jinx—the warmth of her magic in the air, the gentle nudge of energy that felt peaceful and bright. And she wondered how *her* magic felt to Jinx—did it make her stomach both toss and settle all at the same time?

"You are thinking too much," Jinx said.

"How do you know that?"

"Am I wrong?"

Nova flopped over onto her side to face Jinx in the dark. "No."

"What are you thinking about?"

"What am I *not* thinking about?"

"Need a distraction?" Jinx asked.

"Please."

Nova heard the quiet fall of feet in the dark and then the end of her bed sunk as Jinx climbed on with her. Nova's heart clenched hard, then set off at a speed that had her feeling dizzy.

"Up," Jinx ordered.

Nova froze, suddenly nervous in a different way than she normally experienced. She was hyperaware of her body and the space around it, but for once it had nothing to do with her fire.

"Come on. Up," Jinx insisted, grabbing Nova by the forearms and hauling her inelegantly upward. Nova flopped forward, and Jinx laughed. Nova laughed too, glad the other girl could not see the heat rising on her cheeks.

"Let's practice. Hands out."

"Umm . . ." Nova hesitated. "I am not sure."

"Then tell me your most embarrassing secrets."

Nova's jaw dropped, and she sucked in air.

"Now magic does not seem so bad, eh?"

"Sleep does not seem so bad."

"Too bad. You have me awake now. We might as well take advantage of the quiet hours."

There tended to be less guards on the overnight, and while Nova knew the guards were out there, they rarely spoke or moved in the nighttime hours, which gave her at least the illusion of more safety.

"What would we practice exactly?" Nova asked.

"Well, you seem to be doing much better with your balance. I'm curious to know how that will impact your control over the actual manifestation of your magic. How often do you actually use it?"

"Only when I must. In the days before you arrived, I used to rip pieces from the hem of my skirt to burn when I began to feel too full and worried I might slip accidentally."

"That must have been stressful." Jinx's voice was warm and soft in the dark.

Nova shrugged, even though she was not sure Jinx could see the motion.

"I have never known a fire witch myself," Jinx said, "but the crew I travel with had one before me. They said she had precise aim, that she would sometimes use the campfire to tell stories, shaping the flame into a tiny stage with people and places and storms and battles. She helped them build a massive carriage, the likes of which you have never seen. It is all carefully shaped metal that can withstand even the fiercest storms of the wildlands. I did not know the witch, but they speak of her fondly, and of her powers with awe. So it is possible for you to find that kind of control, for you to live without fear of lapses."

"I would like that," Nova said. She had hesitated to let the words out, afraid of even admitting that she wanted such a thing, because then it would hurt so much more if she never got it. But she was having difficulty holding back. Maybe because she had let her magic go, because it flowed through her freely, and instead of the world falling apart, she felt more alive than ever. The temptation to continue loosening the reins was near impossible to resist.

"Then let's try it. Cup your hands together, and attempt to make a small flame, only the size of a candle's wick."

Nova sat more upright, and pulled her legs up, situating herself more comfortably. That left more room for Jinx, which she filled, scooting until she was face-to-face with Nova as they had been a few nights before.

"Start very small. Think of it as expanding the circulation of the magic you already have going in your body, instead of pushing it out with nowhere to go, which might result in some, ah, unexpected trajectories. Imagine the loop expanding outside your hands just enough for a small flame, but then returning to join the rotation again. No magic will actually leave your body, you are just expanding your control of it into the world beyond your flesh and bones."

Nova cupped her hands together as suggested and closed her eyes, letting herself fall back into the rush of the magic inside her, following it through the circulation of her body several times as she had been practicing.

"You are doing well," Jinx told her. "Really, you have taken to this much faster than I expected. It took me years to come to terms with my magic and establish the balance you have found in a few days."

Nova kept her breathing steady, and let her shoulders settle back, finding a straighter posture. "I have a lot of practice with mental focus. This felt like a natural extension of that."

"Mental focus? You mean from trying to control the fire?"

"No. Well, yes, that too, but my mother always said I was a nervous child. She said I would make myself sick with worry." Nova gave a small laugh. "The fire did not help. But it was merely one consequence of many I feared."

"What kind of things did you fear?"

"Oh, anything and everything. Some of which were reasonable—being caught, not having enough money, disappointing my parents, not being able to control my magic. For those, I would catch myself playing out elaborate worst scenarios, torturing myself again and again under the guise of being prepared. Some fears were harder to explain. Sometimes I would convince myself that things were my fault. That a storm had come because I had stitched a button wrong, or been too slow with my work duties, or talked with too many people that day. Some days I would wake up convinced that something awful was going to happen—and I would wait with this gnawing ache all day, feeling too ill to eat, certain that something dire was sure to occur. I constantly wavered between *feeling* to the point of exhaustion and shutting myself away with the goal of avoidance—neither of which helped."

"What did help?" Jinx asked.

"Honestly?" Nova asked. "This helps. This balance. Before, I used to go to a quiet place in my head and breathe, try to let the thoughts pass without engaging. Sometimes I would count. I would try to distract myself from falling down those endless sinkholes of agony and paranoia and never being *enough*."

"Wow," Jinx breathed. "That's beautiful."

Confused on how any of what she said could be *beautiful*, Nova opened her eyes and found that she had produced a tall, thin flame from the valley of her hands.

"See if you can manipulate it. Make it shorter, then taller."

Nova took a deep breath and fixed her gaze on the eerily still flame. It did not flicker, nor swirl about in her hand. It stood as straight as a blade, still seamlessly flowing with the rest of her magic. Slowly, she did as Jinx asked, shortening the loop until the flame was as small as a fingernail, then pushing it back out even farther than she had loosed it before. She let it grow to the length of a dagger, and wondered if with enough practice she might craft a sword of fire for herself. If she could, that meant she would never be without a weapon, never be helpless again.

Jinx cupped Nova's hands with her own, and she stared in wonder. The shock of the touch broke Nova's concentration, the flame flickered wildly, then disappeared altogether, casting them back into sudden darkness.

"Scorch it all," Jinx uttered. "Sorry. I distracted you."

Nova was still thinking about the look on Jinx's face the moment before the flame went out, the way shadows had played over her prominent jaw and cheekbones, both emphasizing her fierceness and softening it too. Novaya had never been one for creative endeavors. She had sought out the position on the seamstress's staff because she was a fair hand with a needle and it was a step up from being a maid, but it was merely a means to an end. She had always been so busy worrying about how to survive that dreams were not something that often had time to take root and grow in her mind. But that one single memory of Jinx in the light of her flame made her suddenly think of being a painter, of trying a hundred different colors until she found the ones to make it exactly right. It did not seem fair that she was the only one who got to see such a sight. It was too beautiful not to want to share.

"Do you think I could shape a sword from fire?" Nova asked. "Or something smaller to start? A dagger?"

"Goddess, please do. I can imagine it already. You will be glorious."

Nova's stomach flopped in that way again—anticipation and anxiety rolled into one mess of confusing, overflowing emotions.

Jinx lay back onto the bed, kicking her feet up against the nearest wall, and they began chatting about the possibilities of different fire weapons, and what Nova might eventually learn to conjure.

Eventually, while Jinx was debating the merits of a fire whip and some weapon she once encountered that could be thrown and would return in the air to its master, not through magic, but design, Nova began to yawn.

She pulled her pillow closer, but did her best to prop herself up on her elbow, not wanting Jinx to stop talking; but the other witch noticed her fading. She leaned over Nova's knees and pushed her shoulders into the pillows.

"Go to sleep if you are tired," Jinx said. "I can imagine that bit of magic was enough to settle your mind."

Nova did not know that it settled anything, but she was always calmer when Jinx was close by, even when she was nervous. Nova liked that about her. Once her shoulders hit the mattress though, there was no pulling them up again. Jinx was still leaning on her knees, and the earth witch reached out, pushing a long strand of black hair off Nova's face that Nova had been too tired to address herself.

Her heart clenched, the heavy beats plunking like unsuccessful skipping stones into a pond.

"My mother would have loved to meet you," Jinx said. "She was a witch too, and she . . . she would be proud, I think, to see what we are doing."

"Even though we are locked away?"

The weight lifted from Nova's knees, and she heard the tiny bed creak as Jinx sprawled herself out over the other end.

"Better than what happened to her."

For the first time, Nova heard bleakness in the other witch's normally indefatigable tone. She sat quiet for a moment, too cowardly and unsure of whether Jinx wanted her to ask.

Finally, she said, "Do you want to talk about it?"

Nova stretched her hand out over the bed, reaching until she found what might have been the other girl's knee. Then Jinx's hand was there too, curling around her own, fingers squeezing tight.

"Not tonight. I think we have had enough thinking for now."

Jinx released her fingers, but held onto her hand, turning it over the same way she had when they had been working before. With Nova's hand on top, and Jinx's cupped underneath, the other witch asked, "Do you think you can do the fire? Just one more time?"

Nova did not ask why. She simply lengthened the loop of her magic in that one hand until a tiny pearl of fire appeared in the center of her palm. When it did, she found Jinx's eyes not on the flame, but on her own. The two looked at each other, both curled awkwardly on their sides in the bed so that their bodies fit and claimed diagonal territories, leaving a narrow border in between.

"Is this okay?" Jinx asked after a long silence.

Nova swallowed, and nodded, the flame growing just a bit brighter without her trying to do so. The other witch searched her face, and Nova never looked away, not even when nerves roiled in her stomach like storm-tossed waves.

"Well, then." Jinx smiled, letting her hand fall away from the one place they touched. "Good night, my fire witch."

Nova let the flame go out, and settled down against her pillow, feeling far less tired all of a sudden.

"Good night, Jinx."

Then she did her best to sleep, but it took a long time for her heart to slow to a normal beat.

They met in a part of town with which Aurora was unfamiliar, but Kiran knew the way. It was on the outer edges of the city, where homes were scarce and industrial warehouses clogged the streets. They were near the docks, where Pavan's limited shipping industry on the Napatya River was based. The Napatya was the city's main source of water, but also provided an avenue for trade for those merchants who were willing to make the journey.

Zephyr had connections in this area too, it seemed. Though in the dead of night, the small port was empty, and the buildings were dark and devoid of life. The night had gone unexpectedly cold, and sleet had begun to fall, stinging at Aurora's cheeks. She pulled the collared neck of her vest up high, blocking the worst of it, and continued after Kiran.

She could feel the Stormlord out there, toiling away at something; dark souls skulked around the city, lingering in the fields and the small rolling hills, and up in the gathering clouds of the inky-black sky, brushing by the city walls. She did not know what the Stormlord had planned, but she could feel him out there as surely as she could feel the souls he corralled.

When they reached the edge of a dock, Zephyr and Raquim were waiting for them, but no one else was present. The port sat at a bend in the river, where it dipped briefly inside the city limits, but then turned again and continued out into the wilds. The city walls continued on the land surrounding the river with bridges built over each section of water. The bridges were lit with a long line of fire torches, but they were far enough from the dock that Aurora could not see details, only the general shapes of the bridges and the shadow of a guard post on top of each. Aurora slowed to a stop in front of Zephyr, wondering how the woman planned to get them past the guard points. Were the soldiers on duty spies of hers too? Like Taven?

"This won't be pleasant," Zephyr said, interrupting her thoughts. "Especially not with the dropping temperatures."

Aurora frowned. "I am not as spoiled as you think me. I lived in the wilds without basic comforts for quite a time. You underestimate me."

"I don't speak of your temporary exile, Princess. I mean your mode of travel."

"And what exactly is that?" Kiran cut in.

Zephyr gestured to the bridge Aurora had seen before. "There's a guard on duty watching for boats, so the obvious choices are not available. But luckily, I offer a choice that is far from obvious. We have never been caught on one of our shipments," she said, nodding to Raquim beside her.

"Then what is it?" Aurora asked.

Zephyr paused, and in the stretched silence, it became harder for Aurora to ignore the bone-deep cold.

"You will be going underwater."

Aurora looked at the distance to the bridge again, then looked about for some kind of transportation, perhaps a waterborne version of the Rock. She had learned to expect the unexpected, after all. "Just the two of you," Zephyr added. "I'll create a bubble of air so you do not drown, and I will use my magic to propel you through the water until you are out of the guard's sight. From there though, you will be on your own. You will be wet, cold, and alone. Think you can handle that, Princess?"

"She can handle it," Kiran answered on her behalf.

Aurora fought not to shudder at the thought of how cold that water must be, hoping she looked as confident as Kiran sounded.

"Do you have everything you need?" Zephyr asked.

Kiran lifted a satchel that sat against his hip.

"I suppose I do not need to tell you to be careful?" Zephyr asked.

"Seems like you are doing it anyway," Kiran replied.

Aurora sighed and stepped forward. "We will. How do we get in touch with you if we need to?"

"Etel visits the camps on my behalf every other day to give out food and other necessities. Go find her if you need me."

Aurora remembered the little old woman who had tried to sell her questionable wares at the Eye on her first visit. She had not realized Zephyr had her working for the rebellion as well. After a few more instructions, there was nothing left but the how of things. At Zephyr's bidding, they sat on the edge of the rickety dock, and she arranged them how she wanted them—the satchel with the supplies pressed between their chests, and Aurora and Kiran facing each other as much as they could while sitting, their arms wrapped tight around each other.

Aurora could feel the heat of Kiran's breath on her temple, and her own face was near to his jaw, where the woodsy, male scent of him seemed to be the strongest.

"The shock of the water will be cold," Zephyr warned. "But do not panic. Breathe normally. As I promised, I will keep the water from entering the bubble of air you need to last you until you pass the bridge. The most important thing is that you do not let go of each other. I cannot split my concentration between the both of you."

Kiran nodded firmly, the bristle on his jaw scraping against her cheek in a way she had not felt in so long. Aurora tried to nod too, but the movement got lost in the hollow of his throat.

Then Zephyr was asking if they were ready, and there were hands on their shoulders, and Aurora was sucking in a breath, bracing for the cold. The next thing she knew, they were falling, Kiran's arms squeezing tighter as they descended.

The first splash was brutal—slicing through clothes and skin and bone down to her very marrow. The cold pierced like a thousand needles, making her limbs ache with pain and feel numb all at the same time. Despite Zephyr's warning, panic overtook her, and she scrambled, her fingers clutching at whatever they could find, legs kicking, trying to find which way was up and which way was down. Then strong fingers found her jaw, pulling her face down until her forehead pressed against something warm. She opened her eyes, expecting to be bombarded with water, no matter what reason told her, but the floods never came. Instead, she found the deep brown irises of her hunter, staring back at her, urging calm in the only way he could. He pressed his face closer, his nose sliding down beside hers until they were so close that her lips touched his on the next exhale.

She watched him, breathing in and out, vaguely aware that they were moving in a way that was entirely unnatural. Neither of them was swimming nor kicking their legs to stay afloat, and with the weight of their clothes and supplies they should have been sinking down to the riverbed. Instead, she felt a gentle pressure beneath her, gliding them along some unknown current. She was not sure how long it went on, only that she lost herself looking at Kiran, because she could, and because what else was she to do?

He looked tired, though she guessed the same was true for her. Circles hung like dark half-moons beneath his eyes, and she wondered how long it had been since he had had a solid night's sleep. The growth of hair along his jaw was the longest she had ever seen it—a true beard rather than the messy unshaven stubble to which she was accustomed. She took a risk, letting one of her hands slide up his back, over his shoulder, and to the back of his neck. His eyelids fluttered under the caress, but when her thumb found the corner of his jaw, between the lobe of his ear and the greater part of his beard, his gaze fixed on her with a sudden intensity.

She did not speak, though Zephyr had not said whether it was possible with the magic she worked. In truth, Aurora decided the silence had its own kind of magic.

His hand was still at her jaw, though his grip had relaxed to a barely-there touch. He kept it that way as his fingers traced down the underside of her chin and the hollow of her throat. When he could go no lower than that, he returned his hand to her cheek, canting her jaw up so that her mouth sat below his, like an offering. She followed his lead, letting her fingers trail through the beard he'd grown, trying to decide what she thought of it. He looked . . . older. More rugged, not that he needed much help there. His eyes had always been fairly guarded, but they were even more so now.

She had done that to him. With her lies and secrets. She wondered if there was a way to undo that hurt, or if she was being selfish by following this pull again. Her fingers kept exploring, until they found the place where his facial hair gave way to the smooth skin just below his lip. She touched there, once, and when he did not object, she let her finger wander higher, to the full bottom lip above. There was a tiny scar she had never noticed just above his top lip. She wondered how long it had been there, and how she had not seen it before. She met his gaze, wondering if she was brave enough to kiss it, and she found nothing but encouragement in the dark pupils that had taken over the rest of his eyes.

Slowly, Aurora trailed her finger along the curve of his upper lip, then let her hand fall to his chest to rest over his heart. She drifted closer, bringing her mouth in line with his. A simple lift of her chin was all it would take to bring their lips together, but she did not want to make that choice for him.

He had been the one to walk away. And she knew he had his reasons. She had made mistakes, and no matter how intensely she felt, she could not make him want the same things as her. She had not given him the choice the first time on whether he wanted to be involved with a princess. This time, he would know exactly what he was getting.

His knuckles brushed over her cheek, gentler than she would have thought possible. She searched his eyes, desperate to know what he was thinking. She saw no answers there, only a depth of feeling that made everything inside her spontaneously loop itself into knots.

Then he kissed her, and she began to unravel.

It was a slow, glorious exploration of a kiss; she felt the tension inside her loosen in small measures, advancing, only to tighten again when his tongue brushed hers in a way that felt new and exciting. By the time he pulled away, she felt like they had been reintroduced. And every knot inside her had been untied.

She looked at him shyly, and Kiran stared back as fierce and proud as he had always been. She wanted to kiss him again, do a little more reintroducing of her own, but before she got her chance, the bubble around them burst and water came rushing in from all sides.

She sucked in a breath, and got nothing but freezing cold blades across her tongue and down her throat. She slammed her eyes shut against the burn of the water, and chaos overtook them. She was jerked sideways and up and down—or maybe none of those directions were right. She could not be sure. Distantly, she was aware of a weight holding on to the back of her clothing, but all her limbs were free and flailing, searching for the surface, which was nowhere to be found. She turned around and around in a current that was rough and wild, nothing like the gentle pulse they had been traveling on before.

Finally, her head broke free from the rapids, and she came up coughing and gasping, her hair covering her face and eyes, which mattered little for there was naught but darkness where they were.

Something hard collided with her back, and that's when she realized the thing clinging to her clothes was Kiran's hand. As soon as his head pierced the surface, he wrapped a strong arm around her, pushing her higher out of the water at his own expense.

But it was a useless gesture. The two of them were moving fast down the river, toppling through rapids, nowhere near finding purchase enough to get free. Aurora yanked at her vest, pulling haphazardly until enough of her chest was bared that the glow of her skyfire gave them some light in the night.

They were in the middle of a fast-moving, rocky river that did not appear to ease up farther down the line. Together, Aurora and Kiran swam toward the nearest bank, fighting against a current that wanted to sweep them this way and that. More than once, Aurora felt her limbs smack into something unseen beneath the water—trees or shrubs or something else she could not identify.

She had no idea how long it took them to get out, only that it felt like it would never end. When they finally reached water shallow enough for their feet to touch bottom, they grabbed hold of each other for strength, and charged out of the water with as much speed as they could manage. Then they collapsed on the shore, exhausted and soaked and trembling. Aurora coughed up water she had inhaled and pressed her cheek to wet soil that felt warm by comparison.

Kiran was the first to drag himself to his knees. The tunic he wore clung to his chest like it was part of him, and the jacket he wore over that was logged with water too. He still had the satchel, thank the skies. She had completely forgotten it in the madness of the current. He did a quick check, and he did not mention any issues, so she assumed they'd made it with everything intact.

Then he looked at her and his mouth lifted in a halfhearted grin. "Enough adventure for you yet, Princess?"

Slowly, she climbed to her feet, feeling sore and stiff all over. "That? Child's play."

He laughed. "Come on. We need to find shelter and get out of these wet clothes, and hopefully start a fire."

For once, Aurora did not argue. The wind was biting, and the temperatures were no more kind outside the city than they had been inside. She knew they risked illness the longer they stayed like this.

Using the skyfire storm in her chest as a lantern, they wandered into the nearest copse of trees and began gathering kindling and wood for a fire. Aurora held it out from her, not wanting her wet clothes to dampen the wood and make the fire harder to start. They were lucky to stumble upon a rocky area in the woods. It was not quite a cave, but it provided flat ground on which to sleep, and just enough of an overhang to block the wind and any rain that might start in the night.

They fell into an easy rhythm, laying out their materials for a fire, pausing occasionally to shuck off the wet outer layers of their clothes to make things simpler. Aurora was down to her pants and a light undershirt when she heard Kiran curse under his breath as he tried to start the fire.

She stopped to peer over his shoulder and saw his hands were shaking so badly that he was having trouble striking the flint with enough force to create a spark. She laid a hand on his already bare back. He jumped at the touch of her frigid hand, but did not move away. "Let me."

Before, he likely would have argued, would have insisted that he knew perfectly well how to light a fire, but whether it was the exhaustion or simply the long journey they had been through together in recent months, this time he said nothing, only stood and made room for her to work.

She ignored the flint he offered her, and instead held out her hand over the flame. She too was shaking, but her intentions required less exact skill, and more brute force. She took a calming breath and reached for the part of her soul that was hers, but not. It answered, frenetic and charged and hot to the touch. She pulled, letting it roll down her arm toward the carefully arranged pile of wood, and she fixed her eyes on the kindling at the base.

With a quick jolt, her arm seized with the changing pressure, and from her palm came a small streak of white-hot skyfire. It blasted the kindling she had been aiming for, charring the ground around it. But it did the deed. Several of the larger pieces of wood burst into flame.

Kiran grabbed her by the shoulders, dragging her back a few paces and out of the reach of the popping, crackling fire that had sprung to life in moments. He grabbed a few heavier logs he had stored nearby, throwing them atop the flame, and in no time, a roaring fire blazed before them, pouring off heat that slowly began to work past the cold that had claimed every inch of Aurora's body.

They laid out the clothes they had already removed over the large rocks that surrounded their sanctuary, and when there was nothing left to do, she turned to Kiran. He rubbed at the back of his neck, unclothed but for the pants he still wore.

He cleared his throat. "It would be best if we took off all our wet clothes."

Aurora nodded, knowing he was right.

"We can stay in separate places," he offered. "I will stay behind that rock," he said, gesturing to an area farther away from the fire that would leave him cold for much of the night, she guessed. "You can stay on this side. Hopefully by morning at least some of these pieces will be dry enough to wear again."

"That is silly," Aurora answered. "You need to be by the fire. You will catch your death all the way over there."

"Then we will sleep on opposite sides of the fire. And I promise not to look."

"Now you are being ridiculous. You know very well that the smartest thing to do is for us to share body heat. Besides, it is not as if we have not slept side by side."

Not to mention the kiss in the river, which neither of them had mentioned since they managed not to die afterward.

"Yes, well, that was before. And we were never . . ." He made a gesture that she guessed referred to their soon-to-be states of undress.

"Before what?"

"Before you were a princess."

"I was a princess the entire time, Kiran. Every time you kissed me, held me, made me run until I wanted to die," she continued, trying to lighten the suddenly heavy mood. But there was no changing the way the air had grown thick and charged between them. They had been apart so long, and now every biological instinct they had was driving them together. Perhaps a few less biological instincts too. Aurora wrapped her arms tight around herself, fighting off a shiver. "I have the same lips. The same body. I am the same person."

"And what would your mother say if she knew you kissed someone like me?"

"Last I checked, we left my mother fairly cozy with your mentor, who is a hunter also."

"You know that is not the same. He is a lord, apparently."

Aurora was not quite through processing that herself. She had gleaned during their travels that Duke had been a sailor in his past. But for him to be *the* sailor, the one on whose story she was raised and inspired and still in some ways modeled her life after? She was not sure how she felt about that. She had spent so much of her youth imagining the true end to Finneus Wolfram's story— waffling between nihilistic visions of a sunken ship somewhere at the bottom of the sea and fantasies of a paradise island where life was simpler and safer and so different from here. Now she knew the end of the story, and it was nothing like she could have ever imagined.

But she was not thinking about that now; she was focused on Kiran. "Do you hold his title against him even after all your years together? Will you leave his crew? Set off on your own? Will you leave him behind the way you threatened to leave me?"

Kiran huffed out a breath and sat down near the fire. "If we are going to have this conversation, we might as well get warm while we do it." He began pulling off his boots, and Aurora inched closer, doing the same with her own shoes.

"Well?" she asked, when both their feet were bare and pushed toward the crackling fire. "Will you run from Duke like you ran from me?"

"I did not run from you."

Aurora raised a challenging eyebrow. "Did you not? I seem to remember a door slamming and me being left alone with my heart practically in my hands."

"I am here now, aren't I?"

"You are. Though I have no idea why. You told me you did not belong, did not meet me when I asked you to, then showed up as part of the rebellion anyway. Your actions have not exactly been clear."

Kiran huffed, his face pulling into a grimace. "I cannot say my feelings have always been clear either."

Aurora swallowed, her throat parched despite how much water she had accidentally swallowed. "And are your feelings clear now?" she asked. "They felt clear back in the river, but if they are not, please do clarify."

Kiran looked at her, the smoke from the fire turning their little alcove hazy against the night. "I still do not belong in your world."

"Some would say I do not belong in my world either."

Kiran's hands flew up from where they had been clutching his knees, and the words burst out of him like a creature finally set free. "Which is why I could not leave. Skies help me, Aurora. I wanted to walk away. I wanted to be able to make that choice." He swallowed and his face turned serious as he leaned closer to the fire, closer to her. "But as long as you are in this world, I want to have your back. I want to make certain you are safe. I want to help you do the wild, improbable things you dream of doing. I want to stand beside you as you turn this place upside down and build it anew."

"I want you there too. I always have." Her voice wobbled slightly as she continued, "So where have you been?"

He sighed. "I will never be good enough for you, Princess. I can do those things without tying you down to someone who brings nothing to the table. I know how royal marriages work. You have to marry someone who is your equal, someone who brings land or skill or riches, and I have none of those things. But I could be your guard. I could be like Taven. I would lay down my life to keep you safe, to see you reach the heights I know you can."

Aurora had had enough of this talk.

She stood and peeled the wet undershirt over her head, tossing it to land on a rock nearby.

"Wh-what are you doing?" Kiran asked, quickly averting his gaze.

Aurora did not answer, turning her attention instead to the pants she wore, tearing at the buttons.

Kiran was on his feet in a moment, protesting, but she ignored him, pushing the pants and undergarments she wore down in one fell swoop. Kiran cursed, spinning to face away from her, much the same way he had at the Rani Delta outside Taraanar when she had been bathing. Aurora had been vulnerable and afraid then, in need of comfort. He had held her together when she felt like a thousand loose threads. His arms had provided a safe place for her to stitch herself back together. And now she intended to return the favor. With his back turned, she deposited her final pieces of clothing on the rocks, and then she went to him.

She started with a hand on his back, finding the place between his shoulder blades where muscles gave way to the straight line of his spine.

"Aurora, you don't have to—" Kiran trailed off when she replaced her hand with her body, pressing skin to skin.

"I am cold," she answered. "And I am tired. And I have missed you so much it feels like I am splitting apart sometimes. I have heard your reasons. I understand them. Now you will hear mine."

He did not object, but she could feel through his back the way his breathing had picked up. She ran a hand down his muscled arm to the clenched fist at the end, and smoothed her fingers around the hard stone his hand made.

"I might be a princess, but I have no intentions of following in the footsteps of those who have come before me. I intend to listen to my people, all of them, and make decisions for the best of the majority, not just those with influence. I do not wish to become swayed by power like the ones before me, nor directed by fear as my mother was. I will not be taken in by greed, nor taken advantage of by those with ill intent. The best way I know to do this is to be true to myself. And I have never known myself better than when I am with you. Who else would I trust to tell me when I'm behaving too much like a high-handed royal than someone who loathes high-handed royals? I have no intentions of trying to make myself fit into this world you despise. I intend to make it fit me. And you. If you will stay. And I do not mean as my guard."

After a moment, Kiran's body still remained rigid, and Aurora began to fear the boldness that had come so easily before. As good as it had felt to kiss him again, she was determined. He had to be all in or all out.

She dropped her hand from his fist and began to back away, but before she had even finished peeling her body away from his, his fingers had found her wrist, and had pulled her back. Her chest landed against his back once more, even more firmly, for this time he had brought her arm around him, pressing her palm flat against his sternum.

"Are you sure?" he asked, still facing away from her. Aurora's body surged with heat everywhere their skin touched, a stark contrast to where her bare legs touched his still-wet pants.

Aurora wrapped her other arm around his large body, resting it low on his hard stomach.

"I am rarely sure," she told him, and she felt the muscles of his stomach strain beneath her hand. "But of this, I have no doubt."

In a fierce whirlwind of excitement, Aurora found her arms flying as Kiran broke her tender hold, then she was flying too, up into his arms as he lifted her. His mouth met hers moments before he guided her legs around his waist. Aurora wasted no time being tentative, instead pouring every moment of longing and doubt and fear she had experienced into the kiss.

Every sweep of her tongue, each gasp of breath passed between their open mouths, every indent left by her clutching fingernails on his neck was another lesson she meant to teach him. The world could get no kinder, unless you made it so. Life could get no easier, unless you had something worth outlasting the hard moments. And hearts were always more likely to be broken if you assumed it was inevitable.

"I love you," she whispered between frantic, needy kisses. "As you are. I need no other version of you."

Kiran slowed their kisses, pulling away, and he lowered her feet to the ground. She squeezed his shoulders, worried she had said the wrong thing, going back over her words to determine what might have upset him.

Kiran cupped her face, waiting until she looked him directly in the eyes. "I love you. Every version of you."

A small breath escaped her lips, and her mouth trembled into something like a smile. She laughed as a tear escaped her eye, and then swatted at his hip, still clad in wet clothes.

"Then take those off, and make me warm."

He dropped a short, soft kiss on her mouth before doing exactly as she commanded.

Witches of air can vary widely with regards to intensity of power. Some were only observed to make minor manipulations in wind, while others have the power to affect air enough to create immense damage, stop someone from breathing, or even fly.

—*An Examination of the Original Magics*

17

Aurora expected everything to feel different when she woke the next morning. She thought the world might look entirely new after her experience the night before, but when the sun rose through the trees and the warbling song of a flurry of birds in the forest woke her, she found the world unmoved, unaltered. Her body too was the same, albeit a bit sore, though it was honestly hard to tell where the soreness from their journey through the river gave way to the soreness from their *other* activities.

Carefully, she lifted her head from where it rested on Kiran's bare chest and looked up at his still-sleeping face. The world might not have changed, but some things had. The doubt that nipped at her heels like a ravenous wolf slumbered somewhere, leaving a contented feeling that was entirely foreign to her. For once, there were no more secrets hanging over her head, no more regrets. There was still much to worry about, of course; their journey was far from over. But at least now she felt like she was swimming, rather than swept away in rapids too strong for her to do anything but try to stay alive.

Aurora Pavan was *living*, and that had been her dream all along—to take ownership of her choices, to unravel the secrets and fear that hemmed her in like mountains. The change had begun the day she wandered into the Eye. That was when the seed had taken root, and she'd broken past the soil the day she left Pavan. Each day in the wilds had seen the change in her watered and pruned and carefully grown. But if Aurora were honest with herself, from the moment she had returned to Pavan, she had been waiting for the inevitable, waiting for her stem to break. Because in this city, in this world, in her home, she was so used to feeling weak and inadequate. When she had lost Jinx and Nova, it had been shattering; it reduced every bit of confidence she had to rubble.

But last night, Aurora had realized something. There were some things in life she did not get to choose—who she loved, how she hurt, or what she was born. But she could not run anymore when things became too painful. Kiran had tried to run from her because he thought it would not work. Aurora had spent her life running from what she was and was not. She had faced that now, but that did not mean she was through. Now she had to stand toe to toe with all the pain those memories held, and she had to feel it. Even if right now was the most inconvenient time imaginable to dig up the weight of scars unhealed. But she owed it to herself, and she owed it to Pavan to come into this with a clear slate.

Ready to face the day, and their mission, Aurora leaned down and placed a kiss on the center of Kiran's chest. She followed it with another and another, each moving higher and higher until she reached his jaw and he stirred.

He hummed quietly and said, his voice raspy, "I do not think I have ever slept that well."

She smiled and propped herself across his midsection. "You are lying on rocks, the fire is nearly out, and the air has more bite than a bear."

"Yes, but you were beside me," he replied, folding his arms around her, and hauling her entire body on top of him.

She squirmed, laughing. "This cannot be comfortable."

"Who said anything about comfort?"

He caught her mouth in a searing kiss that made her forget all her intentions for the day. Almost.

She let the kiss go on as long as she dared, then pulled back, the cold air rushing in to numb her swollen lips.

She sat up, folding her arms around her bare chest to try to fend off the cold. "We should get our bearings, find the best place to do our storm work."

Normally, they scouted areas that they thought were likely to produce a storm, but now they needed to find a place that would keep their activities as private as possible, and hopefully somewhere isolated enough that there was little chance of any damage spreading.

Kiran sat up too, throwing his arm over her shoulder and pulling her closer to his natural warmth. "Right you are."

That did not stop him from ducking down to kiss her again, lingering longer than a peck, but not seeking to deepen the kiss. When he did pull back, it was with a sigh.

"We are going to freeze our arses off the moment we step away from this fire," he said.

She snorted. "My arse already feels halfway gone."

Kiran gave a look of mock horror and pulled her across his lap, planting her as close as possible to the simmering remains of the fire. "I will not let any damage come to your royal behind on my watch."

He left her there, laughing, as he darted naked for the rocks where they had left their clothes the night before. He made a grand show of presenting her clothes to her, and she could not help but giggle, not over the clothes, but the fact that he had done the entire thing unabashedly bare as the day he had been born. Though he looked decidedly grown. Aurora's cheeks flushed, recalling just how adult he had made her feel the night before.

Their humor quieted as they put on their clothes, some of which were still damp from the day before. It would make for an unpleasant day, but they did not have much of a choice. Kiran caught a rabbit, while Aurora gathered berries and greens for their breakfast, then they set out from their camp, being careful to mark their journey by placing piles of rocks or large fallen tree limbs to help them recall their way back.

They found their way back to the river, and followed it farther from the city until they came upon an area where the water slowed and spread out into a calm pool before traveling on again in a small, more winding stream. The area around the pool was large and open enough that it would provide them ample space, but it was slightly lower in elevation, giving them some cover. Aurora guessed it was the best they would do, unless they wanted to travel even farther from the city.

Kiran knelt over the satchel, unpacking supplies for both him and her, laying them in two neat piles. For him, he had numerous empty vessels with which to collect magic. Aurora did not know whether these were jars they had had on hand that had already been enchanted by Jinx before her capture, or if he had sought out another witch—Zephyr, perhaps.

In her pile, he laid a series of Stormhearts, some of which belonged to him, others duplicates from the crew's collection.

Still kneeling over the supplies, he looked up at her and asked, "What would you like to try first?"

Aurora searched the pile of Stormhearts, waiting for something to jump out at her, but her stomach was a jumble of nerves.

She shrugged and asked, "Where would you like to start?"

"Maybe something simple to begin? Wind? Or rain?"

Aurora nodded immediately, glad he had not jumped to something like a firestorm first. For while she was fairly confident now in her ability to call a storm, she was still unpracticed in her ability to control them. And it was just the two of them alone out here. If something went wrong . . . she could not think of that. Starting small did indeed seem the best option.

"Wind," she said. "Maybe it will dry our clothes the rest of the way."

He grinned. "Wind it is."

He offered the Stormheart up to her, and she took it, turning it over in her hands. "How much do you think we need?"

He shrugged. "Wind is moderately useful. It can make a good distraction."

"It is also good for clearing fog in a pinch," she added, frowning at the memory of that day in the palace, the last time she had seen Jinx and Nova.

"I think we can get a mix of things to send to Zephyr. Then if she wants more or less of anything, she can let us know."

Aurora nodded, then looked to Kiran. He was looking at her, and she realized she was stalling. With a sigh, she took a few steps back and closed her eyes. She began preparing to lower her walls, but this time she remembered what Sly had said about focusing on the boundaries of herself, not just keeping intrusions out. She worked to find those edges, and at the same time she let the walls she held up between herself and the world fall.

The barrage of sensation and souls was immediate, but the advice from Sly did help. It was not another barrier, per se, but it held her apart just enough to keep her from getting lost in the chaos.

Then it was time to find a soul. Aurora could have picked any of them, could have forced the bonding of soul and storm, but she thought there was a better way.

Focusing, she tried to pinpoint exactly the way it had felt when she had been trapped in Pavan with no options, no future but the one decided for her. She remembered the claustrophobia of it, the way she would open every window in her rooms to let in the breeze so that she might pretend that her world was not so closed off. Once she had that feeling, once she had shaped every nuance of helpless frustration in her mind, she sent it out into the wilds, searching for a soul that knew that same ache.

It did not take long for one to rise up from the pool of water nearby; it came at her gasping, as if it had been drowning for eternity and she was the only rope that had ever been offered. She took hold, offering comfort and assurance.

I know, I know, she crooned. *I felt the same.*

The soul sent her fragments of a life—not enough to piece together any true identity, but enough to know it was a woman whose soul she held. Her husband had worked at the dockyard. And he had not been a good man. His wife had feared him a great deal.

Aurora was bombarded then with flashes of a young boy, of the Pavan gates, and a panoramic view of the wildlands, storms flashing dramatically in the distance.

You felt trapped.

She was still trapped, by the memories, perhaps by the son she had left behind.

I would like to give you a taste of freedom, if you would trust me.

"Aurora?" Kiran's voice sliced through her concentration, breaking the bond, and she barely managed to hold the woman's spirit in place. She held up a finger in frustration, and focused back on the woman.

I promise, I mean you no harm. Will you trust me?

Aurora laid her soul bare for the spirit, trying to show she had no malice. Finally, the spirit accepted, submitting completely to Aurora's control.

Carefully, Aurora did as she had only a few times before, drawing the soul through the stone she bore in her palm. This time, there was no gust like there had been with the soldier soul in the palace. A light breeze lifted the hair off Aurora's neck to start, then swept through the trees, rustling the leaves. Aurora felt a prickle of excitement in the air as a stronger gust turned and blew over the river, causing a few waves on the previously still surface.

She heard Kiran murmur something nearby, but the words passed by unrecognized.

That's it, Aurora encouraged. *Stay close to me, but you can blow as fast as you would like.*

She felt a flurry of wind whirl around her, and opened her eyes to find herself in the midst of a wondrous vortex, dotted with leaves, burgeoning with warmth and relief that only Aurora could feel. She too felt a little more free having experienced it.

Cassius did not bother trying to disguise his identity, not for this venture outside the castle. And from the moment he entered through the swinging tavern door, the volume of the establishment grew quiet and eyes followed his movement.

Groups of soldiers who had no doubt been carousing only moments before seated themselves sedately around wooden tables, suddenly on their best behavior. But it was not them he came to seek.

His gaze roved over the room, and he was impressed by the crowd. From what he heard, The Mermaid Tavern drew similar numbers nearly every night. The room was cast in a blue tint, and he heard the sound of running water somewhere. Waitresses moved throughout the room in long shimmering skirts, no doubt meant to reference the tavern's mythological namesake.

Growing up near the sea, Cassius had gone through a fascination with mermaids himself as a boy. He had read the stories of their unrivaled, irresistible beauty, and that alone would have piqued the interest of most young boys. But it was not only that which had drawn Cassius to the stories. His father had instilled in him the spirit of a conqueror from the time he could walk. No accomplishment was ever enough, not when it could be done faster or to a greater degree. So a young Cassius had contrived a plan to capture a mermaid, the first step toward conquering the inhospitable seas. It was how he had found the lagoon that eventually became his sanctuary away from Locke. As a young boy, he would spend day after day there, setting up traps, devising new ways in which to lure a creature of the sea into his control.

Then one day a hurricane had come in unexpectedly fast from the coast. The water had disappeared from the lagoon as he worked on one of his traps. He turned to see the very ocean disappearing, drawing away from the land as if someone had pulled a plug. For a moment, he had panicked, worried that a mermaid had somehow found out his plan, and was taking the ocean away as punishment.

Then the skies had turned black and the winds had begun to change. He had barely made it back to the palace before a hell like he had never known descended upon the city. That was the first time he had helped his father with storm duty—because the winds were so strong, the storm so vast, that it battered the entire peninsula for days before the storm's heart was near enough for his father to challenge. Every Stormling in the kingdom worked in shifts in an attempt to contain that storm. But still the flooding and winds brought significant death to the city.

That was when Cassius changed his idea of what it meant to conquer. Unlike his father, he stopped caring about land, about riches and status. Cassius Locke wanted to control that which would not be controlled. He wanted the kind of power he saw in that tempest, the kind that could pull the very ocean from where it rested. He wanted the ability to conquer death, or as close as he could come to it.

He hated to admit it to himself, but he wanted what the Stormlord had.

But for today, in this tavern, Cassius would settle for answers to a few of his questions from the tavern owner he had heard so much about. As he approached the bar, one of the sparkling waitresses intercepted him, bending courteously as much as her costume would allow. "Your Highness, may I escort you to a private table upstairs?"

Cassius lifted his chin, trying to peer at the upper level. It could be seen from downstairs, so the danger of an ambush was minimal. And he knew some of his commanders did business here, meetings with soldiers or informants and the like.

"Only if the owner will meet me for a drink."

The girl's smile stiffened, but she did her best not to let it show. "I am not sure the owner is in, but I can certainly find out for you, Your Highness."

He pressed his lips into a stern line and said, "You do that."

Cassius let the girl lead him up the stairs to the private area, where he was seated at a large booth meant for a party of five or more. He ordered a strong drink and sank back into the cushions, inspecting the environment around him. Upstairs was more elaborately decorated with hanging vines and plants. Combined with the blue light and ocean sounds, the decor kept drawing his memories to the past, to shores where he had wandered as a child and then grown into a man. A peculiar twist pulled somewhere below his ribs; it was not overly painful, more like the smallest of blades had been slipped between the bones there. Smaller even, a needle perhaps. But every time he breathed in the air in this place, he felt it pinch a little more. And with it came simple, innocuous memories—his bare feet sinking into the sand, the constancy of the waves that crashed against the bank, the otherworldly quiet of his little lagoon, broken only by the occasional call of a bird or croak of a frog.

The emergence of memories had become disquieting enough that he was considering leaving when another woman arrived, setting a drink on the table. Something dark, two fingers deep in a small glass. This waitress was not wearing the same costume as the other, but her dress was equally as appealing. Draped in expensive maroon fabric, the waitress had generous hips, and skin a shade darker than his own. He guessed she was of coastal origins, like him.

He nodded his thanks, and took a sip of the drink. It went down smooth; the burn did not start until a few moments after he swallowed, when he could already feel the warmth spreading in his stomach.

"Good," he commented.

"I am glad you like it," the woman said, her voice deeper than he would have guessed. Then she slid into the booth across from him.

He stiffened. He was not in the mood for this kind of attention. He was well aware that this place was popular for the female companionship it provided, but that was not why he had come. He looked at the woman—her eyes were dark, but not quite as dark as the sable hair that poured over her shoulders. There was so much of it that even with the dozens of braids she wore, there was still more than enough loose for two false wigs, should she ever be in dire enough straits to sell it. Her brows were thick, almost mannish, but it somehow all balanced out when combined with her wide, red-painted lips.

"I mean no offense, but I am not here for company. I only wish to speak to your boss."

Those red lips pursed as she blew out a breath, then pulled wide as she gave him a chagrined smile. "That might prove difficult."

"Why?" he demanded.

"I have no boss."

"Your employer, then."

"I am the employer, *Your Highness.*" As Cassius looked at her, dumbstruck, she continued, "I was told you have questions."

He was quick to recover, shifting his evaluation of her to note the unreadable expression on her face, the unintimidated tilt of her head, and the single black silk glove she wore on her left hand. He had miscalculated indeed. This woman was a mystery. *She* was the tavern owner? The Pavanian nobleman he knew had described someone with their finger on the pulse of the city, with the ability to pull whatever strings needed to get a man the information or item he needed. He took her in again—from the elegant dress to her thick fall of hair to the shrewd look in her eyes.

She smiled and spoke. "Forgive me, Your Highness—I am, of course, happy to cooperate in whatever way the crown may ask, but you have caught me in the midst of a busy night. Is there something you needed?"

Cassius was unsure how to continue in his quest. He had been planning to threaten the man he encountered, but now . . . he was not sure if that was the course of action he wanted.

"I pride myself on my ability to garner information."

The woman's shoulders stiffened for the briefest of moments, but she did not hesitate to meet his eyes.

"What kind of information?" she asked.

"Every kind. You never know what will be useful."

The woman nodded thoughtfully. "Sounds wise."

"I had heard once upon a time that the proprietor of this tavern had some connection to the Eye."

No reaction that time. Well, that was not quite true. After a moment's pause, she smiled. "I cannot tell you anything about that, Your Highness. The Eye is long gone, or did not your brother tell you?"

He stared at her, wondering if she could possibly know the open wounds she was dragging mud through with her flippant comments.

"I know that. But did you . . . have a connection?"

She laughed. "Can't say that I did."

"I am not looking to punish you for some crime you may or may not have committed in the past."

"You don't say? Well, don't I feel ever so much better."

"As I said before, I am only looking for information. I had heard that the person who ran this tavern was who I should go to if I ever needed information that was difficult to obtain."

"And what information is it that you need?"

"I have it on some authority that there is . . . a magic user in the city."

She stared at him, unflinching. "A magic user? Would you not qualify as that?"

"You know what I mean."

"I am afraid I do not. If you want information from me, you will have to spell it out clearly."

"An earth witch. I am looking for an earth witch," he snapped.

The woman inhaled, considering. "I hate to disappoint you, Your Highness, but there are no earth witches running around the city that I know of."

"Have there been?" he demanded.

"I did hear rumors of someone like you are describing, but she has not been seen for quite a while." He searched her eyes, and she did not flinch under his gaze. She stared right back, her eyebrows lifted, almost in challenge.

Cassius cursed and threw back more of the burning liquid. Whoever the witch was, she must have left the city right after she rescued the queen. He thought about asking about the princess directly, but he could not trust the woman with such a direct question. Not yet.

"What about newcomers? Anyone new to the city who sticks out?"

She gave him an exasperated look. "There are about a thousand newcomers camped outside the gates, but inside? No, Your Highness, I have not noticed anyone new inside, other than your soldiers."

She stood from her seat across from him, the fabric of her dress falling artfully down her body. "If you have any more questions, you know where to find me."

It was not until she had disappeared down the stairs that Cassius realized he still did not know her name.

The tempests came without ceasing. As soon as the king engaged one in battle, another emerged to bear down on the city. After days of torment, the water breached the first walls. As the floodwaters ravaged the lowest levels of the city, Finneus stood high atop the castle's battlements with his uncle, the screams searing his soul.

—*The Tale of Lord Finneus Wolfram*

18

Kiran had always preferred the wildlands. But the wildlands alone with Aurora? That was more of a blessing than he ever could have dreamed. During the day, he watched in absolute awe as she brought storms to life before his eyes. And at night, they kept each other safe from the cold, wrapped up so completely in each other that it was torture to untangle themselves come morning.

But he did it anyway, because the sooner they were out of bed and fed, the sooner they could start their walk down the river. It was a long journey, and Kiran was determined to soak up every moment he could. He asked her every question he could think of. Some were silly—things about food or colors or animals. Others were more introspective—regrets and accomplishments and hopes. Anything that she would tell him, he wanted to know.

"Do you like it?" he asked, as they made their way to the pool for another day's collection.

"It?" she asked, her eyebrow raised and a provocative smile pulling across her mouth.

He tugged on the hand he held, pulling her close enough to steal a kiss. "Not that, Princess. I mean your magic. Now that you have it mostly figured out. Do you *like* it?"

She considered the question as they walked, their intertwined hands swinging lightly between them. "I think I *do*." She continued,

"It is still odd, of course. And I would rather avoid the darker souls altogether. But the rest . . . it is heartbreaking how many there are, and how their lives—full and real and detailed—have been reduced to a series of impulses and emotions. It is as if someone made a shaded copy of an etching on a piece of paper. And then copied that paper, and the next, again and again until all but the most pronounced designs of the original etching had been lost. That is what so many of these spirits are. They are holding onto trauma from memories they no longer have. I feel like I get to provide them an escape. And I do not know, maybe . . . maybe a few of them will find their way to the next life through it."

"You think that possible?"

Aurora shrugged. "I do not even know if there is a next life. I only know that these spirits are stuck here, and they should not be."

"Have you thought . . ." Kiran hesitated, unsure how she would react, then decided not to censor himself with her. "Have you thought about whether you would ever take another storm? Like with the skyfire?"

Aurora swallowed. "If you had asked me a few weeks ago, I would have been outraged that you even asked. It would have been a firm no. I still want the answer to be a no. But . . ." She sighed. "But . . . things are complicated, and compromises have to be made. I cannot expect everyone else to fight a war, while I stay clean. I—I do not know."

He squeezed her hand. "You do not have to know. We can take things one step at a time. On every front."

He regretted the turn down which his questions had taken the conversation, for she was somber as they arrived at the area where they worked. Like all the days before, he set out their supplies. He had learned to let her take her time. In truth, he could barely even call what he was doing hunting.

So far, most of the storms she had conjured had remained calm, not at all like the predatory tempests to which he was accustomed.

Often, Aurora was even able to direct the spirit toward him and asked it to remain still while he collected magic, then she would send it off to gallivant on its own for a bit, before drawing it back in for the next collection. It was more like corralling a distracted child than a storm.

But he was not complaining.

Aurora was nothing short of resplendent while she worked her magic. Whatever emotion she was feeling, she radiated it outward like she was her own sun. Most of the time, she was happy, which made him feel like he was always just shy of bursting. But in the beginning, when she first connected with a spirit, she was often forlorn. The grief rolled off her in drifts that made him feel like he was back in the freezing river again, fighting not to drown.

Today she laid a hand comfortably on his back as she bent to look over the Stormheart options. They had already collected a fair amount of wind, rain, and skyfire. All their options from here on out were decidedly less simple. She knelt, running her fingers first over the smooth, shiny black of the twister Stormheart. He glanced around, thinking they might need to find a larger open area if they were going to try for twisters today. The water put them at too much of a disadvantage.

But then her fingers left that heart, brushing past a few more before touching the crystalline red shard of a firestorm heart. In truth, they did not need firestorm magic. They needed firestorm hearts to help when natural firestorms hit, but he was not sure how she would feel about providing them, considering it would mean the destruction of the souls she called.

She wavered, her fingers drifting over to the gray fog Stormheart that lay next in line. His stomach clenched. He knew they would have to do the fog eventually, but that did not mean he was eager for the moment. He did not have a fog Stormheart of his own; this one belonged to Duke. But they had only enough powder left for one use, so he would have this one day to collect as much magic as possible. This though was another storm where they needed hearts as badly as they needed the magic, so they could grind them down into more powder. So he would also finally have to face his fear and take the heart of a fog storm, even if the mental invasion it would take made him uneasy.

He saw the knowledge of what had to be done in Aurora's face when she looked up at him, her expression torn.

"I know you do not want to," he murmured. "But perhaps there is a compromise. You can call any soul you like. You do not have to choose the ones with redeeming qualities. Instead, maybe you could use one of the darker souls. I know you hate them, but if I took the heart of one of those storms, it is one less malevolent spirit out there for the Stormlord to use."

"That is true. But . . . I am not sure I will have as much control over the spirit. You will have to be careful."

"I am a hunter, love. Careful comes with the territory," he said, chucking her under the chin with his knuckles, determined not to show any of his nerves.

She took a deep breath and said, "Okay. But we will go with fog, then. I am not risking a firestorm breaking free from my hold on my first try."

They split the fog powder they had left on hand, giving each of them as much immunity from the storm's mind-altering magic as possible. Then they prepared for battle.

This time was different from all the ones that came before. As Aurora closed her eyes and began to wander away from him into whatever world it was that she felt and saw that he could not, she had none of the calm, peaceful demeanor she normally had. Her shoulders were stiff, and her fists clenched. A sweat broke out on her forehead within minutes, and instead of the grief or pity or compassion he was used to seeing as she drew a soul toward herself, her expression tightened into a grimace, her nose wrinkling up in what he could only guess was disgust.

He watched her struggle, and he nearly called the whole thing off. He had come to love the way she looked when she was using magic—ethereal and effervescent and everything that was good in this world. But this . . . this was not like that. As she gritted her teeth, a tingle of magic began to spread through the atmosphere. It felt . . . *tainted*. The air turned thick and sticky, like he was breathing in tar, and even though it was morning, a dark gloom seemed to shadow the sun long before any storm ever took shape.

Then, he saw it. Like creeping fingers bursting from a shallow grave, long tendrils of a dense, milky-white fog had begun to extend from the woods around them. He looked to Aurora, whose face had gone red with the effort of control she was exerting, and knew it was his turn now.

Kiran marched forward, prepared to meet the sinister storm halfway.

Aurora was shaking. Her attention was split between controlling the storm itself, lest it decide to turn in another direction and seek out others for destruction, and maintaining the integrity of herself. Those boundaries Sly had told her about, they had become more and more clear over recent days as she worked through her own emotions alongside the souls she helped. She had presented each of her calls to the souls as an opportunity for cleansing, the chance to break free from the emotions that bound them here. But the experiences had been cleansing for her too. Each time, she poured out the emotions she had been holding onto as well, letting go of old hurts, long-held guilt, and unspoken fears. And each time she had repeated the process, the edges of her own soul had become more defined.

They were not always pretty. She had her ripped and tattered places, the rocky spots where it was only safe for her to tread, but by being honest with herself, those things had lost some of the power they once had, giving her more of the control she needed.

And she was glad for it today, because she was not sure she could have touched this soul, brought it so close to her own, before now. It twisted and writhed under her care, either trying to break free or latch onto her like a leech. It was a delicate balance to keep it close, but not so close that it could permeate her own thoughts and desires.

She felt the moment that Kiran entered the fog, because the storm surged with fury at its inability to affect him. As if it knew she was somehow to blame, it turned all its attention on her instead, pummeling at the barrier of her mind. It swarmed her, clenching around her, gouging at any perceived weak spots, trying to force itself into the space that was only her.

Her jaw dropped in a gasp, but she struggled to lift her chest enough to actually draw in air. She had tried to choose a spirit that was corrupted, but not necessarily the most dangerous option. It appeared she had underestimated the soul's determination to cause harm. But as long as its attention was focused on her, that should make Kiran's task easier. A soul divided would be easier for him to defeat.

She concentrated on all the things she had gained of late—she had her confidence back, her mother was safe, she and Kiran had repaired their relationship, she knew more of her magic than she would have thought possible a few months ago. Skies, she *had* magic. That alone was more than she could have dreamed a few years ago. She was not just Princess Aurora. Nor was she the hunter Roar, who had lied to her friends. She was someone completely different who had taken all of those experiences and come out the other side whole and better, and she would keep doing that, no matter what this world threw at her.

The storm's assault suddenly halted, and she felt a smoldering scream of rage tear through her mind. Aurora was finally able to draw in a much-needed breath, and she knew the real fight had begun—Kiran had gone for the storm's heart.

All the pressure that had been slowly crushing closer and closer disappeared, leaving her dizzy at the change. She opened her eyes to find the clearing completely immersed in fog. She lifted her hand, noting that it disappeared as soon as her arm stretched to its full length. She knew the water was to her left, but she could no longer see it. Kiran was somewhere up ahead. She felt the intensity of his soul, determined and strong. Unlike their night in the desert, she was not afraid this time. He was winning this fight, and she knew it. It was only a matter of time before the fog surrendered its heart.

She was focused so intensely on the battle, on Kiran's nearing victory, that she stopped paying attention to the rest of her surroundings. It was too late to do anything by the time she felt a presence at her back, one whose soul was complex and large and knit together from mismatched pieces like a patchwork quilt.

A hand clamped over her mouth, jerking her back hard enough to lose her footing. Another arm wound around her, constricting her movements, and hot breath invaded her ear.

She shuddered as a low, male voice said, "Come easily, or I will call another storm for your friend while he is distracted. What do you think will happen then? He will either die by my storm or lose focus and die by yours."

Aurora's heart crumpled, sinking somewhere into her stomach. Then she did the only thing she could do. Aurora nodded her agreement, and she let the Stormlord take her.

The waters continued to creep higher—claiming more of the city, more innocent lives, and the last vestiges of Finn's faith in his uncle. The king continued to withdraw, leaving more and more of the fight to the soldiers who were too tired to hold the storms at bay. Finneus could not watch the slow destruction of his home for another moment. That night he began recruiting for his mission. He would save Calibah, or he would die trying.

—The Tale of Lord Finneus Wolfram

19

The door to Nova and Jinx's room flew open without warning. That was how it always was, even for meals; the soldiers made a point of showing them that they could never get too comfortable here, even if their prince had ordered the girls be fed and treated with a modicum of respect.

Luckily, they only did their dangerous work at night, practicing with Nova's magic, which more often than not left the two of them huddled close in one of the four beds in the room. Neither of them spoke about their tendency to sleep in the same bed after a round of practice. It did not happen every night, but when it did, they fell into the same routines without fail.

But today they were on opposite sides of the room when the door swung open—Jinx doing complicated stretches that she did every morning, and Nova watching her surreptitiously, while picking at what was left of her breakfast.

"You," a soldier said, pointing to Nova. "Come with me."

Jinx was out of her stretch and on her feet immediately. "Where are you taking her?"

"Nowhere that concerns you," the soldier sneered. "You stay here. The prince only asked for her."

Nova tried not to sink back into the bed in fear. She had been doing so much better of late. Her anxiety had not gone away; she did not think it would ever do that. But with control and acceptance of her magic, the spells of anxiety had lessened. It had become easier to pinpoint when anxiety was interfering, and she was learning to let it pass, to live around it.

As the soldier crossed the room toward her, Jinx put herself in front of Nova, cutting him off. "No. You can take us both or not at all."

The man shoved Jinx hard, sending her crashing into the bed opposite Novaya's. Leaping off her own bed, Nova prepared to fight back, but someone else stepped into the room, cutting her off.

"That is enough," Prince Cassius snapped. He waited as Jinx climbed to her feet, and when he saw that she was unharmed, he continued, "I mean Novaya no harm."

Jinx scoffed. "Like we would trust anything you say."

"You should. I have decided to release her."

Nova stood in stunned silence, certain she had heard wrong. "Release me?"

"Yes. I have decided that I believe your original version of events surrounding the princess's kidnapping. I believe that you had no part in the scheme. As such, I will be releasing you from detention, effective immediately."

Nova shook her head. "I do not understand."

He looked at her like she was as simple as a child who had not yet learned to read. "You are no longer to be kept here against your will. I am afraid your position with the seamstress has already been taken, but you will be granted the opportunity to pick up your duties as a maid exactly where you left off. Your old room will be provided to you again. You may continue your life in the manner you lived it before this unfortunate series of events."

This unfortunate series of events. That's what he called her imprisonment?

"And what about J—" Nova stopped herself before she said Jinx's name, gesturing toward her instead.

The prince frowned and shook his head. "I am afraid she is a different matter entirely. She broke into the palace illegally and assaulted a number of my men. And I imagine there is a great deal more to her that I have not yet discovered."

Nova hesitated, unwilling to trust that things were as simple as he made them out to be, and even more reluctant to leave without Jinx by her side. "She was only trying to help me. And since you have now decided I was likely wrongfully imprisoned all along, her only crime is trying to right your mistake."

The prince's lips drew into a flat, hard line. "I suggest you take the generous offer I am making you, Novaya. Before I decide to investigate why someone with possible rebel ties was so interested in freeing you."

She knew he did nothing out of generosity. He had an angle, of that she was certain. He likely hoped by releasing her, she would lead him to the rebellion. Maybe he planned to watch her and use her as bait.

"Go, Nova," Jinx whispered, moving to stand beside her. "I will be fine. You know me."

That was the problem. Nova had only just begun to know the other witch, and she did not want it to end now. She would rather face imprisonment in this room with Jinx than reenter the world of the palace without her.

Jinx caught a few of Nova's fingers with her own, squeezing gently. The earth witch's body blocked their connection from the prince's view, but Nova felt her fires rise up in answer. They could fight; the two of their magics combined would give them a chance of making it out. But Jinx squeezed her fingers one more time and released them.

"Go," Jinx whispered. "You have been locked up long enough.

Be free. Get back to work. Reconnect with your friends. You will see. Everything will be fine." The words were light, her tone careful and casual, but Nova heard the message behind them. Outside these walls, Nova could keep working on her magic. She could find Aurora, once she had found a way to slip the prince's watch, of course. And together . . . together they would come back for Jinx, for Prince Cassius, for all the things left undone.

Finally, Nova nodded and let herself be led out of the room where she had been prisoner since her near escape. She did not resent that room, not the way she had the cell down in the dungeon. It was not a place of suffering for her. It was where she had been awakened. And she was going to miss it desperately.

She paused at the door to look at Jinx one more time. She already missed their nights together, and she had not even left the room yet.

"See you soon," Nova told the witch, before stepping back and allowing the soldier to close and lock the door behind her, this time with Nova firmly on the outside.

The prince walked with her all the way back to her old room in the servant's wing, where she found a bed already made, and many of her old belongings just as she had left them. The bed on the other side of the room, however, was empty.

"For caution's sake, you will be confined to the palace for now. You will attend to your work, as well as meals and any other activities of interest inside the palace. But until you have fully earned the trust I am placing in you now, you will not be allowed out into the city, lest you prove me wrong and involve yourself in *questionable* matters again."

Nova forced a thin smile. So, it was simply a different type of captivity then.

"For how long?"

Cassius smiled. "Until I say otherwise. If anyone wishes to see you, they will have to visit you here."

With the barest bend of his head, he turned and left her room, leaving her alone, in a place that should have felt like home, but did not come close to the supposed prison she had just left.

Aurora came awake slowly, disoriented and with her head pounding. The sunshine coming in through the trees was like fire to her eyes. She tried to look away, to take in her surroundings, but the world was so bright, and her head felt as if someone was hammering away at her skull from the inside every time she moved.

Pieces started coming back to her gradually—the fog storm in the clearing, Kiran battling for the heart, and the Stormlord catching her off guard. Goddess, his soul was unlike anything she had ever felt before. As he had marched her away, she had tried to make sense of him with her magic, to understand him the way she did other souls, but he was beyond comprehension. She did not know how much of the seething darkness in him was the souls he had taken and how much was the person he had been before. Aurora was not sure that was even a distinction that existed any longer.

She had cooperated with his demands for a while, until she was certain that they were far enough from Kiran that he was out of harm's way, then she had fought to get free. She had kicked and screamed and punched, simultaneously pulling on every decent soul she felt nearby, ready to set off a hundred skyfire storms if she needed to in order to get loose. He was strong and lean, and he wrapped an arm around her throat from behind, cutting off the scream in her throat.

Before she had managed to pull even a single skyfire storm to her aid, something solid and heavy hit her on the back of the head. She was not sure what had happened after that, or how long it had been since she had taken the blow. She only knew her head rang with pain, and every light, every sound was overpowering.

She tried to listen for any signs of the Stormlord, but she could only hear sounds of nature. There was a babbling brook somewhere nearby, and wind blew hard through the trees, hard enough that it had sounded like distant rainfall at first, before she felt the cold bite of it herself. There were a few birds, but even they were quiet, as if they knew they were in dangerous territory.

Eventually, Aurora chanced opening her eyes again. And though the pain was searing, and water filled her eyes, she managed to keep them open long enough to determine that she was alone, and that both her hands and feet were bound with iron manacles and attached to metal stakes hammered deep into the ground. The bindings had just enough give to let her roll from side to side, but not enough to allow her to sit up.

Aurora took a deep breath, and when that was not enough to stop the panic welling inside her, she took several more. She would not cry. She would not lose her mind to fear. She was *not* helpless.

She could not use her skyfire against her manacles; it would likely only heat the metal and burn her. She supposed she could call a skyfire storm now while her captor was gone, and hope that she was strong enough to defeat him when he returned. But she was weak and weary, and he had far more varied storms at his disposal, while she had just the one. He could kill her in an instant.

But if that was what he wanted, why not do it exactly where he found her? Why go through the bother of kidnapping her at all?

She could call a storm not for her defense, but to draw attention to the area. Maybe if they were close enough to the city, someone would see. Maybe Kiran would see and send help.

But Kiran did not even know what had happened to her. She would be drawing him directly into the most dangerous ambush possible. Or the Stormlord could have taken her far enough away that no one would see.

In the end, she did the only thing she could think of. She asked for help. Lowering some of her mental barriers, she sent out streams of anguish, trying hard to visualize the area where she was. She begged for a brave soul to come to her aid. This was not a project for a timid, hurting spirit. She needed a warrior, someone who would help her fight, someone who could find a way to help her send word to her friends.

Please, please. My name is Aurora, and I am in danger. I need help. If you can, please come find me.

Again and again, she sent out the message, changing it occasionally, hoping to lure anyone to her aid. She had no idea how far she was from the city, or in what direction the Stormlord had taken her, so she tried pushing her message in every direction, as far as her abilities would let her reach.

And though she could feel the usual hum of spirits around her in nature, most of those spirits had already found a measure of peace and were not willing to leave it. She could try to force one, but she was not sure that would work.

When someone finally came, it was not a spirit who meant to aid her, but the man who had captured her, and Aurora got her first true look at the Stormlord. He stomped out of the woods, his eyes settling on her as soon as he emerged. And with him came a crush of other souls that followed in his wake.

He looked . . . *familiar,* and yet she was certain that if she had ever seen this man in her life, she would never have forgotten it. His hair was black as oil, cut in short uneven spikes. His skin was not pale—it was nearly as dark as Kiran's, in fact—but there was still a sickly pallor about him that made him look . . . unwell. His eyes were black pits, made all the more fearsome by the large scar that cut through his right brow, over his eyelid and down to the corner of his mouth. His body was long and lean, and he moved with a slight hop in his step, as though he knew some grand secret that everyone else did not.

"You should know," he said, "when you send out those blasting pleas for help, you might want to be more discerning. Anyone bothering to listen can pick up what you are sending."

He smiled at her, and the expression made her stomach turn. She wanted to throw up, but she did not think there was anything inside her to give. She yanked hard on the manacles bound above her head, knowing they would not budge, but unable to stop the impulse.

"Relax," he sighed. "I am not going to murder you, if that is what you think."

"No?" Aurora said, her voice wobbling. "Then why stake me to the ground?"

"To make you stay," he said matter-of-factly, as if it was a perfectly reasonable thing to do. He crossed closer toward her, then dropped a dead fox in front of her. "I brought food."

Aurora watched in perplexed silence as he set a fire, not using flint or any other method, but the same way she had, with a few sparks of skyfire. His were smaller and more controlled; he did not scorch the ground as she had, only sparked the flame he needed. Then he set about skinning the game he had caught and roasting it over the fire.

He ignored her through most of the work, but he was not entirely solitary. She watched him move about the camp, noting when he would pause and stare intently in a direction, as if having a conversation with someone that she could not see. He did that again and again, sometimes for long periods, other times only a brief, meaningful look over his shoulder. And though she could not hear the discussions he was having—he had shrouded his mind too well—she was aware of the swarm of dark spirits that collected around him. They moved with him like an entourage, clinging to him as if he were their god. And she supposed in some ways, he was. They wanted nothing more than death and destruction, and he offered them that opportunity.

She strained to maintain her shields against the sheer intensity of the souls around her. Some of them had to be centuries old. The decay she felt went so deep, it would be impossible to excise. It was no wonder that the Stormlord's conjured tempests always affected her so strongly, if these were the souls he was using. And from what she could feel, he had dozens upon dozens more. If he let these souls loose, the whole world would burn, not just Pavan.

Eventually, he took the meat off the fire and carried the stick over toward her, kneeling beside her. Her tore a piece of flesh off with his fingers and held it up to her lips. She waited for the catch, but he only held the piece of meat closer, an impatient look crossing his eyes.

It was humiliating, but she found her stomach rumbling fiercely in response, as if she had not eaten in days. She was reminded that she had no idea how long she had been unconscious. And it was safer in the short term if she did not openly question his kindness. She needed to understand why he wanted her. So she opened her mouth and took the meat he offered, chewing slowly. He sat back on his haunches, pulling off a piece for himself.

She took a second piece of meat, pleasantly surprised to find the ache in her head lessening, if only a little. As he took his bite, she gathered the courage to ask, "Why are you doing this?"

His head tilted to the side, and the change drew her eyes to the open neck of his shirt, where she could see the barest hint of a flicker across his chest like her own. Only his was not just skyfire. It flashed between a multitude of colors—the red of a firestorm, the black of a twister filled with debris, the brilliant white of a snowstorm. Again and again, she saw that flicker, the order varied and of no pattern that she could discern. She wondered if all the souls he had taken, all the others he had added to his own, fought for dominance inside him. It would explain the chaotic nature of his soul. It felt too complex, too big for her to fathom. And it was filled with broken pieces and gaping chasms that on another spirit she would have done her best to heal. But she was certain these were not the kind of wounds that could or should be mended.

"I do as the goddess wishes," he finally answered, returning to their meal, tearing off another piece and holding it out toward her.

She hesitated and asked, "The goddess?"

He shoved the meat at her, and she took it, chewing as quickly as she could.

"Surely you, who have been granted her greatest gift, are a believer?" he asked, staring intently at her, a dangerous warning in his gaze. She tried not to let her eyes flick over to the scar that surrounded his eye. Intensity crackled in the air around him, and she had a feeling if she could see the storms over his heart, they would be flickering wildly.

"I believe," she said, regardless of whether it was true. Honestly, she was not sure what she believed any longer. She had been raised to believe the goddess a superstition of the past, a myth, but everything else she knew to be true had been turned upside down. She was not sure of anything any longer. "I believe there is something bigger than us, something bigger than the petty things the world becomes so focused on. But do you mean . . . do you *speak* to the goddess?"

He sneered. "I do not need to. She gave me an ability that only gods have had before me. To pour out storms according to my will. The last time such a skill was needed, it was the Time of Tempests, and the goddess had been betrayed by the very followers she had blessed. Now, all these years later, the same is true again. Those who are goddess-blessed have forgotten their origins, forgotten where their powers came from. They have given in to greed and perversion and cruelty. It is time to set things right once more, to cleanse the world of those who shame the goddess, to rid the world of Stormlings once and for all. I am the weapon she sent to do it."

"And what am I?" Aurora asked, her heart thundering.

The Stormlord had forgotten their meal in his long speech, and now he went back to it, offering her another piece of food with a shrewd, narrow-eyed look.

"That is what I am here to discover. You are like me. I felt you from the day you approached the city. I have been waiting, watching to see what the goddess would have you do. When I felt you pull one of my souls in the forest, I could wait no longer. What brought you here?"

Aurora swallowed, knowing she had a careful line to walk. "The same thing as you. I have been working with the rebellion to overthrow the Lockes. That is why we were in the wilds, gathering magic. We were preparing for an attack."

His head tilted to the side, his eyes sliding off to stare somewhere over her shoulder, and she knew that he was having another one of those conversations.

"Why not use your abilities?" he asked, turning to face her directly again.

"I-I was. But by sending magic to the rebellion, more people can do the goddess's work. Don't you see? Even now, ungifted humans could be attacking the Lockes without me, because I gave them the means."

His lips flattened into a line, and she knew she had to do more to sell her story. "I am not as advanced as you. I only recently discovered my abilities. I have only skyfire at my command right now. I am dependent on Stormhearts to call any other kind of storm."

He tore off a large chunk of meat with his teeth as he stood. He walked back over to the fire, chewing, his expression unreadable. Once he had laid the stick down next to the fire, he turned and looked her over again. His eyes flicked to a few spots in the air around her, before he finally shrugged. "I suppose I could teach you. There must be a reason the goddess sent you. She means for us to work together in this mission."

Aurora nodded emphatically. "Yes, that has to be it. How else would two people with such rare abilities end up in the same place?"

"True. I had planned to attack again tonight. Perhaps, you can join me, and show me what skill you have with skyfire."

Aurora's heart beat so hard, it felt like it took up her entire chest.

"Remember, though, what I said about the rebellion? There are people in Pavan who hate the Stormlings as much as you. We do not need to hurt them to get to the Lockes. In fact, I already know for a fact that the rebellion has kidnapped Casimir Locke with the intent to hand him over to you."

His face turned hard, the scar on his face pulling taut.

"Is that so? And how might I reach this rebellion of yours?"

Aurora tried to keep her voice calm, not to let any eagerness show. "I could contact them. I know of a secret go-between they have in the camps."

He folded his arms over his chest, and though his eyes did not leave her face, his head tilted slightly to the side, and she wondered if another spirit was whispering to him, if they could all see straight through her.

"No," he declared after some time. "I do not think I will be letting you go quite so easily. Not until I am certain I can trust you. If the rebellion is of use, I will decide that myself."

Then he turned and walked out of the woods, leaving her alone again. But alive, at least.

Days. That was how long Kiran had wasted. He could not think of all the things that could have happened to Aurora in that time. He thought at first that maybe she had not taken enough powder, that somehow, the fog had gotten to her. Because when he had come to, fog Stormheart clutched in his fist, Aurora had been nowhere in the clearing.

The dense clouds had still surrounded him, even though the magic that had controlled them was long gone. He thought she might have wandered off, her mind altered by the fog storm's magic; so he had searched for her, calling her name loud enough that his voice went hoarse. He searched through the night and into the next morning. When he still could find no trace of her, he went back to their camp, thinking maybe she *had* wandered off, but had come to her senses, and when she went back to the clearing, he was not there. It was reasonable to assume the next place she would go would be their camp. But she was not there either. As far as he could tell, it had not been touched.

He wandered the wilds for another day, fearful every moment that he might stumble upon her body. There were so many ways to die in the wilds. He knew them all, had seen so many of them up close and personal. He used to pride himself on the fact that none of it scared him; he was ready to meet death however it came.

But the thought of finding Aurora in any of those ways? It was worse than death, worse than any torture he could devise. When he had walked for nearly two days without sleep or any sign of her location, he gave in to the foreboding twist that was knotting up his stomach, and turned back for Pavan. Kiran needed help. He needed Duke and Ransom and Bait and Sly, and gods damn it, he needed Jinx. She would know what to do. With her earth magic, she always had some way of learning things that the others could not. She would listen to the trees or touch the soil, and somehow know things.

He needed his family.

By the time he made it on foot to the remnant camp outside the city gates, night had fallen on the third day since Aurora disappeared. There was some kind of commotion going on in camp. Soldiers were out in full force, but they were still having difficulty holding the crowds of remnants back as they gathered around something in the center of camp.

Kiran pushed closer. Weary as he was, his large body made it easy for him to weave his way through until he reached the front line of the crowd. An enormous number of Locke soldiers were fighting to push back the crowd enough to prevent them from viewing what lay beyond, but there was no blocking out what Kiran saw, no matter how many soldiers lined up to push the crowds back. For there, just at the edge of the camp, was a pile of bodies, all of them wearing blue Locke uniforms. They had been stacked into a grotesque mound, and at the top, a pike stuck out, a white flag waving from the top with bloodred writing too small for him to read covering the surface.

He leaned down and asked a older woman, "Do you know what happened here?"

"'Tis the night guards. They were all in their positions last night when we went to sleep. Then this morning, they were like this."

"Do they have any suspects?" he asked.

"Oh, they would like to blame it on all of us here, ye bet on it. They would love the excuse to get rid of us all. But he signed his name like it was artwork. Called it a gift."

"Who did?" Kiran asked.

"You know," the woman whispered, pointing a finger up at the sky. "*Him.*"

Kiran nodded, that awful, foreboding sensation in his gut magnifying tenfold. He had to believe this was a coincidence. There was no reason to believe this was connected to Aurora's disappearance. He kept telling himself that. And yet . . . he could not shake the terrible fear that was taking root inside him.

He left the crowd to their gawking, and set out looking for familiar faces. He found a few people he recognized from their brief stay in the camps upon their arrival in Pavan. As carefully and quietly as he could, he asked around about Etel and her visits until he found someone who kept regular contact with the old woman. Her last visit had been two days ago, so she had technically been due for a visit today, but the high security had likely kept her from coming, which left Kiran with nothing to do but wait.

And hope.

The Time of Tempests was a long, catastrophic period of storms unlike the continent of Caelira had ever seen up to that point. Records from that time are sparse, but it was estimated to have lasted nearly ten years. When it ended, none of the original magic users were believed to still be alive.

—An Examination of the Original Magics

20

It was another two days before Kiran made contact with Etel, and by then what little hope he had managed to scrounge up had been ground into dust. It took the rest of that day for them to arrange to smuggle him back into the city that night through the same route he had gone out.

He packed up all the new magic they had collected, and tried not to fall apart at the idea of stepping into the river without Aurora in his arms. When he arrived at the dock, it was not only Zephyr and Raquim waiting for him, but the rest of his crew too, excepting Jinx.

He had rehearsed in his mind what he would say during the journey through the river; he had thought out all the facts, all the most immediate problems. But as soon as his eyes fell on Duke, everything in him started sliding out of place.

"I lost her," he croaked, a sob wrenching in his throat. "She was there and then she was gone. How could I have *lost her?*"

His friends were by his side in a moment, pulling the heavy weight of the satchel off his shoulders and steadying him with hands on his arms and shoulders and everywhere. River water still poured from his drenched clothes, and his limbs shook forcefully from the cold.

"Slow down, mate," Ransom said.

Duke was in front of him, his face stark and worried. "Take a deep breath, and start at the beginning, my boy."

Kiran told them everything. None of it came out in the ordered, logical way he had planned during his journey. Instead, it was a jumble of memories and emotions and guesses and fears pinned together in no sensible order.

When he finished they all stared at him, not one of them moving to speak.

"Well?" he demanded. "I came for your help. I looked everywhere I could think of, but I could not find her. I need more bodies to help me search, unless you have any other suggestions."

It was Zephyr who finally broke the silence on their side. "Kiran, there is something you should know. There was an incident in the remnant camps a few days ago. A large number of on-duty soldiers were killed."

Kiran waved a hand. "Yes, yes, I know. I arrived the morning the bodies were discovered. It was because of them I had to wait so long to make contact with Etel. We cannot afford to waste any more time."

"The attack was committed by the Stormlord," Zephyr continued.

"I said *I know*."

"Do you know he left a note? For the rebellion?"

Kiran froze. "What? What did it say?"

"It said he knew we had a gift for him, and he wanted to offer a gift in return. We assume he means Casimir, but with the increased patrols, no one on our side has actually attempted to make contact with the Stormlord yet about offering him the Locke prince. We had thought that he had gathered the intelligence another way, perhaps using magic. But . . ."

"But . . ." Kiran trailed off, piecing things together. "Now you think Aurora told him?"

"It would make sense. Why she went missing, why you could

find no trace, and how the Stormlord learned of something that was supposed to be top secret. Maybe Aurora brought it up as a bargaining chip."

Kiran needed to sit down. There were no chairs available on the dock, so he gave in, and sat himself on the wooden planks, needing to feel something sturdy beneath him. He needed to know that the world was not falling away, no matter how much it felt that way.

"Can we do that?" Bait asked. "Trade Casimir for Aurora?"

"We can try," Zephyr said. "But truthfully, we do not even know if he has her."

"He has her," Kiran murmured, finally giving in to the dark, churning dread that had been stalking him for days.

"You do not know that," Duke said, clapping a hand on Kiran's shoulder.

"I do. We did something different that day. She had been using only benevolent souls to call storms, but that day I needed to take a Stormheart, so we decided it would be better to use a darker soul. One less monster out there. It must have led him right to us." He climbed to his feet, his adrenaline pumping even though fatigue clung to every part of his body. "We have to do something. I brought magic. We need to start planning an attack, a rescue."

Zephyr held out her red-gloved hand. "Take it easy, Thorne," she said. "Let's start with bargaining and see where that gets us."

His eyes strayed from the water witch to the members of his team, and he was glad to see determination and courage staring straight back at him. They would find her. They would not stop until they brought her home. He was certain. That was what family did.

Time twisted in on itself. Long hours passed with Aurora alone and the Stormlord off doing goddess knew what. With her body stretched and bound, she was at the mercy of the elements. The flesh around her lips grew dry and cracked. She could not remember the last time she had been given a drink of water. Yesterday? Maybe the day before?

Her pale skin was no match for the blazing Caeliran sun overhead. It felt like she was baking. She tried to focus, to keep her boundaries, search out a trustworthy soul, and keep it all hidden from the Stormlord, but her ability to concentrate deteriorated rapidly.

The first day, she had done so much thinking, so much worrying, but now she tired so quickly. She slept more often than she was awake. Dark spots marred her vision, and hunger had turned her belly into a gnawing, rumbling beast. Every moment she felt on the verge of tears, but she was fairly certain there was not enough liquid left in her to cry. She recognized the signs of dehydration from her first tangle with Zephyr, only this time the symptoms did not come on suddenly. They overtook her slowly, making her jealous of the quick misery she had experienced at the water witch's hands.

It was the helplessness that was the most maddening. She could not scratch an itch or adjust her position when her body ached or avoid the sun blazing overhead when her head pounded. She tried to force her mind to go somewhere else, to forget about the pain and thirst and hunger, but the constant hum of spirits around her was too distracting. She worried if she let herself get lost, she might never find her way back. So she lived with the pain, every single moment.

She never would have expected to yearn for the Stormlord's appearance, but she did sometimes. He was rarely at camp, and when he was, he still was not entirely with her. He existed in a reality she could not see; he interacted constantly with the souls around him, but he was so much more skilled than she that he blocked her from hearing any of it. Then he would march off with a determined look in his eyes, and she never knew how long he would be gone. The first time, he left her for nearly two full days.

She had still been aware and rational enough then to worry about all the things that could go wrong in his absence. She was easy prey for any animal that wanted to wander along. If a natural storm occurred, she would have no way to seek cover, no way to protect herself at all. The sheer madness of not being able to swat away bugs that landed on her eyes and nose made her want to scream and beg for his return. Maybe she did, mentally, and she did not even realize it, because he came again not long after that. His clothes had been smeared with blood, and he had not even bothered to look at her. He simply trudged straight past her and into the river to bathe.

She tried not to think about what that blood could mean. Was Kiran still out there, searching for her? Had he gotten too close? Goddess, the cramping hunger pains combined with the wrenching discomfort of fear, and she realized she still had tears to cry after all.

When the Stormlord rejoined the camp, he had donned the coat of a Locke soldier, though it was charred black in spots, and littered with holes. She did not want to look weak, but her desperation outweighed her calculation. "Water, please," she croaked.

The Stormlord jerked at her interruption, as though he had forgotten her presence entirely. But he did as she asked, pulling out a waterskin and stalking toward her. He held it up to her lips as she drank. She was weak and clumsy, and water dribbled down her chin, but she did not mind. It felt good on her sunburned skin. She drank until the skin was empty, and she only barely resisted the urge to ask for more.

"I-I thought you were going to teach me," she murmured, falling back against the earth, exhausted just by the act of lifting her head up to drink.

"I will," he said. "When it is time."

"Can you free me? If only for a little while. You have been gone so long, and I need . . . I need . . ." The list of what she needed was endless, but the only thing that popped into her head at that moment was Kiran, and the blood-soaked clothes the Stormlord had worn as he strode into camp. She *needed* to know he was safe.

"You *need* to feel helpless and alone," he snapped. "That is how it starts. It is only when you are truly alone, when you have been given up by those who love you and left by the ones who should protect you and abandoned by your companions . . . that is how you will learn the worth of your gift."

"Is that what happened to you?"

"The Lockes made certain of that. Left me to die in the jungle. They did not know I am never alone. Thanks to the goddess."

He left again before she got the chance to ask for food, and her stomach contracted sharply in protest. She waited and waited, hoping he would come back with another fox or a rabbit or a bird, but when she gathered her energy to search the souls in the surrounding area, she did not find his distinct and confusing signature.

That was when she screamed. She howled up to the sky, her throat raw and everything in her spasming with unrivaled fear and fury. She screamed until the birds flew from the surrounding trees, and the maelstrom in her chest dwindled into exhaustion. It felt good. But all it did was draw her into sleep again.

When she woke next it was to darkness and rain, both of which were trying to swallow her whole. The earth had grown muddy beneath her, and the torrent was so strong, she felt like she was drowning on land. Every time she tried to breathe, she was inundated with water instead; she turned her head to the side, gasping, but that only worked for a little while as a puddle began to form, rising higher and higher until her entire body was nearly underwater, and she had to strain her neck up to breathe.

Did he mean to kill her? If that was his aim, she wished he

would do it and be done. What kind of person left someone tied up like this, completely vulnerable, and then disappeared for days at a time?

A madman, that was who. She had heard the rumors the same as everyone else. But calling him insane seemed like a way to excuse his cruelty and all the fear and destruction he had wrought. Yet, nor had she been able to think of him completely as the evil villain. In truth, she'd tried to think of him as little as possible before all of this. Because that meant she had to question her own similarities to him. Was madness the inevitable result of someone who spoke to the spirits more than they spoke to the living? If so, what did that mean for her?

The pound of rain against her body and face kept her alert, and had her blood pumping fast in her veins. It was the most awake and alive she had felt in days, so she directed all that desperation at something worthwhile.

She thought back to the soul who had helped her in the palace, the one who had been bold and strong and honorable. He had not given her much. She knew not who he had been in his life, nor why his spirit had not moved on. But she remembered his fierceness, and she needed that now. So she focused on those memories, on every detail she could remember about the spirit's presence, and then she called to him, only him.

Aurora called to her soldier soul again and again throughout the night, every time the cold wracked her body, or the fear climbed as high as the water that washed around her, but she heard no answer.

When the rain died down, she slept in fits and starts, but none of it provided any real rest. It was merely her body giving out when it reached the point where not even her misery could keep her awake.

When next she woke it was daytime, the soil beneath her was still soggy, but the sun was shining, and the warmth felt like salvation against her skin. It took a long time for the heat to seep down to the layers of cold that had claimed her so completely the night before. She could hear the clank of the manacles every time a shiver coursed through her body.

The Stormlord was by the fire, some kind of game already roasting above it. Her stomach seized painfully, and her mouth began to water. He looked up at the air, talking to another soul, she guessed, then immediately turned his head to her.

"You are awake."

She did not know how to respond. So she nodded, the world spinning dizzily with that simple movement. When her vision settled, she eyed the meat with naked desperation. The smell of food so near had nausea rising in her throat, and she knew it would only take one bite to make it go away.

Finally, he took the stick on which the roasted animal was skewered and came toward her.

"Today, you have your first lesson. So you need to eat."

He held the stick directly in front of her face. She waited for him to release her hands or tear off a piece, but when he did neither, she gave in to her hunger. Craning her neck upward, she tore at the meat with her teeth. Juices splattered over her face, but she was too hungry to care. Again and again, she gnawed at the food he presented, tearing big strips away with her teeth. Her jaw was tired after only a few bites, but she kept chewing.

Whatever his idea of a *lesson* was, she knew she would need all her strength for it.

When she had eaten enough that she began to feel ill, she stopped and nodded for him to take it away. He did, throwing the entire thing back on the fire rather than eating any himself.

Then to her surprise, he knelt and began undoing her manacles. The first touch of air on her wrists burned, and she pulled them down to find raw, red abrasions where the irons had been. The

Stormlord moved quickly and efficiently, standing to undo the manacles at her ankles next. When he had freed her completely, he stood up and looked at her.

She curled her legs up to her midsection, her bare feet scraping through the dirt.

"What's the lesson?" she asked and was relieved when her voice barely shook.

He gestured toward her chest, and she looked down to see the frenetic flash of her skyfire through the material of her shirt.

"If you are going to be any use to me, you need more than one storm at your call."

Aurora froze, trying not to let the horror show on her face.

"You—you want me to take another soul?"

"Yes. And I have selected the perfect one."

At his words, a chill stole through the air, followed by a soft, slithering hiss of sinister intent. The wind grew around them, building to a howling crescendo, and Aurora forced herself up onto her feet. Her legs wobbled painfully beneath her weight, and the rapidly dropping temperature sliced at her bare skin. The wind grew fiercer, tearing at her clothes and hair and bringing tears to her eyes. Above them, the sky was churning, clouds darkening as if they had been beaten and bruised.

Slowly, she began to notice tiny tufts of white caught up in the gusts of wind. She squinted, trying to discern what they were, but after a few moments, she did not need to see. She could feel. The cold kiss of snow touched her forehead, then her cheek, then her bare hand. She blinked, and the scant little flakes became an avalanche.

Bits of snow and ice claimed the wind, turning the furious gusts into reaching arms of piercing cold. The ground around her was covered, and her bare feet felt as if she had walked into a pile of needles.

She sucked in a breath, and the cold burned deep into her lungs. Her eyes and nose too felt like she had stuck her face into a fire instead of a snowstorm. The air around her had been swallowed up by white, and she could barely see more than a few paces in each direction.

She tried to search out the Stormlord, but she could no longer see him in the hazy winter he had created. Her body shook violently, the thin layers of her shirt and pants doing nothing to stop the stabbing pain of the frigid air around her.

Aurora tried to think of what Kiran would do in this situation. She needed to find the storm's heart or she would never be able to end this. And given enough time, these temperatures would kill her. She was not sure if the Stormlord would interfere before then, but considering his tendency to disappear, she did not plan to rely on him for help.

Find the heart.

How did she find the heart?

She had to either get to the middle of the storm, which was impossible considering the apex of the storm was high in the sky above her, or she needed to trick the heart into coming to her. The hunters did this by convincing the storm that another tempest was nearby with the use of Stormhearts. She did not have one of those. But she had something better.

Closing her eyes, she tried her hardest to shut out the cold and focus on the electric heat of the skyfire storm inside of her. It leaped to her attention as soon as she reached for it, and she let it fill her. For a few moments, it completely drove away the cold.

She opened her eyes, skyfire sparking from her hands, and screamed into blustering wind, "Well? What are you waiting for? Come and get me!"

She stretched out her arms and used what little strength she had to send bolts of skyfire streaming up toward the seething storm above. In response, she felt a searing rush of hostility and hatred bear down on her from overhead.

She ignored it, blasting another round of skyfire into the air, though this time she could only manage one. A savage shriek carried on the wind, but when she looked up, she saw something incandescent in the sky above her coming closer.

It was so different from the last time she had been this close to the heart of a storm. Then it had been an innocent, cheerful skyfire storm that bore the soul of a child. This soul . . . the closer it came, the more she wanted to run. The spirit's presence was foul and potent—she did not feel anger or greed or bitterness or any of the other usual emotions that rolled off the darker souls. Instead, it exuded a cruel curiosity. This soul wanted to cause pain not out of revenge or envy, but because it *liked* it.

She did not want this soul inside her, to become *part* of her. It would rot her from the inside out. But what choice did she have? If she refused, the Stormlord would know she had no intention of helping him and he would have no reason to keep her alive. He might even send the storm he had already created toward Pavan. If she managed to take it, and that was a big if considering how weak and cold she was at this point, that would mean one less dark soul for the Stormlord to put to use in his war against Stormlings. Though she knew he had many more.

As the gleaming heart approached—swirls of luminous light mimicking the larger storm that raged around her—she knew what she had to do.

In the desert, she had been able to control the skyfire storm to some extent. When a hunter took the heart of a storm, it was an all-out battle to see which heart was stronger—that of the human or the tempest. But with her first soul, she had ordered it to submit, and it had listened.

She did not know if the same would be true today. She had a

feeling this soul would put up a much stronger fight. But all the same, she took a step forward, her bare feet sinking painfully into the drifts of snow.

"Come to me," she commanded, drawing on that indefinable otherness inside that she used to communicate with spirits.

The storm's heart moved even closer, hovering just an arm's reach above her head now.

"Closer," she demanded, pushing her will outside herself and toward the twisted, poisonous soul that controlled the still-falling snow.

As soon as the orb dipped low enough, Aurora used her last reserve of strength to jump, shoving her hand directly into the storm's heart.

Her first thought was that the cold she had felt before was nothing to the icy frost surging through her now. Last time, the heart she had taken had been shocked and sad, even afraid. This time, the other soul was nothing short of ravenous. It wanted everything she had—life and power and freedom—and it would do whatever it took to get them.

Strongest heart, Aurora reminded herself. It did not matter if she was cold and tired and weak. She did not need the strongest body to win this fight. She only needed the strongest heart. And the other soul might be hungry for victory, but it was only fighting for its own greed.

She was fighting for so much more.

Aurora had to win so that she could get back to Kiran and tell him she loved him. She had not said those words enough. She needed to see her mother and Duke again. She had so many questions she wanted to ask them about their time together when they were young. She wanted to know everything that Duke would tell her about his life as Finneus. She had to survive to save Jinx and Nova. It was her fault that her friends were in such danger, and she absolutely could not die here and leave them alone. She wanted to hear Ransom and Bait bicker some more, and she wanted to finally get to know Sly better. The wary hunter had been her rock in the palace after Jinx and Nova had been captured, and she had never properly thanked her. She had to do that.

Crying out under the strain, Aurora pushed her hand deeper into that pernicious soul and demanded, "Submit to me. I control spirits, and you *will* obey."

The world ruptured with light, and the fierce pressure from her opponent disappeared. Aurora had a moment of wild relief before something new and *wrong* slid into place inside her. She tried to scream, but her legs gave out, and the world fragmented into darkness around her.

A new type of magic emerged with the coming of the tempests, and its users called themselves Stormlings. But as decades passed in this changed world, the original magics that disappeared did not stay gone forever. Rumors began to circulate of young children with gifts over the elements. The question was whether those powers came from the goddess or if some of the original magic users had survived the Time of Tempests after all. Because the storm seasons did not ease, many believed it was the latter, and that the storms would never truly end until every witch was eliminated. Stormling cities outlawed the use of elemental magics, and those born with the gifts learned to live their lives in secret.

— *An Examination of the Original Magics*

21

Upon waking, Aurora's hands and wrists were once again bound in the manacles, and there was no remaining evidence of the snow that had blanketed this entire area before. Her throat was parched, and her stomach had that hollow empty feeling that went deeper than hunger. The last time she had taken a soul, she had slept for days afterward.

She looked around, trying to find some way to gauge how much time had passed. The Stormlord was nowhere to be seen, and the fire was long out. She did not smell even a hint of smoke or ash.

Out of the corner of her eye, she saw the usual lightning flash of the storm in her chest, only now the pattern had changed. Between flickers of skyfire, there were billowing spirals of pearlescent, snowy flecks that looked as if they were caught up in the wind.

Hesitating, she searched inside her for that new addition, and jerked back when she felt that same voracious, seething presence that she had sensed in the storm. It was weaker now, but it was there all the same, woven inside her own soul.

She squeezed her eyes tightly closed, tears chasing each other down her temples as she lay prone and shackled and forever changed in the dirt.

Eventually she became aware of someone approaching—two

someones, in fact. Her heart leaped into her throat and for a moment she dared to hope.

Please, please, please.

But as they drew nearer, she felt the mass of dark spirits that could only be following the Stormlord. She was too weak to ascertain who the other person was, not without making herself vulnerable to all those spirits. Her heart hammered, fearing the worst. If he had captured Kiran too . . . She swallowed, trying not to be swept away by panic, and failing miserably.

When the Stormlord ducked out of the trees, dragging another half-conscious man with him, it was not Kiran he brought. But she did recognize the man. He had dark curly hair and bronze skin. Blood marred his nose and mouth, and the last she had heard, he had been captured by her friends.

Casimir.

The Stormlord had made contact with the rebellion. The question now was whether that contact had been amicable. He hauled Casimir closer, the man's legs struggling and failing to keep up with his pace. He kept pulling until he drew even with Aurora, then he threw Casimir to the ground.

"Stay or you die," the Stormlord growled, holding up a hand crackling with skyfire in threat.

Casimir's jaw was locked tight, and his eyes shone with disdain, but he made no move to get up from the ground as the Stormlord crossed to Aurora, bent over, and began to unlock her manacles. Her heart faltered, then bounded off into a sprint as one leg came free, then the other. Without a word, he crossed to her hands. Hard breaths sawed in and out of her mouth as he released her, and gingerly, she pushed herself upright, her muscles protesting at the change after such a long time in one position. She looked warily between the Stormlord and the Locke prince. Her captor squared off between them, his arms crossed over his chest, and he stared at her.

His scarred eye narrowed slightly, and he said, "Well?"

"Well, what?" she asked, her voice a barely-there husk.

"You said you support the goddess's will. It is time to prove yourself." He stretched out his hand, and in his palm lay a knife.

Aurora's hands trembled, and the days of dehydration made her mouth so dry she felt as if her throat were closing up. Or maybe that was just her unwillingness to speak.

"You want to be free," the Stormlord continued. "You want to earn my trust and defeat the Lockes. Do this, and you will have taken a step toward all three."

"You want me to kill him? *Now?*" She searched frantically for a way out of this, some escape.

The Stormlord shrugged. "If you want me to continue to teach you the ways of the goddess, I need to know you are on the right side."

He offered the knife again, and this time she took it, wondering if she could use it against the Stormlord instead before he called a legion of tempests against her. She stood, her knees shaky from disuse. And she knew if she tried to run, she would probably fall. She was so weak.

Aurora looked at Casimir. He had been jovial when she first met him, but that had all been an act. She had heard him talk with Cassius behind her back, and he did not seem nearly so good-natured then. She'd seen the cruelty with which he treated the remnants, and knew he had been behind the burning of the Eye, but was that enough for her to justify harming him, potentially taking his life? What did she expect when she was queen? She would have to make these kinds of decisions—the hardest kind, of who was guilty and what they deserved—but she would not be the one to mete out the punishment. Did that make the blood any less on her hands?

Casimir lifted his chin and stared at her, blinking rapidly.

Aurora saw the moment he recognized her, his narrowed gaze going wide with shock.

She tried to convey with her eyes that she did not plan to hurt him.

Not like this. She thought she had accepted the rebellion's plan to hand Casimir over, but now that she had spent goddess knew how many days in the madman's company, she knew there was no justice in that kind of fate, only cruelty.

She opened her mouth to tell the Stormlord no, but his attention broke abruptly away from her to the way he had come. He cursed, and a moment later the sky ruptured. From a clear blue sky an explosion of wind spread in every direction. A pinhole of darkness grew into a vortex of thick dark clouds that pulled at the universe around it, dragging in clouds and trees and everything nearby. A twister began to form as darker clouds bulked up in the sky, and the roar of it on the wind drowned out everything.

She did not even hear the Stormlord move. Everything happened so fast. She only felt him jerk the knife from her hand, saw the glint of the blade in the sun, and looked up just in time to see him drag it across Casimir's throat. She watched the prince's eyes go wide, felt the spray of blood across her face and the front of her body.

She did not know when she had started screaming, only that she was. But it, like everything else, was lost to the monstrous twister that was sucking up everything in its path not far away.

The Stormlord tucked the knife away at his belt, and then crossed toward her. She scrambled backward, her hands scraping over dirt and rocks. She managed to push herself to her feet, and then she ran. Impossible as it was . . . she ran toward the twister. She only made it a few paces before a hand caught her wrist, hauling her back.

She sent out a scream for help—audible and inaudible—and jerked hard, the socket of her shoulder twisting painfully. In the distance she saw that the twister had expanded in size, and for a moment, she could have sworn she saw a person caught up in its vicious winds, but then the shadow rotated beyond her view, and she could not be sure.

Something rumbled ominously in the distance, and the Stormlord growled in frustration behind her. As she watched, the rotation of the twister began to slow. The winds screamed as if in protest. In the moment of distraction, Aurora used her free hand to grab the still-bloody knife from the holster on the Stormlord's belt. And with unflinching surety, she plunged the blade into his chest.

His fingers loosened around her wrist and she broke free, running for the trees. She did not stop until she made it to the edge of the clearing, and only then did she glance back briefly to see how close her captor was.

The clearing where he had kept her was empty, except for the prone body of the dead Casimir Locke.

She clung to a nearby tree, unsure whether she should keep running, or whether she should turn now and run in the other direction, considering the twister tearing through the forest ahead. She had her answer a few moments later when she felt a burst of magic, and the forest went quiet—no more howling winds, no more whirlwind of debris. Only the calm after the chaos.

Someone had dismantled the storm and come to rescue her. And even though every muscle in her body wanted to give up and slide to the forest floor, she pushed herself off of her current tree and toward the next. She did that again and again, stumbling over tree roots and past shrub bushes, determined to set eyes on the loved ones she had missed so dearly.

Soon, she heard the crack of a twig up ahead, and her breath caught, tears preemptively falling down her face. She searched the trees, waiting for the moment Kiran would appear between them, praying to the goddess that no one had been hurt in the fight with the storm.

There were a thousand other things that shadowed form could have been besides a person caught up in the twister's winds. She had to believe that. It had to be true.

Another crunch of boots, and then a tall form appeared. Aurora clutched at the nearest tree, giving up on walking the rest of the way.

But for the second time that day, the person who walked out from the trees was not who she expected. He was tall, with dark hair and eyes and light brown skin not unlike Kiran's. And the moment he laid eyes on her, he started running, yelling commands at someone she could not see. She lost her grip on the tree, sinking to her knees, but he was there to catch her before she hit the ground.

"Aurora. Gods, Aurora, are you all right?"

She looked up into the face of Cassius Locke, and she told the truth. "No. I am not."

Cassius fell to his knees, dropping his sword completely to cradle Aurora Pavan's thin, bloody form as she crumpled into unconsciousness. He felt as if his mind had been swept away by the twister they had encountered moments before, because he could not seem to grasp what he was seeing. She was here, in front of him, after all this time.

Her clothes were ragged and muddy, and she was splattered with blood. Her hair was shorter—tangled and dirty. Her cheeks looked hollow, like they had long forgotten their last meal. He searched furiously for any injuries that could be the source for all the blood, but after a few moments determined it was not hers.

The neck of her shirt was torn open, and he could see mud-streaked skin and what looked like flashes of light. He stared, entranced and confused, as displays of magic he had only ever seen in the sky moved where her heart should be. It was impossible;

only the Stormlord bore those kinds of marks. It was him they had come seeking, after all. One of the remnants had reported seeing a suspicious man with someone she was certain was Casimir Locke. Considering his brother had made it his mission to torture the remnants into leaving, he did not know why anyone would want to help, but it was the first real lead they had had on his brother.

And now he found Aurora here instead? It made no sense.

Someone called out ahead of him. Then more shouts followed. He hefted Aurora into his arms and went toward the noise. She was too light in his arms, her skin too cold, but a warmth he had not known in a long time began to spread through him at the certainty of having her safe in his hold.

Then he came into the clearing and saw what had drawn his soldiers' attention, and what little warmth he had gained left him.

His brother lay strewn across the grass, his neck open, a crimson puddle forming below him. He looked away, blinking hard to rid himself of the sight. But that red pool lingered on the black of his eyelids.

He had never been particularly close to his brother. That was not how his family worked. But gods damn it, he was so tired. Violence lived beneath his very skin, it was part of who he was, but that did not mean he did not want to claw it out sometimes. He wanted to turn that violence inward and burn it all away until there was nothing left but ash and he could finally rest.

He forced his eyes open and scanned the rest of the area around him. His eyes landed on a pair of manacles staked in the grass, about two strides apart. He looked down where Aurora's arms lay limply in her lap and saw the raw abrasions around her wrists. He tilted one arm up and saw the same was true of her ankles.

Then that violence he knew so well came screaming back— black and burning.

If she had been held captive out here too, then the bastard still had to be out here somewhere.

"Search the woods," he demanded. "Search every bleeding tree if you have to. Find him."

He took a deep breath, his thoughts torn in too many directions—wanting to be in on the hunt, knowing he needed to get Aurora to a nurse, and dreading facing his brother's lifeless body again.

He turned to two soldiers who were still kneeling by his brother and gave them instructions. "Wrap the body, and return it to the palace. Somewhere discreet until I can break the news to my family."

The men nodded their assent and set about fulfilling his orders.

Then there was only the girl left in his arms, who was entirely too still.

She, he would be seeing to himself. He set her down for a moment, shucked off his coat, and settled it over her, taking great care to hide the slim slice of flesh that glowed with inexplicable light. Then he lifted her back into his arms and began the walk back toward home.

He wanted to run, to get her to safety and help as soon as possible, but he knew the distance was too far—he might hurt her more by jostling her. So he held her with as much care as he possibly could as he walked back through the area where he had defeated the twister that had come out of nowhere. He would have to send more men back to search here too, for he was certain men had been swept up in the winds.

For now though, he ignored the twisted and downed trees and the mangled mess that the storm had left behind. He was having trouble tearing his eyes away from the thin bones of Aurora's arms. Had she always been so frail? In his memories, she was strong and confident, but the girl in his arms now looked withered and so very breakable.

He wanted to turn back around and hunt that Stormlord bastard down and make him pay.

He would. Cassius swore if it was the last thing he did, that monster would pay.

Aurora could not remember the last time she slept so well. She stretched, her arms and legs reaching across smooth, cool linens. The mattress and pillow beneath her were made of such heaven that she never wanted to move. She reached out, expecting to find Kiran's hard, bare shoulder nearby in this magical dream world, but all she found was an empty bed.

Slowly, she opened her eyes, and blinked in confusion at the familiarity. The bed was wide and extravagant, with plush white linens that reminded her of clouds. It had been a very long time since she had dreamed of being back in her old bed. She smiled, stretching into the soft mattress until a wincing pain at her wrist caught her attention. She pulled her hand closer to her face, staring at the red marks she saw with bewilderment for a moment before recent events came back to her like a horrid nightmare, and she realized she was not dreaming.

Immediately, she jolted upright in bed, her stiff muscles protesting the movement fiercely. Her eyes widened as she took in the room around her, *her room*—it looked exactly the same, and yet it felt completely different. She could not explain how the room had changed. It had always been this decadent, always slightly cold with the stone floors and walls and the dramatic windows. But it no longer felt like hers.

A knock at the door set her heart racing. Her last memories were hazy. She clearly recalled the Stormlord slitting Casimir's neck and fleeing as someone approached. She remembered he'd sent a tornado to slow them down, and she had been so worried that someone had been hurt.

Then . . . then she remembered Cassius. And nothing else at all.

The knock sounded again, and she glanced around wildly, unsure what she could do other than see what he wanted. She was here now. There was no changing that. And in truth, she would rather be here than back with the Stormlord. But she had no idea what would come next.

She lifted her chin as bravely as she could manage and called out, "Come in."

The wooden door creaked open, and again it was not who she was expecting, though the person who slipped through the door was one she had seen come through that entrance many times. Instead of the tall form of the Locke prince, she saw the tentative smile of her best friend.

A sob was out of her mouth before she even knew she had made a sound. Aurora tried to scramble from the bed, but her limbs would not cooperate, and she stumbled, nearly sprawling on the floor.

Quickly, Nova closed the door behind her and hurried across the room.

"Stay in bed. Rest. You need it."

Aurora sat back on the bed without arguing, mostly because she was dumbfounded. "How are you—how?"

"The prince sent me."

Aurora gaped. "From the dungeon?"

Nova's mouth slanted, and she shrugged. "He returned me to my room over a week ago."

Blinking, Aurora asked, "And Jinx?"

Nova shook her head. "He said by participating in my attempted rescue, she was a known affiliate of the rebellion, and he could not release her."

"But he wanted to release you?"

"Not immediately. Eventually he said he believed me that I had nothing to do with your kidnapping, so he did. But he banned me from leaving the palace, or I would have come and found you. We have to get Jinx out. They did not hurt her while we were together, but I know nothing of what's happened to her since."

Aurora grabbed hold of her friend's hand, and when that steadiness felt good, she wrapped her other hand around Nova's too. "I know. I will fix this. Do you understand? Whatever I have to do. I am so sorry I did this to you, Nova. There are no words for how much I regret the hurt I have caused you."

Her friend climbed up on the bed beside her and pulled Aurora into a tight hug. She had not realized how desperate she was for the contact until she had it, and then she was clutching at Nova, so glad to not be alone anymore. Then, the whole story came pouring out of her—every good and awful thing that had happened to her since she had left Nova behind months ago with her fool's idea to fake her own kidnapping. She told her friend about all the incredible things she had seen that she had wanted to share with her oldest friend. She talked about how it felt to fall in love with someone who did not know anything about who she was or her family or the expectations she was supposed to fulfill.

Nova asked her endless questions about her feelings for Kiran, and Aurora told her about their fight when he discovered her true identity, and she blushed hotly when she glossed over how they had made up while out in the wilds.

"So the two of you are back together then?" Nova asked.

"Yes," Aurora answered. "Well, technically, I am here, and he is out there somewhere, probably worried sick because I have not seen him since the Stormlord kidnapped me."

"We will find a way to get word to him," Nova promised. "I am watched frequently, but perhaps I can get a friend of a friend to smuggle a message out."

At some point, there was another knock on the door, and Aurora tensed again, fearing Cassius, but it was only a maid bringing up food. The cavern of Aurora's empty stomach echoed painfully as soon as the smell hit her nose. They moved into her sitting room to eat, and Aurora noted that there were still lingering signs of Cassius's presence around the room. She had not noticed anything of his in the bedroom, and she hoped that meant he had slept elsewhere, using only her sitting room in her absence.

As they ate, Aurora continued with her story while gorging on the small feast that had been brought for them. Strangely, she felt as if she had been plucked out of time. All the pain and stress and worry of the last few weeks melted away in the presence of her friend, and for just a little while she felt normal again. She told Nova about her magic, and what she could do with it—the good and the bad, filling in the specifics that they had not had time for during the rescue attempt. She did not hesitate to peel back her shirt and show Nova the shifting likenesses of the two different storms she now carried inside her.

Aurora almost told Nova about the darkness of the second soul she had taken, but could not bring herself to break the happy mood of their reunion. Someday she would tell her friend how much she feared the soul that was now part of her own, that she worried it would taint her, manipulate her, prune her into something she did not want to be.

But that could wait for another day.

"And you?" Aurora asked. "You do not have to talk about what happened to you if you do not wish. Especially to me. But if you want to . . . I am here to listen."

Nova's large eyes lowered, and she smiled. "It was not *all* bad."

A deep, rosy hue began to spread up her friend's neck, but before Aurora could pounce with questions, there was another knock at the door. Assuming it was another maid, Aurora called out, "Come in."

The door swung inward, and as soon as she heard the thud of a heavy boot on stone, she knew this was no maid. She was still wearing a simple dressing gown, something she did not even remember putting on for herself the night before, and she was sitting at a small table with Nova, her plate scraped clean of food. She clenched her fists around the edge of the table, and sat ramrod straight as Cassius Locke appeared in the room.

He was different from how she remembered him.

He was still handsome—though his short cropped hair had been left to grow slightly wild, and he looked tired. There was still a brooding menace to his presence that reminded her this man was capable of terrible things. But the way he stayed at the door, almost *unsure* . . . that was entirely new.

"How are you feeling?" he asked, remaining near the open door.

"Better," she answered honestly. The sleep and food had done wonders, though she would not be against crawling back into bed for another day or two if she were not potentially in grave danger. Too tired to tiptoe around the subject, she asked him outright, "What do you want with me?"

His brows lifted in surprise. "To save you? It's all I have been trying to do from the moment you were taken. I searched for you everywhere, for months. Anywhere I thought you could be, I sent soldiers there."

She knew that. She had met a few in the small village of Toleme before they had been wiped out by a twister she had accidentally called.

"And my mother? I do not think you were trying to save her by drugging her into unconsciousness."

He took a step farther into the room, his long legs eating up too much space in that one stride. "I had nothing to do with that. It was my father, he—"

"Oh please. And Nova? Was it your father who had her imprisoned for my kidnapping too?"

Cassius gritted his teeth, the muscles in his neck jumping with strain. His eyes flicked behind her to where she knew Nova still stood. "No. That was me. I was trying to find out what happened to you, and—"

"I ran away because I did not want to marry you! There was no kidnapping. I left of my own volition because I saw just a glimpse of the coldness and cruelty you and your family are capable of, and I decided I deserved more. But I am the fool who did not realize until too late that I was leaving my mother at the mercy of wolves."

"Aurora, I never meant for any of this to happen. I *wanted* to rule beside you, not let my father run another city into the ground. Once we were wed, I could prevent him from attempting a coup. I can still do that. My father could not stand against you and me together."

Aurora gathered the dressing gown tightly around herself and shook her head. "I did not want to marry you then, and I will not marry you now. Not ever."

"Then I guess there is no point in keeping you, is there?" The voice came from the still-open doorway, but when she looked no one was there. A moment later Cassius's father leaned around the corner, his gaze hard, and his lips fixed in the same sneering smile she had seen on Casimir.

"Welcome home, Aurora," he said, stepping into the room, and closing the door with a quiet snick. "You caused quite a stir with your disappearance, though I can't say that I minded. It worked out rather well, in fact."

"You are deplorable."

The Locke patriarch shrugged. "Someone has to be." Then he turned to his son and asked, "Do you want to kill her? Or shall I?"

Aurora's mouth went dry, and she knew if either of them looked closely enough they would be able to see the light of the storms flashing furiously in her chest. Let him come. She was not helpless. If he touched her, she would pump enough skyfire into him to stop his heart or char him from the inside out, whichever came first.

When Cassius did not respond, the older man turned to her, crossing the room with a calculating look in his eyes. She let her arms hang loose at her sides, but she could feel the buzz of energy already collecting at her fingertips.

He lunged at her, and she raised her hands up, bracing for impact, but it never came. Instead, Cassius tackled him from behind, and the two men crashed into a table, sending a vase and other knick-knacks crashing to the floor. Aurora gasped, and Nova grabbed her hand, pulling her back toward the wall, and out of the way of the brawling father and son.

They rolled over and over each other, grappling for dominance, and eventually Cassius ended up on top. He reared back and landed a hard punch across his father's jaw. The king grabbed one of the broken pieces from the vase, slashing it across Cassius's cheek with an enraged snarl. Streams of red splattered the rug, and Cassius scrambled back, out of reach. The two stood, breathing heavy, circling each other.

"You would fight me over *her*?" the king growled.

"I have been waiting to fight you all my life," Cassius said. "It is what you built me to do—to conquer whatever stood in my way."

"I am not standing in your way. I am trying to give you a kingdom without another powerful heir to challenge your claim."

"You do nothing but destroy. You will ruin this kingdom, like you ruined ours. I do not need or want your help."

The king lunged again, and Cassius grabbed the arm holding the shard that cut him before, spinning and bending the arm back painfully until his father's grip loosened, dropping the makeshift weapon. The king reached back with his free hand and grabbed Cassius's hair, and then the two of them smashed into the wall—twisting and punching and trying to gain the upper hand.

The king broke free and grabbed the water basin nearby, dumping the contents, and then swinging the piece of pottery at his son's head. Cassius ducked and rammed his shoulder into his father's midsection, sending them sprawling on the floor once more.

"You ungrateful—"

A hard punch cut off the rest of his words, then they were rolling again, knocking into furniture and ripping at each other's clothing. The king ended up on top, his fist connecting hard with Cassius's face, once, then twice, then several more times, each with an almost joyous bark of glee, and just when Aurora was about to run over and throw herself into the fight as well, the older man stiffened, and jerked, his arm hanging in the air for a moment where it had been poised to strike again. Then his whole body was shoved sideways, sprawling flat on the bloodied rug with a dagger buried to the hilt in his chest.

Cassius, bloody and breathing heavy, sat up to look at her—his face swelling from his father's punches. Between heaving breaths he said, "He made me paranoid as a child. Now I keep weapons stashed everywhere. Including here." He thumped a hand underneath the settee next to where they had been fighting. Cassius reached up and wiped away some of the blood that had been running down his face, then he looked at her with purple, swollen features.

"Now will you believe me when I tell you I mean you no harm?"

Aurora stared, stunned and relieved, and a part of her—that new, dark, hateful part—relished the violence she had just seen, that had been done *for her*.

She jerked, horrified by that feeling, and quickly declared, "I am still not marrying you."

"Fine," Cassius grunted, climbing to his feet with a wince on his bruised face. "But maybe a different kind of partnership? You might have more gifts than I realized," he said, gesturing toward her heart with a knowing look. "But I am willing to bet you cannot take on the Stormlord on your own. Face it, you need me, Aurora."

What she needed was Kiran. And her mother. And Duke. And Jinx. And every other member of her newfound family. But she looked at him, at the earnest expression on his face, and the blood he wore like a badge of honor. He had killed his father to protect her. That had to earn him at least some measure of trust.

Finally, she answered, "I'm not looking for a partner, but I'll take a soldier, if you're willing."

She held out her hand, and Cassius took a step forward. He towered over her, and even covered in blood and bruises, the man *looked* dangerous. He ignored the hand she offered and knelt before her instead.

"As you wish, my Queen."

ACKNOWLEDGMENTS

Wow. Where to start? If you follow me online, you know the last two years have been rough for me. I was diagnosed with epilepsy in 2017 after several years of a variety of unexplained health issues. The diagnosis was a complete shock. I had likely been having seizures for several years (if not longer), but because they were not the typical convulsive seizures you see on TV, I never would have guessed. Even once I had a diagnosis, it took a long time (and an intense hospitalization) to find medications that would curtail my seizures. In a strange way, I felt like past me had written *Roar* knowing what was coming. Because I felt very much like I was caught up in a never-ending storm, and it was completely outside my control. For a while, I was not sure I would ever be able to have a life resembling the one I had before.

But after a lot of time and patience and help from my loved ones, I've managed to reclaim my life, albeit with some limitations. I owe more than everything to my parents, who sat with me in the hospital, and while the meds made me miserably sick. They filled in all the gaps of my life when I could no longer drive or do simple things like go to the grocery store or take myself to the doctor or even walk my dog. They gave and gave and gave, and I honestly would not have made it without them. The same is true of my sisters and my cousin Jared and my best friends—Jay

Crownover, Lindsay Ehrhardt, and Bethany Salminen. You guys held me together when everything was falling apart. More love to friends Joey, Victoria, Shelly, Meredith, Heather, JLA, Ana, Megan, Val, Amber, Kami, and so many more. I have to thank my neurologist, Lakshmi Mukundan, who diagnosed me, and who is the kindest, most nurturing, and truly caring doctor I have ever met. I am so glad you came into my life. Tara Ryan, you were an oasis in the chaos, and I am so grateful.

And God bless Tor Teen. I missed deadline after deadline because my brain just did not work the same way anymore, and they were so patient and caring and understanding. I was under a tremendous amount of stress, and they were always looking for ways to build me up and support me, rather than add to that stress. That is remarkably rare in this business. So thank you to everyone at Tor who worked on my book in any way—my new editor Melissa Frain, and my original editor Whitney Ross, along with my publicist Saraciea, my copyeditor MaryAnn, my cover designer John Blumen, and of course, the queen of it all, Kathleen Doherty. Thank you doesn't seem big enough, but it's all I have.

Similarly, the team at New Leaf Literary have always been fierce champions at my side. Thank you to Suzie Townsend, Sara Stricker, Cassandra Baim, Mia Roman, Veronica Grijalva, Dani Segelbaum, and everyone else. Also to KP Simmon—you might be my publicist, but you were my friend first, and I'm so glad for it.

For the Stormlings, my Roar street team—thank you all so much for loving these characters and this world with me. It was such a huge deal to me to fulfill this dream, and you guys worked so hard to make it the best release it could possibly be. And you're just crazy cool people. And to all of you reading this. I know it was a long wait for this book. Thank you for your patience and your support and all the kind words and encouragement. You got me through so many hard days.

ABOUT THE AUTHOR

CORA CARMACK is a *New York Times* and *USA Today* bestselling author. Since she was a teenager, her favorite genre to read has been fantasy, and now she's thrilled to bring her usual compelling characters and swoon-worthy romance into worlds of magic and intrigue with her debut YA series. Her previous adult romance titles include the Losing It, Rusk University, and Muse series. Her books have been translated into more than a dozen languages around the world. Carmack lives in Austin, Texas, and on any given day you might find her typing away at her computer, flying to various cities around the world, or just watching Netflix with her kitty, Katniss, and her puppy, Sherlock. But she can always be found on Twitter, Facebook, Instagram, Pinterest, and her website www.coracarmack.com.